THE EMPTY QUARTER

Also by David L. Robbins:

Souls to Keep
War of the Rats
The End of War
Scorched Earth
Last Citadel
Liberation Road
The Assassins Gallery
The Betrayal Game
Broken Jewel
The Devil's Waters

For the stage:
Scorched Earth (an adaptation)
The End of War (an adaptation)
Sam & Carol

THE
EMPTY
QUARTER

DAVID L. ROBBINS

f THOMAS & MERCER

Published by Thomas & Mercer, Seattle

www.apub.com

Amazon, the Amazon logo, and Thomas & Mercer are trademarks of Amazon.com, Inc., or its affiliates.

ISBN-13: 9781477824023
ISBN-10: 1477824022

Cover design by Chris McGrath

Library of Congress Control Number: 2014902144

Printed in the United States of America

To Bruce Miller, Phil Whiteway, and the Virginia Repertory Theatre family; Adam Lebovitz of Unique Features; and Ron Keller of VCU, for believing in my other voices.

And to Neil and Sara Belle November, and Jane and Edgar Wallin, for believing in me.

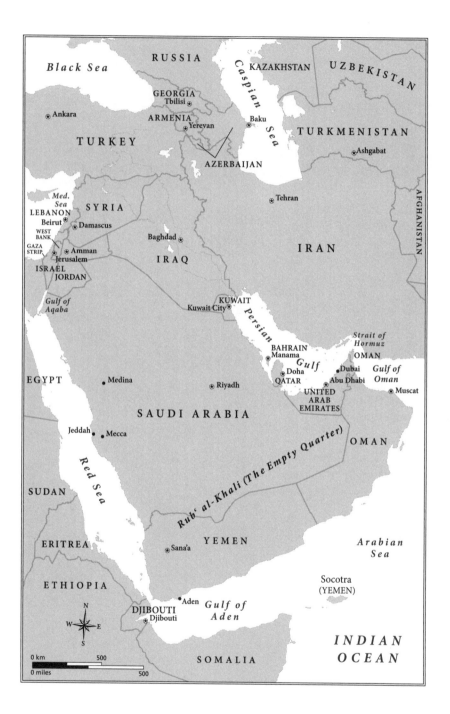

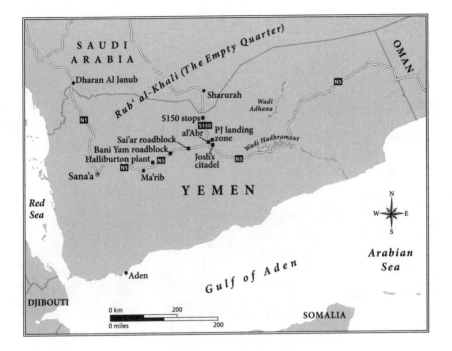

"Expel the infidel from the Arabian Peninsula."
    a *hadith* (tradition) of Islam,
    attributed to the Prophet Muhammad

"When disaster threatens, seek refuge in Yemen."
    The Prophet Muhammad, to his small band of followers after
    being chased out of Mecca

"Charlie Mike."
    US military phonetic alphabet for "Continue mission."

Two Years Ago

Lashkar Gah district
Helmand River Valley
Afghanistan

There'd been no time on the ground to scrub *Pedro 2* of blood. The pair of marines two hours ago in Lashkar Gah district, both hit in the chest, and before them the Ranger this morning who'd taken a round in the gut in Musa Qala—all had left stains on the chopper's metal deck. The PJs never delegated this task to Camp Bastion's ground crews but cleaned the blood themselves, a way to keep faith with their soldiers. LB and Doc did this now, under way on their third mission of the day, with towels and hydrogen peroxide.

As they tossed the towels into a corner, Juggler hailed over the team freq from *Pedro 1*, the other tandem-flying Pave Hawk. Juggler was Capt. Wally Bloom, the team's lead combat rescue officer. Wally got his call sign last year from surviving a helo crash and five somersaults in the Hindu Kush. He didn't lose his sunglasses or drop his coffee mug.

All five squad members in both choppers transmitted, "Lima Charlie." Loud and clear.

On the floor of *Pedro 2*, the primary medical bird, LB and Doc settled shoulder to shoulder, so tired, supporting each other without thinking. Exhausted, the team had left Bastion ten minutes ago not even knowing where they were headed, or why;

they'd just shuffled behind Wally back to the choppers, spun up, and lifted off again.

From *Pedro 1*, Juggler crackled in their headsets.

"There's a twelve-man LRP[1] from the 42nd Royal Marines taking fire in Nad Ali.

Call sign is Bengal. We'll be there in fifteen minutes. We got the job instead of the Brits because the landing zone is hot. Repeat, LZ is hot. Mission intel is scarce, but there are three wounded. I've got no tango status,[2] but all three are isolated and in contact with the enemy. Terrain is open and rocky, within a kilometer of a village, a road, and a field. I want the whole team on the ground. Choppers will drop and circle. Team leader."

LB got on the freq to remind the PJs of their protocols. Stay together. Cover fire. Move to the closest wounded first. Assess, treat as needed, exfil to the casualty collection point. Move to the next.

One by one, the PJs responded. "Roger that."

Wally transmitted a heads-up from the pilot of *Pedro 1* to the team.

"Ten minutes."

LB's lower back ached from the rigid, jumpy helo decks he'd ridden on all day and from running bent and burdened under seventy pounds of rifle, body armor, and med ruck. His feet were hot, swollen in his sandy boots, his emotions drained. The rise and fall of adrenaline many times in one day took a toll in LB's own blood. He wanted a swallow from his canteen but left it for the battlefield. Low on stamina, he figured to keep himself fueled on aggravation. He changed out the magazine in his M4. Beside him, Doc, a marathon runner and a former marine, catnapped. He and LB were the only PJs on the team in their forties, Doc the only one gone bald. Back home in Vegas, he had four daughters and an ER nurse for a wife. Nothing outside his own house upset Doc.

---

1 long-range patrol.
2 severity of wounds.

At Wally's radio call of "One minute out," the two lowered their goggles and rose to their kneepads. *Pedro 2*'s gunner dropped his visor, spread his legs behind the starboard minigun, and latched onto the grips. At a hundred feet altitude, the chopper leaned back on its cushion of air. LB and Doc unclipped their cow's-tails, poised for a fast drop in the middle of a firefight.

Doc shoved open the door just before the chopper set wheels down tiptoe, light and quick. He leaped first into spirals of dust and stinging gravel. LB got close on his butt. The big HH-60 bounced back into the air. The second bird raced in behind her.

They ran crouching to a squad of Royal Marines waving from behind the low cover of a stacked stone wall. LB and Doc joined eight commandos with rifles on top of the wall. LB didn't know where to aim.

The Brit leader was a slight but leathery lieutenant, gray-eyed above a blond mustache the same sandy color as his commandos' camouflage. He seemed in control, and the marines flanking him looked rugged. The fingers of the commando beside LB were flaky with dried blood.

LB nudged him.

"You okay?"

"Yeah, no worries. Go get my mates."

This was the battle LB and his team leaped into with every combat rescue. They brought calm to the frantic, order to the chaotic. They stood their training and their own courage beside the wounded and frightened, the isolated and the dying, and together they fought their way back to safety and life.

LB had never been to this spot in Nad Ali district, but he knew well the Afghan landscape, a drab vista broken by gullies and ancient stone walls. Half a kilometer north, a mud-hut village squatted on the cusp of a wheat field. Goats and camels stood tied to posts. Mulberry trees lined a skinny paved road running east-west over weedy ground. All of it baked in the afternoon heat. Distant orange mountains hemmed in the village under a sky so clear that an early moon peered down.

Why did this Brit patrol draw gunfire? More than likely, some bad guys were operating out of the nearby village. They'd appealed to the local tribal chief's duty under Islam to protect them, and bribed him for good measure. The tribesmen were just earning their pay, calling it religion.

The lieutenant nodded to LB and Doc. "Sergeants, thank you."

They waited seconds for Wally, Quincy, and Jamie to reach them at a dead run. Thirty meters off, *Pedro 1* lowered her brow to zoom away. Quincy and Jamie exchanged hurried nods with the English commandos, then added their carbines over the wall. Wally arrived, skidding beside the Brit team commander.

Wally pulled down his sunglasses, showing the crow's feet of fifteen years in harsh climates. Green-eyed and steely, he let the lieutenant see the measure of confidence his commandos should have in the American Guardian Angels.

"What've you got?"

"Right, Captain. An hour ago we came up on that village. When we got near the road, my point man tripped an IED[3]. The blast took him out and one other. The rest of us drew small arms fire. Not sure from whom—villagers, Taliban, they've bloody all got guns. I called to regroup, nine of my twelve came back. I've got one man seventy meters there, west. I saw him go down. The other two are north, toward the road. I can't say exactly where, can't see them from here. My men don't have radios. We can hear them shouting to each other." The lieutenant bit his lip. "We've tried. We can't get to them." That was rough for him to say.

Before the big chopper could gain altitude, she took small arms fire. Bangs snapped out of the field across the road. Kalashnikov rounds whisked above the wall, driving down the heads of the commandos and PJs. The HH-60 banked sharply

---

3 improvised explosive device.

away, blowing dust over the men hugging the wall. Grit clung to the sweat on LB's neck.

Returning his weapon over the wall, he stared down his M4, swinging left and right. Nothing presented itself for a target but a dry landscape dotted by tufts of wild grass and the debris of old farm machines. With the beat of *Pedro 1* fading, a thin cry rose from the flats to the west.

"Over here."

Wally slid his shades back in place. He touched a finger to the young lieutenant's camouflaged chest.

"Stay on freq 252.9. Got it?"

"Roger."

Wally pushed the finger again into the lieutenant's chest, as if hitting "Record."

"You provide cover fire on my orders."

"Roger."

"I want 360 security for a casualty collection point. Right here."

"Will do, Captain."

Wally pulled his finger off the commando to point at Jamie. The young PJ hardened his grip on his weapon.

"Jamie takes point. Then Quincy, me, Doc, LB." Wally gestured west to the shouting, downed marine. "Him first."

The bloody-handed marine beside LB rapped him on the shoulder. LB winked, then dropped off the wall to huddle beside Wally.

"You're going?"

"I can direct close air support better if I'm with the team. And we'll need all five of us to bring back three. Problem?"

The CRO considered LB through his mirrored sunglasses. Wally hardly ever took them off, which meant his eyes rarely betrayed what he was thinking. LB preferred, when looking a man in the face, not to see his own reflection. This was why Wally insisted on wearing them.

Jamie, the team's youngest member, was also their best rifleman, fearless in the field and affable off it. He already had his back turned, primed to dash out to the first wounded marine. Doc and Quincy had no opinion, and they showed it by lining up.

LB was of a mind to question Wally's decision, but the wounded marine's urgent voice left no time.

"Fine."

Wally pivoted to the commando lieutenant. He patted Bengal on the arm.

"Cover fire now."

The Brit slung his SA80 into his hands. He straightened his legs to sling the rifle into play over the stones. His eight commandos followed suit.

"Lads. Fire."

All nine guns opened on the wheat field, the wall became a firing line. LB wasn't sure the marines had real targets in their sights, but that didn't matter. The point was to keep the bad guys' heads down. Above, *Pedro 1* and *2* were on spin cycle over the village, weapons hot and waiting.

Jamie lit out from behind cover, nimble across the uneven earth. Quincy lumbered behind him. Wally and Doc stayed close at his broad back. LB brought up the rear.

Two hundred meters north, on the cusp of the field, puffs of dust and busted rock perked under the commandos' bullets. Jamie led the team into the open, all scampering in a bent-over bunch. LB's back smarted; he growled to keep himself going.

After fifty grueling meters, a spray of bullets whistled above their heads. The team dove to the dirt as another volley missed, ripping by no closer than the first but near enough for Wally to yell for Jamie and Doc to find cover. The two pushed off the ground; Wally, Quincy, and LB stayed on their stomachs to fire at the rusted hulk of a tractor, where Quincy had spotted two figures duck out of sight.

Doc called out.

"Twenty more meters. Found a ditch."

Ahead, Doc and Jamie opened up to suppress the tractor. Wally leaped first to his boots.

"Moving."

The three dashed headlong to tumble into a narrow culvert, an old irrigation ditch. LB hunkered low to rest his barking back. He went for his canteen. After he'd taken a swig, he joined the team with rifles up to secure their position.

One of the HH-60s hammered past, then the other chopper, low and menacing. Under the din of rotors and the commandos' guns, Wally hailed the Brits.

"Bengal, Hallmark. Hold fire. Repeat, hold fire."

The Brits' weapons went silent. Their reports soared off to the surrounding red mountains.

In the trench, all five caught their breath. The wheat field, weeds, and wrecks lay dormant on their long shadows in the windless heat. The mulberry trees did not rustle. The enemy stayed hidden. A faraway goat grazed. The pair of helos circled, waiting for Wally's beckon. LB raised his goggles to swipe a finger across his dust-caked forehead.

Wally lifted a gloved hand for silence. In seconds, he got what he was listening for.

"Over here."

The wounded commando sounded closer. His weakened voice gathered Jamie's legs under him in the culvert. The young PJ coiled, a Labrador for rescues. Quincy held him back.

Wally asked who had a smoke canister. LB groused while Doc, Jamie, and Quincy raised fingers. Wally held up two digits.

Wally tapped Quincy, then got on the radio.

"*Pedro 1*, Hallmark. Call for fire."

"Hallmark, send it."

"*Pedro 1*. My position marked by purple smoke."

Quincy tossed his canister to the team's left, in the direction of the downed marine. After a five count, the grenade burst into a billowing, wine-dark cloud.

"Target northwest my position, burnt out tractor, hadjis in the open."

"Copy, Juggler. Visual you. Tally target."

In the air a half-mile away, the trailing HH-60 sideslipped to rush its big guns to the target. *Pedro 2* maintained distance.

"Bengal, Hallmark."

"Hallmark, go."

"Direct fire on the tractor to my northwest. On my mark. Copy?"

"Hallmark, I copy. On your mark."

Wally let *Pedro 1* close in.

"Mark."

The commandos' rifles opened up on the wreckage, tattooing metal against metal. At the same time, the chopper's big 7.62 targeted the wreck and the surrounding earth. West of the PJs, velvet purls of smoke fattened along the ground with little breeze to thin them.

Quincy thumped Jamie on the shoulder. The young PJ tore out of the trench, into the haze. The rest followed, darting blind through the oily smoke.

The instant the PJs burst into the clear, a blast of automatic fire stitched the earth ten meters shy of their boots. LB's instinct was to throw himself to the ground, but Jamie, on the scent, did not slow. The team galloped on Jamie's shadow another twenty meters. The young PJ ran behind his raised weapon, straight to the downed marine.

The commando lay in a scoop in the earth. He greeted the diving PJs with a grunt, one hand clamped over his right hip, the other clutching his rifle. The instant the PJs spilled around him, the marine released his clench on himself, his head and gun wilted, relief plain in his collapse.

Quickly, the team arrayed along the lip of the depression, weapons turned in four directions, while Jamie assessed the wound. The gouge in the Afghan earth where they crouched didn't look natural: probably a Russian crater from a quarter century ago, the last time someone else tried to tame this country. LB eyed a rusted-out pickup truck eighty meters west, abandoned in a mulberry grove.

While Jamie sliced away the marine's camo pants to expose the wound, the Brit tugged at LB's boot. He rasped.

"Hadjis. That way."

LB gripped the shaking hand. He squeezed to give the downed boy strength, and to reinforce his own.

LB turned Wally to the west.

"I think we got hadjis in that old truck."

Wally jumped on the radio to *Pedro 2*. Doc and Jamie worked out how to exfil the marine. Doc reached for one of the rolled-up Skedcos they'd lugged along to tow the commando off the field to the CCP[4].

Quincy rattled his head.

"That'll take too long. We still got two more to go. Just shoot him up."

Doc wasted no time. He nailed the marine in the thigh with 15 ml of ketamine while LB probed the exposed wound alongside Jamie. A slug had drilled a hole in the commando's hip, probably shattering bone. The kid was in a lot of pain. LB brought his face close to the commando's.

"What's your name, marine?"

"Elroy."

"Elroy, you're good. I've seen worse."

LB said this without actually considering what else he'd seen. He was trained, and in turn trained other PJs, to blinker himself to the task at hand. He had no focus or memory for anything beyond this mission, the men on this battlefield. LB didn't think

---

4 casualty collection point.

about getting shot himself, only that he hadn't been yet. He didn't mull over what might happen, only what was happening. Long experience had taught him that fear lay in the next moment, not in this one.

He asked Elroy where his wounded buddies were. The marine wiped his lips with trembling fingertips. His breathing stuttered.

"Forty meters northeast. They were walking ahead of me into the village. Brooks stepped on an IED."

"How bad?"

"He got a foot blown off. Hallett got hit running to him, but he's okay. He dragged Brooks into the ditch by the road to wait for you lot."

"Okay, good job. You relax. We got you."

Elroy winced, done talking. Overhead, the drone of *Pedro 2* swelled as the chopper bounded to Wally's call. Two hundred meters out, on Wally's mark, the Pave Hawk unleashed its starboard gun on the grove left of the PJs' position. Instantly the trees splintered into chips. The jalopy pickup rocked on its bare rims under the onslaught of the six-barreled machine gun. While the grove screeched, Quincy stood to his full height. He shouted down to the commando.

"Pal, this is gonna suck. You up for it?"

The marine raised a middle finger with the dregs of his strength.

Quincy dug behind the commando's backpack for the handle on his rear body armor. Like a bear, he hauled the wounded Brit backward, over the lip of the crater. Quincy took off in a powerful jog, dragging the ketamine-limp commando behind him.

LB lost sight of them in the last of the purple smoke.

Along with Bengal's squad, *Pedro 1* continued to blast at the tractor, pelting the ground with a cataract of tinkling casings.

Now that Quincy was away, Wally called *Pedro 2* off the pickup truck and mulberry grove. The chopper climbed to resume circling.

A haze of dust and gun smoke drifted across the open ground while the PJs waited for Quincy in their headsets. Wally let *Pedro 1* and Bengal's boys keep peppering the tractor.

The team freq crackled.

"Juggler, Yogi. We made it to the CCP."

"Yogi, Juggler. Good job."

Wally switched to the ground-air freq.

"Bengal, cease fire."

"Hallmark, copy."

The commandos' guns stilled. Wally called off *Pedro 1*, routing the bird to the CCP to pick up Quincy and the commando.

In the stunned aftermath of the barrage, only creaks came from the pummeled pickup and mulberry grove. The tractor showed the hammer blows of a few hundred rounds, oozing black fluid into the dirt. Behind the wheat field, the mud village had not entered the fight. Her camels and goats stayed on their feet.

LB scooted around the rim of the crater to squat beside Doc, Jamie, and Wally. The four squared off at the road, fifty meters north.

The downed marines were hard to pick out of the landscape, lying in the shade of a mulberry, flat in the ditch beside the lane.

LB cupped his hands to his mouth.

"Hallett."

"Here."

"Sergeant DiNardo, 46th ERS, US Air Force. How you holding up?"

"Been better, Sergeant. Both of us."

"Hang on."

Wally shook his head.

"You think they're bait?"

"Dunno." LB spit grit off his teeth. "I can think of only one shitty way to find out."

Hallett called again.

"We could use a ride out of here."

Wally reached for his canteen. He swigged, using the time to compose his orders.

"All right. Two teams. LB and Jamie first. Get up there and mark. I'll call in CAS[5], then Doc and I will move up. We'll go from there."

"Roger."

Wally cupped his hands.

"Hallett."

"Yeah."

"Can you lay down cover fire?"

"No one's dead up here, mate. Say when."

Wally indicated LB's web vest. "Where are your smoke canisters?"

"I already used them this morning."

"No you didn't. You forgot them."

"You want to lecture me right now? Seriously?"

Wally tugged two smoke canisters off his own vest.

"Later."

LB stowed the pair of grenades. Jamie squatted beside him on the rim of the crater. Hip to hip, the two waited for Wally's signal.

A hundred yards east, behind the stone wall and Bengal's guns, *Pedro 1* touched down. The bird drew no enemy fire and in under a minute was airborne again with Quincy and his commando aboard.

Wally worked his radios, coordinating both choppers. Until LB and Jamie reached the two marines and marked their position, neither Pave Hawk could come into play, nor could Bengal, with no visual on Hallett and Brooks. LB and Jamie would have to make the dash covered only by Doc, Wally, and the two wounded Brits.

---

5 close air support.

A mile downrange, both choppers thrummed through a flawless sky. Unseen dead lay in the busted mulberry grove and riddled tractor. LB surveyed the ugly ground between him and the road. Were there more buried IEDs? Where were the rest of the villagers hiding? In the wheat field, in more craters? Had they gotten their fill of the two Pave Hawks and gone home? Or did they have a bead on the ditch, and were waiting for someone to come get Hallett and Brooks?

"Ready?"

Wally patted Jamie on the backpack. The young PJ tucked the stock of his M4 to his ribs, rose slightly out of his crouch, and took off. In turn, Doc rapped LB on the back for luck. On Jamie's six, LB burst out of the hole.

Behind them, Wally and Doc fired blind bursts across the road, into the wheat field. The two wounded marines tore into the stalks at closer range. The bullet-mown wheat wavered as if men were moving inside it. Jogging hard, LB kept his finger on the trigger, eyes flicking to the ground for trip wires.

Halfway to the road, no resistance came from the field or surrounding ground. Jamie put on a burst of speed, rising out of his crouch to cover the last twenty-five yards.

LB shouted for him to stay down, but too late.

Bullets zinged around them. LB buckled to slide on his stomach and bring his M4 to bear. Jamie kept to his feet, bolting fast and straight for the two marines over ground that buzzed and popped around his boots. LB unloaded a long volley into the standing stalks until Jamie skidded into the ditch.

The bullets out of the wheat stopped. LB had picked out the cheap rattle of only one Kalashnikov. Some bad guy did stay back; the marines in the ditch were lures.

Jamie and the commandos laid down a blanket of cover fire, Wally and Doc, too. LB bounded off the ground. He ran like a bull, head lowered as if to ram through the danger. The hadji inside the stalks tried for him. Several rounds whizzed past and one skipped off the ground to slice through the leather and laces of his right boot. LB plummeted the last twenty yards, again growling to himself, pushing until he slid into the ditch with rifles going off all around him, still not hit except for the loose boot.

Jamie had flattened beside the marines, shooting with them into the wheat. LB snatched the pin out of one of Wally's smoke canisters, then heaved the grenade across the road to the bare expanse on the rim of the field.

Still in the air, the grenade pulsed its first coils of smoke. In the instant before the canister landed, a last shot zipped out of the field. The canister rolled to a standstill, spewing a barrier of smoke; on the other side the wheat fell silent again. Jamie stopped firing. The commandos quit, too; fifty yards back Doc and Wally quieted. A stillness spread over the battlefield with the welling smoke, the only sound the onrushing beats of *Pedro 1* and *2*.

LB knelt behind the two commandos and Jamie, training his M4 into the smoke. Brooks lay in the middle. The bottoms of five boots faced LB, who shook his head at the English boy's ragged pants leg and, extending from it, the pink and white of meat and bone.

Both Brits had eased their rifles. Hallett's chin lay in the dirt. Jamie moved to tend to the footless Brooks, but the young commando pushed him away. He rolled his buddy over.

Hallett flopped onto his back, lifeless. Crimson painted the marine's lips. His jaw hung loose, a dark puncture glistened in the flesh of his cheek. Below his chin, more blood seeped from a ragged exit wound left of the Adam's apple. That last hadji bullet out of the wheat field had found him.

Brooks scrabbled on his one foot to wriggle closer to his buddy. He called Hallett as if he might wake him. Brooks reached without knowing what to do, then pulled back. Madly, he whirled on Jamie, who treated him roughly, yanking the commando backward and out of the way. Swiftly, Jamie tugged down Hallett's ruined jaw to peer into his bloodied mouth.

"Tongue's been hit."

Hallett had one minute to breathe on his own. His tongue was going to swell and block the airway. LB kept back, staying sharp on his rifle to defend their position, while Jamie furiously doffed his med ruck.

LB hailed Wally. "Juggler, Lima Bravo."

"Go, LB."

"Position is marked. Get up here now, we got a tango one. Then call in CAS."

"Moving."

On his back, the unconscious Hallett coughed a red spray out of the hole in his neck. In addition to his expanding tongue, his fight for breath was worsened by blood draining into the trachea and probably bits of jawbone or teeth blocking the airway. Hallett began to thrash, choking.

LB came off his knees.

"Brooks, you good?"

The kid seemed startled. He'd lost a lot of blood and was likely in the early stages of shock. He glanced down quickly at his truncated leg, chewing his lower lip, in grief and pain, wanting to say no.

"Yeah, yeah."

"Okay. Put your gun on the smoke. Shoot anything that moves."

The commando, pale as the blanched earth, scrambled back to his rifle. He took it up, breathing fast through puffing cheeks. Young Brooks had lost a foot, a tourniquet squeezed his calf, and his buddy was hemorrhaging beside him, but he put his hands on his weapon to do the job. LB was impressed, but there'd be time later to tell him that. What he had to do now was get Brooks out of this ditch and into a chopper, to a prosthetic foot and a long life back in the UK of having been a hero in a faraway land.

Hallett blew more blood, drowning. LB pressed him down by the shoulders. He found the marine's other bullet wound, a rip in the tunic and a furrow through the meat of his left biceps.

LB checked his own boot. The leather was grooved and the laces snipped, but the round had missed his sock. His skin prickled from another adrenaline rush.

Jamie tore into his med ruck with practiced hands. The pack was organized like every PJ's, segmented into MARCH compartments: Massive hemorrhage, Airway, Respiration, Circulation, and Head/Hypothermia. From the A pocket, Jamie snatched a sealed cricothyrotomy kit and tossed it to LB. From R, he tugged a breathing bag, then from the surgical kit a scalpel and swabs. Jamie set the ruck aside to take over pinning Hallett down. The unconscious marine gurgled, spitting up blood again.

Wally and Doc sprinted forward, jostling under their loads. Behind the smoke, they drew no fire. Wally arrived first, collapsing to a prone position next to LB. Doc dropped beside Brooks and talked to the marine softly.

Behind the M4, Wally turned his sunglasses on the wheat. He was one of the best rifle shots LB had ever seen. If a head poked up in the field and Wally saw it, he could hit it.

"What've you got?"

"One hadji in the wheat. No visual. This kid needs evac fast. Bring a chopper in tight."

Keeping one hand on his weapon, Wally got on the ground-to-air channel. While Jamie restrained Hallett in the ditch and LB tore into the crike kit, the battlefield renewed itself. High over the village, the pair of Pave Hawks banked in formation, speeding toward them, louder by the moment. A hundred yards off, Bengal and his team traded more rounds with unseen Afghans. The diehard in the wheat field wouldn't quit; he and Doc and Brooks swapped potshots through the smoke screen. Wally instructed *Pedro 1* to set down close to the ditch. He warned the pilot twice that the LZ was very hot.

Jamie tossed a second smoke canister to buy them another shrouded minute. LB swabbed as much dirt, blood, and sweat as he could from the young commando's throat. He needed to work fast; Hallett hadn't drawn a full breath since the bullet, and his wounded tongue was filling his mouth. Because the kid was lights-out, LB didn't sedate him. He'd do that last. Jamie would inject him with the paralytic in the chopper.

"Got him?"

Jamie put all his weight on Hallett's shoulders.

"Do it."

LB nested his thumb in the sternal notch at the base of Hallett's throat. He pressed up to feel for the small ligament between the cricoid and thyroid cartilages, below the Adam's apple, beside the weeping exit wound. Finding the ligament, he laid the scalpel to the spot. The workings of Hallett's throat gulped under the blade as the kid's body groped for air. LB clamped his left hand under Hallett's chin like a strangler, locking him in place to push the scalpel into the skin. Blood broke on both sides of the blade, but LB worked on feel, sensing the cartilage under the edge. He gave the scalpel pressure, slicing through the membrane, then drew it downward, cutting an inch-long vertical fissure. Instantly a moist suck wheezed into the slice, straight into Hallett's windpipe.

LB twisted the scalpel sideways to widen the flaps, then pushed his left pinky in to landmark the cut. Around his little finger, Hallett's trachea panted in warm gasps. With his free hand LB shook out the plastic tube. He threaded the plastic into the cut, past the membrane, directly into the trachea, then far enough down to reach the tracheal branch between the lungs. He inflated the cuff at the bottom to secure the tube in the airway.

Then Doc got hit.

It was a lucky shot through the barrier of smoke. Doc cursed, seizing in the ditch like he'd been scalded. He slapped a hand over his right butt cheek and pulled back ruby fingers. Doc got control of himself fast and put his hands back on his weapon.

Wally barked past Jamie.

"You all right?"

Doc clenched his teeth, stung and badly teed off. He returned fire through the haze.

"Just a graze. But son of a bitch."

No hands were free to check Doc out. He was on his own until the chopper touched down.

Overhead the two HH-60s winged closer. *Pedro 2* slipped into firing position over the wheat field. The other Pave Hawk circled behind the ditch, dropping altitude to line up an LZ on the open ground. Wally worked the frequencies between both helos and Bengal.

With blood-tacky hands, LB snapped the ventilator bag onto the end of the crike tube. Three times he filled Hallett's lungs; the kid did a good job exhaling on his own. When white mist clouded the inside of the tube, LB judged the seal was tight, the tube in the right place. After a quick stethoscope check to hear both lungs working, he bobbed his head at Wally.

"Let's roll."

Wally cleared *Pedro 1* to land and *Pedro 2* to fire.

Pedro 2 surged forward to scythe the field. The HH-60's starboard minigun lit up, mowing the stalks around the sniper, showering him with shards, chaff, grain, and 7.62 rounds.

Jamie unrolled the Skedco while LB taped the crike tube in place. LB gave Hallett an IM shot of ketamine to keep him knocked out for the rest of the evac. With Jamie, he lifted the commando onto the sled and strapped him in place as *Pedro 1* put wheels down, blowing away the purple smoke. *Pedro 2*, banking tight in a vulturelike circle, didn't let up pounding the field.

Wally leaped across the ditch to Brooks. He lifted the kid by an arm, lapping it across his shoulders. Below the tourniquet, Brooks's pants leg hung empty, ragged, and wrong. The young commando's remaining boot gave way. He was dizzy from blood loss. Wally propped him up, but the kid's good leg firmed under him. Wally pulled him away.

"Doc. Chop chop. Let's move."

Doc grimaced, trying to roll over in the ditch. The strain on his face and a stream of cussing said that he was in pain, stuck on his belly. Standing now, with *Pedro 2* clipping the wheat field and Bengal's squad exchanging volleys with ducking targets, LB got a good look at the bullet hole in Doc's ass. He quashed a string of remarks to use later, when guns weren't going off.

"Sit tight."

"Who's sitting?"

Jamie peeled off his camo tunic. He tucked it over Hallett's face to protect the hole in the marine's throat from the whipping dust under *Pedro 1*'s blades. Jamie grabbed the handle at the head of the skid; LB took the rear grip.

Wally and Brooks hobbled to the helo's open door. Jamie and LB trucked fast behind them. As they entered the gushing wind of the chopper, the noises of the battlefield disappeared. Wally guided his commando to the open door, where Quincy hauled him in. He helped Wally and Jamie heft Hallett into the chopper, then Jamie jumped in behind the sled to join Quincy and the three wounded.

Wally spun on LB. He mouthed the question.

Where's Doc?

LB pointed at his own butt.

Wally banged on the side of the chopper. He tossed a thumbs-up to the pilot, who'd turned in his seat to watch his helo loaded. Quincy slid the door shut. The pilot wasted no time, lifting off the moment LB and Wally cleared the blades and doubled back for Doc.

Pedro 2 continued to rake the field. Acres of wheat bordering the road had been barbered down to yellow stubble. The low sun winked on thousands of spent casings lying in the debris and on the road. In the late afternoon, between the red mountains, the land was golden.

Wally got on the ground-to-air. He called *Pedro 2* to swing around for a pickup.

The minigun quit as the bird pulled away from the field. Nearby, *Pedro 1* climbed to take over guard duty.

When Wally and LB reached the ditch, Doc still hadn't moved off his stomach. They dug under his armpits to put him on his feet. Doc howled as they set him in motion. He would put no weight on his wounded right side.

LB lacked sympathy. "It's just an ass wound."

Doc, arms spread over both sets of shoulders, smacked LB in the back of his helmet.

"Ever been shot in the ass?"

"Yes."

"It fucking hurts."

"Quit whining about it."

Wally yelled across Doc.

"Lighten up."

Pedro 2 descended rapidly into the bowl of dust she reared. With Doc hanging between them, Wally and LB pulled up short to let the chopper swoop down.

LB had to shout.

"You ever been ass shot?"

Wally shook his head.

"Then what do you know?"

"I know now's not the time."

Doc squeezed both their necks. "Both of you, shut up."

When the chopper's wheels touched, the door was flung aside. LB and Wally urged Doc toward the dust storm under the rotors.

Sparks flashed off the Pave Hawk's fuselage.

In the window, the chopper's gunner swept the 7.62 side to side, searching for a target. Then, like everyone on this mission, he strafed the wheat field blindly, and the road, the mulberries. Another flurry of incoming bullets bit the dirt around LB's loose boot. Again, the locals had lain in ambush, this time for a rescue helo. Why wouldn't they just take the rest of the day off? LB didn't know, didn't care. He'd done three missions today, the sun was setting, and he wanted to get on this bird. He tugged Doc forward to cover the last distance to the chopper's open door.

Wally dug in his heels, screaming. "Get down."

Wally collapsed, pulling the helpless Doc down with him. LB tried to tug Doc back to his feet and press onward; their ride out of here waited twenty yards farther. Another spark off the spinning rotors left LB no choice; he dove to the dirt beside Doc, who'd landed on his backside and was bellowing loud enough to be heard over the gales from the chopper and the minigun.

On all sides, the battlefield erupted. Overhead, *Pedro 1* coursed past, taking its turn battering the wheat. Behind their wall, Bengal's commandos popped off at shadows that returned fire. *Pedro 2*'s spinning six barrels flailed at every hiding place, the field, orchard, roadside ditch, the already-riddled wreckage in open ground. In the distance, one of the innocent, tied-up goats was felled.

Pedro 2, a big target, wasn't going to sit on the ground long and tolerate being shot at. Plenty of cover fire was going on. LB wanted to move, now. He scrabbled to his knees, grabbing for one of Doc's wrists.

"Come on, get up."

Wally shook his head and wrapped Doc in both arms, pushing him over to lie on his back. Doc, in too much pain to resist, flattened. Wally hurled himself across Doc's chest to shield him.

LB belted at the two of them. "You're kidding me."

Pressed under Wally's weight, Doc howled. "Get off me, get off, goddammit."

LB hauled on Doc's arm. "Then get up."

Wally held Doc to the ground. "Stay down."

Doc batted at Wally. "Get off."

LB tugged on Doc's arm. "Get up."

Wally kicked at LB. "Get down!"

Today

Chapter 1

The Empty Quarter
Six miles east of Ma'rib
Yemen

Arif stood on the crest of a high dune lit orange by the horizon behind him.

The desert was not empty. Like the sea it was vast, with waves that rolled at the pace of years. Yet standing alone, facing the endless ribs of it, Arif's sense was of emptiness. The great desert was not for the eye or ears but for the heart. If a man himself was empty, this was not the place for him. The desert kept a still tongue, and when it did speak it came for your life. But if a man was full, if a man had found his own voice, the desert was the most intent of listeners.

At the end of his evening walk, approaching the time for prayer, Arif turned northwest to his lost homeland and to Mecca inside it. The setting January sun pressed his cheeks like warm, open hands. One mile away, the distance Arif had walked, the light cast his pickup truck into silhouette. Six miles farther, the shanties, old city, minarets, and fading homes of Ma'rib gleamed amber against the perfect sky. Ma'rib bore the history of a prince fallen to beggar. Once the land of Sheba, a crossroads in the Ramlat al-Sab'atayn desert between the Orient and Mediterranean, she'd been the site of a marvel of the ancient world, the huge dam to fill the Wadi Adhana. For two thousand years a man-made lake fed fields of sorghum, wheat, frankincense, and myrrh. Along with the plants, prosperity and influence took root in Ma'rib. She became a center of knowledge and riches, lasting for millennia. Then, as they will, the riches overtook knowledge, and the people lost the ways to keep their wealth flowing. In the year of the Prophet's birth, the dam was overtopped, and Ma'rib found she'd forgotten the skills to repair it. While Muhammad grew into a man in Mecca, the desert reclaimed what had been kept from its reach in Ma'rib. Many fled; the city withered with the roots. Most of those who left were foreigners, the non-Arab merchants and tradesmen who'd flocked here for business. Their exodus began with the Prophet's birth.

Closing his eyes to begin the sundown prayer, Arif was grateful for Ma'rib's fall into poverty. He was not Yemeni but Saudi; this was not his people's tragedy. Ma'rib was no longer a jewel of temples and silk but a small mark on a worn map, beneath notice, a place for him to hide.

"I offer *Maghrib* prayers, seeking nearness to God, in obedience to Him."

Arif raised his open hands beside his ears.

"*Allah hu akbar.*"

He uttered the first *rakaat* to the blazing horizon and the sun dousing itself behind Mecca six hundred miles away. Arif spoke into the sand as he bent from the waist. He whispered through his beard, into the dune, with his forehead touching.

Arif flowed through all three rakaats, bending, bowing.

From his knees he muttered the final Salaam. He spoke this not to faraway Mecca but to the outline of his little village on the eastern rim of the city, bathed in sunset. There Nadya would be rising from her own Maghrib.

Arif got to his bare feet, peckish and thinking of the evening meal. He wondered what Nadya would prepare. A Yemeni *ogdat* stew, a chicken, or lamb shank she'd picked up on the drive home from her women's clinic? Milk tea and a sweet afterward. Before taking the downward slope of the dune, he reached into a pocket of his white *thobe*. It was an oddity of Ma'rib that some of the best cell phone reception could be found a mile east in the desert.

He flipped the phone open. As he had done almost hourly for the past week, Arif checked his email.

He caught his balance on the edge of the dune and rocked. The message had come. One wait had ended; another would begin. He slammed the phone shut. Arif hoisted the long hem of his thobe, not to trip over it as he ran.

· · ·

He skidded the pickup to a stop, flinging gravel inside the mud walls of his little courtyard. Arif slammed the truck door, rushing to the back of his earthen-brick house, shouting for his wife.

He lifted the lid on the generator box to fill the tank with diesel so that he would not be interrupted if the power went down, as it often did. Nadya emerged from the rear door. Stepping outside, she lifted a silk scarf over her head.

"You're driving like you're in the movies now?"

Arif tilted the diesel can higher to pour the last of the fuel.

"I can still move fast."

"You drive fast, that's all. Was there news?"

Needing both hands, Arif waited until he set the can down empty. He closed the generator box, then produced the opened cell phone.

She ran a fingertip across the face of the phone, the email notice.

"Allah hu akbar." She shifted her hand to his big chest and patted. "Patience."

The Prophet said the world rests on an ox and a fish. The ox meant farming, the fish hunting. A farmer sows seed and waits. The hunter leaps when the prey leaps.

Arif stood on Yemeni ground, not his birthplace. He'd been the ox for two years now.

"I've already been patient. Will you bring me dinner?"

"Eat with me properly. I won't see much of you for a while."

Inside, Arif washed his hands in the kitchen, praying silently. A candle flavored the air cedar. Was this a romantic touch, or a celebration? He joined her in the alcove, where she waited on the carpet. A heaping plate of *kapsa* steamed between her folded knees; beside it, a wheel of freshly baked *kimaje*. Through the windows, the last daylight smoothed the crinkles around her coal eyes, softened the grey in her long black hair. Arif did not need these concessions of the dusk to find her lovely.

She poured milk tea while Arif descended to the carpet and pillows. Nadya held out the full cup. "What will you find?"

"I don't know."

"Whatever it is, I understand."

Arif sipped, watching Nadya. She blinked at welling tears, drawing the flickers of the candle into her eyes.

"You are a warrior, my wife."

Together they said their *du'a* before eating.

Because she had cried, Arif did not fidget during the meal to hurry away to the tug of his computer. He tore the kimaje, using the flatbread in his right hand to scoop up chunks of chicken and rice. Hints of cinnamon and cardamom on his tongue played with the piney aroma of the candle and the rising youth of his wife in the settling light. Arif let himself be fully in the alcove with her because she was correct; she would not see much of him once he left the meal.

He let the conversation drift from the hot weather and his afternoon walk on the dunes to her day in her women's clinic. A pregnant *qabil*[6] girl had come in malnourished. A village matron with chlamydia. An elder who found a lump in her breast paid for her exam with the chicken in tonight's kapsa. More than a

---

6 tribal.

physician, Nadya counseled the village's newest bride-to-be on the secrets and surprises of the wedding bed.

She cleared the plates, then set between them a bowl of honeyed figs. Easing down to her pillows, Nadya mentioned that a woman came to the clinic today to schedule the abortion of another man's child. Under the *hadiths* that the woman lived by, the abortion was allowed within the first four months. But the adultery was perilous, and she begged Nadya to keep her secret. Nadya hid from Arif the woman's name, but because she'd mentioned her while setting down the figs, he assumed she was the young wife of a village fig farmer he knew to be a bully.

With the last fig, the meal ended. Hands steepled, they said together, "*Alhamdulillah.*" Allah be praised.

Arif rose to boil another pot of tea. He fetched his wife's cigarettes and kneeled in the alcove to light her first smoke. He stayed close beside Nadya while the teapot heated.

She reclined against a pillow, the shade of night drawn outside. On the eastern edge of the village, the homes were sparse, only dogs made noise after dark, and lanterns and fire pits cast as much light as electricity. The desert beyond the road spawned a mute rising moon. Nadya blew a patch of smoke against a windowpane, facing away from him, perhaps crying again. Arif pushed the hair off her neck to run his thumb up the tendon there. Her skin was slick. She'd bathed and oiled before the meal, expecting a different evening. Arif leaned into the mist of her cigarette to sniff her perfumed throat. He kissed the tendon, nuzzled her neck with his beard, and cupped her breast as the teapot whistled.

She did not turn from the window but pinched the cigarette at her fingertips, smoking like a starlet. Nadya took a somber drag. So she was crying again.

"The tea, Arif."

He let loose her bosom.

He shut off the burner on the stove and set the teapot on a trivet beside her.

"I'll go."

Nadya blew out the candle.

"I don't want to know what you find."

She tapped another cigarette from the pack. Arif left her in the alcove surrounded by haze and moonlight.

• • •

In his dim second-floor office, Arif turned the power on to boot up his computer. He tossed the white thobe over the back of his chair and pulled on a black T-shirt and khaki shorts. After flicking on the window fan, he bound his hair into a ponytail. In the chair, Arif slid his hands under the spotlight of the lamp bent low above his keyboard. With a pause to mark the clutch in his chest, he logged in to his offsite command and control server in Al Hulaylah, United Arab Emirates. With the link established, Arif opened the message from Jaffar bint-Ahmed al-Saffar.

The email had as its subject "High-Paying Network Engineering Jobs." Two days ago, Arif found a list of Saudi ISP network engineers who'd attended the International Conference on Network Security in Dubai the previous week. To those two hundred names, Arif sent an email with an attachment touting the benefits a few lucky job seekers could expect with an exciting start-up Internet company in Sana'a, Yemen. Among the Saudi technicians, Arif went phishing for the one who was not just underpaid and malcontent but careless.

This evening, while Arif prayed in the dunes, Jaffar bint-Ahmed al-Saffar opened the email, then the attachment, and let Arif in.

The malicious software had leaped into Jaffar's computer, boring deep into the privileged kernel ring while Jaffar read an apology email that all the engineering positions at the new company had been filled. With the malware in place, the payload wrapped itself next around Jaffar's keyboard driver, capturing all his keystrokes, including passwords and user IDs. A separate thread in the rootkit checked to see if Jaffar was running any network monitoring tools and, finding none, established a covert secure socket connection between Arif's server in the Emirates and Jaffar's office computer at Saudi Telcom, a private Internet service provider in Riyadh. From that moment, Arif could monitor everything Jaffar's computer did, peruse anything it contained.

Jaffar had sent a politely disappointed reply, asking to be kept informed of any further openings with the start-up in Yemen. He sent along his résumé.

Arif had left his wrists hovering above the keyboard near the hot lamp. He pulled his hands out of the light to rub them and accept the gravity of this moment.

"*Masha'allah.*" God's will.

With a keystroke, he linked to his command and control server via the Onion router that would randomize and mask his connection. He selected the tunneled link to Jaffar's computer.

Arif spent only moments on the first glimpses of Jaffar's computer. He familiarized himself quickly with the trivialities of how the technician managed folders and files, then moved past them. Arif dove straight for the network shares on the file servers available to all Saudi Telcom software engineers. He selected three gigabytes of files, all email messages, for upload to the c&c server, then downloaded the files to his own computer's hard drive. Before logging off, Arif covered his tracks by deleting the source files and event logs.

He converted the files into flat text to load them into an indexed database in order to make them searchable. Lastly, Arif initiated a Boolean search for records and email addresses from all members of the House of Saud—over two thousand in the royal family—sent to Prince Hassan bin Abd al-Aziz, the head of the Saudi General Intelligence Presidency. The quest exploded into an uncountable number of hits, arranging themselves into subject lists, ordered by date. While the search worked, Arif walked onto the balcony of his office.

He lit a cigarette from a pack left on the lawn chair. He should go lie with Nadya under their quiet roof. Loving her, marrying her, bringing her here, these were all acts of defiance. One more would be to go to her.

He gave himself until the end of the cigarette to make up his mind, but when it was done he remained on the balcony. The half-moon rose above the desert as if floating on the heat. An old man in a white bamboo *kofia* strolled past on the road, humming, unaware he was being watched. Arif would make his choice once the man's song faded.

The passing stranger moved in the gray light like a ghost of Arif's old father, who used to hum to himself. He would not see his father's simple grave again so long as he remained in exile. The tune disappeared with the hat into the village.

From the balcony, the milky desert lay smooth like skin. This was no *jinn* or mere metaphor, but a pull to Nadya's side.

Arif spun on his bare heels to return to his computer. Let it begin. How else to make it end?

• • •

He jerked awake in the chair, head on his arms around the keyboard, his ear warmed by the lamp. The sunrise *adhan*, called from the minaret deeper in the village, put him on his feet. Arif shuffled to the balcony, joints creaky from his awkward, short sleep.

Half-awake, he completed the *fajr* prayer on his knees, then stood to light a cigarette. Dawn lay prettily on the sorghum fields between his home and the desert. Irrigation pipes began to soak the soil; by the rosy light and spraying waters, his morning view was cool and placid. The village awoke with Arif. Horse carts bore goods to the market square. Women in flowing *abaya*s walked in groups to fetch the day's groceries; some wore pointed straw hats to keep their heads cool working in the fields or herding goats in the palm groves. Below Arif smoking on the balcony, Nadya left the house in the pickup without looking up.

In his office, Arif clicked off the lamp to study his computer screen by sunlight. During the long winter night, he'd scanned more than a thousand records, recent emails to and from the royals, with transparent usernames and passwords. Most of the messages were commonplace: meetings, chitchat, and official emails. Arif saw the sameness of concerns: Saudi men carping over money and women, women remarking on fashions and parties, officials mewling over schedules and petty slights. Some messages carried darker content: wild nights in Abu Dhabi, trysts in Qatar, drunken car crashes by royal sons, clannish dealings among brothers to fox outsiders.

Through the evening hours and height of the half-moon, Arif read of the hypocrisies and excesses of the royals, a river of debris from the House of Saud drifting by. He could pluck out one or two of the nastier stories, flog them about the Internet, but that would accomplish little. The profaneness of the royal family was well known, poorly plastered over. Arif had no intention of setting off a minor scandal, one more crack in the Saudi monarchy. That was all he'd been able to do in the two years since he'd come to Yemen, small things.

He settled into the chair, wondering if Nadya had made him coffee before heading to her clinic. He'd go downstairs in a minute, after reading a fresh email isolated by the text search engine that snagged his eye.

The sender was Mohammed al-Bakr Sudayri, a royal second cousin. The search engine identified this email as the first in a queue of messages sent back and forth, beginning yesterday at 3:10 p.m., between Sudayri and Abd al-Aziz.

The subject read *Fatima*. The message ran only two lines:

After you left, Fatima handed me her number and asked me to give it to you. Do you want it? She seems classy and discreet.

Arif instructed the search engine to put in order, by date, all emails between Sudayri and Abd al-Aziz in the past month. This done, he pushed away from the desk.

Downstairs in the kitchen, Nadya had left coffee warming, and bowls of olives, soft cheese, honey, jam, a round *chipotti*, and a bar of *helwa* for a sweet. Arif dunked the chipotti in his coffee and ate alone in the brightening alcove. He stared at Nadya's pillows, glad she was not home. She knew to leave early today, to let him come downstairs to an empty house for his breakfast. She'd told him she didn't want to know, but like any wife and daughter, she would have tried to read his face or hands for what he was finding out about her father.

Chapter 2

Major Torres looked good.

Hands on hips in the middle of the Barn, feet spread, she looked like an ad for women in the air force. Surrounded by walk-in lockers stuffed with hi-tech gear for skydiving, SCUBA, mountaineering, combat communications, motorcycles, wave runners all kitted up to be pushed out of airplanes, and racks of weapons, Torres dabbed a bead of sweat off her brow from the Horn of Africa sun. LB changed his mind; this was an ad for men in the air force.

Wally rose from a worn leather recliner. The rest of the team stayed seated. In OD T-shirts, boots, and camo pants, the PJs took an informal attitude toward rank inside the Barn.

Wally approached the major briskly. They shook hands to continue the fiction that they didn't know each other well. Torres curled a finger at LB.

"Master Sergeant DiNardo."

She repeated the gesture at Jamie.

"Staff Sergeant Dempsey. Join us."

LB and Jamie got to their feet. Like Wally, the two of them perpetuated a lie, that they weren't sore, recently wounded. Seated next to Jamie, Mouse pushed on the young PJ's rump to help him lift off the sofa; Jamie swatted the hand away. Doc muttered at LB's back, "Uh-oh, Mom's pissed." The new CRO, Berkowitz, a Manhattan kid, watched expectantly. He'd been in HOA[7] a week and hadn't gotten down the rhythms of the team yet. Berko, muscular, with an early receding hairline, stood for the major. Passing close, LB whispered for the young officer to sit back down.

Wally led the way to the briefing room. Torres stayed at the front, leaning on the table while the three took seats on the tiers. Wally eased into a hard desk chair. Three days ago, he'd had 101 stitches removed from his neck, upper back, shoulders, and right biceps.

"It's been two weeks since the cargo ship."

"Yes, ma'am."

"How's the rehab going?"

All three fidgeted.

"I need to know. I have to decide whether to send you stateside or keep you here. Lieutenant Berkowitz seems capable of taking over the team. We have replacement PJs waiting to deploy. They're sitting on my word and I need to decide. Now."

While Torres glared, LB scratched absentmindedly at his right calf, where his own twenty stitches had been removed. Jamie, who'd taken bullets through both thighs, flattened both palms over where the holes had been, as if to hide them.

"Boys?"

LB gestured at Wally.

"He doesn't bring it up at dinner?"

Wally's chin sank. Torres folded her arms to give LB a brown-eyed, dark-haired Latina shake of the head.

"No, Sergeant."

"We're good to go, ma'am."

"Is that so?"

LB slept in a tent on top of a high, broad shelf here in the Barn. Doc camped next to him. The two liked having the Barn

---

7 Horn of Africa.

to themselves after hours, the Ping-Pong table, TV, fridges, and saline IV bags available to ease a hangover. The rest of the team lived in cramped CLU trailers around the dusty camp. Yesterday was the first day in two weeks that LB could haul himself up the ladder to his rack; he'd been sleeping on the sofa. The first time he saw Jamie walk without a limp since the mission against the Somali pirates was when Jamie stood for Torres. Two days ago, Wally took off his sling.

Most nights, at 11 Degrees North, the camp canteen, LB, Jamie, Doc, Quincy, and Mouse defied orders never to discuss what happened on the CMA-CGM *Valnea*. They talked quietly about young Robey who died on that freighter, the twenty-three pirates they killed up close, the three pirates LB took out with a knife, including the Somali chieftain on the sinking ship, how they all were just one minute from being blown up by their own government, along with the crew. Their many wounds were mending, but there were no sutures for the images of two dozen corpses, a dead comrade, the ship's murdered skipper, PJs running through corridors of blood. No one wanted to break up the team, no one wanted to give in to their wounds or *Valnea*, and it definitely wasn't a good idea to leave the team to the untested Berko. LB assumed that Wally, on those nights at a separate table with Major Torres, was talking the same stuff, healing himself the same way, breaking his orders.

"Yes, ma'am. That is so."

Leaning against the table, arms and ankles crossed, Torres beheld LB while he stood.

"Anything else, ma'am?"

"Oh, yes."

"Ma'am."

"I want a PT test for you three. Today."

Wally rose to his feet.

"Today, Major?"

Torres didn't budge. "As in right now."

Wally was clearly blindsided; that meant Torres just got the orders herself this morning. With LB and Jamie watching, she could give Wally no sympathy. All she could do was stonewall.

"Captain, you've had two weeks to rehab. Anyone else, and I mean anyone else, would've been sent home by now. I'm down to seven PJs. I need you three fully operational. Or gone."

Wally needed to keep his face blank, as well. He had all of LB's reasons for wanting to stay at Lemonnier, plus another, the one now facing him, who might have to send him away.

To punctuate Torres's point, the hangar roof of the Barn rattled to the roar of big engines rumbling down Lemonnier's flight line four hundred yards off. With Yemen and Somalia heating up, over fifty flights took off from the base every day, at all hours: HC-130s, a squadron of F-15E Strike Eagle jets, choppers, Predator drones. Bulldozers and contractors flooded the camp, expanding the HOA facility and its importance in this theater. The PJs had been lucky not to have a major rescue mission while Wally, Doc, and LB were laid up. They'd pushed the envelope. Torres was right to push back.

Wally headed for the door, LB and Jamie close behind.

"Ten minutes. In the Barn gym."

$$\bullet \quad \bullet \quad \bullet$$

LB gutted out twenty-one pull-ups in a single set. Thick-chested with short arms, he was the team champ for pull-ups and could have done twenty-five without the wrenching sting in his left shoulder and right forearm from the thirty stitches needed to close both knife wounds. Still, twenty-one was good. Dropping from the bar to his boots, favoring his left calf, LB mimicked snapping a whip at Torres and her clipboard.

Jamie followed. He was athletic and lean, and all his injuries had been to his legs. The kid banged out eighteen.

Wally reached the bar just by raising his long arms. His T-shirt sleeves slid back to reveal the scar a pirate's bullet had left across his right biceps—a pink, puckered grimace. Wally's cheeks flushed while he gutted out a dozen pull-ups, mostly with his left side. The best athlete on the team, Wally should have been able to do twenty.

Sit-ups were hellish for Jamie. He gritted his teeth against the searing in both thighs where bullets had tunneled. Though the skin had knitted, his damaged quad muscles must have been smarting viciously. Grunting from the start, Jamie managed thirty-five sit-ups in a minute, with LB shouting into his straining face every time he bobbed up, for one more, one more. Wally got back on form with seventy-two. LB struggled to make sixty; he'd gained a few pounds from inactivity and nightly beer sessions at 11DN. Torres stood apart, scribbling notes, observing more than the numbers.

Push-ups became another ordeal for Wally. On the pirate ship, he'd dived across LB to protect him from an RPG blast in the ship's passageway. Wally's body armor caught a lot of the shrapnel, but every exposed bit of his back took a hit. With each press off the gym floor, the scabs, new skin, and red welts across his hundred small wounds stretched and flexed. Wally bared his teeth through twenty-nine push-ups in sixty seconds. With a secret nod, LB and Jamie sandbagged to make Wally's number look better, each recording push-ups in the thirties for Torres's chart. All three should have been north of sixty.

Without letting them change out of their blue shorts, gray Ts, and combat boots, Torres led the way to one of the Barn's fridges for bottled water, then outside to a waiting all-terrain cart. The African sun stood on girders of midday heat, and the temperature had reached an easy ninety. Torres drove through the camp, headed for the dirt track along the security fence. Wally sat on the front seat beside her, left hand resting on the bench. LB wanted Torres to reach down and cover it with her own, give some signal that they all weren't up shit's creek. Torres drove on, wordless and unglancing.

At the start of the dusty path, LB tried to stretch his calf and hip. Jamie glared at the trail as if it were a mountain slope, nodding to himself, looking defiant, as though he knew he could do this with two freshly healed bullet holes in his legs. Wally seemed stoic, perhaps sad, behind his sunglasses. Humidity from the Gulf of Aden dripped into every breath, a sopping blanket of air.

Torres tattooed her pen against the clipboard, giving the men time to gather themselves. She pulled her cap low over her eyes, then tapped the board hard once.

"Three miles. You first."

LB didn't budge.

"What?"

"I said you first."

"We run together. A team."

"Not today."

"Every day. Trust me, I learned that one."

Torres cocked her head like a dog trying to understand something it can't, like LB's disobedience. Torres looked past him to Wally.

"Captain."

"It's her call, LB. Stand down."

"You stand up, Captain."

Torres cut him off.

"This is not a hill to die on."

"It's a hill."

"All right. I understand the PJs well enough. But I can't have any more fake results. I need to assess you, each of you, one at a time. Those are my orders. That makes them yours."

Her head righted, mind made up.

"Get on the line. And to be clear, that's an order. On your mark."

Torres held her stopwatch in plain view, thumb poised.

"Get set. Go."

Torres clicked the stopwatch. It ticked with the audible urgency of a bomb. LB shook his head.

Wally cursed and took off, arms pumping. His heels kicked high. A strong runner, he sprinted hard; the team would have at least one good time on Torres's notepad.

"Staff Sergeant Dempsey. You're next."

Silent, Jamie waited while Wally disappeared down the track. Torres gave him the go. Jamie dashed off, looking good for the first hundred yards, until his limp caught up with him downrange. He ran on gamely. Torres made a note.

"You can't send us home."

"You think I want to? Honestly?"

"No."

"Then shut up and go balls out so I don't have to."

"Can I say one more thing?"

"Which part of shut up did you miss, Master Sergeant?"

Torres showed him the stopwatch.

"On your mark."

• • •

In swimsuits beside the swimming pool, they circled each other, whistling at scars, scabs, and cherry-stained flesh. They'd not seen each other's wounds since the fight against the Somalis, and the bloodbath returned in their marks. Knitting cuts and nicks crisscrossed Wally's back and hamstrings. Jamie's thighs each showed the two red coins of entry and exit wounds. All of a sudden, Wally shook Jamie's hand. LB patted Wally's naked shoulder because every slash and stitch Wally bore would have been LB's.

Torres cleared the twenty-meter pool, telling a group of marines it was closed for the next hour. The jarheads didn't say a word on their way out, only nodded and dipped their heads at the diced-up PJs they shared the Djibouti base with.

Torres sat on a bench, clipboard in her lap. Jamie approached.

"How're we doing, ma'am?"

"We'll need to pick it up, Sergeant."

"Normally I can do that run a lot faster."

"I know."

"It was just tough this time."

"Of course."

They moved to the edge of the three-lane pool, Wally in the middle, Jamie on the far side. Torres stood, stopwatch in hand and said, simply, "Go."

All three dove in. An endurance swim of 1,500 meters was the last stage of the PT test. Despite his squat physique, LB was one of the strongest swimmers on the PJ team, indefatigable and powerful through the shoulders. His first strokes didn't bother him and he reached the far wall in quick style, thirty-seven laps to go.

He swam fast, leaving Wally and Jamie behind after the first turns. The pounding of the three-mile run had made LB's calf sear, causing him to finish with an awful time, thirty-two minutes, just ahead of Jamie's thirty-three. LB narrowed his focus to the concrete pool floor, controlled his breathing, and surged through the water.

The ache in his shoulder didn't slow him until the tenth lap, then grew as the distance reeled off. The pain, working like a spear twisting in his gashed shoulder, drew his focus tighter, away from the rest of his tiring body, to become a spur. He swam faster, racing the hurt to see if he could finish before it peaked. With eight laps to go, kicking into the next turn, he arrived at that place where the pain was so great it couldn't increase. He windmilled his left arm into another stroke; the flesh quit.

Stymied, clamping his teeth to keep from bellowing, LB rolled onto his back. He frog-kicked to keep advancing, with his face out of the water. He trailed his left arm, letting it burn. At the wall, he ducked under the surface and screamed, then kicked off.

He stretched his arm not into water but agony. He swam on like this, fending and fighting with the pain, moving a distance and time that Torres couldn't record or evaluate. LB himself couldn't measure it. He pushed through the barrier of his body and didn't stop, doing all of his yelling underwater, until Torres stood at the end of his lane shouting that he was done.

He dropped his feet to the shallow bottom, cradling his left arm as if it were not attached. Turning from Torres and her ticking stopwatch, LB bit his lip hard. Crimson threads spread in the water beneath his dripping elbow, dissolving into a rusty cloud. Torres headed back to the bench to watch the last laps of the other two.

LB hoisted himself out and fetched a towel to stanch the reopened slit in his shoulder. Catching his breath, he faded to a seat against the cinderblock wall next to the major. She spoke without turning, as if she wasn't supposed to address him.

"Did you know you were bleeding?"

"I was busy. How's it going?"

"Not good."

Wally appeared winded; a hundred small wounds slowed him, stopped him from reaching fully into his stroke. Jamie crawled ahead, his legs barely propelling him. He finished three laps behind LB. Torres noted his time. Still dripping, Jamie limped alongside the pool, urging Wally on.

Wally completed his final four laps; when he emerged from the pool, Jamie tossed him a towel. Torres scribbled while the two sat against the wall next to LB.

Torres let the clipboard loose in her lap. She twined her fingers over it, pressing her thumbs together.

"The numbers aren't good enough."

Jamie hung his head. Wally ground his palms into his eye sockets.

"I'm sorry, gentlemen."

LB shot to his feet, flinging the bloodied towel against the wall.

"Then call it a pretest. We'll do it again in a few days."

Torres licked her lips, deciding whether to respond. A trickle warmed the back of LB's arm. Wally motioned him to back off.

"Major?"

"Yes, Captain."

"Are we close?"

"I can't determine close. Just go or stay."

"Maybe there's something else."

"I don't know what you mean."

"Something else we can show you."

LB bled on the tiles. Jamie tossed him back the towel he'd thrown.

"That's bullshit, and you know it. How many times do we have to prove ourselves? Huh, Wally? This kid here."

LB stabbed a hand at Jamie.

"He took rounds through both legs and got the job done. You went through a meat grinder and still captured that damn ship. Robey wasn't even supposed to be on board. He saved all our asses and got killed for it."

LB made no mention of his own role on the freighter.

"Next time you send us on a mission, Major, tag along. See for yourself. Then you can tell me what you know. Those numbers don't mean shit. *Never quit* is what fucking counts, Major."

"LB, sit down."

"Nah, I'm going home."

Torres matched LB's glare, containing herself where he did not. She faced Wally.

"Suggestion?"

Wally stood, clearly worn out. Next to him, just as tired, Jamie rose, not because he knew what Wally might say but to have all three of them on their feet before Torres when he said it.

"LB's right. Sixty meter underwater swim."

Torres blinked, taking in the challenge. She set aside her clipboard and walked next to the pool where Wally had just dared himself to swim three lengths without surfacing. She kept her back turned long enough for LB to determine that it couldn't be done. Sixty meters was longer than anything they'd had to do to qualify at Indoc[8], ten meters more than the SEALs' underwater swim at BUD/S school. Torres, who managed Special Ops teams every day, would know this.

Without a bleeding wing and a cut-up calf, LB could probably have gutted out fifty meters by the skin of his teeth. Wally and Jamie, too. But today, after a grueling PT test that all three of them had failed, not a chance.

Wally addressed the back of Torres's head, her black ponytail.

"I'll swim for the three of us."

Torres stayed fixed on the pool. LB stomped around to confront her.

"I'll do it. I got this."

Torres raised her eyes from the water.

"No, Sergeant." She pivoted. "Captain. In the water."

"Thank you."

LB insisted.

"This ain't fair. He finished last, he's beat."

"That's why he's the one to do it. Sit down, Sergeant. Or stand. Captain, it's on you."

Wally climbed into the pool. Jamie and LB, pressing the towel to his shoulder, walked to the edge to stand over him. Jamie stayed erect on his bad legs. Some of the scabs on Wally's back had softened during the swim and wept diluted blood.

LB took a knee. "Can you make it?"

"Can you?"

---

8 The pararescue indoctrination course conducted at Lackland AFB, Texas. Indoc is an intense ten-week physical training program. Graduates qualify for entry into the two-year pararescue Special Ops training program known as "the Pipeline" and "Superman School," recognized as one of the most demanding training regimens in the military.

"Not a chance."

"Then it might as well be me."

"Yeah. Might as well."

Wally lacked so much right now, the sunglasses and cool manner, even confidence. He reminded LB of the cadet he first met at the Academy seventeen years ago, the kid who followed him into the Rangers, then pararescue. He liked that kid.

Jamie said "Good luck" and stepped back.

Torres called "Ready."

LB spoke soothingly, to calm Wally. "Listen. Long smooth strokes. Glide as much as you can."

Wally tugged his swim goggles over his eyes.

Torres called "Set."

"You got one shot."

"Nothing new."

"Roger that."

Wally sucked in four fast, deepening breaths.

Torres gave the signal. "Go."

Wally gulped a last lungful, ducked under, and pushed off the bottom. LB strode alongside while Jamie stayed in place. Under the surface, Wally flowed into the first strokes at a good rate, not rushed, frog-kicking between pulls. LB had to move at a good clip to keep up. Wally reached the wall with five strokes. LB checked his watch: twenty seconds, on target. Wally's back trailed bloody wisps like smoke from an engine.

The silence in the pool area felt wrong for the stakes. LB began to chant, "Come on, come on." Jamie joined in. Torres, too, was on her feet.

Wally spun around at the first turn, lunging off the wall. He pulled and coasted three times, steady, past the middle of the pool. Two more strokes brought him within range of the wall. Instead of gliding into the final turn, Wally stroked again.

He pushed off the wall for the final lap but didn't coast forward as he should have. He took another stroke, then another, hurrying, not slipping through the water any longer but dragging himself, fighting the water. Wally released bubbles to ease the CO_2 in his lungs, then burned up two more desperate strokes to pass the halfway point. Extending his arms for the next stroke, with just eight meters left, he was done.

Wally went into slow motion, clumsy and muddled. He spread his arms and legs, trying to push through the water one more time, and left them there. His momentum faded. He sank to the bottom four meters from the finish.

Torres spilled her clipboard with a clatter.

LB jumped in.

Wally lay spread-eagled, eyes open behind the goggles. LB lifted him by the armpits. Wally sagged heavily with no buoyancy, lungs empty.

Torres helped haul him out of the pool, flat on his back. Jamie reached under Wally's shoulders to put him in a sitting position. Torres smacked him across the face.

"Wally. Wally. Wake up."

Wally stared with unfixed eyes. LB moved the major aside. He lifted Wally's chin, then slapped him again, harder than Torres, beneath his blind eyes.

"Wakey wakey."

Wally gasped, jerking his head out of LB's palm. His gaze revived and wandered for focus, then centered on LB.

"You blacked out."

"No I didn't."

"You did."

"Did I finish?"

"No. Gave it a hell of a shot."

"How much?"

"One more stroke."

"Shit."

"Yeah."

Torres stood erect, both hands covering her mouth. She turned away, retreating to the bench for her dropped clipboard.

Wally got to his feet, teetering while Jamie supported him.

"Major. I'm sorry."

Torres cleared her throat. She spun on the three of them standing side by side.

"What just happened?"

"Apparently, I passed out."

"Why didn't you come up for air?"

"Stubborn."

Torres rattled her head. She hugged the clipboard as if to shut it out of the conversation.

"Did you know that was going to happen?"

"It seemed likely."

The major surveyed them, Wally and LB slowly bleeding, Jamie on his last legs.

"I suppose it wouldn't have mattered which of you was in the water."

"No."

LB chimed in.

"It's how we train."

"To drown?"

"To never quit. Ever."

Torres threw an unmasked look of concern at Wally, then caught herself. She hid behind her hand, caressing her own forehead. She spoke before lowering the hand.

"Fine."

Torres walked away from the pool with long strides.

Wally called after her.

"Fine what?"

The major tore the top sheet from her clipboard. She crumpled it and left it on the floor behind her.

Chapter 3

Village of al-Husn
Ma'rib
Yemen

Arif shuffled in line on the dry road. In front of him the sandals of
two hundred men, another hundred behind, took the same short
strides. The eldest of the mourners, the deceased's three gray-
bearded brothers, led the way with their long walking sticks, and
the procession moved at their aged pace.

Arif dressed as a Yemeni for the burial, in *futa* skirt and
brown *mushadda* head wrap. In his belt he'd tucked an onyx-
hilted *janbiya*, the short, curved ceremonial knife particular to
Yemen, and tucked behind that a well-worn pocket Qur'an. At
the beginning of the long, slow march, he'd unraveled a portion
of the mushadda with others in line, to cover his mouth and nose
against the dust and climbing sun.

The path to the cemetery wended through a quilt of crop-
lands and sere open spaces. Terraced coffee trees and qat shrubs
mingled with emerald pastures of barley grass. In the bare
ranges, litter blew loose on the breeze, inevitable in a country
used to tossing its refuse out the window, still unaccustomed to
Western goods that did not decay. In the distant foothills, a patch
of oil pumps nodded without cease.

Far ahead, the cloth-wrapped body of Shaykh Qasim Tujjar
Ba-Jalal rode on the upraised hands of his seven sons, spelled

by grandsons and tribal leaders. Shaykh Qasim had owned the house where Arif and Nadya lived. It was Qasim two years ago who'd granted the Saudi couple protection and sanctuary in al-Husn. Qasim found the building for Nadya's office. She'd supported the women's clinic from her own funds for the first year and a half, until her family froze her accounts, then Qasim found the money. The old man had never met Nadya, but every woman in the shaykh's household and those of his sons deemed her wise and kind. When Qasim died last evening after prayers, Arif had been reading emails, checking his traps. Nadya soaked in a scented bath to clean away the odors of the day's sick. A knock came at the door to tell Arif that the shaykh's grave was being dug by lamplight. Mourning prayers would be held in the square at dawn.

Arif kept his eyes lowered and his face masked, speaking to no one in the snail's-pace line. Though Nadya was well known and admired in the town's markets, by the water wells and pumps, all the places for women, very few Yemenis knew Arif. He left it that way. There were other Saudis in Ma'rib and the Wadi Hadhramaut, other expatriate *mujahideen* like him, plus a dozen old al-Qaeda who'd escaped in a prison break in Sana'a years ago. Arif would gain nothing by associating with them. They were either tired jihadis who couldn't go home because of blood on their hands or young radicals seeking to dip their hands in more. Arif lived without attention now, anonymously, with no urge to be found or thought notable at all. And his enemy was not so numerous as the enemies of the others, only the Al Saud.

The village grave site lay east of al-Husn on the cusp of the desert, ringed by date palm trees. The large Ba-Jalal family plot sprawled in the shade, fortunate for the imam and family but sunny and harsh for the rest of the crowd. Arif loitered on the outer edge of the men pressing close to the imam's final words. He kept his head bent and let himself be present, away from his computer.

The funeral prayer finished quickly; most of what was said over Qasim had already been intoned in the square after dawn. He'd died in his mid-eighties, still a powerful man, father of seven living sons, outlived three wives. He was being buried a shaykh of the Abidah tribe, pious and faithful to the Prophet.

When the words were done and the imam dropped his arms, Qasim was lowered into his grave without a coffin, on his right side to face Mecca. Working fast before the shade shifted, servants filled in the hole. The three hundred mourners began to file past the sons who arrayed themselves shoulder to shoulder.

Arif moved in the last quarter of the line. He'd only visited Qasim three times in his two years here. He'd seen the brothers more frequently but rarely spoke to them on the streets, in the souk or the mosque. He passed the time in the slow line rubbing a thumb over the keys of his cell phone hidden in a pocket of his futa.

When at last he stepped into the slanting shade of the fig trees, Arif unwrapped the mushadda from his face. He walked with both hands crossed over the janbiya, a pose of grief. Passing the grave, he tossed in a bit of broken pottery, which an old man in line was handing out, a reminder of the frailness of life. Qasim's grave would have no flowers or headstone, only a small stone marker bearing his name and these bits of clay.

The first and oldest of the sons greeted Arif with a flaccid hand, palm downward, as if Arif was expected to kiss it. His white hand was a sign of Yemeni wealth; this qabil did not work in the fields.

"I will remember Allah and pray for your father."

"*Shakkran.*"

The son withdrew his hand to extend it to the next in line. Arif sidestepped to the next brother, and the next, each of the seven progressively younger.

The last one dressed in finery beyond his brothers or any mourner. His black turban gleamed like coal. His hands, the softest of the seven, reached to Arif from the belled sleeves of his ebon robe. Gems studded the sheath of his janbiya beneath a hilt of rhino horn, tucked into a belt stitched in green, silver, and gold.

Arif had seen this youngest son around the village. He drove a car resplendent like his clothing, a dark Mercedes SUV. Unlike his brothers, he kept his beard trimmed to a goatee and wore no rings. Without gray or wrinkles, he was likely in his early thirties, the tallest of the brothers, as tall as Arif. The man covered Arif's hand with both of his own.

"I will remember Allah and pray for your father."

"Shakkran, Arif al-Bahaziq."

The son let Arif's hand slide free.

"You know my name."

"You were my father's tenant. You are now mine. I should know your name. Walk with me."

"There are others still in line."

"I have six brothers. My father will be mourned well enough. Come."

The last shovels of dirt fell on the shaykh, and more shards of pottery were tossed into his grave. The youngest son turned Arif by the elbow.

"I am Ghalib Tujjar Ba-Jalal."

"*Merhabba.*"

"Merhabba, Arif."

Ghalib rested his hand in the crook of Arif's elbow as they strolled away from the graveside. At their backs, more men of al-Husn gave their condolences, while the servants tamped the grave level with the earth.

Ghalib patted Arif's arm.

"Muhammad tells us the services due from one Muslim to another are six. If you meet him, greet him. If he invites you, accept. If he asks your advice, give it. If he sneezes, tell him God bless you. If he falls sick, visit him. And if he dies, walk in his funeral."

"I did not come from duty. I admired your father. I am grateful to him."

"Of course."

Ghalib stopped at a fig tree to pluck two ripe fruits. He handed one to Arif.

"These are now my brother Ahmed's trees. My brother Salah owns the fields there to the east, and my brother Hussein owns the irrigation machines. And so on, you understand. We are many, thanks to the will of God."

"And you own my house."

"Your street, yes. My father was more wealthy than people knew. Oil has come to much of our lands."

"*Subhanallah*."

Arif and Ghalib bit into the sweet figs. Neither spoke until the fruits were eaten. Ghalib put his hands before his face to utter a prayer of thanks, then clapped.

"And so, Arif."

"Yes."

"You may not know this, but my father took an interest in you."

"I cannot imagine why."

"Modesty is the true wealth. I like you."

"I'm honored."

"I hope you will do me one more service and pay me a visit. I believe we have much in common. Much we can speak about."

"I'm a simple man. I live quietly."

"Yes." Ghalib spread his great black sleeves. "Exactly."

Arif folded his hands once more at his waist, over the janbiya. He inclined his head, a suppliant posture. In Saudi, he'd had twenty years' experience of speaking to those considered his betters.

"With respect, I am not seeking friends."

Ghalib tucked his thumbs into his ornate belt. He bent backward, lifting his goateed chin. He laughed like a rich man.

"Nor am I."

Ghalib quelled his glee. He reached into a pocket for a small gold case, to extract one calling card.

"Ring me today after *dhuhr*. I will give you instructions to my home. It is easy to find. We will chew qat and talk, yes?"

Arif took the card. The youngest son swept away, his dark robe feathering around him, shining like a crow.

• • •

Arif's house stood empty. Nadya had driven away at dawn, before he rose to attend the funeral ceremony. The call to prayer had brought the village to Qasim's swaddled and scented body lying in the open dawn in the square, but Nadya would not attend. She refused to close the clinic. Oddly, Qasim had smelled of her. She liked aromas, of candles, coffee, cooking herbs, incense, skin oils, the flavored mists of the water pipe. Their little house smelled of her always, even with the windows open to the Yemeni heat. But on Arif's return home, he caught no whiff of his wife at all. She'd left nothing baked for him before she left, no sweet rolls or bread on the counter, no coffee to heat. Last night in bed, after her floral bath, he went to sleep breathing his wife, as every night. Holding his cell phone in the silent kitchen, Arif felt empty of her. He feared that he stood at the boundary of a place she finally would not go with him.

Arif set the phone on the counter and imagined leaving it there as an offering. He thought of walking two miles in the sun to her clinic as a feat for her. He wanted Nadya to tell him to stop, he wanted her beside him to nod her assent before he went up to his office.

Years ago Arif had stood on the edge of battlefields like this, wondering what lay ahead in the fight, what would happen if he turned back? Everything would change with the direction of the next step.

What did Ghalib of the Ba-Jalal want with him? What had Arif ignited with the email that had alerted his phone? And at what cost? He had little left in his life to pay but his wife.

He lost track of how long he stood like this, a steadying hand on the counter, doing a martyr's math. When he became aware of himself, he snatched up the phone.

He thought of calling Nadya but for what? To ask forgiveness? Permission? She'd given both already.

Arif headed for the stairs. With every rising tread he shed his hesitation. He was not alone nor was he wrong, and he rebuked himself for believing otherwise just because Nadya had not left him a treat or a burning candle.

Before sitting at the computer Arif changed from the funeral clothes to the T-shirt and shorts he'd left in his chair last night. He slid back the door to the balcony to ease the stifling room and put on the fan. Miles away the midmorning desert flushed red.

Arif sat before the screen, opening the covert link from his c&c server to Jaffar's computer. Jaffar's keystrokes showed him busily tapping away; Arif ignored the engineer's diligence, instead boring in on the network email file share he'd singled out last night. After loading the file into the text search engine, he quickly found the one message he sought.

At 0743, Prince Hassan bin Abd al-Aziz had answered his cousin al-Bakr Sudayri's mention of Fatima. He'd typed a simple *Yes.*

Sudayri had not yet replied.

Arif entered the email account he'd spoofed using Sudayri's ID and password. Any email Arif sent to Abd al-Aziz would appear to come from the Saudi ISP.

In the heat of his office, to the sounds of a mule cart creaking past beneath his balcony and a knife sharpener shouting his trade, Arif leaned back in his chair. He had to wait for Jaffar in

Riyadh to take a break from his industriousness and send out his personal emails. When he did this, Arif would slip in one more.

• • •

The engineer was an honest man. He did not take time for personal business until his lunch break exactly at noon. The instant Jaffar sent an email to his sister in Medina, a lament that he did not have money to fund her son's visit, Arif hid inside his shadow and sent Sudayri's answer to Abd al-Aziz.

Subject: Photos
Message: Fatima asked me to forward you these pictures. See attached.

Arif's wait was short. An answer came back within ten minutes.

Subject: Re: Photos
Message: The attachment was empty. Re-send.

Arif waved to his computer screen, a good-bye to Jaffar, who would not know why or how he'd gotten into so much trouble.

The command and control server indicated that it had Abd al-Aziz's computer under its control. The malware had launched itself when Abd al-Aziz opened the attachment. Arif arrived seconds later.

A surge flowed from his hands on the keyboard and up his arms. The image on his screen was the same as the one in his father-in-law's home office. Arif now owned the prince's computer; he had access to its hard drive, could edit any data he found, capture every keystroke, dive as deep as he chose into Abd al-Aziz's records and the secrets stored inside them.

Arif could not guess how long the link would last. His father-in-law was the chief of Saudi Intelligence; his personal computer wouldn't be like Jaffar's, naïve and poorly protected. Abd al-Aziz could have tiers of cyber-security trip wires, any one of which may already have been activated without Arif's knowledge. Arif pushed back against the temptation to snoop through the full electronic world of his father-in-law. If he did, he might find perfidy, plots, all the impieties of the House of Saud. But it was too great a thing to contemplate, to catalog in the time before he was shut down—perhaps a day or only hours—until Sudayri explained that he did not write these last few emails, until the lowly engineer Jaffar was arrested. Curiosity was too blunt an instrument. Arif turned instead to his anger, honed over decades.

He drove for the place where every member of the Al Saud was most vulnerable, what every royal most guarded and feared. Arif went for Hassan bin Abd al-Aziz's private bank accounts.

Chapter 4

Turkish embassy
Sana'a
Yemen

Many in the ballroom spilled their pomegranate juice when the boom shook the chandeliers and windows. Women gasped to look down at themselves, then patted their gowns with napkins, while their escorts complained about the jet. There should be rules, groused a few diplomats with stained shirts and cummerbunds. A mustachioed Yemeni army officer, elegant in all white, said there were.

Josh handed a Tunisian woman his own handkerchief. She brushed the darkened bosom of her dress. Her portly husband bustled up to take the kerchief from her and return it to Josh. He led his wife away.

Josh moved across the parquet dance floor, slipping through the diplomats and spouses packing the ballroom. He ate from several traveling trays of lamb kebab.

He parked alone at the foot of a curving stone stairwell beneath a two-story-tall banner of Kemal Ataturk. The founder of Turkey's blocky jaw and farseeing eyes watched over the embassy's celebration of Independence Day. The Turks put on an opulent party this afternoon for the Sana'a diplomatic community. Velvet and bunting softened every table beneath a hundred tulip vases; pipers and drummers played native music; and the servers wore caftans, pantaloons, slippers, and turbans. A large ice sculpture of the Blue Mosque anchored the event.

Josh motioned to a costumed waiter for more skewers. The little Yemeni hustled over, his tray of beef kebabs held high.

"I prefer lamb."

The waiter cocked his turbaned head, surprised to be addressed by a tuxedoed Western guest speaking Arabic.

"Sir. Yes, sir."

"Could you find some lamb?"

"Sir, yes, sir."

The waiter left as he'd arrived, hustling.

Josh exhaled a worn sigh, a flute of juice in one hand. The formal backs of chatting diplomats bunched around him. He sampled their conversations, covering those in English and Arabic. The gathering sparkled in the eclectic dress of sunbaked Arabia and those who'd come to influence it. Italian-cut suits and business couture flattered the Europeans; pastel *bubus* draped the West Africans, embroidered dashikis for the North Africans, fez caps and *sufis* on the East Africans, and *dastars* on the Sikhs; and the Saudis glided along in floor-length white thobes and headdresses wrapped in the double rope *agal* of camel herders.

Josh surfed on snippets of talk, little of interest: the social calendar in Sana'a, a new UN fund for sub-Saharan agriculture. Checking his watch, he saw he had another hour of handshaking and banalities. He'd already stood aloof too long under Ataturk. It would go noted if he left early.

Josh inhaled as if preparing to dive from a height. Before he could stride back into the crowd, an older man, prominent in a formal cutaway tux, watch fob across his gray vest, headed his way. The man was short, shaved bald with skin baked golden brown. Coming to rest beside Josh at the staircase, he seemed twitchy, patting his coat pockets.

"Damn. Can't smoke inside. Can't leave."

Josh stood still, not sure what to say.

"You could step out for a moment."

"No. The Turks take everything to heart. You'd think, of all people, they'd let a man light a cigarette indoors. Who smokes more than a Turk?"

Josh offered a guess.

"An Egyptian."

The diplomat extended a hand. Josh took it. The shake was light, noncommittal.

"Ahmed Elghul. Egyptian embassy."

"Joshua Cofield. American embassy."

Elghul lifted a stubby, manicured finger between them. He leaned in, eager, almost conspiratorial, as though he'd had an insight about Americans and had waited a long time to share it with one.

"You have a Biblical first name and an Anglo-Saxon last name. I make a study of these things."

"Interesting."

"What is your middle name?"

"Darius."

"Persian. That is perfect. Very American."

"I suppose."

"Where are your people from?"

"Father from Louisiana. Mother from Baltimore."

"You understand, this is your strength. If I may."

"Please."

"It is a law of nature. The mixture of breeds is always strongest. The mongrel."

Josh paused, laying back to see how Elghul intended this, offense or jest. The older man let the observation hang between them, undeciphered. Josh laughed first. Elghul's cheeks pinched.

"I did not mean to amuse you."

Josh tumbled to his normal speaking voice.

"It's an odd way to put it, that's all."

Elghul nodded, lips pursed. It appeared that Elghul wanted to speak his mind more. In the tedium of another embassy party, Josh could do with some candor to help pass the time. He reached out a palm like an usher. Elghul blinked slowly, owlish.

"This is no secret, my friend. This issue of American strength, it occupies the entire world. How will you use it under this president, then that president? Who will you defend, who will you target? It is Monte Carlo with your country, always."

"Like you say. Mongrels are tough to predict."

"And that makes you difficult to trust. I say this with affection and friendship. The rest of us, we wait for you to grow up to match your strength. You will be a young people for another thousand years."

"At least."

The Egyptian's manner would have been no different if he were discussing the weather or the results of a cricket match. He smiled without condescension, waggled a finger without chastising.

"Look at your names. What was yours again?"

"Josh Cofield."

"Where is your father in that name? Your town and tribe? I am Ahmed al-Barudi Elghul. From the village of Barudi, of the el-Ghul. You, in America, you start over with that name, Joshua Cofield. Always an infant. This is what I am saying."

The costumed waiter had found Josh a tray of the lamb kebab. He neared, but Josh gestured him away.

"May I reply?"

"Of course."

Josh dug both hands in his pockets, an attempt to remain casual.

"First, not every old way's a good way. I would've thought the Arab Spring taught you that. Second, sometimes it takes a child like America to show the way. Sometimes a brother, like the Turks here, or the Iraqis. And sometimes, you just find the right way after going all the wrong ways first. That's what I'm saying. With affection."

"You compare Egypt to Turkey? To Iraq?"

"They both have constitutions. They both respect democracy." Elghul fluttered his hand primly.

"The Turkish generals guarantee their constitution. America's generals guarantee Iraq's."

"Who guarantees Egypt's?"

"The people, of course."

"Good to know. We'll be watching for that."

Elghul tugged out his pocket watch, a neat gesture to break their time together.

"With apologies, I must return to the party. You will excuse me."

"Certainly."

"Before I go, if I may observe."

"About?"

"You, sir."

"I'm all ears."

Elghul tucked away the watch. He left his thumb pushed inside the little vest pocket, to pat his belly with the dangling fingers.

"You have a grating manner." Elghul said this with the same delicate touch as his handshake.

"I'm sorry. I meant only to be frank."

"It might be better to save your frankness for more political venues. This is a social event. I should suggest diplomacy, young man. Good day."

The Egyptian lowered his brow for a parting nod. He walked off stylish, without haste or cantankerousness. In seconds, he was part of a new conversation.

Another tray of juice glasses floated nearby. A couple fingers of scotch would have done better to pass the next hour. Josh beckoned the waiter.

Before the server could reach the stairwell, he was inter-cepted by the tall, mustachioed Yemeni soldier decked in white dress uniform. His shoulder boards told his rank, the twin stars and brass eagle of a full colonel. With grace, the officer snipped two flutes off the tray, then ferried them to Josh.

"With my compliments."

The officer spoke in Yemeni. Josh accepted the offered glass.

"Shakkran."

"You're not very good at this, are you?"

"At what?"

The colonel swept a hand across the panoply of diplomats, spouses, global attire, food, décor, posturing, ice.

"This."

"Good enough, I suppose."

The colonel switched to a British-flavored English.

"I think not. You quite butchered that with the Egyptian. He's a bored old buzzard. He goaded you as an entertainment. You took him seriously."

"No I didn't."

"My friend, never compare one country to another, espe-cially as an American. It's shaming for you to tell us how much better we could be doing things. Especially among Arabs. You speak adequate Arabic. I should think you would know this."

"He started it."

"Are you a child?"

Unlike Elghul, the colonel did not let his words hover between them but flashed broad white teeth to cue that he was kidding. Josh grinned in response, to wrap his reply in the same clothing: a joke, and not.

"I'm way too damn big to be a child."

"That you are. What are you, six foot two?"

"Six three."

"Excellent. Then are you a *siyasi*?"

"A spy? No. Why would you ask me that?"

"Nothing. Ignore it."

"First that guy tells me I'm rude, then you tell me I'm a spy."

"Perhaps you are having an off day."

"Maybe. But you're the one eavesdropping."

"Yes, I suppose that is what spies do. But no. I simply happened to be standing nearby and your conversation interested me. Though I think spies enjoy these events more than we. There's no such thing as idle talk."

Josh put out a hand for a shake. The soldier's grip was firm, rare among Gulf Staters, not hesitant to project himself through it. Josh returned the squeeze.

"Joshua Cofield. American embassy."

"Colonel Khalil Yahya al-Din. Military attaché to the vice president."

"Colonel."

"Joshua. What is your role at the embassy?"

"Public affairs officer."

"Ah."

Khalil chuckled behind his rising flute. After a sip, he dried his mustache on the back of his hand.

"So it's your job to attend these ordeals. How sad."

"And ribbon cuttings. Visiting universities, writing the ambassador's speeches, talking with the press."

"Why on earth would your embassy put a man like you in that position?"

The server had hovered nearby with the tray of lamb kebabs. Josh gestured him over to put a gap in the conversation. He and Khalil selected skewers. Josh's better judgment told him to eat silently, bid farewell, then walk off. But he did want to learn diplomacy beyond stamping visas; he was posted to Sana'a to do just that. This blatant, toothy colonel clearly had some sort of agenda. He seemed to know the game. Josh sipped, to give himself a few more seconds. "What sort of man is that?"

Khalil spread his hands, to say Come now, we both know.

"Go ahead. I'd like to hear this."

"If you insist."

"Apparently I'm the kind who does."

"As you wish. I note the American South in your speech. Most of your foreign service fellows iron out the regional accents from their speech, but not you. You're intelligent, so this may indicate you are hardheaded. You're blunt. I suspect you're former military. You barely flinched at that sonic boom. You carry yourself apart, with the upright feel of a soldier. And you're removed. Something about you wishes you were elsewhere, doing something different. You may not be cut out for shaking hands."

Khalil snared another skewer from the tray, Josh did not. The waiter departed. The colonel chewed on the first bit of meat, pleased with himself.

"I did well, didn't I."

"You read a file on me?"

"No. All deduction."

"The military thing was right."

"I knew it. What service?"

"Eight years in the army. Rangers."

"Iraq, Afghanistan?"

"Yep."

"Your share of medals."

"Yep."

"So you left the military. The foreign service wanted you for your language skills. You accepted, done with the clash of weapons, preferring the war of ideals."

"You can stop now."

"Two years posted in Riyadh doing consular work, visas and such. Now in Sana'a in your second posting, as a low-rung cultural affairs officer. Shaking hands."

"You read a file."

"Of course. Haven't you read one on me?"

"No."

"Why not?"

"I have no interest in you."

"That hurts."

"You'll get over it."

Once more, Josh sensed the tug of judgment at his sleeve, telling him to wish the colonel *Ma'a salama* and ease into the crowd the way the Egyptian did, classy and final.

"So why the interest in me?"

"I think you might be a spy, Joshua Cofield."

"I'm not. And you have to stop saying that."

Josh considered that al-Din might, in fact, be a spy. The man wore all white to stand out; he laughed loud and often, to be heard; and he was overt and oddball behind the mustache, all to hide in plain view, to make those seeing him catch a mask. The men Josh had known who meant and did exactly what they said, those were quieter men.

Khalil touched Josh's shoulder.

"May we be honest with each other?"

Josh shrugged under the colonel's hand to remove it.

"No."

"I suppose that's true for now. I'll tell you what. I'll be honest with you and you decide whether to repay me in kind another time."

"Go ahead."

The colonel sucked on the finished stick.

"I've seen you before. I've been watching. I've had others watch, as well."

"That's not making me happy. And it's creepy."

"You are awkward as a diplomat. You know this. You are thirty-two years old. And though you had a fine record in the military, you are not a young man to be on such a low rung in the world of diplomacy. That is why I read a file on you."

"Because you think I'm a spy. I'm not."

"Because I think you are a man who wants to get ahead. A man I may want to deal with."

"What do you want?"

"Your discretion. Your trust."

"For?"

"On occasion, I would like to feed you privileged information, but without attribution. Anonymously, you understand."

"That's spying."

"It's also back-channel diplomacy. Done all the time."

"Why would you do that?"

"On occasion, when my country would like to see something in your press or in your ambassador's report, something we can't officially claim, I'd like to know you are a reliable partner."

"Such as."

"Intelligence on terrorists' movements. News regarding Yemeni economics, politics, tribal tensions. Whatever we'd prefer to release without putting a name to it."

"Why not?"

"As you'll learn quickly in Yemen, we dance on the heads of snakes. We balance a hundred competing interests: tribes, warlords, Islamists, reformers, revolutionaries. Look around you. Every person here, every dashiki, robe, and tuxedo, knows Yemen harbors both oil and al-Qaeda. We are a choke point for the Red Sea and the Gulf of Aden. We teeter between democracy and a failed state, like Somalia. This makes Yemen coveted and frightening. The United States operates more armed drones over my country than any place on earth. Much of what we have to say must be uttered in secret, to known friends only. I am trying to make a friend of you."

Khalil backed up a step; he'd moved in close to Josh, almost whispering, wagging the bare kebab stick like a baton. Raising his long, white-clad arm, he signaled for a fresh round of pomegranate juice. When the tray was delivered, Khalil snatched two full flutes.

Josh accepted. He didn't lift his glass until he'd heard it all.

"Of course, there is something in this for you."

"I figured."

"If you are a spy, this will make your work easier."

"I'm not going to say it again."

"It doesn't matter. Either way, you will look good to your superiors when your own reports feature confidential information. You'll look connected. Perhaps this will help you move up the ladder, whichever ladder you're on. Yes?"

This Yemeni colonel might be a clown, or he might be an against-the-grain James Bond genius. Josh could bet either way. But al-Din did have instincts, he'd done his homework, and he knew what to dangle. Josh had no desire to be locked in as a public affairs officer for his whole career. There were five diplomatic "cones" in each US embassy: economics to study the host nation's economy; management of the embassy's staff and business; consular to handle visa applications; public affairs, where Josh was assigned now; and political officer, dealing directly with power and the powerful, the fastest track up. If he was CIA, that would be his cover.

Josh raised his glass. He drained the sparkling juice, privately toasting what might turn out to be his good luck. But wasn't it bad luck to toast with anything other than booze? Too late now. He placed the glass on the steps beside his two other empties. He kept a bottle of Balvenie 15 in his desk drawer at the embassy.

"You know where to find me."

Without hurry, Josh walked away, leaving the Turks' party early.

Chapter 5

Lashkar Gah district
Helmand River Valley
Afghanistan

LB's boots hit the stony ground a moment before the chopper's wheels touched down. The healing gash in his calf yipped but didn't slow him. When Torres put him, Wally, and Jamie back on active status, he'd hoped they'd have more than one day before the next rescue. That hadn't worked out.

Beneath the spinning rotor LB bolted through twirling ghosts of dust, running for the clot of marines. The men kneeled in a circle, guns up in four directions on the high Afghan plain.

LB bowled into their midst on his kneepads. Inside their parting ring, two marines were down. One of the wounded had a stained bandage wrapped around his thigh and a tourniquet at his groin. The second marine lay on his side, seething bloody bubbles through clamped teeth. One of his buddies held him in place by the shoulder. LB patted the back of this fighter's wrist to say I got him, get your hands back on your weapon.

Someone in the circle loosed a volley toward a scraggy line of brush 150 meters away. A few more in the forty-man patrol fired from their positions, spread out and on their bellies, with only rocks, weeds, and natural depressions for cover in the baked-white wadi. The insurgents answered, firing tit for tat, and hit nothing but their own pocked earth.

Pedro 2 was a big target on the ground. She bounded into the air, kicking up more dust.

Two marines scooted sideways to make room. Doc burst into their center, skidding to his knees. Immediately he began to unroll the flexible Skedco litter he'd lugged from the chopper. LB addressed the marine with a bullet in his thigh. The kid was tango two, needing exfiltration within the hour.

"You okay for a few?"

This tough kid sat up on his elbows. "Take care of my buddy."

Doc set to work. He flattened the Skedco, then shrugged off his med ruck. Doc dug in while LB took a sit rep from the squad's lieutenant.

Fifty minutes ago his patrol had walked into an ambush. They took small arms fire from an indeterminate force embedded in scrub to their north and on high ground east and west. The young officer's best guess was two dozen enemies with automatic weapons. A pair of his marines went down in the first seconds under fire; the squad retreated, set up a perimeter and a casualty collection point, traded gunfire with scurrying shadows, and called in the Guardian Angels.

Overhead *Pedro 1* roared an arc over the dry battlefield. *Pedro 2* climbed behind her. Both circled, waiting for LB's direction.

The name tape on the marine under LB's hand read ROME. The kid's comrades had already stripped him of his vest and pack. LB leaned down, nose to nose. Rome was tango one, requiring evac now.

"They call you Romeo, marine? Huh?"

Rome rattled his head, quick and pained, a shudder. "Not Romeo. Just Rome."

"They call me LB. Little Bastard. You're gonna be fine, Rome. Hear me?"

Doc rolled the kid faceup to cut away the buttons on his tunic, then sliced away the olive drab T-shirt. On his back, Rome struggled for breath; blood pooled in his trachea. Moving fast, Doc peeled back the soaked cloth to reveal a neat hole an inch below the left collarbone. The round had punched just above Rome's chest armor, probably tearing off the top of his lung. Judging by his difficulty breathing, the lung had collapsed. On instinct Rome had rolled onto his left shoulder to keep his working right lung above the flood. The kid hacked up more red foam. Doc eased him onto his side again.

He readied an ampoule of ketamine and uncapped a needle. Rome, in a lot of pain, weighed about 180 pounds. He'd need twenty milligrams to cool him out.

"Doc's gonna give you a shot for the pain. Okay? Hear me?"

Inside his helmet in the white dust, the boy's head wagged up and down, blue eyes wide and wild on LB. Specters of fear and death had come uncaged inside this brave boy whose breath had turned red. Shot in a foreign country, defended by his brothers, Rome fought hard to stay brave.

Doc spiked the ketamine into Rome's biceps. Moments later, LB withdrew his hand when he felt the kid sag. Overhead, *Pedro 2* rocketed past in a dogbone pattern, *Pedro 1* seconds behind.

LB slipped out of the marines' circle, leaving Doc heads-down on the wounded. He'd stay heads-up. LB pushed the push-to-talk clipped to his vest.

"*Pedro 2*, Hallmark."

"Go, Hallmark."

"*Pedro 2*, request for exfil. LZ remains hot."

"Copy that, Hallmark. LZ is hot."

Downrange one mile, the big HH-60 broke out of the dogbone to rocket straight for LB. Behind her, the second chopper maintained the pattern. LB hailed this bird to bring her big 7.62 six-barreled machine guns into play.

"*Pedro 1*, Hallmark."

"Hallmark, *Pedro 1*. Go."

"*Pedro 1*. Call for fire."

The helo banked hard. She dropped her nose and came charging at LB.

"Send it."

"*Pedro 1*, mark my position." LB stood to wave his arms at both advancing helos. "Target one five zero yards north my position, in the bushes. Fire for effect."

Both choppers closed at 120 mph, then blasted past. *Pedro 2* did not land; the guns of *Pedro 1* did not fire.

With gunships in the air but no reason to hide from them, the Afghans in the bushes and on the high ground opened up. The marines responded and the firefight flared. Ten steps from LB, several rounds nicked the pebbles. Doc lay across Rome to shield him. LB dropped to a knee to ram his thumb on the PTT[9].

"*Pedro 2*, needing exfil. *Pedro 1*. Shoot."

The choppers zoomed straight away from the embattled wadi, now buzzing with gunfire.

"Hallmark, *Pedro 1*. I saw no smoke. Mark your position."

"*Pedro 1*, my position marked by me getting shot at and waving my fucking arms in the air. Or did you not see that?"

LB didn't wait for the chopper pilot's answer. It wasn't going to make LB happy anyway. He flung himself flat on the ground.

Pedro 2 crept closer, poised to set down for evac but keeping its distance.

"Juggler, Juggler. Hallmark. You copy?"

"LB, Juggler. Go."

"Juggler, get on one of that chopper's guns and fire it yourself."

"LB, where's your smoke?"

"Juggler. I swear to God. I mean it."

"Did you forget your smoke again?"

LB rose to his knees. *Pedro 1* banked slowly, warily.

From his knees, LB pushed the PTT. "Yes. Okay? I forgot it."

LB did not wave his arms this time but held them out, palms up like a beggar.

---

9 push-to-talk.

Pedro 1 leaned steeply out of its turn to charge back to the wadi. The pilot's voice snapped in LB's headset.

"Visual you, Hallmark."

"*Pedro 1*, roger. Brush line to the north. Clear to fire."

"Tally target."

Above the plain, *Pedro 1* swung onto her side, leaning over to widen the gunner's field of vision. The chinking bark of the portside 7.62 cut through the whop of her rotors. Kneeling in the open door, tied in by cow's-tails, Wally and Jamie added the firepower of their M4s. Big Quincy let his legs dangle out.

The chopper opened up hard, shredding the shrubs, pulverizing rocks. A cascade of brass casings trailed her. On the ground, the marines turned their guns on the hills to the left and right. Forty meters away, *Pedro 2* scudded in low, adding the thunder of her rotors to the guns all around.

LB scampered back to Doc and the wounded.

Together they lifted Rome onto the Skedco sled, laying him on his side. The ketamine left Rome loose, eyelids fluttering. Scarlet drool drizzled from his open lips; his breathing was shallow but not labored. Doc finished strapping in Rome while LB tapped a meaty corporal to grab a handle and help skid the plastic litter to *Pedro 2*. Nearby, the HH-60 set wheels down, impatient, pawing at the ground.

Overhead *Pedro 1* broke off her firing. She streaked away to bank for another pass. All the guns on the ground went quiet. The bad guys were hunkered down and would stay quiet for another minute. The plain echoed.

"Doc, move."

Rome was hauled away. Watching him disappear, the circle of marines called encouragement. LB squatted beside the kid with the leg wound. His name tape read BRAUN.

"I think we can beat 'em. You ready, Braun?"

LB hoisted the marine onto his one good leg. His buddies in the ring reached out to say So long, but LB slipped under the kid's armpit to hop him away as fast as he could.

He really wanted to beat Doc to the chopper.

. . .

The bay of *Pedro 2* sweltered. The HH-60 blasted through arid, mile-high desert air under an afternoon sun. Dried perspiration from that morning's casualty evac added salt to the sweat of this afternoon's mission. LB's crotch and armpits itched.

Rome lay dopey on the Skedco. LB pinched a Zoll's monitor over the kid's index finger to track blood O_2 and pulse. Doc plugged both marines into IVs. LB slumped beside Rome, resting his arm on the marine's raised shoulder. Doc eased the tourniquet around Braun's thigh to let fresh blood flow into the leg.

No one felt chatty for the sixty-mile flight. Rome moaned; Braun grew paler. LB and Doc mopped their brows and monitored vitals. After forty minutes, the Pave Hawk set wheels down on the pad at Camp Bastion.

Doc moved first. LB, lulled by the heat and rocking of the airframe, had closed his eyes, drowsy in the last minutes of the approach.

From outside, the chopper door was shoved open. Rotor wash and tarmac heat gushed in, followed by the urgent arms of a four-man fireman team. They slid out Rome's Skedco to hurry him to a waiting ambulance. Another group of firemen darted forward to lay Braun on a fabric litter, then hustled him away.

LB dropped his boots to the concrete. He paused in the shade made by the HH-60. Slipping off his helmet, he lowered his chin to let the wind from the flipping blades gust down his back, past the armor plating. One of Camp Bastion's Irish nurses slipped three bottles of water into his hands. LB gulped one dry, emptied one into his canteen, and the other over his head.

Thirty meters away, *Pedro 1* settled to the pad.

Doc brushed past LB, looking just as worn. He rapped LB on the med ruck, striding toward one of the ambulances. A member of the recovery team had to stay with the casualties for the short ride to Bastion's hospital, to brief the waiting doctors.

"I'll do the handover."

LB lifted a grateful palm at Doc, who followed Braun's litter bearers. He folded to the helo pad, into the long shadow of the Pave Hawk. The chopper began to shut down its turbos, but for a few minutes more the blades would make a giant fan. LB laid down his M4 to slouch against his pack. The concrete was hot; the low sun made the distant mountains and corrugated plains appear Martian. The water dribbling off LB's crew cut in the mechanical wind slackened the heat.

He did not react to the noise of metal landing near him or the tinny squeal of rolling. The sound was joined by another, then two more.

A smoke canister nudged LB's leg. Three more rolled past, all missing him.

Wally raised his fist in triumph, having bowled closest. The loser, Quincy, threw up one great arm in disgust. Even Doc had turned back to roll one at LB. He waved before strolling off for the ambulance.

Limping, Jamie joined LB in the shade, grinning to be sure LB was okay with the jibe. Quincy, who'd missed by the most, fetched the three errant canisters in the sun before folding his long legs beside Jamie.

Wally strode into the shadow. He did not sit. LB cocked his arm to toss him the smoke grenade. Wally raised a palm.

"Keep it. I have a spare."

"This again? Seriously?"

LB shifted his rump on the tarmac, trying to dispel the image of *Pedro 1* scorching past without Wally demanding the gunner open up to protect his PJs on the ground. All because

LB had forgotten, again, to pack a smoke canister, while Wally packed extras. Wally did everything by the book. LB didn't take the book on rescues. After eighteen years together, the two dealt with each other like old boxers, mostly through tired jabs.

Wally took a seat in the shade next to Quincy, under the chopper's flipping blades. The whine of the Pave Hawk's engines continued its slow fall in pitch.

The CRO and three slouching PJs stared at each other. Doc disappeared into the back of an ambulance. Before the truck rumbled off, Wally, with the tireless and cheery vigor that most annoyed LB, held a thumbs-up into their center.

"Good job, guys. All day long."

Good-natured Jamie held out his own thumb.

Quincy, from the open plains of Nevada, didn't talk much. He'd grown up mostly in a saddle, with horses for company. The big man had a nose for nonsense and tried not to get caught between Wally and LB. Even so, he put up his ham-sized fist, thumb raised, a sign of how tired he was.

All eyes and Wally's reflectors turned to LB. He wished Doc were sitting here; he'd have an ally to gripe at Wally. Getting shot at aged a man. Both he and Doc were old enough.

Quincy rattled his head. Nonsense. Jamie flicked the back of his hand against LB's leg.

"Come on. I'll remind you from now on."

Wally smiled, forgiving, the good spouse. The weight of being wronged held LB's hand down. On top of that he was now the one who wouldn't let the spat go, the Little Bastard.

LB didn't raise his own thumb, wouldn't give in. He waited for Wally's response.

Wally ignored him except to lower his own thumb, leaving his hand suspended between them. Behind the sunglasses, Wally's face lost expression.

Quincy dropped his own hand, Jamie followed suit.

LB reeled his ankles in under him to shove off the tarmac. If he was going to make a scene, he'd do it on his feet.

"What the hell."

Wally silenced him with a raised hand. The fingertips shot to his radio earpiece.

LB sat again.

"What is it?"

Wally shoved the open hand again, then pressed his PTT.

"ROC, Juggler. Go."

While Wally listened, the jet engines of *Pedro 2* reversed their power-down mode to throttle up, rising in tone. The bird's drooping rotors stiffened and began to blur again. Both *Pedro* pilots and Wally were on the same freq to the Rescue Operations Cell.

Wally lifted an index finger beside his temple. Panning his sunglasses across Quincy, Jamie, and LB, he spun his finger in small circles. He spoke into the mike curled at his lips.

"Spinning up now."

Quincy climbed to his feet. He offered a mitt down to Jamie to lift him, then to LB. Across the pad, through waves of heat off the concrete, the rotors of *Pedro 1* accelerated also.

Quincy and Jamie hurried away with their packs and carbines. Jamie's gait showed the strain; Quincy dug a big paw under the boy's pack to help him along. LB donned his helmet and shouldered his rifle. Wally stayed seated, on the radio recalling Doc from the hospital.

LB stood over him, reaching down with his good arm.

Chapter 6

Al-Husn
Ma'rib
Yemen

The village market sprawled the length of a shady lane. Whitewashed walls formed the banks of a river of color: lush tomatoes and lettuce heads, white onions, red clumps of radishes and beets, sacks of amber grains and beans and brown coffee, the heather of bundled herbs, all spread on spun flax blankets. Old men with lined faces kneeled beside their wares to make sales and give change. Sons and younger brothers hawked firewood, carpets, used auto parts, fencing wire, and small appliances. At the entrance to the souk, a young qabil held a Kalashnikov rifle above his head shouting, "Ten thousand *riyals*."

Arif wove through the noon market, the smells of man and earth strong and mingled. He moved among the merchants and shoppers who'd spilled out of the mosque following the dhuhr prayer. Arif recognized no one but returned many nods of women who knew him not by name but because of Nadya. Arif waved away proffers of wool, radios, and knife sharpening. He tossed ten riyals into a pot for a man standing on a box reciting poetry.

At the far end of the closed street, in the short shadow of the mosque, a tribesman sat on the tailgate of a battered pickup. Alongside the truck's bed, other men picked through sheaves of qat branches for the most succulent leaves. Emerald bits flecked the yellow teeth of the old salesman; a wad bulged in his cheek while he made deals.

Arif asked for help selecting the best branches. The merchant, with the fiery eyes of the frequent chewer, wrapped three fresh sprigs in newsprint. He let them go for three hundred riyals.

The home of Ghalib Tujjar Ba-Jalal was indeed easy to find. The place was a concrete and stone giant, a three-story citadel adorned with arched windows, wooden shutters, and horizontal belts of white and pink tile. Behind an adobe wall, it towered over a street of humbler homes, boxes of mud and straw brick painted canary, rose, or sky blue and arrayed at random angles.

A taxi jeep clattered along the pebbly street. It let off passengers lugging woven baskets filled at the market. One of the abaya-covered women entered the tall iron gate to Ghalib's house. Arif followed. She did not glance behind her.

The woman floated across a courtyard that was swept and wetted against the dust. Potted lime, fig, and basil trees shaded the flagstones. She opened a great, iron-studded wooden door weathered beyond the rest of the house and hefted her basket inside. She closed the door, ignoring Arif behind her.

Arif banged the brass ring knocker, receiving no answer, then knocked again. A woman's voice called from a watching window above. He did not look up.

"Who is it?"

"Arif al-Bahaziq. I've come at the invitation of Ghalib Tujjar Ba-Jalal."

The door opened smoothly. No one stood in the dim foyer. The same disembodied voice replied.

"Go to the third floor."

Arif slipped inside. Behind him the door shut on its own, operated by a rig of pulleys and lines disappearing into the shadowy recesses of the house.

He took the first steps. Rising on the treads, Arif uttered the warning of a man walking unescorted into a house of women. "*Allah. Allah. Allah.*"

In the surrounding darkness, on the second floor landing and to the third floor stairs, giggles and scurries tracked him behind walls of carved plaster. Children's small eyes watched out of keyholes, and older girls peered past cracked doors. Arif continued to announce his presence in the house, cool and dark in the late afternoon behind its thick walls, until he reached the top floor and the aroma of smoke. From an open doorway, a man's voice issued with the molasses mist of a water pipe.

"This way, Arif the Saudi."

Arif stepped into Ghalib's *mabraz*, the home's entertaining space for males. Shaykh Qasim's youngest son rested against a pile of satin pillows in a room filled with them. A small refrigerator hummed beneath a shelf of jars holding loose tobacco and charcoal, candies and cigarettes. Bright batiks and tapestries decorated two walls. Ghalib reclined under a broad window; tiers of smoke shifted above his bare head, leaching from his lips. He set aside the hose of the *shisha* and jumped nimbly to slippered feet. Ghalib wore a green silk robe, bare-chested.

"Welcome."

Arif shook his hand and offered the bouquet of qat branches.

"From the souk."

"Already you are an excellent guest. You honor me. Sit. Will you smoke?"

"Please."

"We'll have a snack, then a chew, yes?"

Ghalib returned to his pillows. Arif sat in the Yemeni fashion, right knee raised, left leg tucked under. With hands opened to the floor, Ghalib pressed both palms down from shoulder height to his waist, as if patting in place the cushions around him and the worries of the world outside his walls.

"*Fi l-bayt murtah.*" At home and comfortable.

Ghalib spread out the newspaper and qat stems. He pinched off the greenest leaves, rubbing the dust from them with his thumb. When finished, he presented them in a bowl to Arif, then did the same for himself.

Ghalib set between them yoghurt bowls, a red pepper sauce, raw honey, salt, and fresh *kobz* flatbread. He spread his silken arms, beaming.

"In the name of God, the Merciful, the Compassionate. *Esh wa milh.*" The bond of bread and salt.

Arif tore the wheel of bread, handing half to Ghalib. Together, they dipped into the bowls. In the Arab fashion, neither spoke while eating. Talk would follow, with the qat.

The meal done, Ghalib clapped loudly. An *akhdam* entered to clear the plates. The old servant was African, darker than an Arab. He returned to set a new tray on the floor, bearing tea glasses, a steaming samovar, and a smoking incense pot. The black man served and departed.

Ghalib raised his bowl of leaves, Arif did the same. He'd not chewed qat since arriving in Ma'rib. But years back, in Afghanistan beside a hundred Yemeni fighters, he'd indulged whenever they could get the stuff in the hills. The qat stimulated them, kept the fighters awake and their moods high. Arif tucked the first leaves into his mouth; they tasted grassy and familiar.

The chew moistened Arif's tongue, making for a bitter swallow. Ghalib poured tea for them both. Arif raised his cup in tribute.

"Your home is wonderful."

Ghalib accepted the compliment with his own teacup lifted.

"High praise from a Saudi. There are many palaces in your country."

"Your father was generous to me. He was a great man."

Ghalib licked his finger to snare the last of the leaves from his bowl. He chewed on the wad swelling his cheek.

"The Ba-Jalal have been merchants in Ma'rib since the Sabeans."

"Shaykh Qasim must have been a keen businessman."

Ghalib stroked his goatee.

"My father inherited his business and land. The same as my brothers and me. He was clever with it. He was a hard man. A good Muslim."

A cloud crossed Ghalib's face. Arif chewed the last of his own qat bowl.

"As I said. Your father was kind to me."

Arif sipped his tea. The incense pot gave off heat and a sweet haze, warming the mabraz. The chew would take hold better with a sweat.

Like a rain in the desert, the qat pattered in Arif's blood. He raised his chin, as if to a real cloud, and smiled for no reason but for a spreading sense of delight.

"Tell me about your family, Arif the Saudi."

As he'd told Ghalib at the funeral, he was not in search of new friends, not in need of testimony or approval. The qat reminded Arif, too, that if he had bold thoughts, he could speak them.

"May we dispense with this?"

Ghalib stayed silent but nodded at Arif, who set the tea glass aside.

"My father is dead. My mother is dead. You don't care and I don't want to perform for you. Please tell me the reason for my invitation."

The youngest son licked green flecks off his teeth. He extended his empty tea glass.

"Please."

Arif did not move for the hot samovar. Ghalib held out the glass. After an uncomfortable pause, Arif poured, a reversal of hospitality. He had become the server.

"Tell me about your wife."

"She is my wife. Beyond that?"

"I know she's a Saudi doctor, French trained. She runs a clinic for women in the village. She came with you from Riyadh."

"Is that all?"

"She's a princess of the Al Saud."

Arif caught his breath. He did not let the qat speak his mind now that Nadya was invoked. He emptied his face.

"Your father was the only one who knew that. He told you?"

"Yes."

Ghalib reached for the shisha before he asked:

"Do you mind if I smoke?"

Arif minded much more than that. The betrayal of this secret by dead Qasim. His hands curled toward fists, but he knew better. He'd learned in the hills of Afghanistan, when faced with an unknown force, to hide. He made his hands ease.

"Go ahead."

Ghalib set about preparing the pipe, scraping away the spent ashes from the brass bowl on top. He rose from the pillows to fetch fresh tobacco.

"How did you come to marry a princess, Arif the Saudi? Why are the two of you in my village? Saudis do not come to Yemen just to care for our poor, ignorant women. My father promised you both sanctuary. From what?"

With Ghalib occupied, Arif spit the mashed qat into his glass. He spoke to Ghalib's back.

"First, tell me why I should not stand up and go? I already know the answer, but I'd like to hear the threat from you."

"Truly?"

"I live a quiet life. I have no friends or enemies here. If I'm to acquire one or the other, I should like it made clear."

Ghalib sat with the pipe. He did not speak until it was lit and bubbling.

"A man should not be by himself so much. Shaitan whispers to those who are alone."

Arif spread his hands. The gesture said *Just give it to me.*

"All right. I inherited my father's property, not his promises. Your protection is mine to grant now. I will throw you out. I will cut off the funds for her clinic. Whatever it is you are doing in your quiet life with your Saudi princess wife, you will have to do elsewhere. Does that suffice?"

"I know how to pack a box."

Ghalib raised his own hands to silently ask Why do you make me say it? Arif waited him out. Ghalib sighed, shaking his head at the ruin of protocol.

"Kidnappings in my country are not unusual."

"You wouldn't."

"No, I would not. But your wife is a princess of the Al Saud. If word were spread, less noble men than I would line up to snatch her. Rest assured."

"I would kill you."

"I know."

Ghalib drew on the water pipe's hose, puffing in a way that seemed to blow a kiss at Arif.

"But I wish us to be friends. Allies, at the least."

"You threaten my wife to make me an ally? Is this a joke?"

Ghalib tongued the chawed qat ball out of his mouth, into his bowl. He sat up from his pillowed slouch.

"Not in the least."

"Allies in what?"

"Another secret you gave my father, which he left to me. You are a mujahideen."

"Did Qasim leave my secrets to his other sons, as well? Will I be bartering with your whole clan?"

"Only me. You are a jihadi."

"I was. And you?"

"My family's business is in good hands. My six brothers are all wolves, we'll remain wealthy. As the youngest, I have a luxury. I wish to conduct jihad, as well."

Ghalib aimed the shisha's mouthpiece at Arif. The opening leaked smoke, in the way of a fired gun.

"It was my father's wish for me. You understand."

"And what will you bring to jihad, Ghalib the Merchant? A full heart for Allah? Or a full purse."

"One is not better than the other. I can be a great help to you if you'll let me."

"Help me in what?"

"Yes, Arif. Exactly."

Ghalib folded his long legs beneath him. He leaned elbows to his knees and sat like a boy on a magic carpet, ready to go.

"What are you doing in Yemen?"

• • •

Arif had no ready answer.

His thoughts still raced on the qat. He parsed many things, first among them whether to answer at all, perhaps to lie, or to dare soft Ghalib to a blood feud over the threat.

Ghalib prodded. "Do you know the hadith on loyalty?"

"Do you?"

"'My servant draws me near until I *love* him. When I love him, I am his hearing, his seeing, his hands with which he strikes, and his foot with which he walks. Were he to ask something from me, I would surely give it; if he were to ask for refuge, I would grant it.'"

"Am I to be your servant?"

"My friend."

"Do you know the hadith of the friend?"

"No."

"'A friend may be like a perfume seller or a blacksmith. The perfume seller might give you perfume as a gift. You might buy some, or at least smell its fragrance. The blacksmith might singe your clothes. At the very least you will breathe in the fumes of the furnace.'"

Ghalib clapped gently, fingertips into palm.

"Are you a scholar?"

"Of sorts."

"Arif, I have no reason to fight with you. You cause no one trouble. Your wife does much good for the village. I'm a tribesman, and you live in a tribal place. The Ba-Jalal are of the Abidah. You belong here or you do not, there's nothing in the middle. My father gave you shelter. That put you in his debt."

"The shaykh did not collect."

"He left that to me."

"Why?"

"I'll answer that only to a friend."

Ghalib sucked again on the water pipe, settling deeper into the pillows. He nestled inside the smoke, waiting in there like Shaitan.

"Choose."

This merchant's son already knew enough to put Nadya's life at risk, perhaps Arif's, certainly his own. Telling him the rest seemed a small enough leap from there.

"Are you an educated man?"

"I can read and write."

"What do you know of the Kingdom?"

"A little. And what you will tell me."

Arif reached for the rubber hose of the shisha. Ghalib extended it to him. Nadya would smell the flavored tobacco on Arif's futa later and ask him where he'd been. It pleased Arif to have this in his life, a woman caring enough to question.

He puffed. The tobacco, like the qat, swept him away from this room, on the carpet of his memory, to the vivid years in the mountains, fighting and wild, sandals in the snow, stabbing at an enemy, slipping away to do it again. Arif would murder Ghalib if the man touched Nadya. Arif had last killed men twenty-five years ago, but he remembered well enough. He could do it again, if it was *qisas*, retaliation. The Qur'an gave him that right. Arif exhaled his story with the smoke.

"Are you aware of Juhayman al-Otaybi?"

"No."

"He was a fanatic. In 1979, with two hundred others, he took over the Grand Mosque in Mecca. After three weeks of siege, destroying much of the Mosque, the army had to flush him out of the tunnels by flooding them. Juhayman was beheaded."

"Of course."

"Instead of discrediting him as an extremist, the Al Saud embraced what Juhayman stood for. They were afraid, you see."

"Of what?"

"That there were more like him, charismatics demanding a puritanical version of Islam. In other words, men who resisted the Al Saud's right to rule. So, to appease the Islamists and prevent any more revolts, the monarchy turned the public schools over to the *ulema*. All education in Saudi Arabia became religious. Of course, this also worked to the advantage of the royals."

Ghalib reached for the water pipe's hose, then leaned back onto an elbow. Before sucking on the mouthpiece, he twirled it in front of him to say Keep going.

"The Wahhabism the clerics teach makes obedience a pillar. As a boy, I was taught that to obey the rulers of my nation was holy. That the laws of the Al Saud were the laws of God. It has become the Saudi way not to question."

"But, I think, not your way."

By reply, Arif reached again for the shisha's hose. When the rich man's son was slow to give it, Arif snapped his fingers. He'd stopped being the server.

Ghalib, a chubby, flamboyant man on his feet in the market and today at the funeral, did not seem so feckless reclining in his wealth, holding back the water pipe from Arif. Though the youngest son was manicured, Arif knew the makings of hard men. He began to sense a leavening between himself and Ghalib the Merchant, who surrendered the hose with a sideways tip of his face as if the finger snap awoke in him a new appreciation of Arif the Saudi, as well.

Arif smoked and settled into the pillows.

"I was twelve years old when the reforms came. Overnight, all of our learning stemmed only from the Qur'an. No more English, math, or sciences, just rote memorization. We studied theology, the hadiths, Islamic jurisprudence, and the sciences of the heart. I was part of a whole generation of Saudi boys left unprepared to find work outside a mosque. We had no idea of the realities of the modern world. At the same time, oil production in the Kingdom fell. The economy imploded. There were no jobs. And what work there was, few of us were qualified to do."

"So you became a radical."

"This was the time of the *sahwah*, the awakening. Hundreds of thousands of us could find no self-respect. We couldn't raise the money for a dowry, so we didn't take women. Piety was all the state could give us. Qur'an study groups cropped up everywhere. It was easy to believe that television was evil, that Islam was under attack by the West. I joined a Salafist *madrassa*. One night my imam drove me to a cemetery. He had me lie in an open grave. I looked up into the dark while he told me stories about the scorpions and spiders of hell, the two blue angels who would come to my own grave to take me there, if I did not find my path to God."

Arif laughed, not expecting to do so. He offered back the shisha hose and let himself laugh in the barrel of his chest.

"I will tell you about Peshawar."

"Will this require more tea?"

"Yes."

Ghalib refused the water pipe. He clapped for his akhdam, instructing the old man to bring a fresh tray. In these ways, Ghalib restored Arif to the status of guest.

"Please. Continue."

Arif waited on the tea. When it arrived, he sipped to let a bit of time pass between Ghalib's request and his compliance.

"I turned twenty. Like thousands of young Arabs, I took the Russian invasion of Afghanistan personally, as an attack on our Muslim brothers. I wanted to do something, but had no idea what. I had little money."

"Your parents?"

"My father was a third cousin to the royal family. A petroleum engineer. When I was a young boy, he was killed on an oil rig in the desert. My mother worked as an English tutor. She lost her job when the Al Shaykhs took over the schools. She died twenty years ago."

"Our parents will be paid in heaven for the good works of their children. I'm sorry."

"What have you read beside the Qur'an, Ghalib?"

"Nothing."

The merchant's son said this with no hint of chagrin. Why should he read else, when all was given and taken by God? Ghalib sat easy in his great home, his small world, his women around him, a servant and a mujahideen at his beckon. His Arabic was formal for a man of so few letters. Perhaps his brothers were better educated and he'd picked up some of their ways.

Arif would finish his own tale before asking for Ghalib's, as a guest ought.

"The government wanted us to fight the Russians. It was a way to get unemployed and radicalized young men out of the country, to keep the next Juhayman occupied. The state airline gave discounts to Peshawar, near the Afghan border. I landed in Pakistan with no clue what to do, how to be a mujahideen. That's when I met Osama."

"Bin Laden? Truly?"

"He ran a guesthouse in Peshawar. *Bayt-Al-Ansar*, the House of the Helpers. I stayed there. Osama was a gentle sort then, generous. He talked of jihad in a slow, studied way. There was nothing about him that said he would ever go to the battlefield himself. He was just a wealthy Saudi providing a halfway house for Arabs who'd come to fight. He sent machines over the border to build roads for the mujahideen, that was all. In the souk at the crossing, I bought a Kalashnikov for a thousand riyals. I used it for the three weeks I stayed, then gave it to one of the Afghan fighters. I flew home. I found myself suddenly very popular."

Ghalib stroked his goatee.

"This wasn't jihad. It was a vacation."

"Perhaps. But for the first time in my life I felt at peace. I was away from the madrassas, from talk and study. At the front I was very at ease with the danger. If a bullet or a bomb took me, it would be my entry to paradise. Stories flew around about battlefield miracles. Then when I went home, I was celebrated. People in Riyadh held parties and wanted to know what was going on in Afghanistan. I wanted to go back, but I had no money. That was when I met Nadya."

"At one of the parties."

"She was on holiday from school in Paris. Women were rare at these events, so she stood out. She was keen to know what was going on at the front. Nadya believed like I did, that the Soviets had to be pushed out of Afghanistan. I looked for her at other parties, and she for me. She couldn't go on jihad, not as a woman. So she became my patron. She paid for my plane tickets, guns, and food. I wrote her letters. Each time I stayed in the war longer, often for months. One day bin Laden stopped greeting us at the guesthouse. He'd gone off to fight the Russians in person. I saw him often at the front. He was like a piece of leather left outside; he grew browner and craggier. He could move in the hills with the Afghans like a goat."

Arif drank more tea, the qat chew having left him dry-mouthed. Ghalib stroked his little beard in the same manner his father Qasim had stroked his great gray one. Both listened in the same fashion, nudging and looking for their own advantage.

"I saw much fighting."

"Tell me."

"We were always outmanned, so none of us could do just one thing. I fought as a sniper. I fired Mistral missiles, rigged plastic explosives. We used small arms, submachine guns. Knives, even bows and arrows. We hit the Soviets' flanks, where they were weak, never head-on. We learned to live from the land, sleep under bombs, run away, creep back."

"You are a dangerous man, Arif."

Sweat trickled down Arif's brow from the hot tea and incense burner, the hastening day outside, his memories. Ghalib reclined in cool silk, unbothered.

"I have been."

"Go on. This is fascinating."

"Afghanistan was nothing like what any of us Arabs were used to. We weren't in the desert or a packed city, just flat, white plains. There were rivers and mountain ranges. Long and colorless winters. The Afghans we fought next to belonged to warlords and drug kings or the CIA. A lot of them were criminals, illiterate. All were braver than any men I'd ever met. If they took a wound, they bled without a whimper, while we Arabs rolled around like we'd been cut in two. Even after writing her these things, Nadya wanted to come see for herself."

"But that would be *haram*." Forbidden.

"Not if we were married. We were in love by now. So we signed a *milka* that allowed us to be alone in each other's company and to have relations. She gave me the money for her own dowry. I presented myself to her father."

"The prince."

"I was an uneducated man. But I was a mujahideen, one of the volunteers. I had met and fought alongside Osama bin Laden. And my father had been a distant cousin of the royal family.

Abd al-Aziz groaned, but Nadya is just as strong willed. She'd never opposed her father before. The prince agreed, reluctantly of course."

"Of course."

"We married quickly, another thing that displeased him. Secretly, Nadya flew from Paris to Peshawar. One morning I took her across the border into the battle zone. I showed her how to throw a grenade. I pulled the pin on one and squeezed it between us. 'If I let this go, we will die. So tell me I am your king, I am your master. Yes?' 'Yes,' she said, and I tossed the grenade away. Nadya grabbed another grenade. She pulled the pin, just as I had, and said, 'Now listen to me while I tell you who *I* am.'"

"You are fortunate to have one good wife. I have three wives. I think all of mine would have dropped the grenade."

Their laughter eased the tension. On the wall above the jars of tobacco and candy, a golden square of light beamed through the window, climbing to the ceiling from the setting sun. Arif considered how to proceed with Ghalib, who had threatened him. They'd broken bread, shared smoke, qat, tea, some pleasure. Could he now rise and walk away? What would follow him out the door of this house to his own?

Arif let the mood settle in the scented, hazy air between them.

"I'll finish my story, Ghalib. I'll ask you yours. Then I will choose."

• • •

Arif took for his battle name Abu Ansar. For a year he did not go home to Riyadh, while Nadya completed her studies in Paris. He fought the Soviets in the mountains and open ranges, and in between battles helped ready the corpses of young Saudis for the truck rides to Peshawar. The bodies were wrapped and embalmed with sweet-smelling fluids to console the grieving parents who had to convince themselves their sons died martyrs.

But the war against the infidels was being won. Where twenty years earlier the armies of Egypt and the Arabs could not defeat tiny Israel, one of the world's two superpowers was pulling back a bloody stump against the forces of Islam in Afghanistan. The victory was Allah's.

Inside the Kingdom, the people were jubilant. The Saudis had financed much of the war; they also had paid in blood. Abu Ansar was not one of the dead or maimed; he'd not even been wounded, though he was often under fire. Arif credited this to Allah. For a long time he'd made himself ready to die but had done little to prepare himself to live. Nadya had begun to give him this. A missile at his feet finished the job.

The battle of Jaji marked the beginning of the Soviet retreat. The mujahideen had seized control of the city; the Russians bombarded it to take it back. Working at an aid station, a mortar shell landed only strides from Arif.

Glaring at the smoking shell, he sensed no fear, only *sakina*, the serenity that he was not part of this world any longer but linked to God in another place. Arif raised his arms for the bomb to explode and kill him. When the shell fizzled, the door to God was left wide open. He was done with jihad. Arif could go home.

Once the fighting in Afghanistan turned their way, thousands of young Arabs returned to the Kingdom. They lurched home as hardened mujahideen, savvy with weapons, with experiences and ideas all their own. The monarchy did little to reintegrate these prodigal sons into Saudi society and the Wahhabite culture that had become the way and tool of the Al Saud. In the mosques and madrassas, with stories and scars, these young Islamists, often charismatic, added fuel and credibility to the radicalizing of Saudi youth.

Immediately upon his own return, before they could reunite, Arif's father died in an accident on a rig at a remote drilling site.

The man left behind more debt than money, and the sorrow that Arif would not get to know him, as men together. The only family remaining for Arif was his wife's.

He quickly gave up Abu Ansar, eager to be with Nadya and begin their lives together. Arif's father-in-law was now responsible for him. Hassan bin Abd al-Aziz provided incentives for Arif to reform. Arif grabbed at them greedily: a house in Riyadh, cash payments, and admission to King Saud University to study computer and information sciences.

Ghalib sat forward off the cushions.

"Wait."

"Yes?"

"Your wife is the daughter of Abd al-Aziz?"

"She is."

Ghalib guffawed, clapped, and turned his face up. He glanced left and right to address an invisible chorus of onlookers.

"*Mo'jiza.*" A miracle. "His father-in-law is the head of Saudi Intelligence."

"Shall I continue?"

Ghalib pushed his palms at the floor, tamping down his mirth.

"I apologize. I had no idea. Please."

Nadya began residency at a women's hospital. In three years, Arif earned a degree in software engineering, then completed graduate work in IT in two more. He took a job with the government handling payrolls. They lived well and privately. Nadya's family did not warm to Arif.

"Have you no children?"

"We were never so fortunate."

Ghalib took to his goatee again, fingering it sagely.

"That is reason to leave her. The Ummah must grow. I have seven daughters, two sons."

"The next time you mention my wife, we are done talking."

"I meant no offense."

Ghalib the Merchant was unschooled but far from ignorant. He intended every word he said. Arif poured more tea for them both, to help the moment pass and to serve, what Ghalib seemed to want most from those around him. The box of sunlight crept up the wall. Along with the tea, Arif handed to the seventh son the destination of his story.

"We lived in Riyadh for twenty years. I spent the last three of those in prison."

"At the invitation of the prince?"

"I'm sure he was behind it."

Ghalib opened his arms as though to offer an embrace.

"Again, what did you do?"

"Nothing against the law."

"How can that be?"

Five years ago Nadya told Arif she wanted to go on *hajj* alone. She wanted, like him, to have her own experience of God. With a million other pilgrims, Nadya traveled to Mecca. She stood for a day in the plain of Arafat, stoned the devil at Mina, walked seven times around the black cube Ka'aba inside the Grand Mosque, and returned. On the way home from the airport, she ordered Arif to pull the car to the curb.

"She told me that God had come to her in Mecca not as a woman but as a child of the Prophet. She said, 'Enough.' I was told to get in the passenger seat. She would drive."

"This is a crime in your country, yes?"

"It's only custom. The same way that a woman can't hail a taxi, or buy music, or walk the street unescorted. There's nothing in Sharia that prevents these things. It's only the Al Saud."

Ghalib tapped his bare chest between the collars of his silk robe.

"I have seen your wife drive in Yemen. *Wallah*! Arif."

"Yes."

"May I observe without annoying you that your wife is headstrong?"

Arif nodded. She was more than this. Nadya was the epitome of her father, brilliant and determined. The one daughter among three brothers, she alone had permission from the prince to be educated outside the Kingdom. She was his unstated favorite until she married Arif and left his home. When he demanded grandchildren, she concocted the lie that she was barren to spare Arif more of the prince's disfavor.

Ghalib raised a finger beside his head, to announce that he would make a point. The gesture seemed theatrical, artificial, as if Ghalib had seen a wiser man do this, his father or an older brother perhaps, and he did it now.

"But we must control our women, yes?"

"Why?"

"If you let your woman go off with anyone she pleases, that is the end of the tribe. We are a tribal people, Arif. Perhaps the Saudis take this too far. But you agree, yes?"

"No."

"Truly?"

Arif nodded.

Ghalib lowered the finger. He looked at it, disappointed, on its way down.

"How did you wind up in jail? It was not by letting a woman drive, surely."

"That only got me a visit from the Mutaween, the religious police. And a lecture from the prince to do a better job keeping his daughter in line. This I would not do. I've had three awakenings in my life. An open grave. A mortar shell. And her."

"Ah, you've turned into the worst of men, Arif the Saudi. You've become a reformer."

"Only at first."

Prodded initially by his wife, using his computer skills to stay anonymous, Arif began to contribute to international blogs criticizing the monarchy. Through a series of straw-man accounts, he and Nadya sent funds to opposition groups in London. Arif exploited Twitter and social media platforms using a new battle name, Abu Adel, father of the Just. As Abu Adel, he developed a large following inside the Kingdom, despite the many attempts to root him out and shut him down. Like a mujahideen, Abu Adel knew how to hit and run.

Arif drubbed the royals for their hypocrisy. Every weekend after morning prayers, members of the family could be found speeding down the causeway to Bahrain for nights in bars and discos, every amusement they forbade in the Kingdom. They justified their existence as the absolute guardians of Mecca and Medina; they interpreted the *da'wah*, the call to faith, as an obligation to the government instead of solely to Allah. They twisted the laws of the Prophet to benefit themselves and protect their positions. The royals' corruption, oppression of women, support of America's wars against Muslims, repressions in education, the myths of obedience, their Wahhabite claptrap of severity and punishments, Mutaween enforcers patrolling the cities with canes in hand, the suppression of any political opposition—all ran counter to Arif's reading of the Qur'an.

"And I said so online."

"It is not a wonder you ended up in jail. I mean that as a compliment."

"I will take it as one."

"How did you get caught?"

"The way we all do. I had faith in myself one too many times."

To stay in touch secretly with others in the Kingdom who opposed the Al Saud, Arif ran or tracked several private Internet Relay Chats. The IRCs were set up and torn down daily, with a rotating series of passwords and IDs among users. Regularly, Arif hacked into computers just to slave them as chat servers for hours at a time. In response, the government's General Intelligence Presidency played a cyber game of cat and mouse, spoofing servers to fool rebels into signing in and betraying themselves. Often when the GIP snared a target, they swung deals to persuade the hacktivist to switch sides. One man Arif knew and trusted got swept up in such a sting. He drew Arif to a new IRC, but in a last act of defiance included a warning code that he'd been turned. Arif, overhasty and cocky, missed the signal.

One bright afternoon he emerged from a coffee shop to find a ring of men in tracksuits and running shoes. Had he chosen to make a break, they were dressed to pursue. Politely, they took him to his home where they pored through his books and computers. They let him wait for Nadya to come home from the women's hospital so that he could say good-bye, then drove him to al-Ha'ir, the prison of the Mabahith, the secret police. The charge against him was *fitna*, spreading "discord" across the Kingdom. In the Wahhabite view of Sharia, the governing Al Saud had the duty to preserve the state's harmony; they regularly used this to imprison critics without trial.

For months Arif was questioned, always by pleasant men, who argued that he should be respectful of the community, not sow disagreement and subversion. "This is not the Saudi way. It is *takfir*." The act of a nonbeliever. Arif quarreled with them. He'd not taken up arms against the state, used no violence, only expressed a different opinion. He made no headway and did not buckle. Arif was kept in agreeable conditions—the food and quarters were excellent—but he wasn't allowed to read newspapers or books. Arif was not released.

After the first year, it became obvious that other forces were at work to keep him locked away. Nadya went to her father. The prince responded that he could only do what God commanded. *Allahu A'lam*. Only Arif could effect his release.

So Arif stopped debating his interrogators. He took advantage of the policy that any Saudi prisoner could have his sentence cut in half if he memorized the Qur'an. This cost him the next two years.

Ghalib covered his heart with both hands, a gesture of awe. "Magnificent."

Then Arif was allowed to enter Care Rehabilitation, the Kingdom's response to 9/11, after fifteen of the nineteen hijackers turned out to be Saudis. Just as the prince had tried to do for Arif a decade and a half earlier, the Al Saud created a program of indoctrination and incentives to repatriate its young mujahideen coming home from the conflicts in Iraq, Afghanistan, Somalia, Yemen, West Africa, the Philippines, Chechnya, the far-flung horizon of jihad.

Along with forty returnees from Guantánamo Bay, Arif was held in isolation for three months at a complex of former desert resorts outside Riyadh. The guards did not wear uniforms, and the grounds were grassy and open. The men lived dormitory-style, prepared group meals, and were well fed; the ghostly jihadis around Arif regained the weight they'd lost. Every day they played football on the athletic fields; the Saudi boys had been exposed to mujahideen from around the world and picked up many bad habits of the aggressive European-style game. It amused Arif to watch the detainees being coaxed back to the Saudi brand of soccer, meticulous and team oriented. Daily meetings with Wahhabite scholars and shaykhs opened them to persuasion and to debate over the interpretation of Islam. They were reminded over and over that the Qur'an held 124 verses about dealing kindly with non-Muslims, while only one advocated waging war against them. Again Arif was instructed, like he had been as a child, that the Qur'an was the basis for everything in the nation's constitution, that the Al Saud ruled by the hand of the Prophet. He was challenged to find disagreement, but this time Arif simply nodded in agreement. Those radicals who would not renounce their extremism, the militant warriors who'd come home convinced in the power of a gun, the battle deranged, the withdrawn and sullen ones who refused to engage even in the football games, they were held longer.

"On my release, I signed a *taahud* promising to be a good citizen. Not to criticize the Al Saud online. Nadya's father came to the prison personally to open my cell. Before letting me walk out, he asked if I would keep my pledge, since he was responsible for me. I said I would honor it."

"Did you?"

"For two months. Then we left."

"A lie is a sin of the tongue, Arif."

"A man may lie when he speaks to his wife to please her, to reconcile between people, and in war. I had all three reasons."

"I see the Al Saud's rehabilitation of you did not take."

"No."

"And I think you have come to Yemen to break your taahud."

"I came here because I believe the will of God, not the words of oil barons and fat princes, is law. Nothing in Sharia supports an absolute monarchy. Power is God's to give, not the Al Saud's. God desires to give it to my wife, to me, and to the Ummah of his lands. Allah wants no kings."

"Did you tell all this to my father?"

"Yes."

"I see now why he gave you sanctuary. You are indeed a scholar. And a warrior. You're the new Juhayman, with a computer. What have you done since you've been our guest?"

"I've taken down some Saudi censorship sites. I was part of a group that disrupted the Saudi oil company's network."

"Anything else?"

"I've hacked into some archives and corporate sites. There's more than a hundred thousand cyber attacks on Saudi ISPs every day. I am part of that."

Ghalib frowned, trying to grasp.

"This is jihad?"

"I'm very close to something more. Something big."

"Excellent. Tell me."

"We haven't decided if we're friends."

"My father was your friend. Tell me for him."

"I wasn't aware Qasim believed in reform."

"He didn't."

"What then?"

"Retribution."

Arif had answered Ghalib's questions for two hours. The qat finished, the tea cold, the tobacco gone, the sun was falling. The time had arrived for the shaykh's youngest to answer, or for Arif to leave his home.

"Why did you ask me here?"

"At my father's graveside were seven brothers. There should have been eight. Three years ago, the next one older than me, Yasser, was killed."

"What happened?"

"He was incinerated driving west from Ma'rib. A missile strike from an American drone. He was killed with his wife and youngest son. Another car nearby was destroyed also, a local businessman."

"I'm sorry."

"Of course."

"Your brother was al-Qaeda?"

"No. He was only responsible for funneling our family's money to them. My father was al-Qaeda. But Yasser's name was the one on the CIA's list. And so."

Many times in prison, al-Qaeda—the child of Osama bin Laden—had reached out to Arif. Emissaries were sent his way, gifts and quiet persuasions. A man of Arif's talents would be invaluable. Al-Qaeda shared his goal of toppling the Saudi crowned heads. Gently, Arif rebuffed the overtures. Their methods were not his, their aims too broad, and they would replace the Al Saud with themselves, not the people, and not an improvement.

Ghalib's invitation was coming clear. Qasim could spare his youngest son; just as Ghalib said, the family business was in good hands without him. Arif asked a question he already knew the answer to.

"And you, Ghalib?"

"Tell me. Do you have American drones flying over Saudi Arabia?"

"No."

"Your people will not allow it. Would America tolerate drones from a foreign government flying over their cities? What would be their response after the first missile murdered an innocent or child? At my father's wish, in my brother's place, I have taken the *bay'a*." The al-Qaeda oath.

"I see. And what will you do for them? Move money, like your brother?"

"I have taken a blood vow. America is the far Satan. Her allies around us are the near Satan."

Ghalib, foppish and virtually illiterate, knew just enough to quote Osama bin Laden. He talked like a warrior, but he was a jihadi on pillows.

Ghalib rubbed his palms, a greedy, more suitable gesture.

"Arif, this thing, this big thing you are close to. What will you do with it?"

"Post what I find online. Maybe give it to one of the opposition groups in London."

"London? What will that accomplish?"

"Humiliate the Al Saud. Expose them. Defy them."

"And what reforms will you demand? What would you have them do?"

"Share power. Allow transparency. Freedom of expression."

Ghalib chuckled softly.

"Dreams."

Arif drew in his legs to get on his feet and go. Ghalib slowed him with a raised palm.

"Do you think the United States will allow the Al Saud to fall? Truly?"

Ghalib pointed behind himself, out the window, into the gilded sky where the drone had come from, as if America existed there, above them like Allah.

"Do you believe America will allow this? Democracy in the Kingdom? Give the Saudi people freedom to vote, so they can say No, we do not want the crusaders' interests in our country? Shave my beard if it is so."

Arif raised his voice.

"And what would you have me do? Pick up a gun again? This is how I fight now."

Ghalib settled after Arif's outburst. Arif did not release the tension in his legs, remaining poised to rise when he'd heard enough.

"Dissent, Arif? Embarrassment?"

"Yes."

"Your problem is you think too small. You need one more awakening. I am it."

"How do you suppose?"

"You can't get what you want doing it your way. The House of Saud will not topple like that. You need another path."

"That is?"

"*Fawdha*." Ruin.

Ghalib gathered himself on his cushions. He closed his green robe across his chest and folded his legs, hands on knees to sit like a shaykh, a powerful man.

"Think of Juhayman. In the end he got what he wanted."

"His head chopped off?"

"No. Change."

"And what do you suggest I do?"

"I have resources you do not."

"And?"

"This information you will find. Give it to me."

Chapter 7

11 Degrees North
Camp Lemonnier
Djibouti

This warm evening 11 Degrees North was packed. Marines, pilots and aircrews, sailors, National Guardsmen, contractors, all milled around the Armed Forces televisions, dartboards, and pool tables, inside at the bar or out on the terrace.

LB sat alone on the balmy patio, at the rim of the crowd in the fringes of light. He clapped his first beer bottle on the tabletop and leaned back. Beyond the canteen's lights, the clear Djiboutian sky twinkled. Behind the high blackout fence, an aircraft warmed up unseen on the main runway a hundred yards away. LB made up his mind to drink until he counted a dozen takeoffs and landings—a random number, but he figured it would cover his evening.

In the middle of the patio, with people on all sides, Wally and Torres leaned toward each other on their elbows, going public for the first time, and unaware that LB or anyone else was here with them. She wore her dark hair down her shoulders, loosed from her constant bun.

The first flight, a Predator, idled a while, then blared skyward. The big drones operating out of Lemonnier, always ominous to the fighting men and women, both for being invisible and unmanned, raised a distinct, mournful whine. Flying lightless into the night over Africa, the drone seemed witchlike.

Closer to the fence, an HC-130 finished its engine run-up. The cargo plane taxied, then accelerated down the strip to lift off. Like the Predator, only a gray shape rose into the dark; the plane was executing a blackout drill with no external lights, the crew wearing night-vision goggles. On board were Doc, Quincy, Mouse, and a still-gimpy Jamie on a night training jump. LB tracked the plane's rumble until it faded, then walked inside the canteen. He bought a round to be delivered to Torres and Wally plus two beers for himself. He ferried the bottles back to his table.

LB finished one of the beers without ever setting it down. Out of the nighttime west of the base, a marine chopper left the ground, chasing after the cargo plane to practice in-flight refueling, a difficult thing to do in daylight, a hazard at night. After the chopper departed and the patio returned to the buzz of mosquitoes, chatter, and country tunes, LB started his third beer. Through gaps in the shifting crowd, he fixed on Torres and Wally.

Another HC-130 approached from over the black Gulf of Aden and landed. A helo returned from somewhere. To the long winding down of the chopper's blades, LB sipped and in his imagination entered the fuselages of all these aircraft coming and going, even the drone. They carried away men and missions, weapons and cameras, and as long as they brought them all home, LB and the PJs were left to wait and prepare. LB could drink his beers alone tonight in the starry peace of his table, and Wally could gaze into whatever he saw in Torres's eyes.

A waiter delivered to Wally's table the drinks LB had bought. Torres pulled her attention from Wally, listened to the waiter, then started to rise. Wally took her wrist to keep Torres in her chair. Instead, he shot to his feet. Taller than most, Wally scanned the deck until he found LB.

He headed for LB's table, swinging his shoulders to wend through the crowd. LB watched him come, then stop, reconsider, and keep coming.

He arrived with hands out, mouth hanging open and silent. LB indicated one of the empty chairs.

"What are you doing over here? I thought it was date night."

Wally dropped his hands and closed his jaw.

"What's wrong with you?"

"Beg pardon."

"What the hell are you doing?"

"I sent over a couple drinks. You're welcome."

"Why would you piss her off like that?"

"It was a joke. Calm down. Both of you."

Wally pulled out the chair to sit. He laid his forearms flat, leaning in as he had across from Torres.

"You really have no idea half the time, do you?"

"About what, specifically?"

"Other people. Normal people."

"I've known you eighteen years. Got you pretty figured out."

"You think?"

"I do."

"Here's something new you might be missing. I like her. She likes me. I scared her in the pool last week when I passed out. Didn't you see how she reacted?"

"You were fine the whole time."

"That isn't what I asked. Did you see how she reacted?"

"Yeah."

"Like what?"

"Like she didn't understand that people get hurt doing what we do."

"She's the PRCC[10], she sends you and me out. She gets it, LB. But she never figured she'd have to watch me drown myself. I didn't think of that before I did it."

---

10 Personnel Recovery Cell Coordinator.

"Why the hell would you?"

"You're the one who doesn't get it."

"Bullshit. You put the team first, where it belongs. Bravo. You did your job."

Wally loosed a headshaking laugh.

"Man. I just saved your ass again and you don't even know it. Next time I'll let Torres come over here. You want to keep pissing her off, it's your funeral."

Wally surveyed the stars and the canteen crowd, as though searching for a way out, a back door to avoid saying something even more harsh.

"You know what?"

"What?"

"You're right. I was doing my job. But at the moment, over there, I'm doing something else. My life." Wally pushed back the chair. "And that doesn't include you."

He strode into the canteen crowd, not dodging the marines and airmen but letting them move or get bumped.

LB raised his third beer to himself.

"That went well."

The opposite chair stayed out of alignment, a lingering mark of Wally's vexation. LB thought to straighten it, when the seat was filled by the wide frame of young Lieutenant Berkowitz.

The CRO arrived without a drink, on alert tonight. He pointed at LB's beer.

"You good?"

"Yep."

The LT settled in. He looked around the canteen, taking it all in, the eagerness of a first deployment.

"How're you feeling, LB?"

"Emotional."

"Really?"

"No."

Berko grimaced, trying to decipher, then gave it up to slouch in the metal chair. Far behind him, another cargo plane revved for takeoff. The kid was broad shouldered, six feet and chiseled, with keen dark eyes.

"I was asking about your wounds. That's all."

"I know."

The cargo plane lumbered to the runway. In the canteen crowd, a woman saw someone she'd not crossed paths with in a long while and hugs flew around. Somewhere seven thousand feet up, four PJs leaped off a lowered cargo ramp into the blackness. LB took a swig, and Berko snapped his fingers.

"Hey. I heard you wrestled in college."

"UNLV."

"That's big-time. I was at Brooklyn College."

"Good."

"We should take it to the mat sometime. Be fun."

"Don't think so."

"Why not?"

Twenty-one years ago, LB had joined the military. For the first decade, most of the grappling he'd done had been to take men to the ground to silence or kill them; after that, to hold them in place to save them. LB cut his eyes at Wally and Torres, who'd resumed gazing at each other. And he'd done some of that. Not enough.

"I'd cheat."

Berko nodded without understanding.

"How old are you?"

"Twenty-four."

"You got time."

"For what?"

LB ran a hand over the crown of his head, wondering how he might answer.

"Nothing."

Berko winced, still confounded.

"Sure. So why're you sitting by yourself?"

"Why aren't I?"

The young officer didn't scoot his chair back to leave. Instead, in a manner that was not friendly or insistent but simple and loyal, he held his ground. Berko yanked a thumb at Wally and Torres.

"What was that with you and Wally?"

"You watching me, kid?"

"Isn't that what I'm supposed to do?"

"Look, Lieutenant, that's work. I'm not working right now."

LB tapped the table, trumped by himself. It felt low to say to Berko the same stinging thing Wally had said to him.

"All right. Stay. But I'm drinking."

Berko dug into his hip pocket for a small leather case.

"I'll smoke. Cigar?"

"You got two?"

"It'd be rude to only bring one."

This was one of those raised-right kids. LB accepted the stogie and a light. The cigar would slow his beers, and the young officer distracted him from counting landings and takeoffs. Berko lit his own cigar, then leaned back to admire the stars with LB. The kid didn't speak and blew smoke rings better than LB.

"It was a joke. All I did was buy them a round."

"What'd you get?"

"I sent Wally a rye, Coke, and cranberry."

"So?"

"It's a Dr. Pecker."

"That pissed him off?"

"No. It pissed off Torres. You heard about that thing in the pool last week."

"Yeah."

"I got her a Bloody Mary. I told the waiter to call it a Bloody Wally."

"That's funny shit."

"I know."

The ember of Berko's cigar glowed from a deep draw.

"You and Wally know each other pretty well, then."

"That's an understatement."

"That's cool."

"We've been back-to-back as much as we've gone nose to nose."

"Kind of like brothers."

"Like sisters."

"How long?"

"Close to twenty."

"Man."

"Since he was a fourth year at the Academy. I was an LT in the Rangers; he ran the school jump team. My squad stopped in for some high-altitude training. Wally jump-mastered for us. He was the best. Still is. Later on, I had some Spec Ops in Honduras. I requested him to jump us in. He did a good job. After he graduated, he joined the Rangers. Just as I was quitting for the GA."

"So he kind of followed you."

"Kind of."

Except that LB gave up his officer's commission to become a PJ. Wally stayed an officer and became a CRO. And for the last thirteen years, he'd been LB's CRO.

"I'd heard you'd done that. Gave up being a captain to be a PJ?"

"Where'd you hear it?"

"At Indoc. Why'd you do it?"

"What do they say at Indoc?"

"No one knows for sure."

"Let's leave it that way."

"That's cool."

Berko mulled behind his cigar.

"So I get it. You guys are tight. You were just kidding around with him and Torres."

"That's all."

"But you understand. He was just standing up for her. Though I don't think the major needs anybody doing her standing."

LB answered with his own long puff. He cocked his head, inviting the young lieutenant to stop right there. Berko gave no ground and planted an elbow on the table.

"You'd have done the same thing. Same situation. You know, if someone upset your date. Even if they didn't mean it."

LB had accepted the cigar. Now he couldn't get rid of the kid.

"No I wouldn't. He's a GA. One of us. She's not."

Berko pursed his lips and let it go, but with a shrug that showed he really wasn't.

There's more to life than being a PJ. That's what LB read in the young officer's slow fade back into the metal chair, the theatrical way he lifted the cigar to his lips. There's other things to do with your time between deployments than spend it at Indoc training kids. There's Berko's nice Jewish parents and probably a pretty Brooklyn girl. Doc's home filled with a wife and daughters in Vegas. Quincy's cattle ranch in the Nevada highlands. Wally's mom and dad, a sister in San Francisco, a date with Torres in Djibouti.

LB bit the cigar and took the sweating third beer by the neck. He waved the back of his hand at all of this, everything young Berko did not say. What was LB supposed to do, apologize for saving lives? For training hard and pushing others to do the same? In the silence between him and young Berko who had saved no one and given nothing yet, the canteen raised more glasses and voices, the equatorial stars glittered, and more dark planes flew away.

They recite the Qur'an and consider it in their favor, but it is against them . . .

What I fear most is those who interpret verses of the Qur'an out of context.

They will pass through Islam as an arrow passes through its quarry.

Wherever you meet them, kill them.

The one who kills them or is killed by them is blessed.

They are the dogs of the People of Hell.

A hadith of the Prophet Muhammad
regarding those who pervert Islam
for their own purposes

Interlude

The home of Prince Hassan bin Abd al-Aziz
Riyadh
Saudi Arabia

Abd al-Aziz rapped a knuckle against one of the dozen video screens.

"That's him?"

"Yes."

The guard opened a file folder on his desk. He plucked from it a black-and-white photo, a passport-style shot. The Pakistani held the picture up to the monitor so that the prince could compare the likeness; both the still and live images were of a short, hawk-faced, and slender man, beardless, with a beak nose and distrustful eyes.

This confirmed the presence of Walid Samir bin Rajab from Jeddah in the prince's waiting room.

Abd al-Aziz had come the instant he was notified, an afternoon nap interrupted. The small, ragged chap on the screen rocked gently in a cushy chair, hands in his lap. He ate nothing from a tray of hummus, olives, and flatbread set near him in hospitality. He was dressed not like the Saudi he was, in white thobe and agal, but in a cotton tunic, futa skirt, sandals, and *pakul* hat, the traces of Yemen. Walid Samir bin Rajab seemed tense but in no hurry; he was surely aware that armed guards stood on each side of the doors in and outside of the reception room.

"Has he been searched?"

The security guard was a mustachioed man, chestnut dark and fat beneath a burgundy beret. The prince never spoke this guard's name because it was Muhammad, and he didn't like to attribute the Prophet to such a black and foreign fellow.

"He had these on him."

The guard handed over a cheap flip cell phone, a compact Qur'an, and a USB thumb drive.

"Anything else?"

"He says he wants to speak with you."

The prince hefted the items.

"Did he say why?"

"Only that you will want to talk with him."

"Tell him I know that he's here. Ask him to wait."

The guard flicked a switch, leaning his mustache close to a microphone.

"*Sayedi?*"

On the screen, bin Rajab got to his feet, blank-faced and ruffled. He bowed at the voice in the waiting room. The guard informed him of the prince's words. Bin Rajab bowed again. He asked the camera for a bowl of water and towel to wash up.

Abd al-Aziz tapped the monitor once more.

"Search him again."

• • •

The prince traced a finger down the list, though he did not need to. He knew by heart the names of the Kingdom's most wanted men, those who'd plotted or taken part in attacks on Saudi targets in or outside the country. The List of 85 was his profession. He maintained it, crossed names off, added new ones.

Walid Samir bin Rajab. #34. Forger, recruiter, and trainer for al-Qaeda on the Arabian Peninsula. Involved in the fighting in the Nahr al-Bared refugee camp in northern Lebanon.

Planner for the 2006 suicide bombing of the Abqaiq oil refinery. Organizer of fighters for the Afghan war along the Syrian-Iraqi border. Planner for the 2012 suicide bombing of a militia funeral in Jaar, Yemen.

Abd al-Aziz took the little thumb drive in his palm, weighing its nothingness. What was on it so that bin Rajab could say The prince will want to see me?

Whirling to his laptop computer, he plugged the stick into a USB port. Immediately Abd al-Aziz ran an antivirus scan on the contents of the tiny drive. The scan came up clean.

The drive contained only one file: *alAziz$girls.xls*.

The prince bit his lower lip, scraping his front teeth through the thistles of his beard. He clicked on the file; a spreadsheet popped onto the screen.

The header above the first column read: Accounts. Beneath it were listed the numbers of nine different accounts all belonging to Hassan bin Abd al-Aziz: four banking access numbers, one each in Scotland, the Emirates, Lucerne, and Grand Cayman; one stock brokerage in London, another in Tanzania; credit cards issued by private banks in San Francisco and Hong Kong; and the account number for the prince's Amex Black Card.

A second column bore the heading Payees. For each account, a collection of businesses was listed by date and withdrawal amount, extending over the past twenty-four months. The prince read the first few names: Top Hat in Toronto, Paradise in London, KingsMistress in Dubai and Paris, Jînshèn Nǔshén in Hong Kong. The list of escort services flowed well past the bottom of the screen, totaling close to £100,000. Abd al-Aziz did not follow the list to its end. He blanked the screen and yanked out the thumb drive.

He'd been hacked. Someone, who? How?

The prince balled both fists and let that be his expression of outrage. Anything more would do no good, a lesson long and hard learned in espionage. He glared into the compromised laptop as if into a black tunnel, at the unknown trespasser looking back at him. Who was it? Certainly not skinny bin Rajab; the little terrorist had a different set of skills. Who'd burrowed into his private computer? Who? What else had been stolen out of it? The prince's mind raced with the contents of the hard drive, what more personal damage could be mined from it.

Abd al-Aziz closed the computer, unable to look it in the face. He'd have it scrubbed, but until then, he couldn't touch the keys. He slammed a fist on the desk, conceding himself one act of rage. A Tiffany lamp tipped, almost falling over, but righted itself. The prince wanted to clear his desk with a swipe of his arm, throw things, damage something. He put his hands in his lap before he could do this.

• • •

In front of a mirror, Abd al-Aziz donned his *mislah*, the dark, gold-trimmed cloak of the Al Saud. He admired himself, a man of girth and value. He stood in his home office of stone pillars, marble floor, brown leather sofas and chairs, on an ancient woven carpet. His windows looked out on a palm-shaded swimming pool, beyond that to his cameras and walls, and to the cameras and walls of his powerful neighbors.

He had a wife and mistresses and children. Many brothers and sisters, and a vast family beyond them. He had responsibilities to his cousin the king and to his nation. He possessed power and greatness.

Bin Rajab had come to his house to threaten him with pilfered information. Or was it a threat? Why had he come here? Why deliver the thumb drive in person? What trade was he seeking?

Calmed in his royal robe, Abd al-Aziz considered the cost. For his wife, the price would be jewels and promises. To his sons, an apology for his carelessness and a wink. The rest of the family and the press would get nothing but a stony denial and his own set of well-placed threats. The king would insist on discretion, and perhaps a temporary demotion. That would be the worst.

Years ago, while still a young man, Abd al-Aziz had traveled the desert many times on camelback. A distant Bedu cousin took him to the far reaches of the Rub' al-Khali. On one such journey, a servant fell asleep in the saddle, spilled out, and broke his neck. He could not move his limbs. He asked to be shot. The cousin did this. After burying the servant, the Bedouins all agreed they would rather see a man dead than humiliated.

Abd al-Aziz moved behind his wide desk. He chose to sit. He would not stand to shake hands when bin Rajab entered but would rise once their meeting was done and he'd gotten what he wanted.

He opened the file on his desk to imply he'd been reading it. Beside this, he set bin Rajab's cell phone and the little thumb drive. The prince touched a call button.

First through the door came his personal security chief, Tariq, a burly fellow of Israeli blood, the hardest people on earth. Behind him shuffled bin Rajab, hands clasped and face turned down as if already walking down a prison corridor. Last came the prince's secretary and nephew, Kemal, to take notes and learn.

Tariq walked bin Rajab to a chair facing the desk. Young Kemal took a seat against the wall. Before the prince could speak, he was caught on the awful gaze of bin Rajab. The terrorist measured the prince like a man buying a knife. Bin Rajab was skimpier than he appeared on the monitor, an ascetic, judging little man. Reputedly he'd killed a hundred in his time. Abd al-Aziz had sent more men to their deaths than that.

The prince gestured to the plush chair. "Sit, please." The desk between them was very old, heavy, and polished. It had belonged to Abd al-Aziz's grandfather. On this desk was signed the order to behead Juhayman al-Otaybi.

Bin Rajab folded into a leather chair that nearly swallowed him. Tariq stood behind him. Kemal set a notepad on his knees.

With a finger, Abd al-Aziz flicked the little thumb drive forward as if it were a dead bug on his desk.

"Where did you get this?"

Bin Rajab pointed at the closed laptop. "Out of your own computer, sayedi. Of course."

The prince drew a deep breath to hold on to his calm. The long exhale rustled in his whiskers.

"How?"

"I do not know how, sayedi. The data stick was given to me."

"By whom?"

"I did not know the man."

"Do you know what is on this drive?"

"No, sayedi. I was told only that it was your sins. I doubt they are all there."

"Is this blackmail?"

"No."

"Was there more stolen from me?"

"I do not believe so."

"Has any of this been made public?"

"No. But what will happen, I cannot say."

"Then why did you bring this to me?"

"As a warning. As a gift. And it seemed the way to meet the prince."

"What do you want?"

"To come home."

"You want to enter rehabilitation."

"Yes, sayedi."

"I see."

The prince spun the opened file around on the slick desktop. He laid a fingertip onto the List of 85, on top of #34, bin Rajab.

"I know you've taken the bay'a to al-Qaeda."

"Yes, sayedi."

"You have blood on your hands."

"I have."

"Why should I let you return?"

"Sayedi?"

"Why should I not put you out of my house, have you followed and killed in an alley? Then I will scratch your name off my list."

Bin Rajab's lips worked for an elusive reply. Abd al-Aziz pressed him.

"Perhaps I could give you to the Americans. And who knows who they would give you to?"

The prince waited. Kemal had written nothing yet.

"Tell me why I should not do this?"

"Because I am a Saudi citizen."

Abd al-Aziz smacked a flat palm on the List of 85.

"These are all Saudi citizens, too. And none of them have come to my house. Why are you here? Who sent you?"

Bin Rajab licked his lips. His gaze tumbled, cutting back and forth as if scanning the floor for crawling things. The prince turned the folder around to close it.

"Let me help you. You wish for amnesty."

"Yes, sayedi."

Nephew Kemal's pen began to move.

"You wish to recant the aims of al-Qaeda. You renounce your membership."

"Yes, sayedi."

"You will accept a prison term. After you're done, you'll enter rehabilitation. Following that, you will take a new oath, to be a proper Saudi citizen. Understand, I will take a personal interest in you keeping your word."

"Yes, sayedi."

The prince pulled his hands from the sleeves of his thobe. He propped his elbows on the great desk to rub his palms together, causing a hiss. Behind bin Rajab, big Tariq nodded.

"None of this will happen if you do not tell me where you got the information on this drive. You will be escorted from my house. And so you understand. What will happen after that, I cannot say."

This raised bin Rajab's thin face. The tiredness was gone. He seemed resolved, a flush in his cheeks.

"Yes, sayedi."

Bin Rajab drew in his sandaled feet to stand. Behind him, Tariq fingered the grip of the 9 mm at his waist, inching forward. The prince motioned him to hold back. Tariq halted with the gun half-drawn, scowling at the back of bin Rajab's hat, clearly wanting to press the muzzle of his pistol to it.

The terrorist gestured to the cheap cell phone on the desk. "I have a number to call."

"And who will answer?"

"I do not know. I suspect you may."

The prince took the phone in hand. This was a break; he'd not guessed he would actually speak with the one who'd sent bin Rajab. There was still a chance, then, that the damage could be contained.

"Kemal."

The young man, tall and spare, pale for a Saudi male, was the eldest boy of Abd al-Aziz's sister. He spent too much time indoors. Kemal looked up from his note taking.

"Yes, Uncle."

"Get out."

Kemal left with a white flutter of robes. Behind bin Rajab, Tariq did not budge.

Bin Rajab accepted the phone and flipped it open. His right index finger hovered above the keys while his lips moved silently, recalling the number, or praying. Quickly he punched in a long series of numbers, an international call.

Bin Rajab extended the phone at arm's length to the prince.

The phone trilled several times. The speaker clicked. A reedy voice emerged.

"Merhabba?"

Bin Rajab blinked away sudden tears.

The prince came from behind his desk. Around the pistol's grip, Tariq's knuckles whitened. The prince moved carefully, slowly, reaching for the phone bin Rajab held out. Bin Rajab's hand trembled as the prince closed in. Again, the answering voice inquired.

"Merhabba?"

Instantly bin Rajab reeled the phone back in. He hung up the connection.

The prince flexed his fingers. "Give it to me."

Bin Rajab clutched the phone tight to his chest so that the prince could not wrest it away. Abd al-Aziz surged forward, reaching. Tariq drew his pistol fully. He shouted.

"Let it go!"

Bin Rajab screamed back.

"Allah hu akbar!"

Bin Rajab punched one more key, a series of beeps, a speed dial.

A red, wet explosion knocked Abd al-Aziz backward off his feet. He wound up sitting on his desktop, lifted there like a child out of his sandals, bare toes dangling. Warm bits slipped down his cheeks and forehead, clung on his lips and in his beard. His ears rang and his chest hurt from the jolt. Blood marred his vision but he could not wipe his eyes for the red spray on his hands and the front of his thobe. A haze smelling of chemicals, spicy like burning coal, clouded the office, but the prince saw well enough to watch Tariq climb off the floor to a wobbling stance. The big security chief held his arms wide to look at himself, also spattered in shreds of gore, still clutching his pistol. The office had been splashed crimson and brown near the spot where bin Rajab had blown himself up and chairs were tossed about, but beyond that the room was barely wrecked.

Abd al-Aziz slid off the desk into his sandals, left where they'd been when the blast hit. From a drawer he took a box of tissues to clear his eyes and wipe his face. He tossed the carton to Tariq.

"This is what you call searched?"

Tariq opened his mouth to say something. With a raised hand, the prince shut him up. Tariq's failure would be part of the investigation that started now. Besides, Abd al-Aziz would be barely able to hear for a few more minutes, though he was aware of Kemal pounding and shouting at the door.

"Tariq, tell him to be silent. And to keep everyone away until I say."

The prince stepped beside the detonated remains of bin Rajab. The corpse lay chestdown, missing its head and Yemeni hat from a jagged and charred neck. Smoke curled out as if from a gun barrel. The carotid artery dribbled onto the carpet. The tip of bin Rajab's spinal cord protruded; the exposed vertebra was sooty and the meat around the bone had been fried gray.

The prince knelt into the stench of blood and bile. The left sleeve of bin Rajab's peasant tunic lay vacant; scarlet stained it from the empty shoulder socket. Tariq busied himself searching the upturned office for the missing head and arm. The prince lay a hand on the back of bin Rajab's warm blouse. The little terrorist's torso caved under his touch, collapsing like a sponge. Beneath the flesh, the rib cage had been shattered, all the organs popped, containing the blast.

Abd al-Aziz tugged up bin Rajab's futa skirt to expose the man's small buttocks. Using his thumbs, he pried apart the cheeks to peek between them. As expected, he found the dented, silver bottom of a metal tube tucked inside the anus and a tiny wire antenna trailing from it.

The prince stood, moving to his desk. He planted his hands and leaned over them. His left wrist, the one clutching for the phone at the point of the explosion, felt wrenched. He closed his eyes to thank Allah for his life and for the stupidity of bin Rajab. His hands trembled on the desktop. He did not lift them until they stilled.

Abd al-Aziz stood erect, lifting his eyes to the ceiling. His jaw fell. The gathering smoke there slipped upward through a fifty-centimeter-wide hole.

The prince gasped, agog, laughing that he just now thought to look up from the mess at his feet.

"Tariq."

The prince stood again over bin Rajab. He peered up through the blood-smeared hole in the ceiling, past busted plaster and broken boards in the floor above, at the shocked brown face of his Filipino servant gaping down from the dining room overhead. Before Abd al-Aziz could speak to him, the servant turned his own face up to the hole punched in the ceiling above him. The deafening of Abd al-Aziz's ears had eased enough to allow him to hear the screams of his teenage niece from her room on the third floor. There was a mangled head under her dressing table.

Tariq had found the arm. He moved beside the prince with the cell phone from bin Rajab's dead hand.

Tariq nudged bin Rajab with his boot, to dishonor the man's body by touching it with a shoe. Bin Rajab had plenty of shame on his own; he lay decapitated, armless, soft as a stuffed doll with a wire hanging out of his bare *teez*. He or someone had packed a lethal amount of plastic explosive—probably PETN, by the telltale bituminous stink—into a metal tube, perhaps a cigar canister. It had been inserted into his rectum, with the failure to calculate that bin Rajab carried this directional charge. When his phone signal sparked the blasting cap, the detonation followed the shape of the container, jetting vertically through his bowels and chest cavity, blowing into his shoulders, neck, and head. Bin

Rajab's suicide became a grim and comic waste, his skull turned into a cannonball that plowed three stories straight up, to land in Abd al-Aziz's niece's bedroom.

The prince did the same as Tariq; he shoved bin Rajab with his sandal.

"I want the house locked down. All the phones, electronics, everything. No word of this gets out. Tell your men. All the staff. I'll speak to my family."

"What about your computer?"

"Don't scrub it yet. Someone's in there. I want him to stay a little longer."

The prince took the cheap phone from Tariq.

"How long until you know who answered this?"

"One hour. Two at the most."

"And where he is."

"Tomorrow morning."

Down through the two ceilings, past the ringing in his ears, the prince's niece would not stop screaming.

"And get that damned head out of my niece's room."

• • •

Abd al-Aziz stood unwashed in his gory thobe before his wife and niece, to impose the seriousness of what he was going to demand. At the sight of him, they covered their hearts in shock and dropped to their knees to thank Allah for his safety. They cursed the terrorists of the world as cowards and evil. He lifted them both to their feet, thanking them for their prayers and kind words. To relieve them, he made them laugh with the story of the launching of the man's head three stories high, a silly thing; the niece now giggled to report that the head had landed on her bed and bounced beneath her makeup table.

The prince informed them that Tariq would be taking away their phones, tablets, and laptops. They were not to leave the house or contact anyone on the outside until Abd al-Aziz gave permission. Three or four days at the most. His niece threw her arms wide and wailed. No, she had to go out. She needed her phone. The prince's wife hissed like a cat, making the girl recoil. Bin Rajab's body and parts were removed to the kitchen's walk-in freezer, covered, and locked away. The house staff and guards were banned from the first-floor office and surrendered all cell phones and computers. They were told to find cots and cushions to sleep on over the next few days. Tariq rolled up the office carpet, mopped the floor, and laid another rug. He washed down the desk and walls and replaced the chairs, then nailed sheets of plywood over the holes in the floors and ceilings. Abd al-Aziz showered and changed. He smashed bin Rajab's thumb drive with a hammer.

By himself in the office, he sat at his desk, drumming his fingers before his laptop, the cleaned keyboard and computer screen, a direct link to the unknown assailant who'd tried to kill him. He ached to type invectives: fuck you, go to hell, you missed me, you simpleton shit. But with one keystroke, the watcher would know he was alive. The best way to nab whoever was looking back through this black screen was silence, make him wonder, make him sit in place and wait.

The prince was not disturbed for an hour, until Tariq knocked. Even then, with the big guard lumbering behind him, he did not turn from the dark screen, as if facing away from his enemy was to give an edge.

"Do you know?"

"Yes."

Abd al-Aziz spun on Tariq. The advantage was about to shift. "Who?"

Tariq retreated a step.

"Your son-in-law. Arif al-Bahaziq."

The name stunned Abd al-Aziz into slow, blank moments, as if it had lit a fuse. When it did go off, his gut buckled, even seated.

He rushed both hands to his knees to keep from doubling over. The prince bit down hard to stop his tongue. Like bin Rajab, he contained the blast.

He wiped a hand down his face, stopping it across his lips to press them shut until he could speak without screaming.

"Is there doubt?"

"None."

Abd al-Aziz froze. He gazed into the middle distance at nothing. Around him the office blurred and became insubstantial; he was besieged elsewhere, in a senate of angry, passionate voices. They roared from all sides. You knew this would happen! Twenty years ago! You never trusted him, and you did nothing! He took Nadya away, turned her against you! Nadya! You gave him chances, over and over, then this! This!

What does Nadya know? Did Arif show her the files?

Did she know Arif would try to kill her father?

Where are they? Find them!

The prince could not say when Tariq left the room. His head pounded. He caught himself panting. His hands trembled on either side of the laptop on his desk. He pushed back his chair away from the computer, before he could swing a fist at it.

The prince raised both arms over his head to quell the voices, as if they were real and shouting at him what he ought to do to Arif al-Bahaziq.

When they were quiet and he could think, Abd al-Aziz rolled his chair close again to the laptop.

"I want him dead."

He marveled at the statement, how fully he wished it. He was grateful to Arif for no longer skulking in cyberspace, an elusive irritant. He'd become so openly vile, and that made the choice plain.

Abd al-Aziz opened bin Rajab's file and took from it the List of 85. With a pen, he added his son-in-law's name.

He summoned Tariq again.

"Update the list."

Tariq read the addition in the prince's handwriting.

"Of course."

"Get me the American COS on the phone."

Tariq left for his station. With folded arms, Abd al-Aziz sat back to address the laptop's dark computer screen.

"You lied to me. You stole my personal records. You tried to kill me."

He bared his teeth.

"You took away my daughter."

Again, he yearned to type all this for his son-in-law's eyes waiting on the other side of the black glass of the screen. He ached to let Arif the deceiver know he was coming for him.

The phone rang. The prince exhaled a long, hot breath at the computer.

"Sit right there. I'll be with you soon."

• • •

Abd al-Aziz was not fond of the CIA's chief of station in Riyadh. Mr. Fulton was a cheerless man with a difficult job. The Saudi state was a monarchy. As such, the flow of information in the Kingdom, the lifeblood of all intelligence agencies, tended to follow personal relationships, family and tribal links, more than bureaucracy, the way it did in more modern countries. Americans, a people from a democracy, preferred dealing with governments over individuals. This made them reliant on their Saudi hosts for information. The prince made frequent use of the imbalance, and was about to again.

He put Mr. Fulton on speakerphone so that he could walk behind his desk while speaking. His nerves were still jangled.

"Thank you for calling me back so quickly, Mr. Fulton."

"Your man was pretty insistent. I figured it was important. Is it?"

He was not bothered by the CIA man's casual brusqueness. Within the last two hours, the prince had escaped death.

"I will let you be the judge of that, Mr. Fulton."

Abd al-Aziz explained how Walid Samir bin Rajab, #34 on the List, had come to his private home, to surrender.

"Bin Rajab. That's a good haul. He's AQAP. We'd like to have a word with him, too."

"That will be impossible."

"Oh?"

"Let me continue. Bin Rajab arrived at my house with a data stick. This contained some of my personal banking information."

"He hacked you?"

"Someone else did."

"Was it compromising?"

"Yes, Mr. Fulton."

"Jesus Christ."

He gave a disinterested ear to this common American blasphemy. On another day, perhaps, he might react.

"I invited him into my presence to question him, of course. Then he blew himself up."

The CIA station chief gagged.

"He what?"

"He blew himself up, Mr. Fulton."

"Holy—" The man bit off another curse. "You all right?"

"No casualties but the bomber and my carpet."

"Didn't you search him?"

"Of course. But the device was in his rectum. We Muslims are not accustomed to searching there, though that may have to change. Fortunately for me, the charge was shaped. It detonated vertically. Bin Rajab blew off one arm and his own head. That was all."

The secure line stayed quiet for seconds, until Mr. Fulton chuckled. He drew out his words.

"You, sir, are a lucky man."

"What I am, Mr. Fulton, is a faithful servant of Allah. I will report to your office all the details before the day is over. At the moment I have a separate, and time-sensitive, request."

"I'll do what I can."

"I will rely on that. I know who is behind the hacking of my computer, and who sent bin Rajab to kill me."

"You know this already?"

"There was little effort to conceal it from me. The expectation, I suppose, was that I would be dead with the knowledge."

"Who was it?"

"My son-in-law. Arif al-Bahaziq."

"Prince." The American stumbled for words. "Prince, I'm shocked. I'm sorry."

"I've added his name to the List of 85."

"I can see why."

"Here is what you can do for me. You understand, I will be grateful. Personally and officially."

"Tell me."

"I want him added to your country's disposition matrix."

The prince knitted his fingers waiting for Mr. Fulton to reply.

"What you're saying is you want your son-in-law on our drone hit list."

"Exactly."

"You want us to kill your son-in-law for you."

"That is what I am saying."

On Mr. Fulton's end of the secure line, computer keys tapped.

"Okay, let's see. Arif al-Bahaziq. Mujahideen in the late eighties, Afghan war. Longtime computer specialist, so there you go. Entered Saudi prison five years ago. Never formally charged. What'd he do?"

"He is a malcontent. A reformer."

"And you put him in jail for that."

"I am a liberal man, Mr. Fulton. I allowed my daughter, his wife, to be fully educated. She is a French-trained doctor. But the pace of change in the Kingdom does not suit Arif. He has resorted to more expedient methods, like slander and murder. You see?"

"I'm not paid to judge, Prince. All right, let's take a look. He got out of jail two years ago. Disappeared two months later."

"With my daughter."

"That's got to be tough."

"More than I can tell you."

"Did you lose sight of them?"

"They have been living very quietly."

"But you know where he is now."

"I will by tomorrow morning."

"So, what do you think's changed? Other than fighting in Afghanistan, his record is nothing but nonviolent protest. Why, all of a sudden, has Arif al-Bahaziq gone from hacker to killer?"

"Clearly he's fallen in with al-Qaeda. Bin Rajab is proof of that. Mr. Fulton, Arif has made an attempt on the life of the Saudi chief of intelligence. I worry he may have also converted my daughter to his extremism. I suspect there is no end to what he is willing to do to attack me and the Saudi state."

"I can appreciate that. But see, there's the sticking point. Al-Bahaziq has attacked the Saudi state. Not the US. Until he becomes an imminent threat to an American noun, my hands are tied. It's in the drone playbook[11]. You know this."

"An American noun" meant an American person, place, or thing. The wiggle room was in the word *imminent*.

"I know this well."

"So how can I help?"

"I have an idea."

---

11 US government standards and processes, otherwise known as the disposition matrix, for approving operations to capture or use lethal force against terrorist targets.

The quiet tapping noise through the speakerphone was not the CIA man typing, but a more hollow sound. Fingers on a desk.

"Mr. Fulton?"

"All right. Shoot."

Chapter 8

Al-Husn
Ma'rib
Yemen

In the morning, leaving the bed, Nadya kissed him. She'd not done so for a full week. Arif grabbed her wrist to pull her back down. She lay with her head on his shoulder until the rising sun filled the room. She patted his chest when she rose again.

Nadya was gone when he came into the kitchen; he'd just missed her. The pickup truck scrabbled away. A candle flickered on the counter beside flatbread and jam, a paltry breakfast. Even this meager gesture had been absent since Arif had broken into her father's computer.

Like she'd asked, he did not tell Nadya what he'd found. She would have been devastated, without being surprised. Nadya knew who her family was. She loved them and rejected them, and this was hard. Arif had benefited from the Al Saud's generosity, but spent time in their prisons. He didn't struggle with disappointment in the prince, only with how to hurt him and not Nadya.

After breakfast Arif climbed the stairs. He threw open the balcony doors to let in the sun, still rising above the town and the desert beyond. Sitting at his computer, he called up his covert server. Four mornings in a row, Arif expected to find the prince's security had severed their illicit cyber connection. But the link remained.

This was odd. He should have been shut down sooner. Was the prince careless, inattentive, overconfident? That seemed unlikely; he'd known Abd al-Aziz for twenty years and never was the man less than cunning and wary. Perhaps the prince knew his computer was compromised and was staying patient, laying his own snares. Arif didn't worry that the GIP could reverse engineer the malware to find him; he'd put too many fail-safes in place for that to happen. But could the prince trick him, trap him?

Arif reviewed the last seventy-two hours of the hack. For the first two days, the prince had busily used his laptop, typing emails, calendar entries, notes to himself and his office network.

On the third afternoon, after a dull morning watching Abd al-Aziz work and craft common emails, Arif snoozed in the heat of his office. He awoke just in time to see the prince close a spreadsheet and the screen go blank.

The exact banking records Arif had copied out of his computer. The prince had just seen them.

Why did he do this? Did he suspect something?

Arif scrambled for Ghalib's calling card. He dialed the cell number.

"Merhabba, Arif."

"I just saw Abd al-Aziz open the spreadsheet. You sent him the information I took."

"Yes. I did. This is wonderful news."

"We didn't agree to do that."

"No."

"He knows his computer's compromised now."

"Does that matter? You have the information you sought."

"Why did you do it?"

"To vex him. Rob him of sleep. To let him know we are coming. There's nothing he can do, Arif. You have no concern."

Arif contained his tongue, though he wanted to lash Ghalib for this breach of trust.

"Will it be published soon?"

"You will see results very quickly now. A day or two more. Masha'allah, Arif."

With this, Ghalib hung up.

Arif sat riveted to his computer. He let his ire with Ghalib pass. Arif imagined his father-in-law raging at the invasion into his privacy, the disgrace he would suffer, furious that the hands manipulating him were unknown. Perhaps Ghalib had a point; this made the attack sweeter and, without Abd al-Aziz even knowing it, personal.

An hour passed. The prince had not touched his keyboard again. The link between their computers had remained in place, though it couldn't last much longer.

Arif jumped, jarred from his recollection. His cell phone rang. The call came from a number he didn't recognize. After several rings, he answered.

"Merhabba?" No one replied. "Merhabba?"

The caller hung up. Only Nadya had his private number. Arif chalked it up to a mistaken call, but it made him wary that the rest of that afternoon and night, all activity on Abd al-Aziz's laptop stopped.

That evening, the link stayed in place. Expecting it to disappear any moment, Arif used the time to delve deeper into his father-in-law's private records, the man's banking and communications, web-browsing history. He found only common iniquities—messages to a mistress, sly references to business dealings. Little to compare with what he already had. Arif went to bed.

The next morning, still with no keystrokes from the prince, he stopped rummaging. Arif worried he might stray into a noose hidden somewhere in the files and folders and trip himself up. From then on, he kept a passive vigil, sunrise to midnight, observing only. He answered the adhans to prayer, came down for evening meals at Nadya's request, and went to bed long after she was asleep. He waited for the link to be broken, for fresh secrets to spill from the prince's fingers, or for Nadya to declare that she was out of patience. Arif got none of these. Instead, he had more empty watching.

He marked the passage of his day by prayers, catnaps, and refilling his water bottle. Heat climbed in the office. The village clattered past below his balcony. Arif kept an eye on Saudi and international news sites, though nothing yet had come from Ghalib's guarantee. He'd sworn and convinced Arif that if the scandal were put in his hands, it would quickly be posted on al-Qaeda's global online magazine, *Sada al-Malahim* (*Echoes of Battles*), and picked up by every jihadi Internet forum. The Arab television network al Jazeera would follow, the BBC, then the rest of the world's news services. The impact to the Al Saud would be worldwide.

But now that the prince knew what was to befall him, had he somehow managed to quash the spread of his whoring bank records? This was not impossible. The prince was a powerful man, the Al Saud jealous of their name. Had Ghalib's plan backfired?

Arif intended to see Ghalib tomorrow, to ask after the progress.

He slept for short periods in his chair. In the late afternoon, the village *muezzin* called for the *'asr* prayer. The adhan pulled Arif to the balcony. The thermometer had climbed into the low nineties.

The 'asr asked of Muslims to break with their daytime labors and remember the greater meaning of life. Praying on his knees under a high sun, Arif did this only half-focused. Instead he pondered the oddities of the unbroken cyber link, the absence of the story in the Arab press, and the long silence from the prince.

Chapter 9

US embassy
Sana'a
Yemen

A mile and a half above sea level, Sana'a dissuaded the few Westerners who lived here from ever taking the stairs. Josh pushed himself up three flights to the ambassador's floor. He wanted to acclimate and so refused the elevator. Pausing to catch his breath at the landing, he admitted that there were some places in the world folks from Louisiana just should not live. Sana'a might be one of them.

The summons had come in a call from the ambassador's secretary five minutes ago, at Josh's first-floor desk in the Cultural Affairs Office. The secretary did not say what the ambassador wanted. Josh had spent his morning so far reviewing the menu of an upcoming diplomatic dinner for a Chinese trade delegation next month, tasked with making sure nothing served would be offensive or inedible to the Chinese. The Chinese were like the Cajuns back home; they'd eat every part of any animal tail to snout. He expected no problems.

Stopping outside the main office suite, Josh ran a hand over his hair and smoothed his suit coat before entering the double doors. The anteroom was empty; the young male secretary was not at his desk.

Josh took in the panorama from the ambassador's windows. From his own ground-level desk, the view was only of the compound's concrete wall, razor wire, cameras, shrubs, and a cloudless sky. On occasion an armed marine or a Yemeni security guard strolled past.

The ambassador's excellent view ran southwest. A clear afternoon let Josh see a long way. One of the oldest cities on earth, Sana'a stood on a high plain broken by mountain ranges and ashen wadis, dotted by sparse and spindly vegetation. The antique architecture was decorative, mainly mud-brick buildings packed along narrow cobble lanes, gingerbread facades studded with geometric shapes, Arabian parapets, and limestone accents. The streets and sidewalks were dense with pedestrians, vendor carts, three-wheeled *tok tok* taxis, and sputtering motorbikes. A thousand years ago, Sana'a had been an outpost in the center of a forbidding terrain, a destination for caravans on the spice and incense routes to the sea. Today it was a remote place of two million souls struggling on the edges of modernity, staggering between the calls of Islam, the seductions of the West, and the past.

Josh shot his cuffs and rubbed his shoes against the backs of his legs to look sharp. No one else had arrived; this meeting was just between him and the boss.

Three years ago, Josh had been in a different uniform from this warm-weather gray suit. He'd been not in those distant Yemeni hills but hills like them, with the US Army Rangers, talking to tribal chiefs, building goodwill, working to make a difference village by village, changing hearts and minds and spilling blood against the forces that would come to change them back.

The ambassador's young assistant came in sipping from a steel go-cup. "Sorry. I was out for a minute."

"Is he in?"

"Yes. He said he wanted to see you as soon as you arrived. Go on in."

Josh rapped a knuckle against the windowpane at the millennium-old city. Nodding to the secretary, he pulled back the heavy wooden door and stepped inside the large office. Ambassador Silva was on his feet beside his desk, back turned, naked except for the pair of white boxer shorts he was tugging over his bare buttocks. The ambassador was short, hairy, and not a muscular man except for strong calves. Tan lines separated his skin into parts: upper, lower, middle.

Silva peered over his shoulder at Josh and finished wriggling into his underpants. The rest of his suit lay across the back of his office chair.

"Tennis. Be right with you."

Josh backed out of the room, clicking the door shut. He stood facing it, unsure what, if anything, to say.

The secretary put down his coffee.

"What?"

His answer came from his intercom buzzer faster than Josh could provide one. The secretary answered, then flushed in the face.

"Yes, sir. I'm sorry, I misunderstood. Yes, sir."

Josh returned to the windows. Outside, the city buzzed and honked. The far-off red hills remained unconcerned.

The intercom piped again. The secretary answered and hung up.

"He'll see you now."

"You sure?"

"Don't start. Go in."

Josh pulled back the heavy door. Inside, the ambassador was still on his feet, this time behind the desk, fully dressed, extending his hand as Josh crossed.

"Josh. Come in. Sorry about that."

"No worries."

"What I told young Tyler was that I wanted to see you the moment you arrived. That didn't mean for him to let you in without telling me you were here."

For a small man, the ambassador had a firm handshake. Guthrie Silva was a known Middle East expert. He'd served in embassies in Pakistan, Iraq, and Qatar; his posting to Sana'a showed the emphasis the United States put on relations here, particularly in the battle against terrorism in Yemen. Silva, swarthy and intellectual, was a Jew and because of that would not have been ambassador here or anywhere else in the Arab world were he not a consummate diplomat.

"I apologize for not taking the time before now to welcome you to the embassy."

The ambassador indicated the upholstered chair across from him. Josh settled his girth.

Despite the informal and accidental beginning, this was not a social call. Two manila folders and a cardboard carton lay open on the desk between them. Whatever this was about, it had just landed in Silva's lap, interrupting his tennis game.

Josh hadn't been in this office before. His few encounters with Silva had been in the second-floor conference room, always with others. The man's private office was big, clean, sparse, without art on the walls, only maps and certificates. The furnishings were chrome legged and inexpensive, as if built to be abandoned. This made sense in light of recent events: two months before Josh arrived in Sana'a, five hundred Yemenis tried to breach the embassy. The marine contingent and local cops stopped them in the front courtyard. The embassy got some spray paint, busted windows, scorch marks on the pavement from burned flags, and a day of international news coverage.

Silva leaned back, not closing the files.

"You've been here a month?"

"Five weeks, sir."

"You came from Riyadh. How's it going?"

141

"A step up from stamping visas."

"I stamped my share in Beirut. You enjoying Cultural Affairs?"

"Well enough, sir."

"Good. I'm going to ask you a few questions. Then I might have a job for you. Okay?"

A job? Other than Cultural Affairs? Josh had to respond without sounding eager. No sense signaling Silva that he was already raring to do something more than prepare menus.

"Fine."

Silva traced fingertips over a page in one of the files.

"Your parents are both professional aid workers. Your father's in Engineers Without Borders at Virginia Tech. Your mother works for the International Red Cross."

"They met in the Peace Corps. They're both hippies."

"They sound wonderful."

"My sister runs a social service office in DC. She's the toughest one in the bunch."

"And you chose to serve in the military. Graduated VMI, language major. Entered the army. Took more Arabic, got a three out of five. Made the Rangers. Two tours in Iraq, two in Afghanistan. Finished as a captain. Your record shows nothing but outstanding service."

"I gave it my best."

"I see that. So, my first question."

"Yes, sir."

"After all that excitement in the army, are we boring you here?"

Josh's back pressed against the chair.

"No, sir. Why would you ask me that?"

"Don't bristle, son. Nothing in particular. I'd just like a candid answer."

Josh couldn't be honest about this. What had he done for Silva to say this to him? Was he in hot water?

He had to answer, couldn't sit in front of the man mute.

Silva read his discomfort.

"Let me restate. In the Rangers, almost every day, you had an immediate impact on something or someone. An irrigation ditch, a village school, some bad guy or other to hunt down, life and death decisions. Why'd you quit all that to come do this?"

"Same reasons. I just wanted to see if I could do it on a bigger scale."

"Like your parents."

"We're a family of meddlers."

"I understand. My father was in the State Department, too. And here I am. But early on, I had to accept something. To paraphrase Longfellow, the mills of diplomacy grind slowly yet exceedingly fine. Now I ask. Can you make that adjustment?"

"You did."

Silva closed Josh's file to move to the other open folder. He drummed his short fingers on it, contemplating.

Josh tapped his own chest.

"Sir, is there something about me you're unhappy with?"

"No. You're a good worker. Excellent Arabic."

"Then what's this about?"

"I'll get right to it, then."

"I'd appreciate it."

"Are you a CIA officer in my embassy I don't know about?"

Josh's hands went to the arms of the chair. He was not going to rise, but every instinct told him a man got to his feet when he felt like Josh did right now.

"What? No. What?"

Silva patted the open file.

"This request. It's from the Agency. I've been asked to lend you to them for a mission. It actually says that. A 'mission.'"

"Can I see it?"

"No. Young men who've served five weeks in Cultural Affairs are not the subject of such requests. Why would they ask for you?"

Josh shifted. The chair squeaked under him.

"I don't know. I'm not a spy."

The ambassador toted Josh up, nodding to himself when he'd reached a sum.

"To be honest, you're a little abrupt for a diplomat. You've got a direct style about you. I'll chalk that up to your military background. Mind you, these aren't complaints, just snap observations."

"Are these snap observations in my file?"

"A few are. Again, you're young in this business. We like to give folks a chance to settle in. You seem to be taking longer than we're accustomed to. That's all."

Josh flipped his own mental file of everyone he knew in the embassy, every encounter in his five weeks in Sana'a. Who wrote him up? What did he do?

Silva remained blandly judgmental.

"Let me say that if you're not a spy, you'll have to work on your manner."

"I will, sir."

"If you are a spy, you're a bit transparent."

Again Josh was stymied. He couldn't admit that he'd heard this before, only days ago, in fact—and like then, it bordered on an insult. At the same time, he wanted to hear what mission the CIA might have for him, if for no other reason than to change the subject. The ambassador continued.

"On the plus side, you've got a steady nerve. You didn't blink when you came into my office the first time."

"Nor did you, sir."

"I'm entitled to know. Are you a spy in my house, Josh?"

"No, sir. I'm not. And if you don't mind, do you have any other questions?"

"No. I don't."

Someone knocked on the ambassador's door, and it opened. The secretary entered carrying Josh's bottle of Balvenie 15.

Josh's throat seized. Is this what he was in Dutch over, sneaking a bottle of Scotch into the embassy? Booze was prohibited in Yemen but this was a private bottle, and only for after-hours.

The ambassador folded his hands while the secretary set two crystal highball glasses on the desk.

"You prefer ice? Josh?"

"Yes."

"How much?"

"One cube."

"Same for me. Michael, a little ice, please."

The secretary disappeared. In his absence, Silva unscrewed the top to pour for them both.

"I hope this is all right. I ran out a week ago. The diplomatic pouch hasn't arrived. I thought we ought to have a tipple, you and me. Before we tackle this request."

"How'd you know?"

"I don't mind good Scotch in my embassy. I do mind secrets. No different from a Ranger company."

"Point taken."

"I'm pleased to hear that."

The secretary returned with a bowl of ice, then slipped out. Silva and Josh each dropped one cube into their glasses before raising them to the other. Both swirled the Scotch and ice before sipping to let the peat flavors open a hint.

The ambassador set his glass on the desk. Josh held on to his; one Scotch together did not make them equals.

Silva gazed out his windows at bright, antiquated Yemen. He seemed again to be doing figures in his head, adding up caution and prudence, Josh and the CIA, counting the heads of snakes.

Plainly reluctant, Silva sucked his teeth.

"The Agency wants you to ride in a car."

Josh opened his mouth twice before he could speak.

"They what?"

"That's what they've asked me to send you to do. Ride in a car."

"You mean with someone else driving."

"I interpret 'riding' to mean that, yes."

"Why? Where?"

"Where is from Ma'rib to the Saudi border. When is tonight. Why is the interesting part."

The ambassador finished the skim of chilled Scotch. He tipped the bottle's neck at Josh, inquiring if he wanted more of his own liquor. Josh waved him off. Silva poured himself a second highball, adding a fresh cube.

Josh wanted to prod, speed up the facts from the file. Silva had his own pace.

"In Ma'rib, a woman has decided to leave her husband. She's the daughter of a prominent Saudi prince. She has no visa or passport, and now she wants to go home. The CIA needs you to tag along in the car."

"As what?"

"As an observer. There are American interests in play, judging by the involvement of the CIA. You're to be the American on the scene."

"What interests?"

"The file doesn't say. But we can draw our own conclusions. We know the woman's father is a senior member of the Al Saud. Let's assume some backs are getting scratched. The father wants an American in the car. He's getting one. I don't know what CIA is getting in return. Someone's hide, most likely."

"What am I supposed to do?"

"Make sure everything goes smoothly. Be an American presence."

"Why doesn't the CIA just send one of their own?"

"They claim that if something does go sideways, politically it's easier to explain if a diplomat's in the car instead of an intelligence officer. Plausible deniability. Unless it so happens that you're both."

"I'm not. And please stop saying that."

"Of course. But you have the language skills. A military background. You were asked for by name. You should be pleased."

"I'm holding off on that until you explain one more thing."

"That is?"

"What do you mean 'sideways'?"

"You'll be moving at night. The roads out of Ma'rib cross tribal boundaries. It's possible you might come up on a roadblock. It's not uncommon for the Hadhramaut qabili to charge traffic for the right to pass. They still consider parts of the desert their land."

"The government lets them get away with that?"

"The Yemeni government does whatever it has to do to keep the tribes quiet and happy. So yes, they let them get away with it. Charge a toll. Nothing much, a few thousand riyals. Ten bucks. After a few hours, they disappear."

Silva pulled the cardboard box to him. He reached inside, then lay on the desk a sheet of paper stamped and signed under the seal of the Yemeni Interior Ministry.

"This is a *tasrih*. It's signed by the Interior Ministry. I'll make you a dozen copies. It should get you past any checkpoints."

"Should?"

The ambassador dug back into the box. He lifted out ten banded packets of Yemeni currency.

"That's five million riyals. Just shy of twenty-five thousand dollars. In case the tasrih doesn't work, you'll use this as *baksheesh*." Bribes.

"Jesus. Why so much?"

"The Saudis sent the money. They've got plenty. Remember, the princess doesn't have papers."

Josh poked at the stacks of cash. She had plenty of papers now.

The ambassador returned the money to the box.

"And Josh. Please note that I have signed for this."

Josh put a fresh ice cube into his empty glass. The ambassador poured.

He carried the Scotch with him to one of the satellite maps on the wall. There, he measured the distances and routes: a hundred miles west from Ma'rib to Sana'a on the N5; then another 150 north on the N1 to the Saudi border town Dharan Al Janub. On the map, the roads looked good, the terrain sparse, rocky, and rolling.

Tracing a finger over the route west, then north to the border, Josh figured six, seven hours.

The ambassador stirred his whiskey. The ice clinked against the crystal. Silva shook his head.

"They're not going that way. They're heading east out of Ma'rib, then north."

"East?"

"That's right."

Josh retraced the route. East on the N5 another 125 miles, then north on the S150 fifty more. Beneath his trailing finger, as soon as the road left Ma'rib to the east, the landscape turned amber, rippling, and barren.

"That's into the Rub' al-Khali."

"It is."

"Why go into the desert?"

Silva sipped. The silk of the Scotch did not ease the sourness on his features. One more time he tapped the open folder, making clear the blame lay with it and not him for what he had to say.

"Two years back, when the princess and her husband left the Kingdom, they were smuggled out. Disappeared. Her family lost track. The Saudis cancelled both their passports."

"So she needs to be smuggled back in."

"Exactly."

"Why not just send a plane to pick her up?"

"The delivery has to be done overland. The CIA was specific and secretive about this. Not unusual."

If the crossing had to be done by land, the only place to do that was where the border between Saudi Arabia and Yemen wasn't patrolled, or even marked—in the middle of the largest sand desert on earth. The Rub' al-Khali. The Empty Quarter.

Up to a point, this made sense. A Saudi princess had followed her husband to Yemen. Whatever reasons took them there, things had turned ugly enough for her to jump ship. She called Daddy. He said I'll get you out. The old man was cashing in some chips with the CIA. The Agency agreed to handle the transport. But to rate this kind of attention, Daddy had to be very important. And the husband, pretty nasty.

"Does the guy know his wife's splitting on him?"

"He does not."

"I'd like it better if this made sense."

"That's why I'm not comfortable saying yes."

The ambassador eyed him over the rim of his glass. Josh believed he'd sat perfectly still but plainly had not, for Silva chuckled into the Scotch before taking a sip. "You want me to say yes."

"Can you say no?"

"I can. With some consequences."

"Would you?"

"To protect you, yes. You're one of my team. This embassy is my Ranger company."

"Roger that, sir. It's your call."

"Let me show you what else is in the box. Then it's going to be your call."

Silva laid on the desk a black device the size of a pack of cigarettes, with a screen and keyboard. Josh took this in hand. "A Blue Force tracker."

"Have you used one before?"

"Not one this small. But yes."

Also from the box, Silva lifted a memo. He slid the page across the desk.

"Here's the instructions. Once you're in the car, every fifteen minutes you're to send an ID code. Program that in before you leave. At the same intervals you'll transmit an all-clear signal. That's threat level one. If you get into trouble, you'll send threat levels up to four. The GPS will monitor your location."

"Who'll be watching?"

The ambassador left his chair to stride to the satellite map. He indicated a point thirty miles north of the border, inside the Kingdom.

"Tonight, a SEAL team will arrive at the airport here in Sharurah. They'll be on four-wheel ATVs waiting just north of the Saudi line. The mission calls for your car to reach a prearranged checkpoint nine miles south of the border. The SEALs will cross the frontier in the dark, travel off-road, and pick up the princess. They'll sneak her back over the border at some remote spot in the desert. You and the driver will turn around and head back. You may take tomorrow off."

The ambassador returned to his chair. Josh admired the man's walk, measured and straight, as if on a rail. He had bearing, a momentum about him; he carried his country when he walked, like a good soldier.

Josh hefted the blue force tracker.

"What happens exactly if I dial in threat level four?"

"A lot of wheels start turning."

"What wheels?"

"A rescue response team will take over, also sitting alert in Sharurah."

"Who'll it be?"

"A team of air force pararescuemen."

"PJs."

"I've heard them called that. Did you know them in the military?"

Josh had seen the PJs work. They were Special Operators, a small and very elite corps with the mission of CSAR: combat search and rescue. They ran, flew, jumped, climbed, swam, and forced their way into any terrain, hostile or remote, to reach downed or isolated personnel. If you fell in battle, anywhere, and your own guys couldn't get you out, couldn't save you, the PJs got the call. Through hell and high water.

"Everybody knows them."

"Good. If you have confidence in them, I will."

One more sheet of paper emerged from the box.

"Here's the time and place of the meeting tonight in Ma'rib. Memorize this and leave it here. If you're going."

"I reckon I am."

"You're sure? This is not the way out of Cultural Affairs, Josh. You understand?"

"Yes, sir."

Silva poured one more splash of Scotch for himself. "But this will look good in your file."

"Apparently my file could use it."

"All right. The driver will be expecting you. Take one of the embassy cars to Ma'rib."

"That's everything? No weapon?"

"I can't arm you."

Silva spoke into the glass at his lips.

"Of course, I have no idea what you do when you leave here."

Chapter 10

Outside Camp Lemonnier
Djibouti

Quincy jammed his fists to his hips. When he stood like this, he was a colossus.

"No. Dude, no, you do not get to pull rank."

LB swung his shoulders to Berko for the final say.

Quincy kept on. "I grew up in the desert. I know this shit backwards and forwards. LT, come on. He grew up on the Strip."

A mile behind Quincy, under a stark East African sun, a rooster tail of dust dashed across the open savanna, past flat-topped acacia trees and the trash fields. LB couldn't hear the gunning motor or what he imagined were the happy yells of PJs. But he was going to drive next. LB tapped his own chest.

"I'm team leader."

Berko had been reluctant to make the call, but finally gave LB the nod. Quincy kicked at the ground before turning to watch one of the two just-delivered GAARVs, short for Guardian Angel Air-Deployable Recovery Vehicle, tear up the plain.

The dust plume cut a long straight swath, accelerating over flat ground. The GAARV's top speed on level terrain was 55 mph, and whoever was behind the wheel—Wally, young ex-sailor Dow, Mouse, or Jamie—was taking all of it. The vehicle sped one mile, two miles in a straight line, flat out, pushing its limits until it kicked up a billow, marking another hairpin turn to a skidding stop. Berko let loose a whoop. Doc whistled and hit LB in the arm. Berko's radio tweeted; the young officer brought the handheld to his ear, then to his mouth. Team 1 was finished galloping over the Djiboutian plain; Wally was bringing the GAARV back in for Team 2's turn.

The big vehicle turned to barrel straight at them, floating on waves of heat, trailing a yellow cloud on a windless noon. Approaching fast, she looked snub-nosed and squat, grabbing the earth with enormous tires. Painted coyote-tan, the GAARV looked battle ready, with her antennas and dual mounted M-240B machine guns. A rear protective cage for two litters, bulletproof steel skin, tubular impact grill, roll bar, high ground clearance—all made her appear raw-boned and rough. She was the pinnacle of Special Ops combat rescue ground mobility: durable, balanced, fast, and powerful enough for the full range of GA missions in every climate and condition. The GAARV could be dropped by parachute into a mission to ford a stream, push down a flooded street, climb a mountain, race over sand and snow, face an enemy, or, better yet, outrace one.

LB's eager hands twitched. The whole team had spent yesterday studying manuals on the GAARV's operation, capacities, limits, and maintenance. The vehicles had arrived on a cargo plane from AFRICOM last night. This morning the riggers kept one for themselves, while the PJs divided into two teams to field-test the other. Wally and his team had been out on the plain since 0800, with a swap time of 1200. Right now the time was 1230. LB and his team had been waiting in the heat and arguing over who got first crack.

The GAARV rushed at them without slowing; LB, Doc, and Quincy lowered their goggles, knowing what was coming. Doc elbowed Berko to do the same.

Jamie was behind the wheel when the GAARV roared past, barely slowing. Beside him sat Wally, with Mouse and Dow strapped in the rear. When they roared past, all four were hollering and punching the air. Jamie downshifted into a tight circle around LB's team, ringing them three times, trying to choke them.

Jamie rocked the GAARV to a stop. All four grinning airmen inside were coated with dirt. Clapping, they made puffs. The GAARV, too, wore a jacket of dust, initiated.

LB moved first, reaching the driver's door, which Jamie had not opened.

"How was it?"

Jamie shook his head as if to rattle into place the proper words.

"Awesome."

"You got it all worked out?"

"We're good. Everyone drove her."

"Okay. Get out."

Jamie raised his goggles above a sheepish grin.

"Nope."

"What?" LB leaned in over the windowsill. "Wally, come on. Our turn. Let's go."

On the passenger side, Wally lifted a finger for silence. He was listening intently to something LB did not hear, the radio in his ear. He nodded.

"Yes, ma'am. Roger that. On our way."

Quincy kicked the dirt again and turned away.

Berko moved beside LB.

"What's up, Captain?"

"The riggers want her back."

LB stepped up to make a more impassioned complaint than the young lieutenant would.

"This is bullshit."

"Orders."

"You guys have been out here since sunup. We get to train on her next. That's the deal."

Wally shrugged, setting off a tiny dust avalanche down his chest.

"Torres says the riggers want it back in the hangar. Now."

"We don't spin up for another six hours. This sucks. At least give us back the thirty minutes you were late."

Wally replied by lowering his goggles.

"Go."

Jamie shifted, mashed the gas, and threw grit and pebbles. The GAARV growled and leaped away. From the backseat, Dow and Mouse added their raised middle fingers to the antennas and gun barrels.

LB watched her drifting dust. Berko, Doc, and Quincy shuffled back to the ATV, the souped-up golf cart that had hauled them out here three hot miles from camp. Doc and the LT climbed in the back, Big Quincy in the front passenger side. LB pointed at Quincy.

"What are you doing?"

Quincy folded his big arms. "You wanted to drive. Drive."

• • •

After cleaning up the used GAARV, six of the team members went to their CLUs to rest before tonight's op. Doc and LB climbed to their tents on top of the high shelf inside the Barn, close to the ductwork, where rain on the metal roof sounded like drumrolls.

In midafternoon, unable to nap, LB descended the ladder without waking Doc. He didn't favor the notion of deploying with a piece of equipment he wasn't familiar with and hadn't shaken his sense of unfairness out on the savanna. On top of this, over in their portion of the Barn, the riggers were working and noisy.

LB moseyed over, hoping at least to sit in one of the GAARVs, to get the feel of it. Even that was frustrated; all five riggers shouted him away. The pair of vehicles glistened like new, which they were. One was already packed, strapped down, and ready to be loaded onto a plane. Both vehicles looked wrong motionless. These things were made to go, evade, survive, carry the Guardian Angels into and out of a fight. They were designed to be tossed out of airplanes, too, so the riggers coveted them as much as the PJs. LB took a seat on one of the chute-packing tables to study their work. At some point in the future, he'd have to undo it.

On every jump, the rigging team held the GA team's lives in their hands. These men were all experts, and by nature perfectionists. They moved efficiently but carefully; this was their first time with a GAARV, too.

They worked from a TO, a technical order binder that came with the vehicles. The first task was to build for each GAARV a platform to tie it to, which would absorb the impact of a parachute landing.

The riggers were halfway through building the platform for the second GAARV. The pallet was made by laying out a big plywood deck, then overlaying it with a five-inch sheet of corrugated crush board. Another plyboard deck was set on top of this, and the sandwich was secured by long bolts. The bottom of the platform was left smooth, to be rolled on and off the ramp of an HC-130. The base would make contact with the ground first, and the honeycomb crush board was designed to take the blow, instead of the three-thousand-pound GAARV.

When the platform was finished, the riggers started the motor of the second GAARV to drive it on top. LB asked to do this for them and was almost run out of the room.

For the next hour, the riggers packed more crush board around the wheels, axles, machine guns, steering column, head- and taillights. Anything that might suffer from a hard landing or get tangled in the huge G-12 cargo chute's lines. The chute container itself was attached to a release mechanism that would detach the silk once on the ground, to stop the canopy from dragging the load away.

Finally, the second GAARV was strapped to its platform by rolls of tubular nylon webbing and metal fast-release buckles. With the rigging done, both vehicles hunkered side by side, looking like subdued wild things, like they wanted to burst their restraints.

The riggers stood around LB to explain how they'd done their job and how best to free the GAARVs. Because vehicles were involved—ATVs and GAARVs—they'd stowed everything needed for extrication in case of an accident: a battery-powered Sawzall, Jaws of Life, crash axes, and shovels, plus inflatable lift bags that could raise forty thousand pounds. They showed LB the blood cooler, spare batteries, signaling devices. The list of supplies for a wide range of mission contingencies was exhaustive. The riggers had done a superb job, and they said as much. They'd finished up two full hours before the scheduled load time. LB could have spent that time out on the Djibouti plains finding out what these wild things could do. He shut his mouth about this and listened to the riggers brag until Wally called from the doorway.

"Nice work, guys. LB, the major wants us in the Rescue Operations Center. Pre-op brief."

LB hopped off the table. One of the riggers patted him on the back.

"Try to make it back in one piece."

LB pointed at the GAARVs. "You mean them or me?"

All five hooted him out the door.

"Them."

• • •

The Rescue Operations Center had the most computers at Camp Lemonnier. Because of this, it had the best air-conditioning.

In the small waiting room surrounded by air force posters, LB and Wally were met by Torres, black hair in a bun. She wore the same baggy airman battle uniform as everyone else, but while the ABUs made LB look like a blue tiger-striped sugar bowl, the major and Wally brought to mind long-legged animals in their prime. Wally held the door for her entering the op control room. LB spoke to Torres's back. "You coming along on this one, Major?"

Torres halted in the doorway, blocking Wally and LB. She kept her back turned, drew a deep breath of patience.

"Essential personnel only. And I still define what essential means." Torres stepped into the ROC.

Inside the op center, a dozen airmen, soldiers and marines sat at computer stations in front of a wall of glowing monitors. These displayed the Falcon View program, combining satellite maps of Horn of Africa, Persian Gulf, and Middle East regions, with overlays of air asset tracking and weather conditions. At the head of the conference table, in the place where Torres normally sat, an O6 bird colonel leaned on his forearms, fingers knit around a coffee mug. Trim and fit, with a chiseled face and short gray hair, he had the look of a future general. His face bore the squint of an intent man. The colonel did not rise. Torres handled the introductions.

"This is Colonel Hulsey, from AFRICOM. He'll be Chief of Operations for this mission. Colonel, team commander Captain Bloom. And team leader Master Sergeant DiNardo. Gentlemen, have a seat."

Gathered around the table, Wally and LB opened notebooks and set out pens. Colonel Hulsey thanked Torres, then took over.

"We're in a support role on this one. The SEALs are out front. It's a precious cargo pickup. You'll get their backs."

Hulsey left his coffee cup to approach the bank of Falcon View monitors. He pointed into central Yemen, at Ma'rib, a small city in the Wadi Hadhramaut, on the edge of the great Empty Quarter desert. The Hadhramaut region was increasingly known in the West for oil and harboring wanted men.

"The PC is a Saudi national. She's the daughter of a big shot in the government, one of the royal family. She's decided she wants to go back to the Kingdom, but circumstances make that difficult. The US has been asked to lend a hand. The request was made at the highest levels. This is a multiagency op. That's why I'm here."

LB raised his pen.

"Sir, what circumstances?"

"Her husband's a confirmed terrorist. And no, he doesn't know she's leaving."

LB stuck out his lower lip. "Those are circumstances."

"She's got no passport, no travel papers. That's why she's being exfilled through the desert, off the grid, where there's no border control. The op goes down tonight. She'll be taken out of Ma'rib in a civilian car, departing 1830 hours. The vehicle will be driven by a Yemeni official. There'll also be a US State Department diplomat riding along."

Wally piped up next. "Sir, why's he there?"

"He's carrying a blue force tracker. Beyond that, it's need-to-know, gentlemen. I don't need to know. So neither do you."

LB snorted. "Funny how the people who say that are never the ones with parachutes on."

Torres glowered at LB but apparently the colonel had earned his wings and agreed. Hulsey just tapped the map north of the Yemen-Saudi border.

"Your rescue unit will sit pre-position here at the airport in Sharurah. A six-man SEAL team will be there, too. At 2300 hours, the SEALs will deploy along the Saudi border in ATVs, where they'll wait for word that the package has arrived here, on the S150 road ten miles south of the line. They'll cross into Yemen to take possession of the PC, return to Saudi territory at a remote location, then bring her back to Sharurah. A private jet will fly her to Riyadh and her rich daddy. The car heads back to Ma'rib. We'll monitor the op from the Personnel Recovery Center. The diplomat will also be coding in threat levels one through four every fifteen minutes. You'll jump in if you see a four. Which you probably won't. This is pretty straightforward. Questions?"

LB spoke before Wally. Since both would ask the same things, Wally sat back.

"Sir, what are the threats in the area?"

Hulsey came back to tuck himself in at the table. He gestured to Torres, who answered without notes.

"Northeast of Ma'rib is the Ramlat al-Sab'atayn. Beyond that is the much larger Empty Quarter. These are vast, unpopulated sand regions. There are some scattered Bedu camps, but they're hard to pinpoint."

"So where's the threat?"

"It's important you understand something. These deserts are barren, but they're not empty. Large areas are controlled by tribes. The land is not unknown to them. Occasionally the tribes will set up roadblocks along the highway. They collect minor tolls for passing through their territories. The diplomat's been prepared with ample funds and government franked permits."

LB spoke to Wally. "What happens if he's got the wrong change?"

Torres patted the table in front of LB to bring his attention back to her.

"We're not worried about the tolls. The concern is the husband of the PC. He's a Saudi terrorist. Some of the tribes have links to al-Qaeda on the Arabian Peninsula. We can't know how that will affect the mission. That's why you're in backup."

Torres's voice had an overly portentous ring to it. Or was she just putting LB in his place, showing her hard-ass side in front of the bird colonel? Either way, LB didn't like it. Hulsey caught something, too, because he jumped back in.

"It's also why we expedited delivery of your new GAARVs. If you have to go in, do the job and get out fast. This is not a good place to take on the locals."

"Exit strategy?"

"Head north into Saudi territory. Stay off the roads in and out."

"What's our rules of engagement?"

"ROE is you're clear to return fire for defense only. Use your judgment. Evade if you can. The point here is to leave no footprint."

"Roger that." LB added "Sir," so Torres would know he wasn't talking to her.

Wally rapped LB's leg under the table, then spoke next.

"How about the passengers. Any medical conditions we need to know?"

"Negative."

"Anything else you can tell us about the SEAL mission, or the cargo?"

"Negative. Now you know what I know. I admit that's not much. This is pretty hushed."

"Thank you, sir."

"The major will handle call signs and frequencies. You spin up in ninety minutes. I'll be watching. Major."

Hulsey stood from the table. The others got to their feet for his exit from the ROC. Torres opened a folder. Wally and LB picked up their pens.

Torres checked down her list. The SEAL team leader would answer call sign Mako 44. The ground-to-ground freq would be 55.50; ground-to-air with the HC-130 would be on 226.45. Sat comm was on a Naval Special Warfare Channel.

"That's it."

Wally closed his notebook. "Roger."

LB rose quickly, gathering his notes. "I'll get the team together. Major."

"Sergeant."

"There'll be a half-moon over the desert. Very romantic."

"LB."

"Ma'am."

"Rescue yourself. Go. Right now."

. . .

LB briefed the squad. They asked the same questions he and Wally had asked, and LB gave the same answers he'd gotten from Hulsey, mostly "I don't know."

He split the unit into two teams, assigning Jamie and Mouse into his GAARV with Berko because they had experience driving this morning. Wally, Dow, Quincy, and Doc formed Team 2.

Wally followed with his usual amped-up pre-mission speech. Stay together, work together, do the job, everyone comes home. You're the best, act like it. This was young Berko's first op and he sat forward through Wally's quick speech while everyone else slouched. Wally clapped when he was done, like a quarterback. Berko jumped to his feet, charged and ready.

The squad headed to their lockers to gear up. Each locker was the size of a small garage, holding the equipment and outfits for the job of combat search and rescue: high- and low-altitude jumpsuits, gear for mountaineering, jungle survival, scuba, traversing snow, and hot climes. Everything needed to enter and survive any terrain on earth. LB grabbed his soft campaign hat and spare water bottles, extra sunglasses, and goggles. He tied a bandana around his neck.

He checked the compartments of his med ruck, adding cold packs to chill down bottles of water for later. Next, he slid the ruck into an eagle pack; if the PJs had to jump tonight, they'd clip these black sacks to their containers' equipment rings once they were tight in their chutes. This allowed the med rucks to ride in front at their waists, out of the way of deploying lines. Next, LB buckled on the web vest that held his armor plates, radios, and five extra magazines of M4 ammo. He tested his night-vision goggles, attached them to his helmet, then clapped the whole on his head. Lastly, he hefted his field pack across his shoulders, tightened the straps, and snatched his carbine from the armory cabinet. This completed the burden. Out of long habit, LB did a few deep knee bends to shrug everything into place. More importantly, he displayed for himself, again, that he could do this.

With the rest of the team, he grabbed his chute off the riggers' table, then shuffled out of the Barn to the three carts waiting to ferry them to the runway.

The carts hauled them under a violet sky and early stars. The African dusk had dispelled little of the day's warmth. As the team entered the staging area, the big HC-130 with its gate down and engines quiet shed heat from standing in the sun all day. Even the tarmac radiated. LB and the rest of the team dropped their chute containers to sit against them. The heat through LB's pants prickled his haunches. He pulled off his helmet to wipe his brow. He was going from this to a desert.

The ground crew and loaders busied themselves around the cargo plane. A forklift delivered the second packaged GAARV, easing it down onto the ramp's rollers. The forks were withdrawn and the load team shoved the big vehicle into the plane's giant bay. Once it was in place, the loadmaster set to securing both GAARVs behind yellow nylon webbing. None of the reclining PJs chatted; they listened to earbuds or, like Doc, dozed.

Berko sat next to the tireless Wally, going over their comm equipment and protocols. The two men were very different types; lanky Wally and his sun-etched eyes beside dark Berkowitz, thick, a former wrestler. They had dissimilar energies, too. Wally spoke with his hands, all wrists and elbows. Berko used less motion; he soaked things up instead of gathering them. The kid was earnest and, in his own way, commanding.

While the PJs dealt with heavy med rucks, the two CROs wore matching Guardian Angel op kits. The bulging vests were the communications centers for the rescue team. Wally and Berko were bundled inside an array of multiband radios, a modular tactical system that strapped a computer to the wearer's back and a drop-down screen below his chest, and a SADL[12] receiver/ transmitter for real-time positions of the PJ teams and all assets on the mission. Tonight Wally and Berko would be able to track the movements of the SEALs, the diplomat in the car, and each other.

The four engines of the cargo plane fired up and the propellers gained speed and volume. Wally and Berko helped each other to their feet, then went among the PJs to do the same. LB sat in the rising roar of the propellers, to stand last.

He did not see the approach of the slim hand that reached down to him.

"Show time, LB."

Major Torres used both arms and a grunt to get him off the tarmac. Taller than LB, she leaned in to shout above the din and wind of the engines.

"Sorry I can't come."

"Won't be much action. This is babysitting."

"Maybe. But you were right."

"About what?"

"There's going to be a nice moon over the desert. Sorry I'll miss it."

Torres left him standing on the tarmac to walk up the ramp into the cargo bay. She beckoned to Wally, who stood from his seat along the fuselage wall to walk off the plane with her. The two had a quick, private word on the tarmac. Before she left, they squeezed hands.

Night had fallen, the plane's wing lights winked. The ground crew removed the wheel chocks while the loadmaster waved for LB to be the last to climb on.

---

12 Situational Awareness Data Link.

Chapter 11

Sana'a
Yemen

Josh left the bottle of Scotch with the ambassador.

At his three-room flat inside the embassy compound, he changed to jeans, walking boots, and a loose cotton shirt. Along with the cash, he stuffed three bottles of water, a first aid kit, and a sweater and light jacket into his backpack; the January desert could get cold at night, an oddity for such a blistering place, like chills with a fever.

Before leaving, Josh programmed the CIA's blue force tracker, using 0724, his mother's birthday, for the ID code. The all-clear would be **1. Threat levels went up to **4.

A well-worn Range Rover had been assigned to him at the motor pool. Josh drove past the marine guards at the bunker checkpoint, pulling away from the embassy grounds in the northeastern reach of the city. He turned north on Alneser Street, ducking into thick afternoon traffic. Two miles later, before merging onto the Ma'rib road, he stopped at the souk beside the al Ferdos mosque. Josh moved quickly through the market, beardless, dressed like a Westerner, and taller and fairer-skinned than the men around him. He stopped at a food stall for a tin plate of lamb and bean stew, hot flatbread, and sweet black tea. When he finished, Josh headed for the weapons stall.

He stood before a confusion of handguns—vintage Lugers, Smith & Wessons, British police pistols, Czech, Israeli, and Italian makes in a range of calibers and models—arrayed on three walls and tossed in woven baskets like black fruit. After hundreds of years of colonial powers buying tribal loyalty with gifts of weapons, the love of guns had become part of Yemeni culture. In calloused hands the old merchant held samples out to Josh, more eagerly when Josh answered in Arabic. Josh was tempted; he let the grizzled salesman show him several pistols, let him make prices. In the end, Josh didn't select any firearm. He thought of his mother and father, his sister, the things they'd done in the places they'd gone without a gun. A gun was force, and for years, as a soldier, Josh had been a part of that. His mission called for a diplomat. That's what he wanted to be. That's what he'd rely on if things came to it. Plus the tasrih permits, and the cash.

He haggled over a beautiful janbiya with an ivory hilt and carved wood sheath. The tempered steel of the short, curved blade held a marvelous edge. At every public event, Yemeni officials carried these ceremonial knives tucked in their belts. If he wanted to understand this country and his role in it, a janbiya seemed a good step forward. Josh paid the price of a case of scotch. The merchant threw in a black-and-white-checked *kefiyeh*. Josh asked the old man to show him how to wrap his head. When he was done, the merchant stepped back. He flung out his skinny arms.

"These will fool no one. Buy a gun."

• • •

Soon after leaving the city, Josh passed a police checkpoint. One of the tasrih travel permits did the trick, and he was waved on.

The road to Ma'rib wound its way east, and backward in time. A few miles outside Sana'a, the landscape turned rugged and expansive, sparsely populated. The few habitations reflected the will of an ancient people to cling to such a place. The houses in these uncultivated plains and hills had been built from the scraps of the earth, mud and sticks, scrub brush, straw, and rock. Mile after mile, Josh drove by nothing he could call a village, at most a dozen dwellings lumped together at a time, as if the land could not support more at any one place. Ruins were frequent; their ages could have been an eon or a decade. The horizon was always jagged with hills like badly torn paper, sharp peaks and high buttes in brown and ochre.

The roadway ran through valleys and saddles, rarely straightening out but crooking into switchbacks up and down pebbly slopes. Pavement covered much of the road, though potholes and long stretches of gravel and dust slowed the drive to Ma'rib.

Josh passed few passenger cars; flat-faced trucks made up most of the traffic. Struggling in lower gears with the hills, they spit diesel fumes. The warning of the gun merchant, that Josh would fool no one in his head wrap, prodded him with each wary look he got from a driver or spindly old woman beside the road. Even the mules and camels swung their heads at him in disbelief. In the army, he would never be on his own this way, and unarmed. Maybe this was, after all, what it was like to be a spy.

The elevation climbed through the early half of the afternoon; the vistas became magnificent. The temperature cooled, the sky stayed clear, and Josh drove with the windows down. Civilization disappeared in the highest hills; not until the road descended into canyons and rugged greenery did he again see the stacked stones that once were homes or old terraces where a farmer or herder had worked in a different century.

In Afghanistan, too, the land had reflected the people, the harshness and isolation that were theirs. A man of forty could look eighty. A chiseled face could hide a gentle heart. Danger and hospitality shared a thin barrier. The people were ignorant only of others' ways, not of their own. It was always a mistake to underestimate them.

The last ten miles was a slow descent out of the mountains. The road skirted the edge of the Ramlat al-Sab'atayn desert, the western threshold to the Rub' al-Khali. With the sun setting at Josh's back, the shadows on the vastness deepened his sense of isolation. He'd wanted this job more while sitting in Silva's office than he did right now. The closer Ma'rib came, the better his desk in Cultural Affairs looked. There he had no loose ends with the CIA, the Saudi royal family, or some angry terrorist husband. Parties, menus, and speechwriting weren't thrilling, but he'd overvalued the excitement he'd gotten out of the military. Josh's heart had been in his throat a lot of his time in uniform, and he did not miss it.

The road entered Ma'rib from the north, past another government checkpoint just outside the limits. The Yemeni guards were disapproving of an American driving alone and unarmed, then let him pass because the tasrih gave them no choice.

He drove into the city flanked by a dirt airstrip on one side and a string of garages and shops on the other. Josh pulled the Range Rover to the curb to check his map. He'd arrived in good time, an hour and a half before the rendezvous. The designated place was in the eastern outskirts, in the parking lot of a fruit and vegetable market. Josh rolled up his windows. Carefully, he drove south through the town.

In the warm dusk, the long main street was a chaotic mangle. Hastily built cinderblock huts hunkered beside mud-brick business fronts, taller offices of solid and newer construction, and open garages thrown up inside corrugated steel walls and a sliding, padlocked door. Riders sat on their parked motorcycles chatting. Men idled on plastic chairs beside shop stalls. Young men in sandals, Western T-shirts, and short beards moved in packs talking on cell phones. No women were present on the street.

Josh drove away from Ma'rib's center. Two miles south the land quickly opened to crops and groves quilted into the dry countryside. Some grander homes stood inside walled court-yards, gazing at each other like chess pieces. The road led near the ruins of biblical Ma'rib. In the half-light, the high mud walls of the old city took on rusty silhouettes. Josh turned down a tourist track to the site. He parked there, facing the earthen skyscrap-ers of Sheba while the land darkened and the time approached. An ebony Mercedes sedan pulled into the empty parking lot of the vegetable market. It stopped and shut down in the early win-ter night. The two cars faced each other for minutes, until the Mercedes flashed its lights. Josh flashed back. This was not a pre-arranged signal; it seemed a little amateurish.

Josh grabbed his backpack out of the trunk and locked the embassy car. As he strolled across the lot, the Mercedes fired up and, with lights off, eased toward him. Josh was not surprised to find Khalil al-Din behind the wheel.

The Yemeni set an elbow in the open window, breezy. He wore a black parka and turtleneck, dark like his mustache.

"Joshua Cofield. You're on time. I'm happy to see you."

"Colonel."

"Get in."

"Not just yet."

The car's windows were deeply tinted. Josh ducked to peer past Khalil, who withdrew his elbow from the sill.

"The time for questions was before this, Joshua. We need to go."

In the backseat, a woman in a gray *burqa* leaned against the passenger-side door and window. A mesh panel veiled her eyes. Josh addressed her in Arabic.

"Princess. Hello."

She did not sit up or turn her head. Josh stood erect. He folded his arms and looked across them at Khalil.

"What's up?"

"She took a sedative. She was understandably nervous. Now please, get in the car. We can talk after we're moving."

Josh stood beside the Mercedes in balance: he had as many reasons for climbing in as he did for walking away.

"What am I doing here?"

"The Americans have an interest in the princess going home. I don't know what that interest is. You're the American observer. Nothing more."

"Did you ask for me specifically?"

"Yes."

"Why?"

"I tried to do you a favor."

"I'm not a spy."

"Whatever you are, get in the car."

"I'm not so sure about this, Colonel."

Khalil took his foot from the brake to let the Mercedes drift forward.

"Then get used to writing speeches."

Josh jogged alongside, clapping a hand on the driver's windowsill. Khalil braked. Josh leaned in to keep his voice down.

"I'm just a diplomat. You know that, right?"

"Yes. Fine."

"You're the spy."

"Joshua."

"Give me this one."

"Why do you care?"

"Because somebody's got to be a fucking spy."

Khalil ran fingers down his mustache, then dipped his head. He flicked on the sedan's headlights to show his impatience. But this small concession—that through the night each would be in their admitted roles and, just as importantly, there was a bona fide spy along—tipped the scale. Josh moved to walk around the Mercedes's hood. Khalil stopped him.

"Money. Did you bring it?"

"It's in my pack."

"The transit permits?"

"Them, too."

"Good. No more questions. Get in."

Josh climbed in front. In the rear, the princess didn't flinch.

The car crunched out of the market's parking lot onto the road. Khalil did not speak but focused on driving. A pair of motorbikes puttered past, then the Mercedes was the only vehicle on the road.

Josh turned to look at the woman. She was inert, covered head to foot by charcoal folds. Only her left hand lay exposed on the seat.

"Princess?"

Khalil shook his head. "She won't hear you. She'll be out for a while."

Josh watched the princess's covered breast until he caught the slightest rise and fall of her breathing. He wanted to smack the back of Khalil's head.

"What'd she take?"

"I'd like to say this as gently as I can. That is not your concern."

"You want to tell me what is my concern?"

The Yemeni raised and lowered fingers on the steering wheel, a sort of shrug with his hands.

"Why don't you close your eyes for a while? I'll get us on the N5 and wake you both later. There'll be a moon tonight over the desert."

"Tell me one more thing."

"If I can."

"Who is she? I mean, to rate all this."

"A princess, going home to her family. Just like you've been briefed."

The Mercedes left behind the measly lights of Ma'rib. Khalil sped through the last patches of irrigated fields, past a bobbing cluster of oil derricks. In a minute, with greater suddenness than Josh had seen even outside Riyadh, the Empty Quarter lay everywhere.

He plunged into it beside an unconscious Saudi royal, an admitted spy, and too much uncertainty. He tried to appreciate the stars, the comfort of the Mercedes, and the seeming ease of the mission. Just ride. Observe.

From his pack, Josh plucked the blue force tracker. Khalil glanced over but made no comment. The slim thing gave Josh some small confidence. Someone was out there keeping an eye on him—American spies.

Josh keyed in his ID code, 0724. Then **1, the all-clear.

Chapter 12

Al-Husn
Ma'rib
Yemen

Arif woke in his office chair. A vehicle passed below his open balcony, crunching gravel. He rubbed the short nap out of his eyes and walked onto the landing to watch the ruby taillights disappear down the lane. It was not Nadya.

Full night had fallen, the Maghrib prayer finished an hour ago. He checked for the time. 6:31 p.m. Arif scratched his beard, wondering about dinner, the whereabouts of his wife. Normally Nadya locked the clinic at half past five and drove the two miles straight home. He called her cell and office, to no answer. She'd been distant all week, removed while he'd hunted her father. This morning she seemed to have allowed a thaw. Arif had been looking forward to tonight. The link with Abd al-Aziz had given up nothing more in four days, and he did not trust it enough to explore the prince's computer much longer. He was going to shut it down tonight and was eager to tell Nadya, and thank her.

Sitting at the computer, Arif checked his own messages in case she'd emailed him that she was working late. Perhaps she was handling a difficult birth or some unseen emergency of a teenage girl's heart. He roamed downstairs to look for a note he might have missed during the day. He climbed the stairs again, worry mounting with each step.

Arif returned to the connection to the prince's computer. The blank screen made him eager to free himself from the man, then go in search of his wife. But he wanted Nadya with him when he did it, a symbolic return to her. Arif rested his chin in his palm, to decide.

The screen stirred.

Abd al-Aziz had launched a simple word processing program. A blank white page glowed in Arif's office.

The prince typed.

Arif.

The lamp knocked over as Arif recoiled. Breath froze in his chest. Needles shot into his ribs and arms. The lamp lay sideways on the floor, its bulb not broken, beaming a skewed, macabre light into the room.

The prince typed again.

I have taken my daughter back.

Arif leaped to his feet as if the prince had said this to him in person. He could not think what to do except stare at the screen. The link had been reversed; Abd al-Aziz was now inside Arif.

Answer.

Arif's cell phone rang.

He stumbled away from the desk, then crept back for the jangling phone. The caller identity read UNKNOWN. Arif took up the phone, breathing into it for several seconds before answering.

"Yes?"

He twitched, waiting for a voice.

"Arif."

The prince, unmistakably.

"Yes."

"I'm going to kill you."

The computer screen blinked to black. The phone line went dead.

He staggered backward to the balcony, where he could stand in open air. He faced the starlit waves of the desert's rim, the dark street below with no cars on it.

Arif redialed Nadya's cell. He imagined his wife hearing the ring, restrained, unable to pick up, frightened. He set the phone aside and wiped his hand down his T-shirt.

Arif flung both hands to his temples to contain his thoughts. The prince had been staring back at him through the computer; how? For how long? Arif scanned the street again, fast, for black-clad Saudi agents come to assassinate him. Only the crinkle of insects and the far-off thrum of oil pumps reached the balcony. He swiped sweat from his brow into his hair and clutched the back of his head.

How did this backfire on him? When did it happen? Was he betrayed?

His head burst with questions. But the greater pang struck in his chest. He dropped his arms.

Abd al-Aziz had Nadya.

He gave himself a moment of calm to prepare for what would follow. He'd known this day might come, but he'd never predicted facing it without Nadya. The prince had struck back in a way Arif hadn't foreseen. If he had, he'd never have chosen this path.

In the office, he righted the lamp and checked the computer. The cyber link had been severed. Quickly, Arif changed out of his futa skirt and sandals to blue jeans and sneakers.

From a desk drawer he grabbed the loaded 9 mm Makarov pistol he'd taken off a dead Russian long ago, when he was a mujahideen.

• • •

Arif ran into the dark village streets. He had no holster for the Makarov but didn't care if he was seen carrying the gun. After tonight, his time in al-Husn would be done.

Entering the village, he dashed through the market, dodging merchants as they closed their stalls and kiosks, rolled carpets, stowed goods in crates. Emerging from the long market alley, Arif flew past fine houses and hovels lit for the evening meal.

He sprinted east, pumping his arms and legs against the dread in his chest. After a mile, on the outskirts of the village, he stopped to ease his swelling wildness and his lungs. With shaking hands, he dialed Nadya's cell phone again and listened through her message. Never before had his wife's voice pained him like this.

"Call me." Arif searched for more to say. "Please. Call me."

He dashed the second mile. The clinic had been built inside the blockhouse of a run-down and isolated fueling station, near the palm groves on the edge of the desert. Shaykh Qasim had provided the funds; Nadya oversaw the renovation. The small building stood on a stark, narrow lane. Though the building was dark and had no outside lighting, the pickup truck sat in the tiny lot, its driver-side door open and an interior bulb burning.

He galloped to the truck, putting hands on it to stop himself. Panting hard, Arif picked Nadya's keys out of the dirt beneath the opened door. He searched the cab's bench seat and floorboards but found no other signs of her. Nadya's backpack was missing, no cell phone, no more clues.

Arif checked the clinic door: locked as it should be. She'd closed the building at dusk, walked to the truck, opened the car door, and disappeared. Something violent made her drop her keys. On his knees, he glanced beneath the truck. A dark rag had been balled and thrown or kicked under. Grabbing it, Arif sniffed, sensing nothing of her. The kerchief was not Nadya's.

He stood back to take it all in. Every second added to the distance between them, swelling his dread. He jumped in the truck, slammed the door, and started the engine.

As the truck swung around to enter the road, the headlamps swept across two ebon forms squatting beside the clinic. Both stood, women, one taller than the other, fully cloaked by burqas, black gloves, and socks.

Arif braked. The women stood motionless in his headlights. Arif got out and reached back into the truck to shut the lights off, to allow the women the concealment of darkness.

"Did you see what happened here?"

Neither answered.

"She's my wife. Did you see something?"

He held out his arms. He'd not yet put the weapon down, it filled one hand.

"Anything."

The shorter of the women, perhaps an elder, towed the taller figure by her gloved hand out of the beams, away into the open night. Arif called at their backs.

"I beg you. What did you see?"

The taller woman stopped. Against the tug of the other, she pointed north, toward the desert.

• • •

Arif braked at the foot of Ghalib's high adobe wall. Before he realized it, he was on his feet, shaking the locked metal gate. Arif scaled back his wrath long enough to think how to climb the wall.

Stuffing the pistol into his waistband, he stepped up into the bed of the pickup to climb onto the cab's roof. Arif leaped for the top of the wall. He caught it only with his fingertips and let go, loudly crunching the roof of his truck.

Before he could jump again, two men leading a mule cart rounded the corner into the lane. Arif did nothing to duck out of sight. The men stopped closer to the truck. The elder of the pair walked forward, raising a lantern.

"What are you doing?"

Arif showed him the Makarov.

"Go away."

The men and the mule did not budge. A weapon in Yemen was common; no one cowered from them here.

The old man held the lantern higher.

"Should I shout the alarm?"

Arif had only murder in mind, but not for two innocent men.

"I'm going to enter the house of Ghalib Tujjar Ba-Jalal."

"Why do you go like this? Are you a thief?"

"I'm going to kill him."

Shadows from the lamplight shifted on the old man's features as he tilted his head. "What did he do?"

"He kidnapped my wife."

"How do you know this?"

"He threatened it. And it has been done."

The man stepped nearer the pickup, raising the lantern to see Arif better.

"Truly?"

"Truly."

"Is it *tha'r*?" A revenge killing.

"Yes."

The old one kept the lantern high while he studied Arif from below. His tongue worked inside his cheeks, behind his gray beard. In the light, the man was not so old and blue-eyed. He pointed to the big house behind the wall.

"You know who he is? This family, the Bayt Ba-Jalal?"

"I know very well."

The old man squinted. "You have killed before?"

"A long time ago."

"So you understand?"

"Yes."

Slowly, the man inclined his head to Arif as if in the presence of someone exalted.

"*Insha'Allah.*" If God wills.

He turned to gesture the younger one forward. This man came leading the mule. The elder took the animal by the bridle while the younger man stepped onto the pickup truck bed. He was burly and the truck's springs sagged under him. He bent, clasping his hands to make a step. The old man shook the lantern at Arif.

"Up you go, then."

Arif tucked the pistol in his jeans. He rested one foot in the man's big hands, braced on his shoulders, and with a heave was boosted high enough to lap his wrists over the wall. The big man in the truck pushed on the heels of Arif's sneakers to shove him higher. Arif pulled himself up to straddle Ghalib's wall. In the street below, the two men and mule walked on with their lantern. Arif slid both legs over the wall, hung by his arms, then dropped.

Shreds of light from the house lit the courtyard. The only glow came from windows in the rear of the first floor where the kitchen would be, and from the top, third floor. Undiscovered inside the walls, Arif paused to check his rage and resolve. The old man had been clever and right to ask him if he'd killed before, if he understood what it meant and what it took. Years ago in war, first in defense of Allah, then of his comrades, Arif had felt this gravity to violence, the downward slope toward killing. As then, he saw no path other than this, the short distance to Ghalib's door. Arif returned the weight of the Makarov to his hand.

He moved to the thick portal and knocked several times, hard.

Just as it had five days before, an unseen woman's voice filtered down to him.

"Who is it?"

"Arif the Saudi. I need to speak with Ghalib Tujjar Ba-Jalal."

He was left without a reply. Through open windows overhead came bustling and women's calls inside the house, until the voice returned.

"With respect, the *sayyid* says he will speak with you tomorrow."

"It's urgent."

"Tomorrow, please."

Arif lifted the iron latch. The door didn't budge.

He receded from the door into the dim courtyard. Arif lifted a flowerpot off a stone table. He peeled back the shutters from a window beside the front door and threw the earthen pot. Panes and mullions shattered, spilling into the house. Arif snapped away the smashed bits of wood and glass to hoist himself over the sill.

Inside he stood in a murky foyer on shards, dirt, and petals. Two young girls in white robes squealed, then darted into a darkened hall, flurrying like fleeing ghosts.

Down the staircase, a woman's voice screeched, "Sir, no! No!"

Arif took the steps two at a time. Above him scattering females shouted curses on Arif, "*Haram 'alaykum!*" and banged doors shut. He held the Makarov out like a searchlight, looking for Ghalib. He listened through the chaos for a man's voice, a man's footfalls.

On the second-floor landing, a woman opened a door wide enough to hurl a shoe at him, then disappeared. Arif coursed up the stairs to the top floor and the mabraz where Ghalib might be chewing qat after the evening meal.

Arif was met by the smell of flavored smoke. Walking carefully, ignoring the uproar below, he flattened to the wall approaching Ghalib's private room. Arif channeled his temper, to release it in the next few moments.

A shadow drifted across the pillowed floor of the mabraz. Arif gave himself over to Allah and the rightness of vengeance. Gun first, he lunged through the doorway.

Ghalib's African akhdam had his arm cocked to throw a jar of tobacco leaves. Arif surged; the glass sailed close to his head. He grabbed the servant by the blouse, pulling him off balance. The old black man collapsed to his knees. The hookah was lit and smoldering.

Arif yanked the old man upright, cramming their faces close.

"Where is he?"

The akhdam whimpered that he didn't know, a plain lie. Arif slapped him to make him cry out, then tossed the old man onto the cushions.

Arif stood in the hallway before the mabraz. He bellowed into the house to be heard above the shrieking on the floors below.

"Ghalib Tujjar Ba-Jalal! Will you run from your house and leave me with your women?"

Bare feet thudded on the stairwell below. Arif flung himself down the staircase to the second-floor landing. Ahead of him, a skinny teenage girl scampered along the dark hall with a terrified glance over her shoulder. Arif whirled to confront an attractive, raven-haired wife in a yellow housedress, her escape thwarted. Behind her shrank an adolescent girl in a cotton gown and bare arms. A small boy wearing short pants peeked around her skirt.

The woman bared white teeth.

"Turn your face!"

Arif averted his eyes while she shepherded the children into a room off the hall. When they were gone, a touch of fury overcame him. He turned a circle screaming Ghalib's name into the whole house.

The door where the woman had retreated opened. Ghalib emerged into the hall and clicked the door behind him. He wore the same emerald robe and naked chest as before, without the rich man's grin. Facing Arif he blinked repeatedly, shoulders turned as if he might bolt back into the room. He stammered something.

With Ghalib suddenly in front of the gun, a vivid image from decades past asserted itself, an interrogation of a Russian about a massacre; the Soviets had gassed an entire Afghan village. Arif should never have been given the task of questioner; he was too enraged. He'd shot the soldier in the middle of the man's first word. Now, as Ghalib opened his mouth, Arif searched for the clarity not to kill this sputtering *kalb*, this dog, in the same fashion.

Arif leaped, ramming him backward against the door, rattling it, making the women behind it yelp.

"Where is my wife?"

Ghalib gawped for words. Arif crushed him again against the door.

"Where?"

"Arif. Arif. Stay calm. I don't know anything about this."

Arif pushed the Makarov into Ghalib's eye socket. The old vision of the Russian soldier departed; Ghalib had already lived longer than him.

"I won't ask again."

A tremor flowed through the gun muzzle pressed to the man's head. Ghalib sputtered more.

"Please, Arif. Upstairs. Please. Away from the women and children."

Arif eased the pistol enough to follow him up the steps. He held the gun between the man's silken, shaking shoulder blades. Behind Arif, the household's gabbling women flooded down the stairs, outdoors into the courtyard.

Arif marched Ghalib to the mabraz. He pushed him down beside the old servant, who had not left. Arif told the black man to get out. The servant scuttled down the stairs without a backward look.

Arif aimed the Makarov at Ghalib's heart. Ghalib would be found dead the way he'd lived, reclining on his cushions.

"Talk."

"You have to believe me. I don't know anything about your wife."

Every second Arif did not act added to the distance between him and Nadya, and to his own peril; the wives and children outside the house wailed at the tops of their lungs for police, neighbors, anyone to come.

"What did you do with the information I gave you?"

Ghalib licked his lips, blinking faster, concocting a story.

"Good-bye, Ghalib. Shaitan waits for you."

Ghalib scrambled backward over the pillows, into the wall, kicking away from the Makarov. He thrust out an arm.

"Wait, wait. Arif, I'll tell you. Wait. Please."

Arif lowered to both knees but kept the pistol leveled. Beside Ghalib, the water pipe smoldered, a samovar steamed. The room had been prepared for his luxury.

"Speak fast. If you hesitate, I know you're lying. What did you do with the thumb drive?"

Ghalib hung halfway up the wall, pinned there.

"Yes, all right. A moment."

He eased down to the cushions. Ghalib closed the robe over his chest while he crossed his legs under him. Unexpectedly, his fright moved aside and he now seemed committed to something beyond his fear: either telling the truth or dying well arranged. Ghalib blew out his cheeks while he gazed into his own lap. He managed a measure of cool and asked the same from Arif.

"Please stay calm."

"I can kill you calmly."

Ghalib raised both palms, a fending gesture.

"I sent the information on, as I promised. The suggestion was made that more could be done with it than simply embarrass the Al Saud."

Behind his lifted hands, Ghalib paused. Arif prodded with his voice and the gun.

"And?"

"It was decided to kill the prince."

"What?"

Killing Abd al-Aziz had never been mentioned. Even with scores to settle, Arif had not thought it.

Arif threatened again with the Makarov, thrusting as though it were a knife. Ghalib kept talking. He filled in the details, briefly and speedily, as Arif had demanded. Within days, a wanted Saudi bomb maker named Walid Samir bin Rajab was recruited to take the thumb drive to the prince's home in Riyadh, use it to gain entry, then detonate the bomb in his presence.

Arif listened, incredulous; his hand slacked on the pistol. He caught himself and firmed the gun. Ghalib responded by aiming a finger back.

"I told you. You weren't thinking big enough. You only wanted to publish it. This was a much greater strike at the Al Saud."

"At my wife's father."

Ghalib turned the finger to himself.

"I am al-Qaeda. You knew this when you gave Abd al-Aziz to me."

"I didn't give him to you."

Ghalib sat up straighter, nearer to the Makarov.

"A Muslim may kill another Muslim for three reasons. If that man has killed another wrongly. If he is married and fornicates outside his marriage. If he deserts the Prophet and fights against Islam. You yourself have said Abd al-Aziz has done all three. Don't act the child, Arif. You know the hadiths. You know we had the right to kill him."

"He's not dead."

This rocked Ghalib. His jaw dropped. Before he could speak, Arif surged forward off his knees to wrap a hand around the man's throat. He drove Ghalib onto his back, squeezing his windpipe, screwing the barrel of the Makarov into his ribs.

"The prince is alive. He has my wife. Now listen to me."

Ghalib, with reddening cheeks and bulging eyes, nodded.

"She's been kidnapped. Exactly what you threatened. Tell me what happened to her. Then I'll decide if you live."

Released, Ghalib sat up to rub his flabby neck. The blood remained in his face. He croaked.

"How do you know Abd al-Aziz is alive?"

"He sent me a message on my computer."

"When?"

"Twenty minutes ago. He said he'd taken Nadya. Then he called my cell phone to say he was going to kill me, and hung up. I ran to the clinic. Her truck was still there. She's gone."

"Anything else?"

"There'd been a struggle. Two women must have been at the clinic late and saw what happened. They stayed by the truck to tell someone. When I got there, one pointed to the road north, into the desert."

"Bin Rajab failed."

Arif wagged his head. Ghalib had failed.

"Why did you do it?"

Ghalib shrugged, as if surprised at himself. Probably this was the boldest thing he'd done in his life. Arif had no faith that this was the blood vow Ghalib claimed against America. This pampered bit of dung had sacrificed Arif only to curry favor with al-Qaeda, his brothers, his dead and commanding father. Ghalib couldn't admit this even to himself, facing death. Instead, he pleaded again for his life.

"You have to believe me. I had nothing to do with your wife's kidnapping."

Arif checked his watch. 6:50 p.m. Where was Nadya? Speeding away from him.

"Tell me right now. What did you do?"

Ghalib paused to fumble for an answer, and it would be the thing that would get him killed. Arif gave up hope. He would go down from this room, out of this house past the shouting women and boys in the courtyard, the killer of their sayyid. Go where, he did not know.

Drained, burdened by his loss of everything, he tightened his grip on the Makarov. Arif changed his mind, not about killing Ghalib but about escaping afterward. He'd stay in the mabraz, smoke the last of the water pipe, and surrender when the police came. He'd be sent back to the Kingdom, where the prince would keep his word. Little matter.

Suddenly Ghalib gushed.

"I betrayed you."

Ghalib worked his hands, rising to his knees before the pistol, throwing everything into his confession.

"I got your cell phone number when you called me. I gave it to bin Rajab. Before he blew himself up in front of Abd al-Aziz, he was supposed to dial your number. Yes? Did this happen?"

The ringing phone, the hang-up. A commonplace death knell, nothing to alert Arif. He ground his teeth. "It did."

"I don't know how Abd al-Aziz survived. But I was sure when you found out that I'd killed him, you'd be furious. So I gave you away. They've tracked you. I thought the Saudis would have you dead by now. But they took your wife instead. That's what happened, that's everything. I swear."

Incredible. His father-in-law believed Arif was behind the assassination attempt. This explained why he said he would take Arif's life. It was only tha'r. Revenge.

Ghalib's admission came too late. Arif, like a man who'd dropped a stone, could only watch it fall.

Over the barrel of the gun, he eyed the middle of Ghalib's forehead.

"Arif, I can get her back. Stop. I can do it."

Arif did not move the gun or his finger from the trigger.

"You have seconds left. You know that."

"Yes."

"Tell me how."

Ghalib made the same patting motions with his hands that Arif had seen before. The last time, the rich son was growing cozy in his large home. Now he made those gestures desperately, to urge the killer in his house to lower his weapon.

"We'll check the airport to see if there have been any private flights in the last hour. If there were none, then your wife's being taken by car."

"If she's on a plane, you die."

Ghalib rubbed both hands across his face. Outside in the courtyard, his family had not lowered their voices. He stood to raise a window in the mabraz and shout down for them to be quiet: he had the situation in hand. When he sat again before Arif, the Makarov had not moved.

Arif faded off his knees, to sit cross-legged. Hurriedly, Ghalib reached into a silken pocket for his cell phone. He called the Ma'rib airport. No planes had landed or taken off since dusk. No more flights were scheduled for the night. Nadya was in a car.

Ghalib held up the cell phone.

"It's a long way across the desert."

Chapter 13

Sharurah Domestic Airport
Sharurah
Saudi Arabia

Wally and Berko viewed the desert moon side by side. From his seat on the lowered ramp of the cargo plane, LB watched them standing on the starry tarmac, wondering if they were talking about tactics or women, Wally playing the experienced man either way.

A light breeze blew from the west, easing the temperature. The rest of the team sprawled beneath the wings of *Kingsman 1*; no one spoke but tapped out emails, read, or listened to earphones. The big plane rested on a round pad at the end of a runway, surrounded by sand that held its warmth as the air cooled.

The flight from Djibouti had taken three hours. The pilots flew high above the Gulf of Aden, then into Saudi airspace, avoiding Yemen. LB dozed for much of the flight except for the time spent admiring the strapped-down GAARVs, looking at new photos from Mouse's Oakland Raiders cheerleader girlfriend, or listening to Doc worry about one daughter or another. He played crazy eights with Dow and Quincy, then slept again until the plane touched down.

They'd been on the ground a half hour when another transport approached out of the north. A US Navy C-130 Hercules zoomed in and taxied to the opposite end of the runway. There it parked. No sooner had the plane shut down than six ATVs revved and rolled off the plane's lowered ramp. The SEALs roared the length of the runway to buzz the loitering PJs. They drove in a crazy circle around the pararescuemen, kicking up sand. Wally and Berko walked forward to check the ground-to-ground freq and call signs with the SEALs, who then disappeared in arrowhead formation south over the dunes.

In the quiet that followed, the night sky was cut into halves. North of the airfield, the lights of Sharurah obscured the stars; the small Saudi border town was isolated in this southernmost corner of the Kingdom. It was no more than an outpost for oil workers, border control, and desert scientists. To the south, stars winked, and the moon laced the blank immensity of the Empty Quarter. The earth lacked contour and, rare on land, left the curvature of the world visible, spectral in the gray light.

Wally moved among the team members, chatting, giving Mouse a thumbs-up over the pictures of his cheerleader. Berko kept an appreciative eye on him.

LB cracked an ice pack to lay it over a water bottle. Berko dropped on the tarmac next to LB. The kid didn't grunt or creak when he sat; nothing on him hurt. Berko tucked his own water bottle under the ice pack.

"Clever."

"Twenty years. You learn a few things."

"That's a long time."

"Please don't say you were only four years old when I started."

"Okay. I was five."

Berko leaned back on his hands and crossed his ankles. The kid was a specimen, powerfully built. Only Quincy on the team might take him in a fair fight, maybe Wally on a good day.

"Wish I had a cigar." Berko corrected himself. "Two cigars."

With Wally circulating, LB waited until the cold pack faded, then opened both chilled water bottles. A shooting star left a long tail over the desert.

"LT, what are you doing here?"

"What do you mean?"

"I mean, why're you sitting on a landing strip in Saudi Arabia?"

"Instead of what?"

"What's your old man do?"

"Lawyer."

"That."

The lieutenant took a swig, wiped his mouth, and caught LB waiting.

"You don't think I fit in?"

"What I think is that you could be doing anything. Why this?"

"I don't have a great answer."

"Give me what you got."

Berko pursed his lips, considering his options. LB nudged.

"Lieutenant."

"What."

"Nothing you say will be the first time I've heard it."

Berko stirred his hands, stalling to compose some eloquence.

"Okay. It's not romantic or anything. But I didn't want an office job right out of college. I wanted the military."

"Adventure."

"I heard about the GAs. I looked into it and liked the idea of being a combat rescue officer. I figured *there* was a challenge."

"You wanted to be elite, be a Special Operator."

"Roger that."

LB passed a hand across the other PJs arrayed around the HC-130, all sitting in their own worlds.

"I've known each of these guys since they started."

LB pointed at every PJ in turn.

"Mouse was an army medic. His big thing was motorcycles. Dow was navy security, served on speedboats. He's a surfer. Both of them are adrenaline freaks. Jamie wanted to be like the PJs he saw in some air force TV ad. He and Dow are gun nuts. Doc came over from the marines, and that big cowboy Quincy was a SEAL. They both got a look at PJs in the field and thought it was a better fit than what they were doing. Wally was in the Rangers, where I used to be. He knew what I was into and figured it would work for him, too. All these guys wanted that test, just like you, to do all the rescue and recovery stuff. The washout rate for the PJ wannabes is nine out of ten. They all wanted to see if they had what it took to be that one."

Berko looked uncomfortable, screwing the cap on the water bottle and stowing it.

"So why'd you bother asking me?"

LB took his team in, silent and sharp-looking men, sloppily splayed on the tarmac. He didn't intend to smile, aiming for a more somber moment with the young lieutenant. But these men were LB's brothers, his only family, and if Berko was to join them, he needed to hear how he did fit in.

"Everyone's different now. They're not mountaineers or skydivers or whatever, they don't care. That might be why they joined, but that's not who they are anymore."

Wally, Jamie, Doc, Dow, Quincy, Mouse—LB had been present when all had taken part in their first rescue. In those moments, with death screaming at them in a storm, in a battle, in a rage, these men who had been many things became Guardian Angels, PJs and CROs.

"Do they know? The other guys on the team?"

"Do they know what."

"Why you became a PJ. Why you gave up your commission."

"Just Wally."

"So tell me. Wally can't be your TC[13] forever."

"Why's it matter to you?"

---

13 team commander.

The young CRO started to speak, then interrupted himself. He spread his hands again, fumbling. To LB, Berko appeared younger than he had since his arrival.

"Just spill it, LT."

"Okay. I want to be the best. That's you."

LB patted the kid on his broad back.

"Thank you, sir."

"I admire you and I want to know."

"Okay, okay. We're not going to date."

Berko made to stand. He'd taken this as more sarcastic than LB meant. LB stopped him.

"Every man, lieutenant."

Berko settled. LB continued.

"Every man has a cemetery inside him. You don't know how big yours is until you dig in it. Civilians bury their families and friends. That's tough enough. But guys like you and me who go to war, we bury a lot. Friends, yeah, and enemies, too. Trust me on this, the memory of killing someone is pretty fucking keen. I spent eight years with the Rangers doing a lot of covert work. South America, Iraq. I just about filled my graveyard. The PJs gave me the chance to leave some open ground. I get to sleep at night seeing the faces of people who're alive because of me, instead of just the ones who are dead."

The freshest graves inside LB were Somali: the three he'd knifed face-to-face and the three he'd shot point-blank on the hijacked freighter just four weeks ago. He made no mention of them to Berko. That mission would be classified for a long time.

The young lieutenant nodded thanks for LB's trust. He shifted his gaze over the desert, a dim and vacant space, vast enough to see what might be.

"What's that like? To save somebody?"

LB climbed to his feet. "Get up."

Berko followed.

He walked the young lieutenant to Doc, who called Jamie to collect the rest of the team. The squad gathered in a ring on the warm tarmac.

Every PJ told his story. Their missions took place in Iraq, Afghanistan, and Haiti. LB had a turn; in Somalia, a Nigerian captain had been gutshot while serving with a UN peacekeeping force. A year later, the officer sent LB a picture of himself and his six beautifully chocolate children.

All the stories were the same at their core. You know a man will die if you stop: stop swimming, running, fighting, pumping, something. If you quit, if you're beat, he won't make it. That's when all the training becomes real. It's your hands keeping him alive, you pulling him back to safety. In those moments, nothing else matters. Nothing. Not even your own life.

The session went on. The stories shifted to fuckups. LB slipped away from the ring to sit alone against his pack. He chilled another water bottle, drank half, and watched the moon drift higher and brighter above the desert.

Wally squatted beside him. "That was good of you."

LB handed him the water bottle. "The kid's got to find his way."

"You know what I remember?"

"What?"

"When you did that for me."

"That worked out pretty well. Figured I'd try again."

Wally drained the bottle dry, then stretched to his full height. He dropped the plastic empty down to LB. "You were right. Nice moon tonight."

LB tossed the bottle at his back.

Chapter 14

Ramlat al-Sabʻatayn desert
Hadhramaut governorate
Thirty-five miles east of Maʼrib
Yemen

Josh wasn't a desert lover.

Growing up on the Louisiana bayou, spending every summer visiting his mother's clan in Maryland, he'd grown fond of big water. Shrimpers on the Gulf, tankers on the Mississippi, crabbers and sailboats on the Chesapeake. In the immense night of the Ramlat al-Sabʻatayn, he thought of these and not the rolling swells of starlit sand. In the army, Josh hadn't taken to the endless plains of Kansas where he'd trained, or the bleak valleys of Afghanistan where he'd served. Now he was in Yemen, after dry Saudi Arabia. For his next posting he'd request somewhere in the Pacific, though his Arabic would probably keep him in this parched part of the earth.

In the pale glow of the car's dials, Khalil drove with both hands on the wheel, intent on the road. This was his personal vehicle; he had maps and breath mints stashed away. Khalil made no conversation. Josh listened but could not hear one breath taken by the cloaked princess in the rear seat.

The road ran true east with little contour to make it curve or rise. For the third time since leaving Maʼrib, Josh entered the all-clear code into the blue force tracker. Beside him, Khalil showed no interest.

The land and road offered up nothing but great emptiness. One truck passed, headed west on the N5. Its many lights had been visible a long way off, and Josh watched them come, heartened until they were gone. Far behind the truck, a sallow and shivering glow lay on the horizon. Josh let himself be pulled across these next miles while the glimmer revealed itself to be the belching flames of a refinery in the middle of nowhere. After this, the desert stretched interminably, void, and the waves of sand did little but make shadows from the Mercedes and the moon.

An hour outside Ma'rib, Josh keyed in another all-clear code. Khalil spoke for the first time since leaving the town.

"I apologize. I've been a little tense."

"What are you worried about?"

The Yemeni hooked a thumb over his shoulder. "She's very important."

"No one's chasing us."

Josh meant this as humor but Khalil looked in the rearview.

"No."

Josh looked back at the princess. "Her breathing's pretty shallow."

"I'll check on her in a little while."

Left and right of the road, the constellations no longer touched the rim of the earth. The Mercedes seemed to be speeding through a valley.

"The dunes are getting taller." Khalil waggled a finger at the night coursing by in his headlamps.

"How high?"

"Some are five hundred feet. The south faces are the steepest, out of the wind."

Khalil reached to his shirt pocket for a cigarette pack. He lit up and cracked his window to bleed out the smoke. The air that coursed in had a nip to it.

"You know the desert well?"

"Of course. In Yemen, in every family tree not too far removed, there is a tribesman or a Bedouin whipping a camel over these dunes. Every child is taken into the desert to learn it."

"What's your tribe?"

"I am Huashabi, from the south, near Aden."

Khalil spoke of the desert, how to live under the sun, travel the dunes, dig for water. He described the many hues of the sand, how the desert changed colors through the day with the timing of the prayers: dull gray before dawn, the honey of flesh at noon, brick-red in the first shadows of afternoon, yellow-orange under the slanting late sun, and finally the black of sleep.

Khalil brightened with his chatter, smoking in a chain. Cool air flowed into the Mercedes. Several miles ahead in the straight distance, a car's headlamps flicked on. Khalil tapped the brakes. This may have been why the princess stirred.

Khalil slowed, pulling the car off the road.

"Get out, please."

"Why?"

"For modesty's sake, you should not watch."

Josh figured he could just turn his head, but complied and got out. The desert whispered a light breeze, lifting the checkered kefiyeh off his shoulders. The night was warmer near the sand. Khalil cut off the headlights and climbed into the back of the Mercedes to sit beside the covered woman. He closed the car door behind him, shutting off the interior lights. The spy did whatever he intended to do in darkness.

When he emerged, he beckoned Josh, holding open the rear door.

"Please ride in the back."

"With her?"

"I'll explain in the car."

Josh stood his ground beside the blacked-out Mercedes. "You'll explain right here."

Khalil put his hands to his hips. His jacket opened enough to reveal the butt of a pearl-handled Beretta in a shoulder harness.

"Why?"

"I don't like what just happened. She shouldn't be that unconscious for this long."

"She is exactly as she should be. Trust me in this."

"I don't. I want to know what's going on. Right now."

"You have no power in this situation. Why do you insist on exercising it?"

"It's a habit."

"I do not want to leave you out here. Truth be told, you don't want to be left. So please get in the back. I'll tell you what I can."

Khalil was right, Josh had no cards to play. He might be able to hitchhike back to Ma'rib, but he was more likely to find himself isolated out here, an American alone in a remote, tribal, and potentially hostile region. The dangers, the desert cold, the failure of his diplomatic assignment, all this put him in the back of the Mercedes next to the knocked-out princess.

Khalil flicked on the headlights and motored onto the road. The woman in her burqa was again motionless, head against the passenger window, bare left hand still lifeless on the seat. Knifing into the long night ahead, Khalil took a gracious tone.

"I'm sorry to speak to you this way. But your role tonight is not what you wish it to be. You were an army officer, I respect that. Likewise I ask you to respect my command in this car. Can you?"

Khalil fired up another cigarette. Josh clamped down on his own gall. Khalil had nailed it; he didn't easily play the pawn. Even less did he like being lied to. He was finding it difficult to reconcile the Yemeni buffoon he'd met last week in the Turkish embassy with this black-clad, armed secret agent issuing orders.

"Sure."

"Thank you."

"Like I said. Habit."

While Josh had been riding in the front seat out of Ma'rib, the woman in the back had been simpler to ignore. Seated beside her, seeing her motionless inside the folds of the burqa, how strongly she was in the grip of some powerful sedative, Josh couldn't look away so easily.

"Can you tell me her name?"

"Only this. Nadya."

"She's really a princess? Is she going home?"

"Everything you were told about her is true."

"Why am I here?"

Khalil tossed the finished cigarette out the window.

"You are my *rabia*."

"Your what?"

On the road far ahead, the headlights were joined by three more sets of vehicle lights shining in the center of the tarmac ribbon.

"We are now in the Hadhramaut. That is a tribal checkpoint ahead. They will hesitate to trouble an American diplomat with franking permits and cash. You are my passport."

"So why've you got me sitting in the back?"

"Ah. That is the most important part for you to play tonight."

"I'm all ears."

"When we are stopped, I will explain that you are her husband."

Josh jerked forward, to crane across the front seat. Khalil did not turn from the wheel.

"What?"

"How else do we explain an unconscious Arab woman in the back of our car? You are a diplomat in Riyadh. Your Saudi wife ran off with another man to Yemen. You went to Ma'rib to bring her home. She's taken a sleeping pill to calm her nerves. With the tasrih and enough cash, we will be allowed to pass."

"Won't we look like kidnappers?"

"Not at all. She is your wife. You have every right."

Josh sat back. He sensed himself hurtling not over the dark desert but deeper into it, like quicksand.

Khalil raised a warning finger. "Stay quiet. Don't let on that you speak Arabic. I'll do the talking."

Nadya's uncovered hand lay near his. Josh wanted to wake her, get her version of the facts.

"Khalil."

"Yes?"

"Are we kidnappers?"

In the rearview mirror, the Mercedes's white dials robbed Khalil's eyes of color, leaving them with the frostiness of the moon.

"It's getting difficult to hide that, I suppose."

This pressed Josh backward into the leather seat. He sat like the princess, still.

Khalil took his time lighting another cigarette.

"Yes, Joshua. Of course we are."

Chapter 15

Ma'rib
Yemen

Ghalib changed clothes quickly, into dark trousers and a black silk T. Arif followed him down the flights of stairs, out the front door, and into the courtyard, where Ghalib's family clumped, frightened and crying out at the sight of him.

Ghalib shouted to his wives and children that this had all been a misunderstanding. To demonstrate, he turned to put a hand on Arif's shoulder. Ghalib told them to go back inside, everything was well. Arif kept the Makarov hidden against the man's shirt as they left through the gates together.

In the street, in the pickup, Arif trained the gun on Ghalib. Every ticking second drubbed on the truck, urging it to leap forward and pursue Nadya, who was almost an hour ahead.

"Where are they?"

"On their way."

"I won't wait much longer."

"Patience. We can't do this by ourselves."

Upstairs, at gunpoint and begging for his life, Ghalib had explained the need for his brothers. They would bring men, money, trucks, and guns. The pledge of sanctuary made to Arif by Shaykh Qasim had bound them, as well. Even if the tribal elders in the Hadhramaut did as agreed and captured the car on the desert road, they might need more than just a request, or payment, to return the woman, though they did not know she was a Saudi princess.

A caravan of technicals, all Toyota pickup trucks, careened into the street. In a line they skidded to a halt beneath Ghalib's high wall. Their collective headlights lit up Arif and Ghalib. Each of the five trucks had a heavy machine gun mounted on a stand bolted to the bed. Every pickup was filled front and rear with local men, all carrying Kalashnikovs. Many had wrapped themselves in bandoliers of ammo.

"Put the gun away, Arif. You don't need it."

Arif did not ease the snub barrel from Ghalib's rib cage.

"And why won't one of your brothers just shoot me?"

"Because they are here to honor our father's oath to you. Not mine to al-Qaeda. Later, I'll answer for involving them. Believe me."

Without much choice, Arif tucked the Makarov into his waistband. Behind Ghalib, he emerged into the blazing headlamps.

Ghalib's six bearded brothers arrayed themselves side by side in order of age, as they'd done at Qasim's funeral. The Ba-Jalal were a portly family and tall. They stretched across the road with their armed men and trucks idling behind them. Each brother was dressed in loose pantaloons, sandals, flowing tunic, and kefiyeh. All had strapped on belt holsters with handguns.

Ghalib stood beside Arif facing the brothers. The eldest spoke for them.

"Arif the Saudi. We are here to help."

"Shakkran. We need to hurry."

"I understand. I have made arrangements with the tribes of the Rub' al-Khali. The road heading north and all roads to the east will be blocked. Your wife will be found. The kidnappers, as well."

"I will repay you for this."

The eldest shot Ghalib a disdainful glance. On the phone, to summon his brothers with Arif listening, Ghalib was forced to admit his role, his betrayal of their father's pledge to Arif.

The senior Ba-Jalal spun on his sandals.

"Ghalib will repay us for this."

The big man wasted no time, climbing behind the wheel of the leading Toyota. All the brothers did the same in their trucks. While car doors slammed and engines revved, Ghalib looked drained in the many headlights. Arif moved for the driver's door of his own truck. Ghalib roused himself to jump in front of him.

"I know the roads. I'll drive."

"She's my wife."

There was no time for this argument. Arif laid hands on Ghalib to shove him away from the driver's side. Ghalib stood red-faced to have this done in front of his brothers.

Before Ghalib could stride forward or Arif challenge him again, one of the armed Yemenis hustled between them. The man joggled with gun and bullets. His teeth showed qat stains.

"Sayyid Mahmoud says Arif the Saudi will ride with him."

The eldest, Mahmoud, leaned his large head out the window of the lead truck.

"We will go very fast after your wife, I promise. Please. Come with me."

Arif made no more argument. He was at the mercy of the Ba-Jalal. His bitterness against Ghalib would not speed them faster after Nadya. He climbed in the passenger seat of Mahmoud's pickup. The man who'd stopped him from punching Ghalib took Arif's place.

Spinning tires, Ghalib led the pack out of the narrow street, onto the wider paved road. The way north from Ma'rib passed Nadya's clinic. Three miles later, a pair of cloaked and veiled women walked along the shoulder, holding hands in the dark. These were the two who'd waited beside the truck and pointed into the desert.

With the road rolling by swiftly, Mahmoud touched a thick, placating hand to Arif's knee, then removed it.

"I apologize for my young brother. I'm certain I know only half of what he has done to you. I did not believe the two of you would do well in the same truck."

"Agreed."

"We'll sort Ghalib out after we've returned your wife."

Mahmoud drove fast, as he swore he would. With the dark road straightening as it entered the desert, Ghalib pulled far ahead, showing the brothers his zeal to make amends. Mahmoud appeared to be in his sixties, and not accustomed to driving himself. The Ba-Jalal were businessmen, not warriors. Arif looked through the rear window into the truck bed, at the four young Yemenis, their clothes all ruffling in the cool night air. They looked to be poor men who would do as they were told.

On the road behind Mahmoud, the other trucks bunched up. The five younger brothers were eager and able to drive faster but stayed in line behind their elder. Arif clamped his impatience. He worked his hands in his lap.

Mahmoud noted his fidgeting.

"They will not leave Yemen with your wife."

"Can we go faster?"

"I will try."

"Thank you for your help."

Mahmoud gained some speed, but the truck, weighted with six armed men and the mounted machine gun, gained little on Ghalib, who kept his lead into the desert.

"Ghalib says you are a scholar. Is this so?"

"I suppose."

"The Ba-Jalal are not the strongest of Muslims. It would please me if you would tell me something about the giving of help, from the Qur'an."

Arif selected a hadith.

"If a man sees an evil, let him change it with his hand. If he cannot, then with his tongue. If he cannot, then with his heart, but this is the weakest faith."

Mahmoud held one hand off the steering wheel to ball it into a fist and admire it. Mahmoud the wealthy seemed to be rising to the adventure of the night, especially if it was agreeable to Allah.

"Yes. It is not enough to pray for change. Another."

"No. Put both hands on the wheel and drive faster."

Mahmoud laughed and complied.

"I like you, Arif the Saudi. I see why my father did, too. We will talk more after tonight. I am getting old. I should like to be a better Muslim. You are welcome to my help."

"Shakkran."

Soon the line of trucks passed a Halliburton refinery. Vivid orange flames danced on the tips of dozens of stacks inside a long chain-link fence. Spotlights lit the paved yard and great parking lot. The operation seemed self-contained and modern in so ancient a setting, on the silk and incense route to Ma'rib. Mahmoud expressed the same thought.

"If only the old caravans had known of oil, eh?"

Mahmoud raced onward, glancing back at the refinery, perhaps considering more property to buy. Arif cared for nothing behind him, only what lay ahead.

In a while, Mahmoud asked, "Will you tell me one thing more?"

"If I can."

"When we catch them. What will we do with the kidnappers?"

"I'm not sure."

"The Qur'an tells us to command the good and forbid the evil. Yes?"

Arif opened his hands to show he was pleased to hear from Mahmoud this famous verse, the *hisbah*. The older man grinned broadly in the crimson light of the Toyota's dashboard.

"That is true."

"So we will kill them."

Mahmoud said this happily, convinced that this, too, would be satisfying in the eye of Allah.

In the sequined night ahead, one shooting star fell from the sky. The flare did not burn itself out but crashed to earth, far ahead, onto the truck Ghalib drove.

In a blink, a fireball blossomed, lighting the dunes on every side. Mahmoud slammed on the brakes; Arif had to catch himself against the dash. The men in the bed of the truck shouted, frightened by the screeching tires and the sudden orange glow on the desert.

Mahmoud's truck skidded to a stop, sideways, tires smoking. A half mile up the road, Arif's pickup somersaulted out of the fireball, ablaze, tumbling into the sand.

The eldest brother struggled with the car door. He stumbled out of the truck to drop to his knees in the road. Mahmoud faced the rising mushroom cloud that flickered from the flames beneath it.

Arif stood on the road behind him. A chill desert breeze cut through his T-shirt; he'd not thought he would wind up here when he'd run from his house two hours ago.

Mahmoud kneeled and wailed, face buried in his hands. His rounded back was starkly lit by the other pickups stopped behind him. The rest of the Ba-Jalal brothers closed ranks around their elder, eyes fixed on the fire that was Ghalib. Only Mahmoud had gone to his knees, only he wept. The others may have had differing opinions of their youngest brother.

High in the stars, above the silence of the dead desert and Mahmoud's grief, the drone would be slipping away. It must have tracked Arif's pickup by its heat signature. How long had the thing been circling, how long had pilots four thousand miles away kept their fingers on a trigger? Surely Abd al-Aziz had sent the drone. Somehow he'd talked the Americans into it. He'd warned Arif, *I'm going to kill you*. Now, with Ghalib crackling to ashes inside Arif's truck, the prince would believe he'd done it. He was mistaken, as Ghalib had been about him.

The licking flames revealed to Arif the plot, why his wife had been kidnapped. As soon as his father-in-law had made the decision to kill him, then convinced the Americans to do it on his behalf, he stole Nadya to protect her, keep her from becoming collateral damage. Abd al-Aziz knew she would not have left him—even if she were aware she might die beside him—just as he would never have left her. With Arif dead, her father hoped to put Nadya in Care Rehabilitation, perhaps jail, break her and reform her, swallow her again into the Al Saud. But the prince did not know Arif was alive and chasing her down. This gave Arif a slim advantage.

None of the armed men had stepped out of the pickups to look at the glowing carcass of Arif's truck. The two dozen Yemenis leaned from windows or stood in the truck beds whispering to each other. Arif caught the eye of one of the brothers, the tallest, who quietly retreated from Mahmoud and approached to whisper.

"You are a fortunate man, Arif the Saudi."

"I'm sorry for Ghalib. But you need to know I would have killed him if I do not get my wife back."

"I know."

"Please give me a truck to go on."

"We will go on together. Ghalib did not speak for our father in life. He does not now."

With a decisive manner, this brother turned from Arif. He walked around the hood to Mahmoud, to crouch before his older brother. He pulled Mahmoud's hands down from his face.

"We have an oath, brother. We must take Arif's revenge today. Ours will wait for another time. Come."

He tugged the heavyset Mahmoud to his feet. The elder wiped his eyes on his blouse while his brother turned into the headlights to tell the others to get back in their trucks. Mahmoud, supporting himself against the hood, walked around to Arif. The stars and climbing moon were limned in his eyes. With both hands, he squeezed Arif's shoulder. Arif thought Mahmoud might strike him.

"You drive."

The remains of Arif's truck lay scattered across the desert in flaming bits. Fire raged in the tires and wreckage and lapped at spilled fuel blackening the sand. Arif slowed to avoid the crater in the tarmac where the missile had struck, a hole many feet deep. The convoy was forced to drive onto the sand. There could be little left of Ghalib and the man who'd taken Arif's place. Even so, one of the trucks pulled out of line to put its headlamps on the pyre; the deaths had taken place at night and it was not proper to leave the remains in darkness. One of the brothers would sit vigil for the second Ba-Jalal blown to bits by the Americans.

Chapter 16

Hadhramaut
The Empty Quarter
Yemen

Rolling toward the roadblock, Josh keyed in threat level **2. With the signal sent to whoever was watching, he tucked the blue force tracker in his pack.

Khalil slowed to a stop, nailed in the white beams of four pickup trucks parked across the road.

"Remember, say nothing."

The joined headlights lit up the Mercedes cabin. They shined into the veil that masked the princess's eyes. Josh leaned forward to see through the mesh; Nadya's lids were shut.

Khalil rolled down his window at the approach of three armed figures. These were smallish men, shabby and sweat stained in loose-fitting dress and woven vests. Their beards were untrimmed. Two had Kalashnikovs in their hands and qat bulges in their cheeks. The one in the middle seemed clear-eyed, his gun across his back. In his belt was tucked the curved sheath of a janbiya knife, hilted in green jade. No one else was visible in the four vehicles barring the road. Josh assumed they were packed with tribesmen and weapons like these.

The middle qabil spoke first.

"As-salam alaikum."

Khalil returned the greeting. The tribesman rested his elbows on the Mercedes's windowsill. The muzzle of the Kalashnikov on his back nicked the car's roof.

"Papers, please."

From his sun visor, Khalil produced a small booklet, his personal identification, and one of the travel permits. The tribesman did not open the booklet and ignored the tasrih. He leaned in more to peer inside the car. The man's oddly spicy smell entered with him.

"Who is this?"

Josh met the tribesman's dark eyes with a lowered brow. Khalil answered.

"An American diplomat. That is his wife. They have been traveling in Yemen. They are going home to Riyadh."

"Is she asleep?"

"Yes."

"Wake her up."

"She has taken a drug to ease the trip. She will not wake for hours."

"Do they have papers?"

"Can you read them?"

Above the bush of his beard, the tribesman turned the long tip of his nose back to Khalil. With his face close, he spoke without malice, a man in control.

"Do you insult me?"

"No. I simply wonder which papers might get us on our way the quickest."

The tribesman scrutinized Khalil for long moments. Khalil registered a cool manner, a spy's restraint.

The tribesman laughed through his nostrils. "And what other papers do you have which might do this?"

Without turning, Khalil reached backward to Josh. He spoke in English.

"Give me a hundred thousand riyals." Almost $500.

Josh pulled the backpack into his lap. Keeping his hands inside the pack he counted the cash from one of the banded packets, then handed the money to Khalil.

Khalil presented the bills to the tribesman. The man stood back from the Mercedes's window to flip through the money with a fingernail. Perhaps he could not read, as Khalil suggested. The tribesman wadded the tasrih and tossed it aside. Then he held the bundle of riyals at arm's length. A little at a time, the qabil released the bills into the desert breeze until his hand was empty.

The money fluttered away from him like poured ashes. Behind the headlights, car doors flung open. Seven Yemenis leaped out to collect the riyals skittering onto the sand. The qabil who'd dropped them enjoyed watching his men chase down the cash, a game.

With arm extended, palm down, he dropped his mirthful mask slowly, like the money. When none of it was left, the tribesman scowled at Khalil.

"Ah. There is the insult." He flipped his hand over, palm up. "The Bani Yam are not so cheaply bought."

Khalil copied the qabil's posture, reaching out his own open hand.

"That's fifty times the normal rate."

"Normal? Are you Allah, to say what is normal?"

Khalil cursed under his breath, then hissed to Josh. "Give me the whole packet." Two thousand more dollars.

Josh pulled out the rest of the banded pack of riyals. Khalil offered this to the qabil, who stood in the headlights, still with his arm out.

The tribesman did not stride forward. Khalil shook the packet as if the man, like a fish, might take it better if offered with a jiggle. "Here."

The tribesman stayed back. Khalil sighed.

"How much do you want?"

"All your money."

Josh dared an urgent whisper. "We can't do that."

Khalil did not show that he'd heard.

"I have given you half a million riyals. That is all we have."

"You are prepared to cross the desert. You brought permits and baksheesh. I know you have more of both. You may keep the permits. The money you will leave with us."

The tribesman lowered his arm. Like the two who flanked him, he filled his hands with a black Kalashnikov.

Khalil rested an elbow in the windowsill while lifting his other to the steering wheel. It was an easy move, a casual pose to open access to the shoulder harness hidden in his armpit and the pearly handgun under the parka.

In the headlights, the qabil's henchmen continued to chase down loose riyals. Khalil faced three men with submachine guns. He might take down one, two at the most, if he shot first. The next move would be to gun the Mercedes off the road, probably under fire, around the barricading trucks, over the sand. If the big car could power its way back onto the tarmac, it might outrun the Toyotas. But a high-speed chase through the Empty Quarter on a desolate road with dead bodies behind them and armed men after them wasn't a choice. Khalil's bravado had gone far enough.

Josh rolled down his window.

"Sayyid."

Khalil jerked around at Josh. "I told you to be quiet."

The tribesman cocked his head. "Yes?"

Keeping both hands visible, Josh stepped out of the Mercedes.

Khalil started to open his car door. Josh pressed it shut.

"Sit tight."

"Do you know what you're doing?"

"We'll find out."

Josh took the banded cash from Khalil, then moved clear of the Mercedes, well lit and towering over all the tribesmen. He touched his own forehead beneath the kefiyeh, then covered his heart. He addressed the tribesmen in Arabic.

"I know the Bani Yam. You are not brigands. You are masters of the Rubʿ al-Khali."

The qabil laughed, pivoting his stained teeth to both men at his sides. The pair remained stoic while he let his Kalashnikov dangle free at his chest, pleased.

"For an American, you flatter like an Arab."

"Thank you, sayyid."

"But." The tribesman lifted a finger beside his beard. "You are not Arab. And if you want to pass with your sleeping wife, you will pay the masters of the Rubʿ al-Khali."

"Can we talk about this?"

"You want to parlay?"

"Yes."

The tribesman glanced around at his men, who'd gathered all the spilled riyals they could find and now waited for him. He alone carried a janbiya in his belt. Rubbing his lips inside his beard, the qabil accepted the money from Josh, then handed the banded packet of bills to one of his men. He strode closer to Josh and unsheathed his short knife. He raised the curved blade higher than Josh's covered head.

"You are not Yemeni. I will not bargain with you. And I will not speak to your dog of a driver."

Josh lifted his own finger to buy a moment, then spun for the car. In the backseat he pulled from his pack the ivory hilted janbiya he'd bought that afternoon in Sanaʾa. Again, when he stepped out of the Mercedes, he kept both hands in plain view, showing the knife.

Like the qabil, Josh bared the blade and held it aloft, far above the tribesman's reach. The two stood with knives raised to the stars in the bright court of the headlights.

"We are both men of honor. I ask for parlay."

The tribesman lowered his janbiya.

"What honor have you?"

Josh tapped the janbiya's white hilt to his own chest.

"I have been a warrior for my country. I have many medals for courage. I've left that behind to learn the language of the Arabs. To understand your ways. I know the Bani Yam. You are a just people. I ask only for that. I give you this in return."

Josh offered the janbiya and sheath. Amid murmurs from his men, the little qabil accepted them.

"Is this ivory?"

"It is."

The man slid both knives into their sheaths, then handed them to one of his men. He shifted the strap of the Kalashnikov to put the gun across his back.

"You may speak."

"Are there more roadblocks ahead?"

"Of course."

"You know if you take all our money, we will not be able to get through."

"Then keep your riyals and turn around."

"I think you know I cannot do that, either."

"I do."

"Who is paying you to stop us?"

The tribesman swung his gaze west behind Josh, beyond the throw of the headlights, down the dark desert road. To the horizon, no traffic showed.

"You have made some powerful enemies taking this woman, sayyid."

"Who?"

"The Abidah."

"Are they more powerful than the Bani Yam?"

The tribesman screwed up his face, glancing about at his cohort.

"No."

"How much have you been offered?"

He answered proudly. "Two million riyals."

"Are they on their way?"

"Of course. We must be paid."

"I will give you two and a half million."

The tribesman reared back in surprise, then turned away from Josh to open his arms to his men, as though he'd bestowed a great boon on them.

"*Wallah!*"

They mirrored this, and all were happy.

Without dropping his arms or his delighted face, the qabil rotated back to Josh.

"Shakkran."

"*Ahlan wa salahan.*" You are welcome.

The little man reeled in his arms.

"And why should I not just take everything and hold you here a while longer?"

"Because you would be a thief and a servant. I have not been told this of the Bani Yam. Who will block the road ahead of us?"

The qabil seemed stymied by Josh's quick, sharp answer.

"The Sai'ar."

"They are the thieves."

The tribesman broke into sudden laughter, without mockery. He clapped once.

"So. You bargain like an Arab."

The man stepped back to swing his weapon again into his hands. Leveling the Kalashnikov by his waist, the tribesman advanced quickly on Khalil in the front of the Mercedes.

"Make no move."

Khalil put both hands beside his head. One of the men was ordered to fetch Josh's bag from the rear seat. Opening the car door, this one recoiled at the sight of the silent woman. He ducked in to snare the satchel quickly. The bag was tossed to Josh.

The spokesman pointed his gun at the bag.

"Three million riyals. Do not let me see how much more you have. Honor is one thing. Remorse is another."

Josh dug out five more banded packets of cash.

"I'll need a receipt."

The money was taken into rough hands.

The tribesmen retreated to their picket of trucks. All four trucks started their engines. Only the spokesman lingered with Josh in the middle of the road, weapon ready.

The tribesman slipped the gun's strap over his head. He presented the Kalashnikov to Josh.

"Give the Abidah and the Sai'ar greetings from the Bani Yam."

He jumped into one of the vehicles. Single file, the qabili veered away, sweeping their lights with them to leave Josh in the dark. They rumbled east toward the moon, then left the road to dissolve into the dunes.

Chapter 17

Sharurah Domestic Airport
Sharurah
Saudi Arabia

Wally and Berko stomped side by side down the HC-130's lowered gate. Both took the same urgent strides, twins in matching Guardian Angel op kits, padded camo vests stuffed thick with radios and a SADL. Both had lowered the drop-down screens at their chests; both had their heads bent and focused. Their boots made tandem hollow thumps hurrying down the metal ramp.

LB climbed to his feet off the tarmac. Wally and Berko stopped in front of him without breaking formation.

"What's up?"

Wally deferred to Berko, to give the kid some experience leading LB. "Go ahead."

The lieutenant hesitated, reluctant. "You're team commander."

The two stood with mouths open; they'd stumped each other. LB started to sit back down.

"I'll be here. You two go figure this out."

Berko and Wally spoke at the same time to stop him from folding his legs. Wally held up a finger to Berko to say *You do it.*

LB made a show of shuffling his boots on the tarmac to face him.

"Yes, Lieutenant."

Berko angled himself for LB to share his small computer display.

A satellite map filled the screen. Emerald waves of topographic info overlaid the black-and-white terrain. Elevation numbers ticked at the bottom of the screen. One road ran east-west, labeled N5. A single green dot pinged, coursing in near real time east on the N5. Berko touched it.

"That's the package."

The dot was the blue force tracker in the hands of the US diplomat whose presence on this mission no one could explain.

"Where are they?"

"Running a hundred miles south of the Saudi border."

LB shrugged. "Everything looks okay."

"They just started moving again. The car stopped for five minutes, right here." The young CRO slid his finger a short distance behind the car.

LB couldn't figure what the big deal was. "Someone took a leak. They stopped to pay one of those tribe tolls. So?"

Wally stepped in. Like Berko, he shifted his torso for LB to see what they'd been monitoring. Doc came onto the tarmac to come look over LB's shoulder. Wally pointed out a small green digit riding along with the dot through the Empty Quarter.

"Look here."

Wally laid a fingertip just beneath an ominous, emerald 3.

"That popped up a minute ago."

"He had some trouble. Looks like he's out of it."

Wally disagreed.

"He didn't send a one or a two. He's saying three. He's still dealing with it. Or there's more threat ahead. But he's not calling for help yet."

Again, Wally inserted his display into the center. Doc scurried around to get a view. Wally had widened his SADL's scope, panning the map farther east.

Forty miles west of the package's current location, the N5 entered an intersection with another road, the S150. This smaller track turned north through raw desert another sixty miles, making for the Saudi line. The S150 was the package's route out of Yemen; at midnight, the car would be met by the SEAL team and their ATVs ten miles shy of the border.

On the map, Wally indicated a village four miles east of the crossroads, labeled al 'Abr. The display marked a few dozen scattered buildings and huts on the slopes of rocky high ground rising out of the desert. Al 'Abr clung to the base of a spine of mountains that formed the southern bowl of the Empty Quarter.

"After this crossroads, there's nothing but open desert between the PC and the border."

LB asked Berko, "What's the next move?"

Again, the young lieutenant tried to pass the question to Wally, but Wally had him answer. Berko glanced around at the lounging PJs.

"If that three turns into a four, that means us."

"And?"

"I'd get everybody on the plane right now."

Immediately, LB stepped back to shout at the team.

"Listen up. Stow your headphones and shit. I want you all on the bird and ready in five."

Doc jumped away to rally Mouse, Quincy, Dow, and Jamie. Wally switched to the ground-to-air frequency. He walked off barking into the mike at his lips, ordering *Kingsman 1*'s pilots to spin up.

Berko stayed beside LB. He folded his arms across the bulky op vest, ignoring for the moment the tray of his computer screen, the electric green dot that was his recovery mission tonight. He took in the action pulsing through the PJs.

The big cargo plane's propellers coughed and started to churn.

"That was good, Lieutenant."

"What was?"

LB backed away to go join the furor. He shouted over the accelerating props.

"You said 'us.'"

Chapter 18

Hadhramaut
The Empty Quarter
Yemen

A freight truck bound west lit the palms of Mahmoud's hands, opened beside his head. He mumbled. Arif drove through the night as fast as the road would allow. The four Yemenis in the pickup's bed ducked out of the wind. Far behind, the flames of Ghalib faded fast.

The freight truck flashed past. Mahmoud quieted and dropped his hands.

"I do not know the proper prayers. Do you?"

"Yes."

"Will you say the *du'a* for me, Arif?"

"No."

"You are a hard man."

Mahmoud sniffed away a tear.

"Ghalib was like Yasser. Young and flamboyant. Show-offs. They were father's favorites. He was tired and old when both were born. They cheered him."

"They cheered you, as well."

"It's a function of age to love youth as you lose it."

Mahmoud pinched his nose to compose himself.

"He was not evil. Only foolish. Too eager to please, though he never amused the rest of my brothers. Like Yasser, a poor businessman. But clever. A good husband and father."

"I'm sorry. But I will not pray for Ghalib."

Arif sped at the front of the five remaining trucks. The desert had a heavy darkness that barely parted for their passing. The night fell in curtains on all sides, a sheer black that starlight and the half-moon did not lift. Arif had not been this deep into the Empty Quarter before, even in the years when he lived in the Kingdom. It pained him even more to think of Nadya rushing away from him into this, as though she were lost on an ocean.

"Where is the first roadblock?"

From his tunic, Mahmoud pulled a cell phone. He checked for calls.

"We should reach it in thirty minutes."

"After that?"

"There is a crossroads at al'Abr-Alwudayah, where the road turns north. Five miles before that."

"Are you expecting a call?"

"Yes. Drive on."

Mahmoud sat silent in the high-speed rattling of the truck. He'd lost another young brother, this one before his eyes. Arif had lost his wife and was chasing her across a desert because of betrayals, his own against Abd al-Aziz, Ghalib's against him. These losses entwined him and Mahmoud, and made conversation difficult. Each had scores to settle.

Arif tried to focus on the road, looking to the far distance for red taillights, some car he could overtake. The black trail ahead remained empty, broken at intervals only by big trucks rushing toward them.

Mahmoud tried again to pray for Ghalib but was frustrated. Arif's refusal to assist and the elder brother's stumbling whispers added to the tension. With every dark, flowing mile and few lights ahead, Arif's desperation for Nadya and his doubts about the Ba-Jalal mounted.

The time came and passed when the roadblock Mahmoud had promised should have appeared. Arif sucked his teeth. Mahmoud checked his watch and phone. Only stars rested on the road ahead.

"There's nothing here. Nothing."

"The next roadblock is forty more minutes."

"How do you know?"

The elder man turned to face Arif.

"My brother is dead. No matter how fast you drive, there is no rescue for Ghalib. Please respect that I am trying to uphold my family's obligation to you. But do not push, Arif the Saudi. I remind you."

"Of what?"

"The missile that killed my brother was meant for you. They were following your truck. I could say the Ba-Jalal have done enough."

"And I could say the Ba-Jalal have taken my wife."

Mahmoud stiffened in the seat. His beard worked around his lips; he chewed on many words before speaking.

"I understand. And you must understand you are not alone in your grief."

Arif urged the pickup into the featureless night. Close behind him trailed four more trucks, brothers and men sworn to help him because of an oath. Beside Arif, Mahmoud pushed through his own sorrow the way Arif did the dark and his dread.

Arif took a hand off the wheel. He reached to Mahmoud's thick shoulder.

"I do not wish to be alone. Raise your hands again. We will say the *Salat al-Janazah*." The prayer for the dead. "Allah hu akbar."

Mahmoud lifted his open palms beside his ears. "Allah hu akbar." With his hands occupied, he could not wipe away a fresh tear.

Chapter 19

Hadhramaut
The Empty Quarter
Yemen

The Mercedes's headlamps beamed out across the sands, petering to an extraordinary sky that touched the rim of the world in every direction. The Bani Yam disappeared to the east. Standing in the motionless road, Josh checked behind him. No one came for them yet. The temperature dropped, but Josh felt the warmth of the tribesman's hands in the Kalashnikov.

Khalil waited at the steering wheel. On the rear seat, the princess sat like a mannequin. Khalil spoke out his open window.

"Throw the gun away."

Josh rounded the hood of the Mercedes to climb in the front passenger side. Khalil waved to stop him, calling through the windshield.

"No. In the backseat."

Josh got in the front, resting the submachine gun across his knees.

"Drive."

Khalil balked.

"Toss that out the window."

Josh bit his lower lip to compose himself. He was in this predicament because of the lying, spying, kidnapping Khalil.

"Drive or I get out. And I take the money and the permits with me. You can deal with what's up ahead on your own." Josh patted the AK-47 on his lap. "And this big boy means I can do what I say. Now put your foot on the gas. You and me are going to talk."

Khalil relented. The car accelerated and the Yemeni grew more agitated.

"I don't like having it in plain view."

Josh ignored him long enough to key in his identification on the blue force tracker. He punched in threat level 3. He hoped the watchers were, indeed, watching.

"There's another roadblock coming."

Khalil smacked a palm on the wheel. "We need to stick to our cover story. If anyone sees you with a gun, we're blown."

"Listen to me. Those guys back there knew. There was no cover story to blow. The husband must've found out we took his wife. He's al-Qaeda, and he's on his way. The Bani Yam were hired to stop us. The Sai'ar, too. We're driving into a trap. We can't stop, and we can't go back."

"You think a weapon is the answer? I thought you were a diplomat."

"I understand a show of force. These tribes don't like each other. My bet is the Sai'ar won't get in a gun battle with us just for the Abidah's money. If we get blocked again, we offer the rest of the cash and a permit. Then we'll show them we'll fight if pushed to it."

"Typical American diplomacy."

"Fucking A right it is."

The strain between them dried up any more talk. The car slipped through the great night, but the lack of contour in the land slowed the speed and the passing minutes. Alone in the backseat, the princess took on an air of fortunateness, the one in the car who was unconscious and unaware of the dangers ahead.

• • •

When the next roadblock appeared, headlights popped up strung across the road a mile ahead. Like the Bani Yam, the Sai'ar blocked the highway in only one direction, against cars headed east.

Josh did not get in the backseat. Khalil slowed, then rolled to a stop in the collected beams of three pickup trucks.

A fat man sauntered over, odd to be so portly in such a severe place as the Empty Quarter. His sandals kicked at the hem of a long futa skirt, his beard only a thick stubble. He carried no gun or knife and wore rings on every finger. Six men around him held automatic weapons.

The pudgy Sai'ar lapped his decorative hands on Khalil's windowsill and leaned in. He didn't ask for papers, said nothing while scanning the interior, eyes first on Nadya slanted against her rear window, then to Khalil, and finally to Josh gripping the AK. The tribesman lifted his hands off the car to back away.

Josh got out, showing his palms, letting the Kalashnikov hang at his chest. Khalil took the same ready posture as before, easy at the wheel, the Beretta in his left armpit accessible to a fast move. The six Sai'ar formed a firing line; the fat man sank into their rank.

Josh kept the Mercedes between him and the tribesmen.

"We have money. We have a tasrih."

All the Sai'ar shifted in surprise at Josh's Arabic. The fat, unarmed qabil took an unconfident step forward.

"Who are you?"

"An American."

"Are you a soldier, sayyid?"

"I was."

"How much money?"

"More than the Abidah are offering."

"I see the Bani Yam wagged their tongues. Did they wag their tails, too?"

"They spoke well of you. They told us you would be waiting. I will pay you the same to let us pass."

"What price did the Bani Yam put on you, sayyid?"

"One million riyals."

The Sai'ar chattered amongst themselves, admiring the amount. The rotund one consulted over his shoulder before turning back to Josh.

"We accept."

Josh ducked into the car for his backpack. Another one of the Sai'ar, not the fat one, called out.

"And how much for the woman? And the driver?"

Khalil heard this the same way Josh did; Khalil's right hand crept closer to his left armpit. Josh froze, bent over the pack. The Sai'ar weren't going to let them go. They were just pretending to be bribed, taking the available money, buying time for the Abidah to arrive. With dread and haste, Josh ran through his options and dead-ended in a gun battle. What else could he do? Stand straight. Fire the first burst with the Kalashnikov, sweep them, scatter them. Knock out a few, no way to know how many. Khalil would join in. Jump in the car, skid around the roadblock, pray not to get hit bad by the Sai'ar still firing. Drive hard another eighty miles to the Saudi border at top speed trailed by armed tribesmen. Punch in threat level **4 and holler for the PJs.

In the army, during four combat tours, Josh had engaged very little in close-quarters fighting. He'd been a trooper, an officer, an interpreter, a witness to conquest, but the few times he'd pulled his trigger against men this close had left him shaken and feeling lucky to be alive. He drew a deep breath to let caution catch up to him. The courage of a gun in hand could be fleeting and misleading.

Josh reached across the front seat to touch Khalil's back. He whispered, "No." Khalil retracted his grip from his jacket.

Out of the pack, Josh freed one of the banded bundles of cash. He tossed the money over the car; the tribesman caught it on the platter of his gut, then tucked it into a pocket of his tunic. Josh left his open hand in the air, showing it in the many headlights, but eased his other under the Kalashnikov.

"I will give you another million riyals for the woman and the driver."

With mutters and gestures, the tribesmen conferred over the offer. The big qabil gave their reply.

"Sayyid, the Abidah want the woman very much. They also want the ones who have taken her. Another million riyals is not enough for all three of you."

"This is what I paid the Bani Yam. And you have brought fewer men."

"We did not think you would get past them. Clearly they are scoundrels."

"I have no more money than that."

"I will not throw fuel on the fires of the Abidah, not for the same pay they offer. It is not wise."

"Do you not worry about my fire?"

At this, Josh put both hands on the AK-47. The Sai'ar gunmen did the same.

"I do. No one wishes to die here, sayyid. Leave us the woman and your beardless driver and you may go on. We will make your apologies to the Abidah when they arrive."

Josh stood before six weapons in an orb of white light in the middle of a desert. He kicked himself for coming tonight. He should have refused half a dozen times, to the ambassador, to Khalil. Moving up the embassy ladder wasn't even close to being worth this.

The Sai'ar spokesman pointed to the rear of the Mercedes. "Wake the Saudi. Let her choose."

"No."

"Then you must choose."

"What if we fight?"

"Then you will die. Is kidnapping a woman worth your life?"

"Is doing the work of the Abidah worth yours?"

Undetermined moments rose like heat between them. Josh widened his stance behind the Mercedes. The Sai'ar were exposed in the open; he and Khalil had the cover of the car. Josh could take out a couple before being shot down himself, the same for Khalil. This wasn't a good choice. Nor was waiting for an enraged husband and his al-Qaeda posse to come roaring up the road. The tribesmen showed no signs of buckling to Josh's bluster, and he'd run out of tricks.

Khalil broke the silence. He stepped out of the car with both hands in sight.

"We agree."

Josh switched to English. "What are you doing?"

In Yemeni, Khalil asked the fat tribesman if he might speak privately with his sayyid. He rounded the Mercedes's hood. Khalil lowered his voice, speaking English.

"Get behind the wheel. I'm going to act like I'm about to wake her. They don't know I'm armed. I'm going to draw and fire. You hit the gas and go. I'll do what I can."

"That's insane."

"It is also the only chance you have."

"They will definitely kill you."

Again, Josh checked the dark road behind. There was no way to know how much of a lead they had on their pursuers. No white lights crept in the distance, only the gray of moon and star. Every minute they delayed brought someone very angry and dangerous closer. Stalling wouldn't help.

Khalil rested his hand on Josh's arm. "The longer we stand here, the closer the Abidah and al-Qaeda come. We cannot wait, and we cannot negotiate more. If you can come up with something else, I'd like to hear it. If you can't, get in the car. Drive away. Finish the mission."

"Khalil. We should think about leaving her."

"No."

"We're kidnappers. I'm not sure we should put our lives on the line for that."

"I am not a kidnapper. I am a soldier with orders. I expect you to understand what that means. Now get ready."

Years of training tore at Josh. To do his job without asking what part he played in the whole. And to do something, anything, other than leave a man behind. In the Rangers, this was an unthinkable act.

Khalil dipped his head to say his last words to Josh. "Allahu A'lam." Allah knows best.

Josh didn't move. Khalil shouldered past him to reach for the rear door.

The tribesmen opened their arms at Khalil, glad of his decision to relent. Numbed and without a choice, Josh climbed behind the wheel of the idling Mercedes.

Khalil turned his back on the Sai'ar. His right hand crept to his left armpit and the pearl-handled grip of his handgun. Josh made himself ready to peel off.

"Drive away." Josh muttered the words but said them out loud to bring the notion of abandonment into the full world, where he'd have to deal with them the rest of his life. Drive away. You're a diplomat. Khalil's the soldier.

He tried to imagine what his father would say, his mother, and Ambassador Silva, to have him alive, and ashamed. He couldn't hear any of them. They stared and gave no guidance, the question too complex for a civilian. But others' voices asserted themselves in his head, the dutiful men he asked next, all men in uniform.

"Wait."

Khalil flicked eyes at Josh that were steeled for violence. He was primed to spin and start firing. Josh said again, "Wait."

Leaving Khalil with his hand on the rear door, his other at the holster, Josh scrambled beside him for the backpack, for the last two bundles of cash and the blue force tracker. With his keyed-up nerves, he fought not to fumble them. He punched in his ID code, 0724. Then **4.

The princess slept. Behind her in the immense night glowed the bloodred flush of the car's taillights. Josh got out.

Chapter 20

Sharurah Domestic Airport
Sharurah
Saudi Arabia

On a circle of tarmac surrounded by sand, the HC-130 idled, cargo ramp closed. The props turned at a low and uncomfortable rpm, waiting to be either shut down or revved up. The PJs sat in the dimly lit cargo bay on seats lined against the fuselage, rattling with the great airframe.

The men were glad to be out of the cooling desert night. Among the PJs every eye was closed and ankles and arms were crossed, not resting but containing their energies, rocking on the propellers' vibrations. LB stayed alert, riveted on Wally. The signal would come through him.

For the next half hour, Wally kept his attention fixed on the drop-down monitor of his SADL. Beside him, Berko followed along on his own screen.

LB figured he could close his eyes for a bit. All he got was one minute of shaky peace behind his lids before Wally's shout goaded him alert again. LB and the team sat up in their seats.

"The PC's stopped again. Still at threat three."

The situation wasn't deteriorating, but it wasn't improving. The car wasn't moving. Not a good sign.

Another five minutes passed with no more reaction out of Wally or Berko, both monitoring the mission second by second. Cautiously, the PJs relaxed into their rocking seats.

Wally shot to his feet, pressing the earpiece deeper into his head. The team leaned forward; apprehension flooded back in like wind through a window. Wally raised an arm for everyone's attention.

"We have 'Execute.' Repeat, we have 'Execute.'" He turned to every team member and the cargo crew, whirling an index finger beside his head to give each the signal, We're spinning up!

The big HC-130's propellers sang higher and the plane began to roll. Doc moved through the PJs, keeping to his feet in the unbalancing shimmy of the plane swinging around, heading for the runway of the little Saudi airport. He bellowed.

"Jock up. Chutes on. Let's go, go."

LB strapped into his chute container, then clipped on the eagle bag holding his med ruck. He pulled from his vest his night-vision goggles to check the batteries, then stowed them. He touched all three spare ammo magazines for his M4 to be sure they were secure. Doc rounded through the team, inspecting harnesses, tugging on straps. He spent an extra few seconds with Berko, then gave LB a thumbs-up. When Doc climbed into his rig, LB did the check. Wally curled around his radios, listening to Torres in the ROC five hundred miles away at Lemonnier as she gave him and the pilots the mission brief. The recovery team checked their radios with each other.

"Radio check."

"Lima Charlie. How me?"

"Lima Charlie."

Kingsman 1 careened onto the runway, dumping Doc into one of the seats along the airframe wall. He buckled in fast with the rest of the team before the plane gathered speed and sound and sprang off the earth. The pilots banked her south immediately in the air, plainly urgent.

The HC-130 leveled off quickly. This was going to be a nap-of-the-earth flight into Yemen: swift, low, and secret. Wally straightened out of his hunker to stand and address the team. Hanging on, he shouted over the engines.

"Here's the drill. The SEALs' mission has canked. Major Torres has swapped us into the lead. The SEALs are now in support. The precious cargo in the car has stopped on the N5 highway seventy miles south of the border. The diplomat in the car with the blue force tracker has now signaled threat level four."

Mouse lifted a hand. "Any injuries?"

"Don't know."

Quincy asked next, "Hostiles?"

"Unconfirmed but likely. Something or someone has stopped the PC twice. Probably tribal roadblocks. The first time the car got through it. The second time, the situation got worse. Right now the package is stopped and we have to assume under attack. That's all the intel we have. We'll jump static line from eight hundred feet three miles from the signal. I want the whole unit plus both GAARVs on the ground."

Wally stepped out of the center, ceding it to LB, team leader. LB addressed the unit.

"There's not much to go on. You've got your teams. We need to move fast, so leave your chutes on the LZ. Load up on water, we don't know how long we're going to be out. Stay tight, be ready. We're going in after civilians, and that means no one knows what's going on. We'll get down, gear up, figure it out, and do the job."

LB didn't like jumping into such emptiness, with no advance intel of what waited below in the world's largest desert. This mission had been tight-lipped from the start; even the bird colonel Hulsey in the ROC this afternoon had little he could say. Threat level four could mean anything, from a panicked diplomat with a hair trigger to a full-blown firefight with locals or al-Qaeda.

Nonmilitary clandestine ops like this were rare for the PJs. They weren't rare enough.

LB had nothing he could add to his remarks that wasn't a guess. He went with what he knew for certain.

"You're the best-trained and best-prepared rescue team in the world. So screw it. Let's go. Hoo yah?"

The unit as one answered, "Hoo ah!"

Zooming above the dunes at three hundred knots, it was fifteen minutes to the LZ. The loadmasters set to work freeing the GAARVs from their cargo strap restraints, shoving the packed vehicles and cargo chutes over rollers and into position. The GAARVs would be pushed out first, with the team right behind them into the night. LB helped Wally into his container, checked his straps and buckles, then popped him on the shoulders.

LB took a seat beside Berko. The young officer was occupied checking everything twice: his ammo, carbine, radios, parachute, bootlaces.

The lieutenant's smile came quickly, then fled at the same pace. His hands fluttered over his equipment.

LB pushed the young CRO's arms down. "Stop it." He ran a quick check over the kid's gear; everything was in place.

"You're good, sir."

Berko puffed his cheeks and seemed to settle. LB had done this for every pararescueman on the team at one time or another, and many others over the years. Told them they were good, then leaped into trouble beside them to try and make sure it was true.

Chapter 21

Hadhramaut
The Empty Quarter
Yemen

Josh opened the car door and left it open, to rise behind it with the Kalashnikov. In the sand beside the road, the tribesmen greeted him with their six automatic weapons aimed his way. Khalil spread his hands at him to say, What are you doing?

Josh raised the blue force tracker high. He and Khalil were well lit in the spill of the many headlamps, ten yards away from the Sai'ar. Josh steadied his voice at the tribesmen.

"I'm holding a signaling device. There's an armed American force waiting at the Saudi border. I've just sent word for them to come. They're on their way. Before they get here, let us go."

The fat spokesman stepped forward, shielding his eyes from the lights.

"Let me see this device."

Josh held it out. "You can come look."

The spokesman, surprisingly good-natured for the circumstances, waved the suggestion off with a laugh.

"No, no. I will believe you from here, sayyid."

Josh set the blue force tracker inside the car on the dashboard. This freed both hands for the Kalashnikov.

"If the Americans come, none of you will survive."

"And if the Abidah arrive first, none of you will. It seems we have a race, sayyid."

Josh had no idea if the PJs could get here from eighty miles away in time to do anything more than retrieve his body. But he had to play this out.

From a pocket, the qabil produced a cell phone. He showed it. "In fairness, you have called your rescuers. I will call mine to find out where they are. It may help you decide how to wager." The tribesman hesitated before dialing. "Or I will be generous. We will let you and your driver go in exchange for the Saudi woman. The two of you will live."

"No. All three of us go. Here."

Josh tossed the last million riyals at the man's feet.

The big Sai'ar scratched the stubble on his chin. He made no move for the money in the sand.

"I have a daughter married into the Abidah, sayyid. A son who wishes to. I will madden the Abidah enough for letting you two go. I will not make it worse. Now wake her. And leave her."

"We'll wait."

Khalil flung up his arms, frustrated.

"No. I will not die in the desert for a Saudi woman."

Josh didn't remove his eyes from the Sai'ar, or his hands from his gun. Khalil the chameleon was playing some gambit, the rebelling servant.

For the tribesmen to hear, Josh snapped in Arabic. "Be quiet. Get back in the car."

Khalil glared hard at Josh. He uttered in English, "Do you believe the Americans will get here in time?"

"No."

"Then there is no other way."

To wait was to die. Leaving the princess behind was to fail. To escape on his own was to sentence Khalil to death. Nothing presented itself but to fight.

The diplomat's role on this mission had come to an end. Josh licked his lips, suddenly dry. He answered, returning to English.

"All right. But both of us."

"Truly?"

"Yep."

"Then as Allah wishes."

"On your move."

Again, Khalil shouted at Josh in Arabic. "I will give them the woman."

Josh let the moment sink in for the Sai'ar before nodding with pretend disgust.

The tribesmen relaxed, congratulating each other, no wish to spill blood. A few took their hands off their weapons while Khalil yanked open the Mercedes's rear door.

Inside, the kidnapped princess did not stir. Her bare hand, furled on the seat, seemed to beg to be left with the tribesmen. Josh looked away. He couldn't be conflicted right now.

Khalil stepped inside the opened rear door, using it for cover just as Josh had done with the front door.

Khalil straightened, as if he'd forgotten something. With his back still to the Sai'ar, he asked Josh in English.

"What is it you Americans say when you jump out of airplanes?"

Prickles went off in Josh's ribs, in his fingers on the submachine gun.

"Oh shit."

"No, not that."

Beyond the cars' lights, nothing struck Josh's eye but dark desert and armed men.

"Geronimo."

"Yes, Josh Cofield. Geronimo."

Khalil flashed inside his jacket for the pearl-handled pistol. He wheeled in a two-handed firing position. The report beside

Josh's head bashed his ears. One tribesman took the first round in the center chest, staggered, and tripped to the ground.

The Sai'ar were never trained for this; they were just greedy men with guns. They knew only to point and pull their triggers, and this was likely the first time they'd done it at men shooting back. The six Sai'ar remaining stayed in their row, packed and reacting a second too slow.

From the waist, Josh let off a long, deafening blast of the Kalashnikov. He swept across their torsos. The big gun kicked, but he was ready and held the muzzle down. Two more tribesmen collapsed, firing high. Josh released the trigger to duck behind the thick Mercedes door. Khalil stayed erect, emptying his Beretta, trading bullets with the two crumpling tribesmen.

In the middle, the fat, unarmed qabil dove for the sand. His three remaining comrades, jarred to their senses, leaped out of the way of Khalil's firing and lit up their own guns. Bullets bored into the car all around Josh. The tearing steel shrieked, holes punched through the upholstery. One bullet ripped across his midriff, an angry sting, another grazed his right forearm below the Kalashnikov. He'd never been wounded before; that luck was gone. In the frenzy of the fight, Josh gritted his teeth to block the pain and adrenaline shock. Another tribesman dropped to his knees with Khalil's bullets in him. The man went down firing, until Josh silenced him with a short burst. The pair of Sai'ar left standing in the open stopped shooting to turn and run into the night. Khalil squeezed off empty clicks, smoke trickling from his barrel.

"Shoot them."

Josh did not. Khalil's gun arm collapsed to his side. He wavered on his feet, patting his pockets, then stumbled. With a crimson hand, Khalil caught himself on the peppered frame of the rear door. In the sand, with the fighting paused, the fat qabil raised his head. He leaped up nimbly to follow his clansmen into the dark.

Josh darted around the driver's door to catch the failing Khalil, propping him under the armpits. He felt the empty holster in one hand, a damp warmth in the other. He hefted Khalil onto the backseat beside the quiet princess and peeled away the jacket to expose a wound below the right collarbone. Josh grimaced while he lifted Khalil's sweater to peek at the ragged exit wound. Both holes drizzled blood. Josh's own injuries were not as severe but bit at him and bled into his clothes as he kneeled beside Khalil. He yelled over the ringing in his ears.

"You okay?"

Khalil pushed at Josh.

"Drive."

A dozen holes perforated the rear door. Broken glass tinkled inside the frame when Josh slammed it shut. Four dead Sai'ar lay in the sand; in the headlamps of the trucks, on the wasteland of the desert, they looked executed. Their killing gave Josh pause. He didn't know which of the four were his doing, which were Khalil's, and would have stared longer at the dead men but Khalil shouted at him.

He tossed the Kalashnikov onto the passenger seat; a few spent rounds that had bounced off the opposite door rolled on the leather. Josh jumped behind the wheel. His door had been drilled many times, too. The wound in his side asserted itself, raw and pinched when he sat. The groove in his right forearm stung when he shifted into gear. Josh peeled around the parked pickup trucks, then stomped on the gas. He had no window to roll up, nor did Khalil, and the inrushing wind added to his franticness after the shootout.

He'd sped several hundred meters, unscrambling his thoughts, before he realized that his left headlight had been busted. Josh's view of the road was cut in half. This made him think that he should have shot up the Sai'ar's trucks. He marveled that none of the Mercedes's tires were blown, and as his head cleared he wondered, too, that he wasn't dead. He checked the rearview mirror. The road behind stayed dark except for the fading headlights of the roadblock; the al-Qaeda husband was surely closer but not there yet. Should Josh turn around and knock out some tires? If he went back, he'd have to deal with the last two armed Sai'ar. Josh made the strategic choice to keep speeding toward the Saudi line and the PJs he'd called out.

He put his attention on the driving. The gashes in his waist and arm throbbed, nagging. In a few more miles, with enough clear distance behind, he'd pull over to wrap Khalil's wounds and his own from the first aid kit in his backpack. Josh checked the rearview to begin measuring how far and fast the Sai'ar were disappearing.

His heart sank. Miles back in the desert clarity, one of the pickup trucks swung its headlights to the east, and followed.

Josh hit the gas. He looked in the mirror for Khalil but did not find him. Josh glanced quickly over his shoulder. Khalil had slumped toward the princess.

"They're after us. Can you make it? Maybe another hour."

Khalil sat bolt upright. Across the front seat, he thrust a palm dripping blood.

"She's hit."

The Mercedes was speeding at a great clip. Josh couldn't stare but for a moment at the black blot spreading across the rear seat and the lap of princess Nadya.

Chapter 22

Above the Empty Quarter
Yemeni airspace

Only red bulbs burned in the cargo bay to preserve the team's night vision. In this crimson light, the faces of Berko and Wally were bathed in the greenish glows of their little computer screens. LB and the PJs waited, each one quiet and gathered into himself.

The HC-130 powered low over the desert, a smooth, blacked-out flight through unruffled air. The pilots flew by instruments and NVGs[14] without cockpit or wing lights. LB sipped from a water bottle and checked his watch. 2310 hours.

He offered the bottle to Berko beside him, but the young CRO stayed fixed on his screen. LB didn't kibitz and kept his own chin down, gnawing on how little information the team had before leaping into the desert. All they knew was that a green dot had stopped on a desolate road and was engaged with an unspecified and likely serious threat. LB rested his arms across the M4 strapped to his left side, barrel down, wondering how much he'd need the gun tonight.

Berko's head jerked up. Lit from below and wide-eyed, his face seemed spectral. He shouted over the engine hum.

"The package is moving."

Berko scanned the PJs for a reaction and got less than he expected. Wally never looked up from his own monitor, busily

---

14 night-vision goggles.

on the horn with the pilots. Berko dipped his head again. LB leaned over now to look down on the screen with him.

The pinging dot sprinted east along the N5. Speed exceeded 80 mph. While LB watched, another emerald 4 was transmitted. The threat, whatever it was, hadn't abated, even on the move. This looked like a chase.

Berko tapped the screen.

"Things are getting tougher."

LB did his own reckoning but wanted to hear Berko's assessment of his first mission.

"How so?"

"They're moving fast. It could be a pursuit. Wally's talking to the cockpit trying to figure out a new LZ to intercept them. But the GAARVs can't do that kind of speed. If we miss them, we don't get a second shot."

"You think we should do two drops? Split up the GAARVs, double our chances?"

Berko looked up, figuring the tactical question.

"No."

"Why not?"

"The threat's unclear. We don't know what force we'll need to counter it. We should stick together."

On the SADL, the icon marking *Kingsman 1* quickly approached the green dot sliding east. A decision on where to drop the rescue team had to be made in the next few minutes.

"Tell Wally what you think."

"He's got it."

"Tell him."

Berko, a big kid in a lot of equipment, bounced on his seat to turn his shoulders to Wally.

The two conferred, heads together under the thrum of the cargo plane's engines. Wally listened and nodded, patting Berko's shoulder. He thumbed the PTT for the ground-to-air freq to consult the cockpit, then stopped. Wally jerked visibly, looking down at his computer screen. He pointed to his monitor for Berko, who checked his own screen and saw it, too. Berko tried to scratch his head under his helmet.

"What?"

Neither answered LB.

Something had gone off the tracks.

The whole PJ team was watching. Mouse and Quincy shrugged together, dramatically, to also ask, What?

LB poked Berko. The lieutenant raised a finger for patience, but LB dug an elbow into the kid's Kevlar armor. Berko struggled in the seat to turn the monitor back where LB could view it.

He indicated a spot just behind the moving green dot. LB could read a satellite map and didn't need the prod. He pushed Berko's hand out of the way.

The car was doing over 100 mph and had run right through the crossroads. The ping hadn't turned north onto the secondary road like it was supposed to, out of Yemen the way the mission called for. Instead, the diplomat and the princess were dashing farther east on the N5, into the elevated ground that edged the desert, speeding toward the outpost village of al 'Abr.

The package was racing in the wrong direction. Away from the Saudi border, away from rescue.

Chapter 23

Hadhramaut
The Empty Quarter
Yemen

The road ran straight and Josh flew along it. He risked only short glances to the backseat.

Khalil's right hand had gone useless and lay like a child in his lap. With his good hand, he hiked up Nadya's long, blood-soaked burqa. Her calves gleamed white in the subdued light of the desert. Khalil drew the hem higher, grimacing with pain, or perhaps the humiliation of a Muslim man baring the skin of an unconscious woman. Josh, too, felt the invasion on this unknown woman's flesh. But the blood coursing out of her pooled on the gray leather bench, and just like the last several minutes, he saw no choice. Josh turned around to face the streaming road. The gash in his forearm challenged his grip on the wheel. He drove as fast as he dared.

He shouted over the gusts pouring in the open windows.

"How bad is it?"

In the rearview, Khalil stayed hunched over Nadya. When he did not answer, Josh yelled his question again. He centered the Mercedes on the white stripe and looked back.

Khalil gathered the skirt of the burqa higher, exposing the princess's scarlet-smeared thigh. The fabric was sopping with blood; the copper stench of it whipped on the wind in the car.

Josh turned back to the road to correct the one-eyed Mercedes's drift toward the sands, frightening himself even more. He couldn't slow down, not with the Sai'ar on his tail. He chanced one more look backward.

One-handed, Khalil tugged the blood-heavy cloth above the princess's left hip. Just below the pale stretch of her panties, a coin-sized hole bled a rivulet into the crease where her leg joined the torso. Khalil lifted the burqa enough to inspect the exit wound on the inside of her thigh, bleeding even more intensely than the entry. Without attention soon, this looked like a death sentence.

Josh spun to the windshield. Nadya remained unconscious; her hand on the seat rested unaware in a pool of her own blood. Josh racked his brain for what he should do next. Tell Khalil to wake her? What was the right thing, the moral thing? He drove at dangerous speeds ahead of armed tribesmen who'd try to kill him if they caught him. He had no clue how soon the PJs would get there. He was unsure how badly he himself was bleeding, or Khalil. No question, the princess didn't have much time before she bled out.

If they kept moving, she was finished. If he pulled over to tend to her, he'd be in another gunfight in minutes, by himself. Khalil was too badly hurt.

Josh couldn't drive on. He couldn't stop.

He powered behind the Mercedes's one headlight, frantically weighing the dangers, looking for one to tip the balance. A few miles back, the pickup hadn't gained on him; he believed he could outrun it to the Saudi border. But what if another roadblock waited in the desert ahead, more guns and bribed qabili? The Abidah knew they couldn't trust the Bani Yam, so they'd backstopped them with the Sai'ar. Who'd been paid to block the road next, and where?

Where were the PJs?

"Khalil."

In the rearview, the Yemeni had collapsed against the seat, eyes closed.

"Yes, Joshua." Shouting over the wind seemed to tax him.

"I don't know what to do."

Khalil's head tipped back, showing the bottom of his chin. He spoke to the upholstered ceiling.

"The mission."

Josh wanted to punch the steering wheel but the speed of the car and the pain in his arm stopped him.

"There's no mission. It's finished. She's not going to make it."

Khalil's head bobbed down. He leaned forward, pale and sweaty. He drew his mouth close to Josh's ear, to be sure he was heard.

"Then save her."

"How?"

The reek of all their blood, even flowing out the open windows, was growing overpowering.

"Be a soldier."

Khalil eased back, leaving Josh alone to figure out how to do that.

Pull the car over and confront the Sai'ar? Three tribesmen had been left alive at the roadblock. Josh had to figure all three were in the pursuing pickup, and rampaging mad. Could he fight alone against those numbers, with a bad arm and a torn side? The best he could hope for would be to lose more time, while the Abidah and al-Qaeda zoomed closer on the road. At worst, Josh would be killed and take Khalil and the princess with him.

Running for it was the best chance to save his own life. Every white stripe flashing under his wheels brought him nearer to the PJs charging to his signal. If they were in choppers or a plane, his best guess was ten to fifteen more minutes of breakneck driving until he crossed their path. If the PJs were on ATVs like the SEALs, then an hour at least. In either case, Nadya had little chance of surviving in the car.

Josh imagined his rescue, safe with wounded Khalil, the corpse of a princess in the backseat, his assignment in shambles. That scene carried no relief, no honor. Just failure.

Josh, too, was losing blood. How much more time did he have in him for a high-speed chase? How long until he grew too weak for this dark desert highway, faded, and drove off the road or got overtaken by the guns of the Sai'ar?

He pulled the blue force tracker off the dashboard. Flicking his eyes between it and the spooling road, he dialed his ID code and one more **4. Hurry.

The mission was, in fact, over. Silva's diplomatic assignment, the CIA and Saudi kidnapping op—all of it flurried out through the busted windows, lost into the Empty Quarter. Josh centered on his only duty: to keep himself, Khalil, and the princess alive long enough for rescue to reach them.

First, they had to stop being chased. He needed to get off the road somewhere to find cover. A stronghold where he could buy a few minutes to address their wounds, slow some of the bleeding, then hang on until the pararescuemen reached them. The rule of thumb for siege warfare was one defender for every three attackers. If Josh could get inside walls, his odds improved. He scanned the fast-passing desert for a structure, any abandoned building. A few miles back, he'd passed some shacks, unused oil garages, the remains of dwellings. More may be ahead. He searched for anything he could defend.

The wild card was the Abidah and the al-Qaeda husband. How close were they? How many guns would they bring?

Josh had only fired the Kalashnikov twice. With any luck, the thirty-shot magazine was at least half-full.

"Khalil, you got more ammo?"

Hurting, the Yemeni rooted in his jacket. He held up two fresh magazines.

"Sixteen rounds."

"Good. How're you feeling?"

Khalil clenched his teeth in the mirror. The man had grit.

"She's dying."

"I understand. How well do you know this road?"

"Well enough."

"We need to get inside somewhere. I can patch everybody up, then we'll hold out and wait for whoever's coming."

Khalil sat forward again. Josh saw how badly he was blanching.

"A citadel."

"That's the idea. Can you fight if you have to?"

"Yes."

"What's up ahead?"

To prop himself, Khalil gripped the front passenger seat with a hand smirched with the princess's blood. His breath beside Josh's cheek smelled sour.

"In a few miles, you will see the turnoff for route 150 north. Do not take it."

"We've got to keep going north."

"There's nothing north of the crossroads but desert and wadis. All the way to the border."

"You want to stay on the N5?"

"Beyond the turn is the outskirts of a village. We'll find an empty place there."

"How about the villagers?"

"This is tribal land. They will not help us."

Khalil let go of the front seat. He drifted back beside the princess.

"Go quickly."

Josh poured on the speed to widen the gap with the pursuing Sai'ar, buying more slivers of time. He fought against the distraction of his own wounds to push the limits of his control over the car, passing 100 mph behind the lone headlamp. The speed was nerve-racking and he could only hold it for a couple more miles.

He backed off when a reflective sign rose out of the black distance for the upcoming intersection.

Josh neared the sign, one eye on the pickup behind. He tore through the crossroads, past a dilapidated truck stop, where a pair of eighteen-wheelers fueled under jittering fluorescent lights. To better assess the surroundings and find a hideout, Josh slowed the Mercedes to sixty, but this proved too fast. He braked more, and with every lost bit of speed his urgency climbed.

The road entered the ramshackle outskirts of a village. The low structures were few, impoverished, and spread out. Each humble house looked occupied. Two had many white bulbs strung across their fronts like holiday lights. Close to midnight, only dogs walked in the dirt spaces between hovels. Josh drove deeper down the road, as swiftly as he could, swiveling his head for shelter. One dark, small building appeared empty, but the walls were corrugated metal and without windows. He needed shooting apertures and walls thick enough to stop bullets.

"Khalil, find something fast."

The Yemeni set his left elbow in the sill of the rear window, peering into the sparse surroundings. Josh hurtled past a clump of commercial buildings with vehicles parked in front; the doors looked locked for the night. He'd driven a mile past the crossroads and lost track of the Sai'ar truck.

Khalil extended his good arm out the window.

"Turn there."

A chain fence stood without a gate on either side of a packed-sand drive. Josh spun the Mercedes into the lane.

"What's down there?"

"I don't know. But we're away from the main road. Cut off your lights."

Josh did this. He hurried down the bare track, driving blacked-out under the moon. On all sides lay nothing but open, dry land. Fifty yards ahead, the silhouette of a low structure broke the level plain. Josh headed for it, raising a dust cloud.

He shot past a battered sign, barely able to read the Arabic in the little light: Keep Out. Excavation Under Way. The order was under the authority of the Yemeni Interior Ministry. The sign looked weathered and forgotten.

A large mud hut emerged out of the gloom. Josh circled it, skidding the Mercedes past honeycombed digs in the dirt. This had been an archaeological site, the building an antique ruin. He stopped behind the old rear wall to hide the car from the road.

The structure was an earthen square, just four tall mud-brick walls with openings for doors and windows, no roof. The surrounding ground had been dug and panned for antiquities, but the effort appeared to have halted years ago. The ruts and furrows showed the rounding of weather and neglect.

Josh grabbed his backpack and the Kalashnikov off the passenger seat, and the blue force tracker, and threw open his door. His side split; he'd overlooked the wound there to move fast. He almost lost his footing from the pain.

Khalil had climbed halfway out of the car. He'd tucked his right hand inside his belt to hold it still. His other clutched the Beretta. Josh tugged him to his feet.

"Get inside. I'll bring her. Watch the road."

Khalil lumbered into the hut. Josh hustled to the rear passenger door, threw it open, and recoiled from the assault of blood in his nostrils and the sight of the shrouded woman unconscious, dying in pulses. He strapped the Kalashnikov across his back and slid his hands under her, soaking his sleeves. Despite his own wounds, he lifted her out of the car to carry her over the threshold.

Josh set Nadya in a corner of the cool dirt floor and stayed on his knees. He yanked the first aid kit out of his backpack. Before he could open it, Khalil hissed. Josh skidded low beside him to a window facing the front.

The Sai'ar pickup truck approached on the main road. Nearing the fence, it slowed, passed by, then stopped and backed up. Carefully, the vehicle swung onto the dirt road.

The arriving headlights lit the last wisps of the Mercedes's dust trail.

Chapter 24

Hadhramaut
The Empty Quarter
Yemen

Headlights barred the road miles ahead. So the Sai'ar had not abandoned their post like the despicable Bani Yam. Was Nadya up ahead? Were the kidnappers? Arif's heart swelled in step with his wrath and a final burst of speed from the truck. The Makarov tucked at his waist took on its own pulse.

"Mahmoud, check your phone. Have you missed a call?"

"I have not."

Closing in, only two pickups blocked the highway. Arif did not touch the brakes until he was almost on them, outpacing the four trucks behind him. He pulled to the shoulder, jarring Mahmoud and the Yemenis in the bed with his sudden stop. He took the Makarov in hand and walked into the beams, seeing no one.

Arif stood in the middle of the road, simmering in the headlights. At his sandals sparkled dozens of spent casings. He raised the Makarov two-handed and moved more carefully behind it across the road.

As he left the throw of the lights, his eyes adjusted to the sudden dark. Ten strides into the sand, a thin tribesman kneeled before three bodies. The corpses lay faceup, dragged into a line with their arms crossed over bloodied chests. The surviving tribesman's hands were lifted beside his head, and he did not interrupt his prayer. He touched his forehead to the sand. A banded bundle of riyals lay near him.

Arif lowered the Makarov as Mahmoud and four Ba-Jalal brothers joined him. The elder indicated the Sai'ar bowing beside his dead clansmen.

"This prayer is getting a lot of use tonight."

Arif lowered to his knees alongside the tribesman. Quietly, he waited until the man lifted his forehead from the sand. Arif touched him to stop his muttering.

"Who did this?"

The eyes of the grieving Sai'ar were without tears. This was an angry man.

"The American. And his driver."

Arif hurled a glance back at Mahmoud. The old man spit in the desert.

"An American? Are you sure?"

"He shot down my brothers. Yes, sayyid. I am sure."

"The driver?"

"A Yemeni. A city man. He is a killer, too."

Judging by the brass lying in the road and scattered around the dead Sai'ar, there had been a fearsome gun battle at close quarters.

"Was there a woman in the car?"

"In the backseat."

Arif made a hopeful, private fist. He'd found her.

"Was she hurt?"

"I do not know, sayyid. She did not move during the fight."

"Where have they gone?"

"East."

"How long ago?"

"Ten minutes."

Before rising, Arif rested a hand on the body closest to him.

"Your brothers."

"Yes, sayyid."

"I am sorry."

Mahmoud pointed at the thick packet of riyals on the sand.

"Take that."

The tribesman did not shift his eyes from his losses.

"No, sayyid."

Arif curled his hand behind the tribesman's bent neck.

"To whom belongs everything in the heavens and the earth?"

The Sai'ar covered his face.

"To God."

Arif stood the same moment Mahmoud's cell phone rang.

Chapter 25

Above the Empty Quarter
Yemeni airspace

The hydraulic gate dropped, and the desert night rushed into the cargo bay. At first the dry air was cooling, then LB noted a bite to it, a rebuke and a warning that the desert below would not be welcoming.

Bathed in the red bulb and the sickly glow of activated Cyalum sticks, LB stood at the front of his pararescue unit. Like the seven others, he held on to the steel static line strung taut past his helmet. Loaded with a hundred-plus pounds of armor, packs, weapons, and chute, he'd be easily put off-balance by any sudden turbulence. Behind him were Jamie, Mouse, and Berko. The second team followed: Doc, Quincy, and Dow, with Wally at the end of the stick.

The loadmaster poised with a blade to cut away the web restraints holding the two GAARVs from the open gate. *Kingsman 1* zoomed close to the ground; LB crept closer to the windy edge to peek down at the speeding earth. No lights shone anywhere on the fretted terrain, just the silver milk of the moon. LB had trained in deserts before, but they'd been American deserts with saguaro and rock, nothing like the vast badlands and dunes of The Empty Quarter.

Waiting for the green light, he wasn't troubled by the desert; the PJs and their equipment could handle it. But two minutes ago, before giving the order to hook up, Wally announced that the package, after blasting through the crossroads at 100 mph, had stopped again. The satellite map showed they'd parked next to a remote hut outside a village. The signal had gone inside the four walls. That could only mean one of two things: the diplomat and the princess were hiding out, or they were gearing up for a fight.

Wally's voice sizzled over the team frequency.

"Get down fast. Free up the GAARVs and let's move. I think we're dealing with minutes here."

LB answered for everyone. "Roger that."

The red light over the open gate extinguished. The cargo bay paused with the dark. The loadmaster set the edge of his knife to the final web restraint. Unnecessarily, and out of habit, Wally shouted "Ready." No one replied, not even Berko.

The emerald bulb flicked on. The loadmaster hacked away the last web restraint. After the first GAARV pallet got a shove, the rollers in the floor did the rest. The next second, the great parcel slid down the gate into open air and was scooped away by the wind to disappear under the ramp. Instantly the second GAARV followed off the gate. Only seconds later, the two giant gray cargo chutes bloomed, and the GAARVs floated down.

Working fast, the loadmaster reeled in the flapping static lines. Done, he whirled on LB with a thumbs-up.

LB lunged off the edge into nothing. He tucked his chin to his chest and held his legs tight together. He locked his arms at his side and his hands on his emergency chute. The winds behind the HC-130 snatched and yanked him backward. His boots were just eight hundred feet off the ground, a distance he'd plunge in five seconds if anything went wrong. Instantly the static line jerked the chute from the container at his back. The many cords unraveled upward, and the rectangular chute took shape over his head. The force of the opening pushed the air out of his lungs, and he let out a hard, gutty sigh. His plummet became a steep downward drift; LB filled his lungs again, as he did on every jump, with a breath of relief.

Close behind, *Kingsman 1* sowed the rest of the team into the brilliant sky. Each chute popped two seconds after tumbling from the plane. LB gripped the twin toggles that dropped beside his ears so that he could control his position in the wind and follow behind the GAARVs' cargo chutes.

LB thumbed the talk button for the team freq.

"PJ one up."

Above him, Jamie replied. "PJ two up."

Mouse and Berko chimed in, then the rest of the team in order, until Wally at the top of the stack reported his chute had deployed.

The drop lasted forty seconds. The pair of GAARVs landed softly and in good shape, both upright. Both chutes cut away automatically and lay deflated on the sand. The LZ was a hundred-yard-wide wadi framed east and west by higher ground. The PJs could stay in this dry riverbed for two miles, all the way to the package.

LB flew a steep glide slope, hastening for the ground. He made a running landing twenty yards from the GAARVs. Boots down, he released his chest and crotch straps, then the bellyband, and the container was tugged off his back by the chute's collapse. He didn't break stride on the pebbled earth, heading for the first vehicle. LB whipped out his black Benchmade knife, opening it with a quick flick of his thumb.

He attacked the packing straps, snipping two with the honed blade before Jamie arrived and joined him to hack at the riggers' work. Mouse and Berko dropped silently and doffed their chutes, leaving them crumpled with the others in the wadi. The gray night was bright enough for the four to cut the nearest GAARV loose without night-vision goggles. Berko set to tossing away all the crush board packed around the four wheels and the equipment bay in the rear, then he readied the twin M-240B machine

guns mounted left and right. Moving confidently, the young lieutenant opened the ammo trays to both guns, laid the 7.62 belts
into the feeding blocks, slapped the covers shut, and armed the
GAARV.

Little Mouse jumped into the driver's seat. He sliced away
the remaining cushioning around the steering column, then hit
the starter to fire up the GAARV. Mouse buckled in, revved the
motor, and clapped his hands.

LB, Jamie, and Berko stepped back while Mouse drove the
GAARV off the pallet that had absorbed the impact perfectly.
The big vehicle rolled free of its constraints, unleashed and capable. Berko climbed beside Mouse, LB and Jamie already strapped
into the rear seats beside the machine guns. All this was completed in under sixty seconds.

Twenty yards away, Team 2 finished their own tasks. Dow
jumped behind the wheel of the second GAARV, started the
engine, and stepped her off the platform. Quincy and Doc
climbed in back with the guns. Wally sat next to Dow, his SADL
computer screen glowing at his belly.

Overhead, the HC-130 gained altitude. The bird would circle
at several thousand feet above the mission, maintaining a backup
comm link to Torres in Djibouti.

Dow took the lead, Wally pointing the way. The pair of
GAARVs spun rubber in the dry wadi, gunning the teams south
away from their chutes and litter.

Chapter 26

Outside al 'Abr
Hadhramaut
Yemen

Josh slung the Kalashnikov around Khalil's shoulders. He lifted the spy's bloody right hand to rest it near the trigger. He took the pearl-gripped Beretta in exchange and left Khalil sitting below the window, gun barrel on the mud sill.

The Sai'ar's truck drove a slow loop around the hut, keeping its distance, inspecting the Mercedes. When it had finished the circle, the truck settled on the entry track, stabbing the hut from forty yards back with headlights that carved the ochre interior into boxes of light and shadow. The hut's roofless walls, open windows, and doorframes did little to keep the desert chill out. The dirt floor cooled Josh's knees.

He scurried back to the princess in a corner, out of the truck's beams. Already she'd stained the ground with blood. He tore into his backpack for the first aid kit and reached for gauze pads and a rubber hose tourniquet.

He lifted the hem of her sodden burqa. Josh sucked his teeth at the ugliness and placement of her injury. The exit wound lay at the top of the left inside thigh. The puncture bled as bad as anything he'd seen on a battlefield. The princess's right leg was clear—the bullet must have dug into the seat before striking it. The entry wound in her left pelvis bled less but scared Josh more.

His best guess was one of her femoral vessels, the artery or vein, had been nicked or severed. It needed pressure to shut it down and save her life.

Using his teeth, Josh ripped open two sterile gauze bandages and crammed the gauze into both holes to help stanch the flow. He made several turns around the wounds with a gauze wrap. Then, with nothing else to try, he ran the hose under her leg, tying the tightest knot he could across the seam of her groin.

"Khalil, you holding up?"

"Yes."

"Anyone moving?"

"No. A bad sign."

The Sai'ar were waiting for reinforcements. Josh was, too.

He hustled the first aid kit to Khalil. Staying out of the light, leaving Khalil and the Kalashnikov in place beneath the window, Josh peeled back the Yemeni's jacket to lay bare the two wounds. He slapped a pair of adhesive bandages over the punctures, front and back.

"That's all I can do for now. Help's on the way."

"Many people are on the way. Tend to yourself."

Josh touched Khalil's good left arm. He slid back to Nadya.

Quickly he rolled up his own soggy right sleeve, revealing a four-inch-long trough through the flesh. He cleaned it with an antiseptic, stinging swipe. Blood oozed back into the groove. After applying a gauze wrap, he tugged his sleeve down to put the wound out of sight.

Josh pulled up his shirttail for a look at the rip in his right side, above the belt. The gash was short, not deep, and more painful than it looked. He'd have to ignore it for a while. He thanked his luck that he'd not been hit worse and wondered if he'd used the last of it.

The princess slumped in the shadowed corner of the hut just as she had against the window of the Mercedes, unconscious, her bare left hand turned up in the dirt. Josh held her wrist for a pulse.

Nadya's skin had gone cold. He found a beat, weak and distant.

In the ten minutes since the gunfight, she'd lost a frightening amount of blood. Her left leg was cold, clammy, and white. The poor pulse indicated falling blood pressure. Her breathing came shallow. Making matters worse, whatever Khalil had used to knock her out was depressing her heartbeat.

"Khalil."

"What."

"She's going into shock. I've got to wake her up."

"That may not be advisable."

"If I don't, she's got no chance."

"Is she dying?"

"Fast."

Khalil did not turn from the Sai'ar pickup idling in the dirt lane. Josh hadn't let go of the princess's hand.

"Khalil. Now."

"On her right shoulder."

Josh flashed a hand up her right arm. Under the folds of the burqa, he felt a small box. Quickly, he rolled back her sleeve, baring more pale, chilly flesh.

A pump the size of a deck of cards was strapped high on her right arm. A small pane showed a silently spinning reservoir; a clear fluid revolved inside. From the bottom of the machine ran a clear plastic tube taped to her arm, trailing down to a port into a forearm vein. Liquid dripped into the tube, then into the princess.

The truck's lights behind Khalil, her kidnapper, darkened his face, keeping Josh from spotting if regret stained it.

"It's propofol. Pull it out."

Josh slid the port from the princess's skin. He taped a bandage over the hole. The catheter wept another drop before Josh could tug the wicked thing off her and toss it into a dark corner. She didn't stir. Crimson seeped through the gauze around her thigh. The tourniquet wasn't stopping her bleeding. Her pulse stayed feeble.

Josh dug a bottle of water from the backpack. Gently, he lifted the hem of the burqa's veil to expose her face. He rested the ebony cloth over the top of her head.

Princess Nadya showed in her features that she was near death. Her cheeks had sunk. Both eye sockets seemed rimmed with ash. Her smooth forehead was as white as her leg. When pink and flushed, she might have been pretty, with a small nose and long, black lashes. She had the wrinkles of middle age and did not deserve to have only minutes left to her. This was Khalil's doing, and Josh's, and the three nations that could find no better way than stealing her. He cupped her chin to straighten her head and hold it in place. Lightly, Josh slapped her.

"Nadya. Princess. Wake up. Come on."

He added more force to his hand across her cheek.

The princess's brows flexed. She snorted, wrenching out of his palm. She took short, startled breaths before opening dark Arab eyes.

"That's it. Wake up."

He took down his hands. Madly she blinked above colorless cheeks, her breathing spiked. She didn't focus on Josh but flitted her gaze around the empty, roofless hut where she sat on a dirt floor, dazzling light pouring in. Nadya tugged at the burqa as if it were unfamiliar, then saw her own bare right arm and ghostly, naked left leg. Her eyelids fluttered on the Beretta lying beside Josh.

With a sudden gasp, the princess put her hands in the dirt to push herself harder against the wall, away from him. She stammered in Arabic.

"Who . . . who are you? What's happened?"

The burst of energy waned. Nadya slumped against the wall, struggling to keep her chin up. Again, Josh supported her head.

She slurred, "Don't touch me." Her face dipped in his hand, the blood loss pulling her back to unconsciousness.

Josh answered loudly, "Listen to me. Okay? You've been wounded. Help is on the way. We're going to get you home, all right? Stay with me."

Nadya swayed forward off the wall as if she meant to stand. Her hands flopped on the earth, wobbly and struggling. She spoke without raising her face.

"Home?" She fought hard to meet Josh's eyes. Fading, she locked on him. "Arif?"

"Yes. Arif. He's on his way, he'll be here soon. Let's wait for him, Princess."

One more time, she tried to push off the ground. Josh eased her down, then opened the water bottle to pour across her loose lips. She choked down a swallow.

Her weight released backward. The crown of her head fell against the mud wall, baring her pallid neck. Nadya faced the open stars.

Josh rocked back on his haunches. Was that who was coming to kill him and Khalil? Arif, for whom the princess fought to get on her feet?

In small tremors Nadya's throat worked. Her mouth opened and closed. Josh lay his ear closer. In a voice almost too soft to hear, she repeated:

"*La elaha ela Allah.*" There is no God but Allah.

A prayer of the dying.

Chapter 27

Hadhramaut
The Empty Quarter
Yemen

The truck would not go as fast as Arif tried to push it. Carrying six armed men and a mounted machine gun, the burdened truck would not exceed 80 mph. The four Yemenis in the back complained and tapped on the window. When they were ignored, they hunkered behind the cab and held on.

Beside Arif, Mahmoud did not speak. He carried a pistol on his hip but had not touched it and seemed unaware of it. As if reading Arif's mind, the elder took the handgun from its holster. He removed the magazine, checked that it was full, tapped it once in his palm, and returned the load into the grip. The old man pulled back the slide to charge a round into the chamber before holstering the gun.

"You've used that before?"

Mahmoud brushed a hand through his whiskers.

"My family are businessmen. I am my father's first son. We were not always merchants."

The road whined under Arif's wheels, and the immensity of the desert did nothing to slow or divert him. He sped before a convoy of trucks bearing five high-caliber machine guns, two dozen armed tribesmen loyal to the Ba-Jalal, and brothers furious and frightened to have seen Ghalib's fiery death. The Americans had killed their youngest brother, and now there was news that an American had gone to ground in a mud hut outside al 'Abr. At first, the Ba-Jalal had come to honor their father's pledge to Arif. That pledge was no longer necessary.

A road sign emerged out of the darkness, marking the turnoff north to the Saudi border. The kidnappers did not go that way. Why did they miss the turn? Why did they stop running to hole up in an isolated hut outside al 'Abr? Were they wounded? Certainly the American and his Yemeni driver could see the Sai'ar pickup truck facing them; they must know that Arif was coming to kill them.

The thought of his enemies bleeding and desperate behind mud walls led Arif to the fear that Nadya was hurt, too. Many bullets had been exchanged at the roadblock. This vision, the heartache of her in pain or worse, roiled in his chest, breaking his focus from the road. Arif shook his head to clear his heart. He floored the accelerator. Silently he asked Allah to preserve his wife and to give this truck more power.

"Mahmoud. The American and his driver. They are waiting for rescue. That is why they have stopped behind cover."

"I have considered this."

"An American helicopter or plane will get to them quickly."

"You are saying there will be a battle in al 'Abr."

"Perhaps. Yes."

"We have many guns."

"So will they."

As any man would if given the time to stand on the banks of his own death, Arif surveyed how he'd come to this place. Where did it begin? How far back to trace his life to arrive at this moment, to the Makarov at his side and the enemies ahead? He looked for accidents, missteps to say he did not belong here and was destined elsewise, but could not find any. Every choice in life, his childhood into the madrassas, to Afghanistan and loving Nadya, leaving the Kingdom, hacking Abd al-Aziz's computer, even meeting and trusting Ghalib, was a natural flow, a river of a life that could only flow here. In the passenger seat, Mahmoud seemed pensive, stroking his beard, perhaps rowing through his own fate.

"Mahmoud, I must ask."

"Yes."

"If my wife is not alive, I will still fight. Will you stand with me?"

"For your wife? No. Our oath to you is for protection. We will not share your vengeance, that is only for clan. You are not Ba-Jalal."

"Then for your brothers, Yasser and Ghalib."

"To my own death, Arif the Saudi."

Chapter 28

Hadhramaut
The Empty Quarter
Yemen

The two GAARVs rumbled through the wadi. Mouse dropped his NVGs to his eyes, steering behind the vehicle's infrared head-lights. Berko bent over his SADL monitor, keeping watch on the green dot, just as Wally was doing in Team 2's GAARV twenty yards out front. LB rested both gloved hands on his M4. Jamie laid his on the stock of the mounted M-240 beside him.

The crisp desert night blew into the open windows. Constellations sparkled down to the horizon on every side, unhindered save for one glow a mile ahead, the throw of a single car's headlights.

The riverbed was well packed and flinty; the twin vehicles raised no dust. A low table of rock lay in the center of the wadi a half mile from the lights. Dow stopped behind it. Mouse pulled next to him. The GAARVs idled side by side while Wally gave orders over the team freq.

"The package is in that hut with the car lights shining on it. That's not good. Team 1, get up there fast. Stay out of sight. Enter the structure, assess and evac the package and anyone else you determine. If there's resistance, return fire. Team 2 will hold back two hundred yards on overwatch. LB, questions?"

LB, team leader, answered swiftly. "Negative."

"Get in, get out. Go."

Mouse peeled away first, pressing LB, Jamie, and Berko into their seats. Dow's GAARV fell in behind.

For the next quarter mile through the wadi, the vehicles rushed in tandem until Team 2 braked and Mouse drove on. He maneuvered to put the high walls of the mud hut in the way of the single staring car, to approach hidden behind it. In the seat in front of LB, Berko closed his computer monitor to put his hands on his weapon. LB tapped him on the shoulder.

"You and me go inside. Mouse and Jamie stay on the GAARV guns."

"Roger."

LB squeezed the young officer's shoulder to say, You're good. We're good.

Fifty yards out, riding the long shadow of the hut, Mouse skidded to a halt. LB was out of the GAARV before it settled, Berko beside him. Berko reached up for his night goggles but saw that LB had left his on his helmet and did the same. The head-lights playing over the hut would provide enough illumination and blind any effort to see more.

LB led the way, bent low inside the hut's shadow, Berko close on his tail. The two galloped toward the rear wall of the hut, freighted and hauling so much gear and armor. They jostled through a maze of old ditches and trenches, this place must have been some sort of abandoned historical dig. They leaped over shallow troughs and ran onto a dirt path leading to the back of the hut. Reaching the rear wall, Berko and LB flattened their backs against ancient mud bricks. LB let them pause to catch their breath. A black Mercedes riddled with bullets was parked close by. Fifty yards back, in the quiet moonlight, Mouse and Jamie charged the bolts on the GAARV's twin .240s.

LB lifted the muzzle of his M4, nestling near the open door-frame. Berko, panting behind him, patted his shoulder. I'm good. Go.

LB called into the opening.

"US Air Force. We're coming in."

Behind his rifle, LB swept inside. Moving the gun barrel where he put his eyes, he quick-scanned the left half of the hut. Behind him, Berko handled the right. One man in dark clothing sat in a crumpled slouch beneath a front-facing window, Kalashnikov aimed at the watching vehicle. This man lifted both hands off the gun to face LB. His palms were bloody. LB and he exchanged nods.

"Clear."

Behind LB, Berko echoed, "Clear."

LB sidestepped out of the beams flooding in from the car outside. He spun to look down on another man dressed in khakis and sweatshirt, curled beside a woman partly cloaked in a gray, blood-soaked burqa. The pair sat in the dirt against a blank wall. The woman had sunk into a ghastly pallor, her bare left leg smeared in blood. A tourniquet circled her groin but to no avail: a gauze wrap around her thigh was sopping red. She looked dead or dying. The man, like the other, raised two gory hands, with a big pistol on the ground beside him.

LB dropped to his knees.

"You the diplomat?"

"Josh Cofield. US embassy, Sana'a."

"This the princess?"

"She is. Glad to see you."

"Sergeant DiNardo. Same here." LB indicated the man with the AK-47. "He speak English?"

"Yep."

"Good. LT, get a sit rep."

Berko hustled across the open-roofed room to land beside the armed man.

LB laid the princess flat, then snatched her wrist. The arm hung limp, skin notably cool and misty. The burqa's veil had been lifted to reveal her face. Sweat beaded on her upper lip. She drew quick and shallow breaths.

"What can you tell me?"

"She took a bullet through the left hip. Bleeding heavy. I don't think the tourniquet is stopping it."

"How long she been like this?"

"About twelve minutes."

"She responsive?"

"Not much."

"You okay?"

"I can wait."

LB cupped the burqa behind the woman's neck to lift her face to him. He patted her drained cheek two, three times. Her eyes wandered under quivering lids, lips muttered mutely.

"Princess, you with me? Princess?"

LB eased her head against the dirt floor. He couldn't locate a pulse in her wrist, so he tugged up the rest of the drenched skirt to expose the barely pink right leg. Reaching to the inside of the thigh for the femoral pulse, he found it and marked her blood pressure at approximately 70 systolic. He measured the beat against his watch—too fast at 124 per minute. The woman's body was starving for oxygenated blood, and her heart had sped up to circulate what it had. Capillaries were automatically closing down in the extremities to preserve the remaining blood for the torso and vital organs. All the princess's systems were under immense stress and she was running out of reserves. Her body couldn't compensate much longer.

Like the diplomat said, she'd taken a round to the pelvic area, just above the crease of the groin in the inguinal region. That plastic tourniquet wasn't likely to work; the damage was above the limb. Judging from her state of shock, the bullet had either torn or severed one of the femoral vessels, and she was fading quickly.

LB needed to stop the bleeding, right now. Then evac her to a safer spot and a closer look.

LB shrugged off his med ruck to tear into the top pocket, M for Massive hemorrhage. Immediately, he grabbed the kit holding a Combat Ready Clamp, a CRoC, to shut down the bleeding.

Wally's electronic voice over the team freq cut into LB's ear.

"Berko, Berko. Juggler. Sit rep."

Berko shot back, "Roger, Juggler. Wait one."

The young CRO scrambled across the floor to hunker beside LB. "Sit rep."

LB didn't take his hands or attention off the princess. Wally had been right earlier when he'd said they were dealing with minutes.

"Gunshot wound to the pelvis. We need to stabilize, stop the bleeding before I can move her."

Berko slid aside to make his report. "Juggler, Berko. Female has gunshot wound to the pelvis. We need to stabilize and stop the bleeding before we can move her. Two male IPs[15] have multiple wounds tango two and tango three."

Beside the princess, the diplomat looked eager to do something. LB grabbed his wrist to drag it over her soggy bandage.

"Cofield."

"Yeah."

"Press right here, both hands. Hard."

The big man did what he was told, ignoring the feel and stench of blood. He kept his composure well, under the circumstances. When he leaned to push down onto the wound, a grimace flashed across his features, then disappeared. Blood squeezed out of the spongelike gauze.

LB assembled the CRoC. The device was built like a little steel gallows, with a base plate, an upright post, and a crosspiece arm. He screwed a T-handle bolt down into one end of the horizontal

---

15 isolated personnel.

arm, then attached a rounded pressure disk head to the bottom of the bolt.

He slid the base plate under the princess's left buttock, pushing Cofield's hands off the bandage. With a flick of his knife, LB sliced away the useless tube tourniquet. He tore open a fresh gauze bandage to lay over her bared flesh, two inches higher on the torso, toward the abdomen above the femoral sheath. After extending the crosspiece to put the pressure head directly over the fresh bandage, he cranked the T-handle, lowering the big plastic knob, tightening it like a vise.

While LB worked, Berko transmitted the sit rep to Wally.

The package had been badly hit, LB was attending to her now. She was critical, tango one. Two other wounded occupants: a Yemeni national was tango two, and the American diplomat tango three. The truck staring at them had done nothing aggressive, but the Yemeni advised they all evac the hut pronto. Bad guys were headed their way. The Yemeni couldn't say how many or how close, just close. Someone he called the Abidah.

LB screwed the pressure head down until the CRoC pushed deep into the princess's pelvis. With luck, he was on top of the damaged section of the femoral, crushing it shut. Without luck, the woman was good as dead.

In the exchange between Berko and Wally, LB caught that the tactical situation was collapsing. Wally had heard enough and made the call. He ordered Berko and Team 1 to start evac immediately.

LB shook his head at the lieutenant. "Sir, she's got to go on fluids right now. Her blood pressure's too low. If we evac now, she won't survive the ride out."

"Time?"

"Three minutes."

"Try to make it two."

LB tugged from his med ruck a bag of lactated Ringer's and an IV catheter.

Berko got back on the horn. "Juggler, Berko. Preparing to move. Two mikes."

LB shouted to the lieutenant. He lifted one hand from the princess to gesture at her and the diplomat. "Get these two in the GAARV. Bring Mouse to the back door. Send Jamie in with more blood and a litter. I'll hook her up, then we'll put her into the cage and roll. Leave Mouse on the .240."

The young CRO transmitted the order to Mouse and Jamie. The lieutenant's voice and actions were holding steady. He was fitting himself into the rhythm of the mission. Outside, the GAARV raced forward on his word.

LB lifted the princess's right arm out of the dirt to lay it across his lap. He rolled up the burqa's sleeve, searching for a vein. The flesh of her arm, like her legs and face, lay smooth, a span of white without ridges or hue, washed out by her blood loss. LB peeled away a small bandage on her forearm, revealing a tiny puncture, a needle wound.

"What's this?"

The diplomat rattled his head as if he didn't know.

LB tossed Cofield a Velcro tourniquet from his med ruck.

"I can't get a vein. Wrap this around her biceps."

The diplomat secured the strap around the woman's arm. LB tapped on her chilly skin, raising a poor, greenish vessel to his needle. He slid the point in and plugged the fluid bag's line into the cannula. Opening the port, LB handed the bag to Cofield.

"Hold this up."

"All right."

"Long night?"

"Roger that."

"You ex-something?"

"Ranger captain."

"No shit. Me, too."

"Why're you a PJ sergeant?"

"Let's save that for after we get out of here, sir. Get ready to evac."

Across the hut, Berko lifted the Yemeni with the Kalashnikov to his shaky feet. The pickup truck did nothing but watch and beam its brights through the windows. The LT hurried the Yemeni near the rear door while Mouse roared closer.

Cofield lifted the clear fluid bag higher.

"I'll stay 'til you go. I can help."

LB took the fluids from him.

"You'll go when I say, sir. Stand next to the door and get in the vehicle."

LB turned his face to give the diplomat nothing to argue with. The man rose, a much bigger figure than when LB first saw him minutes ago folded and wary in the shadowy dirt. Cofield scooped the big handgun off the ground and shuffled for the door behind Berko and the Yemeni.

LB laid his hand across the princess's brow. She remained cool and wrung out. Her lips had stopped moving, her eyes closed. He checked for a distal pulse in the leg below the wound and found nothing. Shifting his fingertips above the CRoC's jaws, he found a proximal pulse closer to the body core, a hummingbird beat in her pelvis still too fast but firmer; her blood pressure had stopped its decline. LB sliced away the gauze wrapping to inspect the exit wound.

He plucked out several scarlet gauze pads shoved inside the jagged hole. Wiping a clean pad over the puncture, LB waited for another tongue of blood to fall. It did, followed by another seconds after.

The CRoC had shut down the major bleeding, but she continued to lose ground. She still might crash; the fluids flowing into her veins carried no oxygen. She needed rich blood moving through her, lots of it to replace what she'd lost.

The GAARV crunched to a halt in the gravel next to the mud hut's door.

Jamie burst in the doorway, a unit of blood in each hand. These had been stored in a cooler in the back of the GAARV. The instant Jamie cleared the opening, Berko ushered the Yemeni out. Before exiting, the wounded man spoke over his shoulder.

"We need to leave."

LB waved at Berko to get him out of the hut.

Wally chimed in: "Team 1, you got one minute."

LB didn't answer, busy snaring out of the air the first chilled unit of blood tossed by Jamie, even before the young PJ landed on his knees beside him. LB rolled and worked the bag to make sure it would flow evenly. From outside, Berko handled Wally's prodding, replying, "Roger. One mike."

In the doorway, Cofield hung back, pistol in hand. LB had no time to shout and chase him out the door. The guy had paid a lot tonight for the right to stay with his princess. LB let him back in.

The catheter in the woman's arm was connected to a plastic tube that branched into a Y halfway up, allowing another fluid bag to piggyback. LB plugged the unit of O negative universal donor blood into the line, then switched off the fluid. Instantly the clear tube ran crimson.

Jamie handed over the second unit. "I'll get the litter."

"Go."

Jamie, strapped into every pound of metal and medicine that weighed down the rest of the PJs, bounded away as if he'd never had bullet holes in his own legs. The notion gave LB heart that the princess could survive this night and be whole again. But the CRoC, while saving her life, had also choked off all circulation to her left leg, from the hip to her toes. Her flesh could live without oxygen no more than five or six hours before it died; the longer the blood flow stayed restricted, the greater the chance of lethal blood clots, lactic acid—any number of nasty elements—building up in the pool of her leg. If LB got the princess in the GAARV in the next few minutes, and they managed to roar out of here at top speed with no trouble, they wouldn't reach Sharurah for two more hours, three tops. They'd need to stay off the road, travel by infrared lights and NVGs across the sand, salt flats, ridges, and dunes of the Empty Quarter. The flight from the Sharurah airport by private jet to Riyadh would eat up another hour, then an ambulance ride into the city. At best, the princess was five hours from this dirt floor to bright lights and cold steel, the definitive care of a proper hospital. It was going to be a coin toss whether she'd lose her left leg up to the hip.

Cofield left the doorway to kneel by the princess's side. LB gave him the draining unit of blood to hold up.

"All right, Captain. Tell me in twenty seconds. What's happening?"

Cofield rested his free hand on the woman's sleeve, protective. He'd fired and taken bullets for her.

"This is a Saudi princess. There's a tribe from Ma'rib, the Abidah, trying to stop us from taking her out of Yemen. Khalil says al-Qaeda's mixed up in this, too. They bribed two other desert tribes to stop us, the Bani Yam and the Sai'ar. I got us past the first roadblock. Guns came out at the second. She got hit. We all did. I figured our best chance was to get under cover, wait for you."

"That truck out front?"

"The Sai'ar. We killed a couple of them. Then they followed us."

"Who's the local?"

"Khalil. An army colonel. He was the driver."

"Looks like he was great company."

"He's not. But the man's got stones."

Jamie burst in the door with the Stokes litter, Berko close behind. Wally called in.

"Berko, Juggler."

"Go."

"Torres called from the ROC. She's got an unarmed ISR[16] Predator overhead that just picked up a convoy of five light trucks. They're closing in on the N5 turnoff, three miles out. High rate of speed. Time to go."

"Roger. Putting the package on the stretcher now."

Jamie laid the litter beside the princess. Cofield scooted out of the way, keeping the blood and fluid bags high, lines untangled. The first blood unit was already two-thirds empty; a faint blush had crept into the princess's cheeks. LB thought to lower the burqa's veil but needed to keep a handle on the woman's color before granting her modesty. Together, Jamie, LB, and Berko shifted her onto the litter. LB took the grips at her head, Jamie the feet. Together they stood erect, lifting the stretcher with Cofield beside them. LB backed toward the door and the GAARV grumbling next to the shot-up Mercedes. Berko stayed on their six.

LB led the way, careful to tread only in the wedges of shadow cast by the watching pickup truck's beams. Jamie and Berko followed his lead. Cofield, holding the bags, trying to stay beside the litter as they maneuvered for the door, got snared in the spotlight. He was lit up clear as day, sneaking out the back.

A burst from an automatic weapon—distinct pops, another Kalashnikov—drubbed the mud bricks of the hut's facade. Puffs and shards sailed in the windows. Jamie and Berko halted, bent knees to the dirt. Cofield dodged out of the light. No one was hit. LB tugged on the stretcher.

"Let's go."

He edged his backside out the door before another short volley battered the hut. Under the flail of bullets, Mouse shouted from behind the GAARV's starboard gun for orders. That same moment Wally's voice crackled over the team freq. Berko handled the reply.

"Juggler, Berko. Shots fired, no casualties. Loading now. Hold your position."

---

16 intelligence, surveillance, reconnaissance.

"Move it. Convoy is two miles out."

Mouse twirled a hand in small circles. Come on, come on.

At LB's back, the shadows around him shifted.

The pickup's headlights had pulled away from the hut.

Jamie shoved on the stretcher, prodding LB in the thighs. "Let's go. Go."

LB froze in the doorway.

The pickup's headlights led the way moments before the truck came speeding around the corner. Mouse waited for the Sai'ar, ready with the .240. The mission's rules of engagement dictated return fire only; that truck was now a hostile. Mouse hugged the gunstock.

A man in a loose, blowing tunic rode in the passenger window of the moving truck, a weapon clearly in his grasp and aimed at the GAARV. Mouse followed with the nose of the .240. The pickup carved a wide rooster-tail arch around the hut and the GAARV. It didn't fire. The chance was worth taking: LB tugged on the handles of the Stokes litter to load the princess.

He took only one step forward before the Sai'ar opened up. A volley drilled more holes into the Mercedes and drummed against the GAARV, flinting sparks against its armor. Mouse depressed the .240's trigger, answering fire. The mounted automatic blasted to life, and the ammo belt waggled, feeding rounds. Mouse's bullets struck up founts of dirt around the speeding pickup; some bit into the metal panels. The gunner in the pickup's window emptied his magazine at Mouse, who did not cringe behind the .240. Over the banging of the guns and the jangle of spent brass casings, Mouse screamed at LB.

"Get back inside!"

Before he could move, the Yemeni spy burst out of the GAARV, pushing past LB and the stretcher into the hut's back door.

LB surged backward away from the corona of bullets wailing all around Mouse. He heaved against the litter frame to push Jamie and the princess back into the hut. Cofield staggered through the door behind them.

Inside the hut, LB and Jamie set the litter on the dirt. LB took his rifle in hand; Jamie spread himself across the moaning princess. Above their heads, a burst of rounds slammed into the mud wall, ripping off a corner section, flinging it over LB, Cofield, and Jamie in bits and dust.

The Sai'ar truck kept rolling fast, firing until it crossed out of sight behind a corner of the hut. Mouse eased off the trigger. LB lunged outside to Mouse, and to inspect any damage to the GAARV. Over the team freq, Wally barked.

"Team 1, can you evac immediately? Repeat, immediately. Torres has the convoy one mile out and approaching. Confirm and we will engage that truck. Confirm."

Inside the GAARV, Mouse poked up his head with puffed cheeks and a shaking helmet. A trickle of blood ran from his left ear down his neck; he'd lost the lobe. The vehicle wore a dozen dents but had survived the onslaught, too. The trunk of the Mercedes had been hit and come unlatched, to stand on end like a frightened tuft of hair.

Behind the wall, the headlights of the Sai'ar swung around in a loop, lighting long cones of blank earth. The truck halted behind the hut's wall, out of the line of fire but in position to leap to the attack again if the PJs tried to get away.

LB turned for Berko. The young CRO had crawled to a window in the front of the hut. The muzzle of his rifle lay on the mud sill.

"LT?"

The young lieutenant came to his knees, to gaze west up the road. When he reeled his head back in, he shook it at LB.

"Okay. Tell Wally."

Berko pressed his PTT.

"Juggler, Juggler, Berko."

"Go."

The front of the young lieutenant's camo uniform brightened once, twice, again.

"Negative, Wally. Negative. They're here."

Wally went silent. Berko sank beneath the mud sill, rifle trained.

Swirling headlights flooded the hut, bleaching the air and dust. Tires and engines scrabbled over the cinder track leading from the main road. Five technicals rushed into a fast circle around the hut. Every truck had a big machine gun bolted to the bed and a man standing spread-legged behind it; each vehicle as it cut around the hut spilled armed men who jumped out of the beds and passenger doors to take cover in the grooves and ruts of the archaeological digs. Inside a minute, LB's team was ringed by more than two dozen dug-in enemies with automatic weapons. The newly arrived pickups finished their loop to park side by side facing the front of the hut, confronting it with five heavy machine guns and their joined, blinding lights.

LB and Jamie moved the princess's stretcher to a glaring corner, no more darkness inside. Berko squirmed on his belly below the windowsill. Cofield kneeled next to the princess. Khalil hugged his knees in another corner. LB dashed for the GAARV to see if he might dismount one of the .240s and ammo belt. Before he cleared the doorway, one of the Abidah's pickup trucks opened fire.

The reports were not the yips of a Kalashnikov but a different, more frightening tone, a deep-throated metal clatter like speed blows on an anvil. The weapon, likely a .50 caliber, unleashed a long salvo that shook the hut walls.

The team, Cofield, and the Yemeni all burrowed into the dirt floor. LB blanketed the princess with his armored torso. The top of the mud wall facing the gun shuddered and disintegrated, heaping chunks of ancient busted bricks over everyone inside. The interior of the hut dissolved into whorls of dust and spinning debris. Bullets pounded the wall, chewing off its cap. Under the maelstrom, through the zings and mist, Mouse dove inside. Landing next to LB, crimson dripping off his chin, he handed over three more units of blood.

The long, excruciating volley went on. The message in the salvo was: Don't try to escape. Don't even think about shooting back. Or we'll blow your hut to the ground with you in it.

When the firing quit, LB rolled off the princess, careful not to spill onto her the rubble that had collected on his back. His ears rang; his teeth and ears felt gritty. His nerves uncoiled slowly after the barrage. The rest of the team, Cofield, and the spy emerged as if out of graves, shedding layers of earth. The top quarter of the front wall had been shorn off, an ugly and jagged warning of only a fraction of the firepower facing the PJs.

LB collapsed onto his back, unable to see any stars. He shouted into the haze.

"Anyone hurt?"

Everyone but the princess sounded off, coughing. No one had been hit.

The princess's eyes fluttered open. She gazed at the billows tumbling out of the windows and the gray shapes carved on the smoke by the headlights of the Abidah.

She tried to speak. LB brought his ear close.

"What?"

She turned black eyes on him. The princess was wan and weak but conscious and smiling. She moistened her lips to utter a word, a name, just above a whisper.

"Arif."

Chapter 29

Arif swept the machine gun across the hut as if he were carving into stone. *I am here. You have my wife. Give her to me, then die.* His muscles rattled behind the big, quaking gun. Fifty yards away, the spotlighted hut smoked as if on fire. Hot casings somersaulted out of the chamber, piling in the sand and around his sandals on the truck bed. A hand squeezed Arif's leg. Without releasing the trigger, he looked down on old Mahmoud. The elder shook his head. *Enough.*

Arif pulled his hands off the grips. The clamor of the gun had nothing to echo against in the desert. A silent aftermath fell on Arif; all he sensed was his own trembling hands and the withdrawal of Mahmoud's touch.

He hopped down from the truck bed, plucking out the pair of torn cigarette filters used to stuff his ears. Arif worked his hands to expel the vibrations. He stood behind the trucks and their headlights. The Ba-Jalal, pistols in their holsters, waited around him. Their two dozen armed men lay in ditches surrounding the hut, perhaps frightened to have so many bullets flying over their heads. Arif gave them no more thought.

A short, thick tribesman approached. The man wore rings on every finger, a clipped beard, and a Kalashnikov at his chest. Mahmoud introduced him.

"This is Qunbula Hossain of the Sai'ar. Arif the Saudi."

Qunbula's name, which meant "grenade," seemed to have shaped him. He was the one who'd followed the kidnappers from the second roadblock out of Ma'rib.

"Thank you, Qunbula Hossain."

"My duty, sayyid."

The man dipped his head quickly but did not retreat.

"What do you want?"

The Sai'ar thrust a hand at the dazzling hut.

"My revenge, sayyid. I want the men inside dead."

The fat tribesman shook his Kalashnikov to make his point. Arif leaned down.

"Have you been paid?"

The Sai'ar stepped back as if Arif had struck him.

"What?"

Arif pointed at the bulge of what was plainly a packet of bills in the tribesman's tunic pocket. The Sai'ar looked down at Arif's accusing finger.

"Were you hired?"

"By the Abidah." The tribesman gestured at Mahmoud. "By him."

"Two hungry wolves let loose among a flock of sheep cause less harm than a man seeking money."

"You give me quotes from the Prophet? I have lost three brothers." The tribesman shot up three shaking fingers as if Arif could not understand. "Three."

"Brothers you risked for money. Step away, Qunbula Hossain."

The Sai'ar gaped at Arif, speechless until one of the Ba-Jalal brothers led him off.

"Careful." Mahmoud spoke from close behind. "We have all lost a great deal tonight. The Sai'ar and the Ba-Jalal have reasons for being here that go beyond you."

Arif turned on the elder, returning his voice to a gentler tone.

"No, my friend, you do not. You are here because of your father's vow to me. Ghalib was killed by a missile aimed at me. The kidnappers in the hut, the soldiers who've come to save them, they've all been sent here because of me. Tonight will be my revenge, Mahmoud. But I will see that you and the Sai'ar are satisfied."

Arif framed Mahmoud's heavy shoulders with his hands. He held the elder at arm's length, then kissed both gray cheeks.

"I have not been in battle for twenty-five years. I do not like this. I did not ask for it. But I will fight for my wife as I did for Allah. We are old men, you and I. Tell me I have your forgiveness. Then tell me I have your strong hand with me."

"Yes, Arif."

"Thank you."

"And you will be kept to your word, as well."

"I expect that."

"What do you want? I will tell my brothers."

"Spread your trucks around the hut. Surround it, keep it in your lights. Do not shoot unless I do. And when you do, destroy it. Go, Mahmoud. Masha'allah."

Mahmoud conferred with his kinsmen. They assented and returned to their technicals, calling other men out of the ditches to drive or work the guns. Inside a minute, the pickups had circled the besieged hut, ringing it with guns, men, and lights.

Arif stood before the mud building alone, the Makarov hidden in his waistband. He strode toward the bullet-pocked wall.

Inside, men in uniform ducked, aiming weapons at him and in all directions. The soldiers were likely Americans, though Arif did not care who they were. He stopped when he'd walked close enough to speak without shouting. The empty eye of a rifle and a young face behind it stared unblinking at him.

"Nadya. Answer me."

The desert was without birds or insects to ease the answering silence.

Chapter 30

"Shoot him," Khalil hissed. "He's al-Qaeda. Shoot him."

Khalil tried to leave his corner, struggling to his knees. The pain in his shoulder tripped him.

The youngest of the pararescue team slid over to Khalil before Josh could do the same. He eased Khalil down and took away the Kalashnikov. The spy had lost plenty of blood; he seemed drained and disoriented. Khalil continued to mutter that Arif had to be shot. The PJ spoke calmingly.

"It's okay, we got it. Let's take a look at that wound."

The rusty contours of the hut, the men and the downed princess, all shone bright as noon from the lights of the encircling pickups. The open ceiling of constellations made for an unsettling, dark roof. The front wall had been battered and mown short. The mud citadel felt incomplete and vulnerable.

While the PJ tended to Khalil, the stubby sergeant they called LB scooted beside Josh.

"How's your Arabic?"

"Good enough."

"What's he saying?"

"He's asking for his wife. He wants her to answer."

"She's too weak."

The husband called again. "Nadya. Can you hear me?"

Josh translated. LB chewed his lip, his attention suddenly distracted. "Just a sec." He whirled to the young lieutenant lying beneath the windowsill. "Berko."

"I'll send it."

The lieutenant pressed his radio talk button to report their situation.

"You got more assets out there, Sergeant?"

"Another mobile team two hundred yards north."

"That's it? Anyone else coming?"

LB rattled his head. "Not as fast as we're gonna need them."

"So we're surrounded, big-time."

"Yep."

"We're not getting out of here."

"We'll see."

"You want my tactical opinion?"

"If you need to tell me."

"Your other team needs to save themselves."

"Yeah. See, that's not what we do."

The husband outside called again for his wife. Behind Josh, she moaned, trying to reply. LB snapped his fingers at the PJ ministering to Khalil, then hooked his thumb at the princess.

"Jamie."

The young pararescueman, lithe and strong, sprang beside the princess. Instantly he quieted her while checking the flow of her second unit of blood. Nadya was barely able to stay conscious, and her exposed left leg looked white as a cadaver below the clamp. Though she might not keep the leg, her odds of survival seemed on the rise. Josh had fought alongside enough men to know the kind who would lay down their lives to do their jobs. These PJs were that sort. In every case, the ones who did so went down hard.

Twenty yards off, the husband called a last time for his wife. When he heard nothing from her, he gave up. He pivoted away, reaching under his tunic for a pistol. LB nudged Josh.

"Call him back."

Josh rose to a knee, unsure what to say.

"And tell him what?"

"Just stop him from walking off. Now."

Josh got to his feet to lean out from a window.

"Arif."

The Saudi stopped. He didn't turn immediately but sloped his shoulders and hung his head.

"Yes?"

Josh replied in Arabic.

"Your wife is here. She's alive."

The man spun. Josh stepped sideways to stand full in the opening, illuminated and exposed. Bearded Arif was a handsome man, big like Josh, weary like him.

"Let me talk with her. Have her come to the window."

"She can't. She's hurt."

The handgun at the end of Arif's arm knocked against his thigh. Josh considered moving behind cover. He held his place and let Arif see he held a pistol, also.

Arif gazed at the ground between them. It seemed such a small distance to be so great.

"How badly?"

"She took a bullet in the hip. She lost a lot of blood but she's stable now. These men are rescuers."

"They are Americans?"

"Yes."

"You?"

Josh pulled the checkered kefiyeh off his head.

"Yes. I'm a diplomat. My name is Joshua."

"You kidnapped my wife, Joshua. You will give her back to me."

"And in return?"

"That I cannot say. There are others around us, as you know. They have a voice in this. But I will have my wife."

"Come inside. See her for yourself."

"And be your hostage."

"No. You have my word."

Arif raised the pistol, aimed into the stars.

"I have seen America's word tonight, Joshua. How do I know Nadya is alive?"

"I know your name."

"How do I know she is alive right now? Ask her to tell you something only she can know."

"All right. Wait there."

Josh turned from the window. LB blocked his way.

"What were you talking about?"

"He wants to come inside to see his wife."

The stocky pararescueman shook his head, skeptical.

"She's trying to get away from this guy. I'm not sure that's a good idea. She's not in great shape."

The PJs didn't know the true mission. They'd parachuted in, put their lives on the line and, like Josh, had been kept in the dark.

Crumpled in a corner, Khalil spoke. "Tell him."

"Tell me what?"

Josh ignored Khalil, moving to Jamie and the princess. LB grabbed his arm to turn him back.

"Tell me what, Captain?"

"If it wasn't part of your brief, it's not for me to tell. Need-to-know."

Across the hut, the smallest of the PJs taped a gauze pad over his mangled ear. He grumbled. "If I hear that one more time."

LB waved him quiet.

"We've all got TS[17]. And there's forty guns pointed at me. I need to know. And you need to tell me."

"You're not going to like it."

"Compared to the rest of my evening."

"The princess isn't running away. She's been kidnapped."

---

17 top secret clearance.

LB pressed a hand to his forehead. He took a second to open and close his jaw.

"No."

"Yes."

"You did this?"

"Khalil did. He's with the Yemeni government. My embassy sent me along for the ride to the Saudi border. I didn't know either. She was sedated the whole time. By the time I figured it out, it was too late to stop it."

LB whirled on the wounded Yemeni.

"You a spook?"

Khalil fought to lift his face. He showed no shame, just the pain of his own bullet.

"Yes."

"We're Guardian Angels. We don't do kidnappings. Personnel recovery, search and rescue. Period. Son of a bitch, I can't believe we're involved in this. No wonder the guy's got so many guns out there."

The rest of the team tensed at the rebuke. Khalil paid no more attention. LB glanced around the hut, adding up the new circumstances.

"You're right. I do not like knowing this. Shit."

"Told you."

"All right. What do we do, just invite the guy in?"

"He's negotiating."

"He's not negotiating. He's al-Qaeda. And you stole his wife."

"Let go of my arm, Sergeant."

Outside, Arif waited in the spill of headlights, inside the ring of weapons he commanded. Josh kneeled beside the princess. From the stretcher, she blinked up at him while Jamie plugged her into another unit of blood. Her face, arm, and leg were all laid bare from the folds of the damp, reeking burqa. She lay quietly; her agony showed only in a throbbing squint of her eyes. Josh bent close.

"Should I cover your face?"

"No."

"Do you want to see him?"

"Yes."

"Did you hear?"

"Yes."

"What can I tell him?"

"Sorry."

"Is that all?"

"Wait."

She licked her lips. Carefully, the young PJ Jamie lifted her head to pour bottled water across her lips. The princess swallowed, gasping when she was done. Jamie eased her head down to the litter.

"Sorry I left him."

Josh nodded. He began to rise off his knees, uncertain this would satisfy Arif. He pulled away. Feebly, Nadya reached for him and missed.

"Yes?"

"Left him."

She coughed, an awful strain. A vein swelled in her forehead, a sign of returning blood pressure.

Before Josh could stand, she strengthened her voice.

"Left him a beggar's breakfast."

Chapter 31

Arif set his Makarov in the dirt, as he was told to. Approaching the hut, he did not raise his hands. He was not surrendering.

The diplomat came outside to usher Arif in. He'd put down his own pistol and kept himself in full view as an act of trust.

Inside the mud hut were four armed Americans in camouflage uniforms. One, small with a bandaged ear, did little more than turn his head from his rifle aimed out a window. Another, squat and burly, watched Arif with a fighter's eyes. A large man, the one who'd kept his muzzle trained on Arif outside, stepped up beside the diplomat. In a corner, a lean and dark-faced Arab curled, silent and obviously wounded.

None of the Americans moved until the sergeant spoke to the big officer.

"Introduce yourself, lieutenant."

This one, with a young face and an athlete's build, stepped forward to offer a handshake.

"I'm Lieutenant Berkowitz. US Air Force. You speak English?"

Arif accepted the hand. "Yes."

"This is Sergeant DiNardo."

Arif shook again.

"My wife."

The lieutenant led Arif, the sergeant, and the diplomat to the opposite wall. The Ba-Jalal's surrounding trucks had chased every shadow from the ancient hut. Nadya lay partly naked, pale, and deathly in so much light.

A fourth American, another young one, slid aside in the dirt to make room. Arif dropped to his knees beside Nadya. The American held two plastic bags, one of blood, the other clear fluid, for them to drain into her bare arm. Three more bags of blood lay nearby. Arif kneeled into the copper stink of a burqa he'd never seen her wear before. The soaked cloak had been lifted high, exposing her left leg above the groin where the jaws of a contraption bit into her pelvis over a drenched bandage. Her wound must be grievous to have bled this badly. She lay inside a metal basket, a stretcher; the Americans had intended to take her with them before Mahmoud's trucks surrounded them.

Arif touched her bare leg, fighting nausea from the cool deadness of it, the spatters of blood. He rested his palm lightly in the blood, against her flesh as he had done for twenty-five years of marriage, this thigh and this hand.

The young American said only, "Sorry."

"Must you look at her like this?"

The American nodded.

Arif gathered up her hand. Her gaze rolled to him before her head could follow.

"Arif."

"My love." He raised the back of her hand to his lips. "Should I cover your face?"

Her dark eyes had lost none of their depth, their night; they twinkled.

"No. Thank you."

"What happened?"

She glanced at the strangers around her. Nadya walked a razor's edge of wakefulness. The Americans gave her blood, but how much had she lost to be so shallowly conscious? She whispered, Arif lowered his ear.

"At the clinic. Chloroform."

The kerchief beneath the pickup. Her keys in the dirt.

The diplomat crouched beside Arif and spoke English.

"Khalil is a soldier. He had orders and a duty to obey them. These air force men, they're rescuers. They had no part in taking your wife. They knew nothing about the mission. They're not responsible."

Arif clasped his wife's hand harder and answered without looking at the diplomat.

"Who is responsible? You?"

"No. And I don't know who gave the order. Or why."

"Do you even know why you are here?"

"No."

"I do."

Arif set Nadya's arm across her waist. Her eyelids fluttered as she fought not to pass out. The youngest American readied another bag of blood. Arif stood to his full height, taller than any of them. In his corner, the Yemeni shivered alone inside his own arms.

"My wife's father is a very powerful man in the Kingdom. He believes I tried to kill him, and in return has ordered me killed. He went to the CIA to have it done. But they could not send a drone for me unless I posed some threat to an American. So my father-in-law arranged for that Yemeni pig to kidnap Nadya. He gave them a head start, then tipped me off. He knew I would pursue. He planned it. As soon as the Sai'ar told me you were in the car, I knew. You, Joshua. You are that American. You are the bait. I chased you, and now I can be murdered. He has already tried once tonight and failed."

The diplomat sputtered. "You didn't even know I was in the car."

How could this man be so naïve? How could he say none of them knew, not one of them was to blame? Orders were given by others, yes, but these men followed them. For that, ghostly Nadya lay at their feet barely alive, Ghalib was in cinders, three Sai'ar had been gunned down beside the desert road. An unbreakable ring of guns surrounded their mud hut, waiting on Arif's word. Arif would lay blame as he saw fit, and he would take a full measure in return.

He snarled at the diplomat.

"Truly, do you think that mattered?"

Arif bent again beside Nadya. Her face had rolled away from him. He slid his arms beneath her on the litter, to lift her away.

Chapter 32

"You can't do that, pal." LB lapped a mitt over the Saudi's arm before he could lift the princess out of the Stokes litter. "You need to take your hands off my patient."

Arif glared, incredulous to be spoken to, and touched, like this.

"This is my wife."

"Don't make me repeat myself."

Berko closed in, the only one in the hut who'd have a chance in an unarmed tussle with the big Saudi.

Arif removed his arms from under the woman barely aware of the tug-of-war going on above her.

Bearded, dark, in loose-hanging clothes and sandals, Arif fit in this desert world. Standing in the white beams of six trucks, a limitless dark sky for a crown, Arif had the bearing of a king here, one with guns and clans behind him. He shot a look that made LB want to take a step back.

"If I do not leave with my wife, you will all die."

"And if you do leave with her, she'll die."

Arif's features remained graven, as if he didn't comprehend that both paths would kill the princess.

"Jamie."

From his place beside the princess, the young PJ spoke without looking away from his charge. He made his points gesturing over his tools and her wounded body like an instructor.

"She's got a torn femoral vessel in the pelvic region. That's why we're using this clamp, the wound's too high for a tourniquet. She's lost about forty percent of her blood volume. We got her hooked up here but she's still in shock. She needs to be in a hospital as fast as she can get to one. Without a steady stream of blood and fluids, she'll die. Even with that, she might not make it. And she's at risk to lose this leg from the hip down."

Jamie, a sincere boy, looked up from his knees.

"Buddy, that's the truth."

Arif's lips bared his gritted teeth. He balled both fists. Gazing at his unresponsive, uncovered wife, he seemed ready to scream. LB couldn't name what flashed across the man's face, all too fast to fathom. Then Arif's features eased. He seemed only distant, somewhere else. In a memory, maybe.

"You have ten minutes."

Arif turned to leave the hut. Berko barred his way.

"Sir. It might take us a little longer to figure this out."

"I would not advise it."

"Why ten minutes?"

"Because you are Americans. You have more of something coming. Another team of killers, another drone, a satellite. And as you say, my wife needs a hospital. Bring her outside before ten minutes."

"Or what happens? To be clear."

"To be clear. I will not engage you in a battle while you wait for reinforcement. We will simply destroy this hut with you in it. You've seen that this can be done."

"We have."

"Then *as-salam alaikum*."

Arif dodged Berko's wide shoulders. LB called after him.

"What about your wife?"

Arif strode to the end of the hut, past the diplomat, Mouse, and the Yemeni spy. LB trailed the Saudi and, in the doorway, spun him by the shoulder.

"I said what about your wife?"

Arif knocked LB's hand off him. He scraped teeth over his lower lip, chewing on his beard while he corralled his plain urge for violence. LB didn't back off, pointing behind him at the princess swimming in and out of consciousness.

"You so hell-bent on revenge that you'd kill her with the rest of us?"

"If you do not bring her to me, it is you killing her."

"What if we give her to you? You got a doctor or a medic in your crowd out there?"

"No."

LB lit into the big Saudi.

"So you plan to drive her across the desert in the back of a pickup. What happens if the clamp comes loose and she bleeds out? It'll take two minutes, then she's dead. You've got to know exactly where to put it, what pressure to use. We'll give you blood and fluids, but you don't know how to use them. What if she doesn't come out of shock? She's still bleeding, how're you going to keep the wound sterile, the bandage changed? And can your hospital save her leg even if she makes it there? Think this through."

"Why did you come here, Sergeant?"

"To rescue your wife. You need to let me do it."

"Then you," Arif drilled a finger into LB's vest, "will go with her. You'll save her."

"All right."

Berko stalked across the dirt floor. He raised his voice so that it would arrive before his boots did.

"No."

The young lieutenant took long strides through the criss-crossing lights. LB hurried to make his deal.

"What about the rest of these guys?"

"I cannot say. There are debts to pay."

"You're running the show out there. You've got to say."

Reaching the doorway, Berko tried with a quick gesture to shut LB down before he could protest. LB didn't quiet on the first try; Berko shoved a hard finger between their faces.

"Be quiet."

"Sir."

"Right now."

LB bit his lower lip. Berko turned his attention to the Saudi.

"We'll do everything to resolve this peacefully. But I won't let one of my men go with you. You can't guarantee his safety."

"I cannot guarantee it here."

"If you fire on us, we'll fight back. We know what we're doing. Lives will be lost. Not just ours. Can we talk about this?"

"There's nothing you can offer me but my wife. If you return her without one of your men, she will lose her leg, or die. I understand that. And if you keep her, she will die alongside you. What is there to negotiate?"

"Sir, we can't bring your wife outside to you. She's the only thing keeping you from shooting us down in here."

"True. For another ten minutes. At the same time, you cannot keep her. It is difficult, young man. Do you pray?"

"I do. But right now, I've got other things on my hands."

"No. You do not."

Arif swept through the opening in the wall he'd ruined. He picked his pistol off the dirt and walked into the starburst of headlights.

Berko stomped through the hut, returning to the princess as if, from her stretcher, she might help the decision. The lieutenant spoke over his shoulder to LB in pursuit.

"No. Final."

"Then what, LT? You tell me."

Berko kneeled next to Jamie, considering the pale woman in the jaws of the CRoC.

LB insisted. "I can do it."

From his knees, Berko swung on him. "Back off."

"Permission to speak. Sir."

"Quickly."

LB walked around the princess, to squat across from Jamie and Berko.

"This mission isn't what we were briefed. It's not CSAR; this is some spook rendition. We have every right to refuse to stick our necks out for this. We can leave the lady on the ground and fight our way out of here. But she's dead if we do that, kidnapping or not. Some or all of us will be, too. You know it. Let me go. I'm the only bargaining chip you got."

"No."

"Sir. I've done a ton of missions."

"And I haven't. That what you're saying?"

"Due respect. Yes. I'll make it back. Ask Wally."

To calm himself, Berko blew a slow exhale. Beside him, the princess's brow swayed slowly side to side with her rocking head and her low, openmouthed moans.

"I know about you, LB. You did some tough stuff in the Rangers. I admire it, I respect it. Now you're making up for it in the PJs. I got no problem with that either. But you're not working alone. And you're going to keep your goddam death wish in check. Do your therapy some other time, not on my first mission. We ride out together. No other option."

Berko nodded to himself. He'd done that well.

Jamie and LB shrugged at each other. Jamie asked, "Where did that come from?"

"I did ask Wally. He said to tell LB that if he started up."

Jamie tipped his head, masking a grin. Berko rose. LB put his hands on his hips, giving no ground.

"Fine. Now what?"

"I've got an idea. Let me check with Wally."

"You got an idea."

"You sound surprised."

"An idea about what?"

"Arif says he won't negotiate. I think I know a way to make him."

Chapter 33

Josh stood in the mud hut's open doorway. Twenty yards off, in the grooves of dirt, two dozen weapons aimed his way. Behind those guns, the tribesmen's headlights blinded the night; to see the dark with any clarity, Josh had to look straight up. This he did, wishing himself away.

LB came beside him, exposing himself, like Josh, to the guns.

"Captain. You might want to get behind cover."

"It's all right. It's kind of liberating standing here."

"How so?"

"No pretense."

"You losing hope?"

"Aren't you?"

"We're going to get out of here."

"Really."

"Berko says he's got a plan."

Behind them in the hut, the young lieutenant worked his radio.

"The kid?"

"The kid's a Guardian Angel. Like me. And we're getting out of here."

On the other side of the electric and milky spill of the headlamps, Arif conferred with a heavyset, long-bearded man, one of the Abidah. Arif had a plan, too, and enough men and metal to back it up. Arif's ultimatum to the PJs had been a Gordian knot that Josh couldn't see a way to untie: the princess was to die, one way or another. That sealed the fate of everyone inside the walls in eight more minutes.

"I was set up, Sergeant. So were you. So was Arif. His wife. Khalil. All of us."

"It's tough."

"It eats at you."

"I been there. I know."

"What do you do?"

"Gut it out. Do the job. Kick some ass later, if you can. Shut up if you can't."

Josh drew a deep breath of the desert night. The expansion of his ribs aggravated the wound in his side.

"I don't think I'm cut out for this."

"For what?"

"Using people like this. I trusted my ambassador. He trusted the CIA and the Saudis. I come from folks who think saving the world is possible. My dumb ass quit the army to give it a try. I've been told on more than one occasion that I lack the touch for it."

"Big job, saving the world. What else would you do?"

"Maybe see if the military would take me back. Maybe do what you do. Try to save just what's in front of me."

"It keeps you focused."

"You're a little more than focused. You have a family? Wife?"

"Nope. This is all I got."

On his shoulder LB wore the patch of a Guardian Angel enfolding the globe in arms and wings. Beneath the angel read the pararescueman's creed: That Others May Live. Josh pressed a finger to the patch.

"Is it enough?"

"Most nights."

Directly overhead, a shooting star slashed a lengthy silver tail. Josh did not take it as an omen, but LB said it was a good sign.

The young lieutenant hurried up behind them, energized.

"We're ready. Come on. Charlie Mike." Continue mission.

Chapter 34

The trucks lit the red mud hut against the dark like a movie set, isolated and unreal. In the open doorway stood the diplomat and the short sergeant, exposed to Arif's guns. Whether the Americans were fearless or despondent, Arif could not tell from where he waited behind the lights, the Makarov in one hand, Nadya's blood on the other.

Mahmoud had stood beside him a while without speaking, until Arif broke the silence.

"What do the Ba-Jalal ask?"

"Not this. Not the martyring of your wife."

"Then what?"

"Only our portion."

The Americans had killed two of Mahmoud's brothers: one tonight, one two years ago. The elder would see Americans die in return. This was proper. The Sai'ar would require similar terms. None of them would vouchsafe the life of any American returning with Nadya. In his mind's eye, with the minutes draining out, Arif grabbed fat Mahmoud and shook him, Yes, you are asking the sacrifice of my wife.

In that imagined world, Arif walked past the diplomat and the sergeant in the doorway, into the hut to sit beside her. He took Nadya's hand, and she awoke to him pink and fair again. He told her how the Prophet Muhammad had lost eight family members in his wars to defend Allah. The Prophet could not keep his loved ones safe from the battles. Arif could not save her.

Far above the hut, a meteor cut the night sky, a bright and final act.

"Mahmoud, thank you for your loyalty. Your honor. And your loss."

The elder replied with a deep, barrel-chested sigh.

"Obligations."

"When this is over, I will not stay in Ma'rib. My father-in-law will not stop. And after this, the Americans. You cannot protect me from them."

"I will help you find another place in Yemen."

"Do not. I need to disappear. I require only funds."

"Of course, Arif the Saudi."

Mahmoud moved away. What more could he say to Arif with only minutes remaining? Mahmoud hoisted his big heft onto the back of the nearest pickup to stand behind the mounted gun. This was a last kindness, so Arif would not have to do it.

In the lights, the two Americans disappeared from the doorway. To do what, prepare to die? Pray, as Arif suggested? Not likely. These were Americans; they planned.

Arif wanted this from them, some plan to save his wife from him. Do something clever, Americans, outfox me, get away. He tried to muzzle this part of him and wiped his blurring eyes on the back of his hand holding the Makarov. Honor, loyalty, love, vengeance, they tore at Arif like dogs, and he did not hear the airplane until it was upon him.

With a deafening roar and a rumble in Arif's clothes, an invisible giant swooped low over the hut and the Abidah's gunmen. Many of the qabili raised hands to their ears to block out the blaring engines. The plane zoomed by without lights, a colossal *jinn* of the night. It banked tightly, tracing the earth, sowing a din over the Abidah that left room for no other sound. As if by that genie's magic, one headlight of a pickup truck exploded and went dark, followed the next instant by the other. Then the lights of one more truck popped and extinguished.

Tumult ignited among the men in the trenches surrounding the hut; they ducked lower into the dirt, frightened even more, waving at each other because their voices could not be heard. The long gun barrels in the beds of the Abidah trucks swiveled into the air and around to the darkness to find targets. Old Mahmoud looked lost, unaccustomed to the suddenness of battle. Around the hut, the headlights of two more trucks went dark, shot out.

The large plane peeled away. In the easing racket behind it, an unseen and speeding vehicle snarled nearby in the desert flats. A long volley of gunfire ripped from it. Another tandem of shots rang out. The truck bed beneath Mahmoud rocked, then collapsed like a mule on its haunches onto two flat tires.

Arif fixed on the hut, the focus of many lights and weapons. None of the shots had come from there. None of the Americans inside pointed a gun.

"Yes." He strode to the center, saying, "Yes."

With a minute to spare, the Americans had made their move.

Two of the Ba-Jalal trucks began to pull out to go after the ghost vehicle. Arif ran into the remaining headlights, arms high.

"Stay where you are! Do not chase them! Stop!"

The trucks halted, then slowly drove their headlights back around to Arif and the hut. He called to the restive tribesmen in the archaeological ruts.

"Have any of you been hit? Anyone? No?"

The qabili spoke to each other. Heads shook. Arif turned.

"Mahmoud!"

He beckoned the elder into the core of the lights with him, only twenty steps from the bullet-pocked mud wall. Behind it, the quiet Americans kept a close eye.

Fat Mahmoud took his time entering the center. He walked glancing left and right at the big guns around him, even though they were in the hands of his brothers. He arrived a little wild-eyed.

"There are more Americans out there, Arif. We should not stand in the open."

"Calm yourself. No one has been hit. They are shooting over our heads."

"Why would they do that?"

Arif faced the hut. He shook his head at the watchers while he spoke to Mahmoud.

"For four years I was a mujahideen with the Afghans. We fought like this, guerillas against greater numbers. The Americans are trying to make us think we are the ones surrounded. To break our resolve, make us chase them into the night, where they have the advantage."

Two more shots potted out of the dark. Another pickup rocked backward onto popped tires.

"Why are they shooting at our trucks?"

"To take away our lights and our mobility. Listen to me, Mahmoud. Tell your brothers and your fighters to fire into the air. All of them. Do it now, and watch."

Mahmoud moved swiftly, feverish to get out of the lights and the middle of so many bullets. He waved his arms, turning a circle.

"All of you, Ba-Jalal and Abidah! Fire into the air! Fire!"

At once, Arif and Mahmoud stood in the midst of an explosion of weapons, as though on the rim of a volcano. Three dozen muzzles flared straight up; the five .50 cals howled the loudest, a deafening and fearsome barrage. Arif fired his Makarov at the stars. Mahmoud trembled visibly.

Arif let the fusillade go for seconds, then signaled for quiet. The shooting was hard to quash; the tribesmen enjoyed triggering into the air. Arif walked a wide arc, gesturing broadly until the reports petered out on all sides. The final salvos vanished into the desert beyond the invisible Americans.

"Now have your men train their guns on the hut."

Mahmoud shouted again. With the rattle of arms, every barrel bent low, pointed at the Americans peering from the mud windows and doorways.

"Go back now, Mahmoud. There will be no more shooting at your trucks."

The elder Ba-Jalal gazed at Arif as if he were looking at madness.

"What will you do?"

Arif checked his watch, fated to see the second hand tick the last moments of the allotted ten minutes.

"As I said. Watch."

Mahmoud waddled away.

Arif had nothing to wave at the Americans, only his kefiyeh, but it was black. He made a show of setting the Makarov on the earth, as before. He showed both his white palms in the lights, and waited.

From the doorway of the hut, a checkered cloth waved in answer. Bareheaded, the American diplomat stepped into the clear. He strode toward Arif until the harsh sergeant stopped him.

Chapter 35

"Whoa." LB stepped out of the hut to grab the diplomat by the arm. "Where're you going?"

Josh stopped but continued to wave his kefiyeh.

"This isn't combat. It's diplomacy."

"Diplomacy with guns is combat. Get back inside."

LB hauled on the bigger, younger man, pulling him behind the shot-up wall.

Berko flattened a hand against Josh's chest to push him against the mud bricks.

"Stay right there. Do not move. You understand me?"

"Fine."

"One minute."

Berko got on the team freq to Wally.

"Juggler, Berko."

"Berko, go."

"Shots fired, no casualties. It was a message. He can blow this hut down whenever he wants. Suggest you stand down."

"Roger. Quincy, Dow, you copy?"

The pair of PJs, the two best shots in the unit, had been the snipers. Under cover of *Kingsman 1* buzzing the hut, they'd crawled close to the ring of trucks, then shot out tires and headlights.

Both checked in. "Confirm. Standing down."

"Rally at GAARV."

Berko lowered his hand from the big diplomat's breastbone. Josh held against the wall, biting his lip.

"Juggler, Berko. It worked. Arif wants to talk."

"That's the guy in the middle? Arif? Torres wants to know. She's on the satellite."

"Affirmative. I'm going out to parlay."

"Roger that."

"I'll take LB with me."

"It's your call."

"Juggler, any intel on additional resources?"

"You've got the C-130 in place. Torres has CAS incoming. Two armed Predators, thirty minutes out."

"Tell her thanks."

"Will do. Good luck, Lieutenant. LB?"

Berko ducked out of the conversation. LB checked in.

"Juggler, LB. Go."

"Sit rep on the package."

"She needs immediate evac. Stable but still in shock. She won't survive if we give her to the husband. She needs care all the way to the hospital."

"Berko tell you my thoughts on that?"

"Word for word."

"Good. It's a kidnapping. I don't like taking her. I don't like leaving her."

"Roger."

"You and Berko go talk to the son of a bitch. Figure this out."

"How about the SEAL team? They on their way?"

"Negative. It'd take them over an hour to get here on ATVs. We're still dealing with minutes."

"What if Arif wants to fight?"

"Then he'll get a fight. Tell him I said so."

"Roger. Out."

Josh had moved between LB, the lieutenant, and the doorway. He extended his kefiyeh to Berko, then a hand.

"So I'll see you two back here in a few."

LB shook first. "The bad penny."

Berko clasped hands with the diplomat, too. Mouse called encouragement. Jamie said to tell Arif there was a crosshair on his forehead. The Yemeni spy said nothing.

"You go first." LB put the lieutenant in front of him. "Keep waving that thing."

They stepped into the open behind Josh's kefiyeh. Only two sets of headlights lit them directly as they advanced; the lamps on two of the trucks had been blown out by Quincy and Dow. Two other pickups squatted on their rear rims with their back tires punctured, tipping their beams above the hut.

LB slung his M4 across his back, away from his reach. The lieutenant did the same, and lowered the checkered headdress. Arif waited for them thirty strides away, on the dirt track leading from the main road. No traffic rolled in their direction. No one from the village only a mile off was curious at midnight to come see what the shooting was about. This was Yemen, like Afghanistan and Iraq, where shooting was part of the people's lives.

Berko stopped walking to turn on LB.

"Follow my lead."

"What're you going to say?"

"I'm going to threaten him."

LB took in the guns aimed at them, enough to deliver about three hundred rounds per second.

"Nice."

They resumed walking. The big Saudi spoke when they had come within ten yards.

"Go back, Lieutenant. Bring medical supplies. One of your medics. And my wife."

Berko walked through the words to put himself face-to-face with Arif. LB stayed at his shoulder.

"I've got two armored vehicles waiting on my word or your next bullet. That big plane's got two chain guns on it, and if I call it back that's an angry thing, trust me. I've got ten commandos with night-vision goggles and sniper rifles in positions around your men. There's a crosshair on your forehead right now."

Arif blinked. A corner of his mouth curled, a half grin. The rest of him remained stolid.

"I have seen your tactic. I've used such bluffs myself long ago against the Russians. It can be effective against the inexperienced. But in the end, it makes no difference what you have or what you claim. If one more of your bullets is fired at my trucks or my men, we will mow this hut down like wheat. Then we will deal with your ghost commandos and your unarmed plane. And you may trust me."

Arif indicated the PTT button clipped to Berko's vest.

"Get on your radio, Lieutenant. Tell your men."

Young Berko kept his posture hardened, but did not speak or move as he was told. LB weighed the responses, unsure which the young officer might pick. Arif hadn't been fooled by Wally shooting out tires and lights, the shooting in the air. Arif's terms were unaltered: bring out the princess and a PJ, and no guarantees beyond that. With enough guns in place, he had the upper hand. And he'd made his peace with killing his wife in order to get at the Americans inside the hut.

Arif spoiled for a fight. Berko had no counter except to do as Wally said, and tell him he'd get one.

Berko held his tongue, still studying the big Saudi up close. LB readied to stride forward and insert himself. Before he could, the lieutenant spread his arms, breaking the icy posture between him and Arif.

"It's already done. We're standing down. There'll be no more shots."

LB was left off-balance, to swallow his bluster. Berko paid no attention, staying fixed on Arif.

"Why'd you call us out here?"

"For you to bring my wife to me. And for one of your men and his bags of medicine and blood to come with her."

"You knew I wouldn't do that. Something else."

"And what do you believe that is?"

"You need a way out. You need us to help you find it."

Arif chewed on his beard, black strands crossing his teeth. He pointed at LB.

"Send him away."

"He stays."

"I stay."

Berko turned his palms up, offering.

"Let's start with what we both want. Your wife to live. Do you believe that?"

Arif waited, staring as if counting his breaths.

"Yes."

"The only way to make sure that happens is if you let us leave with her right now. We'll get her to a hospital, care for her all the way. We'll save her life, and maybe her leg. Is that right, Sergeant?"

"More than likely."

"Anything else, Arif, anything else, and her life is in serious danger. Let us keep her alive. You can figure the rest out later."

The Saudi gazed to the brown hut where she lay, stymied.

LB slapped his own thighs, time to speak up.

"Man, she's in there dying right now. Make up your mind. If you start a fight, you're dead, we're dead, she's dead. And understand something. We actually do have backup out there. I don't know how good your boys are, they look a little raggedy, but ours are real good and they're not going to let you just kill us and roll out of here. Forget that. And one more thing for you to chew on. You were right. There's an American satellite watching your ass right now, and a couple of armed drones on their way. If the shooting starts, none of you are getting back home either. So what the fuck. Pick something."

Berko did not interrupt, but when LB paused he pushed him back a step away from Arif.

The Saudi licked his lips, considering some internal logic. Berko waited but LB twirled a finger, impatient and done with diplomacy. Drops of blood, dying flesh, Predators and Hellfire missiles, trigger fingers—he stood on the faces of too many ticking clocks and he wanted to get off.

"It is not so simple, Sergeant."

Berko answered for LB.

"Why not? Life or death. Simple."

"The Sai'ar will bury three brothers at sunup. The Abidah have nothing of their own brother to bury. My wife was kidnapped by the Yemeni spy you are protecting. You cannot walk away from this. The tribesmen will not let you."

Berko asked, "Would they if you told them to?"

Arif considered.

Berko pressed.

"Arif, try. There's a bloodbath waiting for all of us if you don't. The one innocent person, the one who hasn't pulled a trigger and didn't come here by choice, is your wife. What'll save her life? Can you think of a way to do that?"

"Perhaps."

"Then do it. And we'll call it a night."

Arif nodded to himself, something he'd thought of that might work. Then he shook his head.

"My wife will leave here only with me. And he must come, your sergeant. Do this, and I will fight for the lives of your men."

"That's not an option and you know it's not."

"Then I see no other way."

Arif glanced around, imagining the carnage, the incredible number of bullets in the air. "You. And us." He turned a wincing gaze to the vast desert sky, the slowly tilting constellations. "And retribution."

He pivoted his bulk, a droop across his shoulders.

"Go back now."

The Saudi took several steps. LB cursed, walking off. They'd have to radio Wally that the parlay had gone badly. Between LB and Arif, both dragging away, Berko held his ground.

"Wait. Both of you."

LB stopped.

Arif lumbered on. "No more talk."

The lieutenant ran after the Saudi to stand in his path.

"What if we can give your wife back without the sergeant having to go with you? What if she'll live and keep her leg? You can take her home."

LB arrived beside Berko. The Saudi mulled the question.

"How will you do this?"

"Will you keep your word? Stop the fight?"

"I will try. And what will you do?"

"Fix her leg."

LB grabbed the lieutenant by the arm. He hoisted a finger to Arif.

"Just a sec."

LB tugged Berko away.

"Do what? Sir?"

"Fix her leg. You can do it."

Steps away, Arif listened intently. LB walked the young CRO farther from the Saudi, lowering his voice. When he was sure Arif couldn't hear, he hissed.

"No. I can't. And you should have asked me before you said anything."

"You're trained, you've got the tools."

"I'm not trained, not like that. You're talking about repairing a femoral vessel. That's surgery. We don't do that, especially in the field. We're pararescue. Trauma and combat evac. Our job is to get them home safe, *to* the surgeons. Come up with something else."

"Something else or someone else? Who's got the best set of hands in the team? You?"

"Who do you think?"

"All right. Now, before the shooting cranks up, if you got a better idea, say it. We can threaten him again, see how that works. But you know I'm right."

LB controlled his arms, to keep from waving them in Berko's face and demonstrating his frustration for Arif.

"Let me get this straight. You want me to just pretend I can do this."

"LB, one of three things will happen. You won't fix her leg and we all get killed anyway. You'll actually do it, and we stand a chance of getting out of here. Or you'll stall long enough for the Predators to show up and we'll see what happens."

LB pressed a hand across his mouth to shut himself up and think. Berko leaned over him.

"You're tough. You're cool. You got this."

"What about your mission? Taking the woman back."

"This was a kidnapping. We're done with it."

LB had no time to consider a response. Arif called across the open ground between them.

"That's enough time."

Berko faced Arif.

"We'll do it."

LB turned for the hut, Berko with him. Arif hung back.

Berko asked, "Are you coming?"

"No."

LB imagined it was *his* wife that was going to get torn into. He might not be able to watch, either. He said before walking on, "We'll keep you posted on how it's going."

Arif drove a hard finger at the dirt under his sandals.

"It will be done here. In the open."

"What?"

Arif lifted his finger to the desert sky. The night chill laced around LB. Arif wore only a T-shirt and cotton trousers. He was thinly dressed, yet he smoldered.

"You have said more drones are coming. If that is true then you, Sergeant, will be standing next to me, not behind the walls of the hut."

Berko raised a conciliatory hand. "I'll ask my commander."

"You'll tell him. I want the American diplomat, as well. And the Yemeni spy."

"Why?"

"Are you still bargaining with me, Lieutenant?"

"Just explain it so I can tell them."

"It is hard to have faith in you. In Afghanistan we were your allies; I saw the CIA at work then. I saw it again tonight. Also I have lived among the Yemenis. They, too, are a treacherous people. I will trust all of you better if you are beside me."

Berko and LB took this with them into the hut while Arif faded into the ring of men and guns.

Chapter 36

Inside the battered mud walls, Josh waited for LB and Berko to step through. The lieutenant was distracted by a radio conversation with Juggler. Josh took LB's elbow.

"What's happening?"

LB told him Arif's demands and reasons. Meanwhile the young lieutenant finished reporting over the radio. He pulled off his helmet to brush a hand over the crown of his head. The kid, honestly trying to figure out the right things to do, had a chiseled All-American look, and Josh patted his shoulder.

"Lieutenant. Sometimes on the bayou we rode alligators. It's just like this here. You can't hold on. You can't let go."

Berko strapped on his helmet, finding no insight from rubbing his pate or from Josh's try at empathy. LB walked close, the other two PJs flanking him. The princess lay unattended, and no guns pointed out of the hut. Berko shook his head.

"I can't send you out there, LB."

"You don't have to. I'll go."

"You think Arif will do what he said?"

"I don't know."

Berko gestured to Josh.

"Any ideas?"

"He's given his word in a lot of directions. We'll see which one he keeps. Either way, I'm in."

Josh turned on the Yemeni in the corner.

"Khalil."

The spy would not look up. He pulled his jacket tighter as if it could protect him.

"No."

With both hands, Josh hoisted the spy off the dirt floor. Khalil swayed, unsteady on his feet. Josh drove him against the mud wall, ignoring the sting of his own wounds. None of the pararescuemen intervened.

"Walk out or get dragged out."

"I did my job."

Josh shook him against the wall.

"And I did it with you. That's why we're both going."

Josh didn't let the Yemeni loose but kept him upright with one fist balled in the jacket. He swung Khalil into the doorway and propped him there, like forcing a child to face the mess he'd made. He let Khalil go but rammed a hand before his eyes to warn him to stay. Josh turned for LB.

"Let's get the Stokes."

Berko shucked his M4 across his back. "We got it."

"You're going?"

The young lieutenant flung a quick glance at LB, who nodded, curt and visibly proud.

"We don't work alone."

Berko got on the radio, advising Juggler of his tactical decision and handing over command of Mouse and Jamie. He trailed LB to the rear of the hut to prepare the princess.

Josh moved behind Khalil, edging him into the open, where tribesmen gathered and headlights swirled.

Chapter 37

Arif created a smaller ring of trucks, men, and guns.

He ordered one of the pickups with its lights shattered to move to the center of the dirt track. He dropped its tailgate. This he lit brightly with the headlamps of the two remaining technicals that had their bulbs, plus all four tires, still intact. Arif collected the five Ba-Jalal brothers, two dozen Abidah tribesmen out of the trenches, and Qunbula Hossain of the Sai'ar from the roadblock. He conducted them into a circle around the open surgical theater he had made. The rest, he left to guard the mud hut front and rear.

The American sergeant, the diplomat, and the Yemeni emerged as Arif had ordered. The large lieutenant came out with them. He and the diplomat bore Nadya's litter between them, the husky sergeant walking beside her carrying bags of blood and fluid.

The ring parted to let them through. The men, all Muslims, gasped at Nadya's nakedness, her left leg exposed above the groin, her arm and face bare. They muttered over the strange clamp biting into her hip and the vermillion-stained wrap. It could not be helped that she would be viewed openly this way by the tribesmen. Motionless inside the litter, white in the garish light, she seemed made of marble—a fallen, broken statue. The Americans lifted the basket onto the lowered truck gate. The sergeant who would do the operation doffed his helmet, rifle, and backpack and set another pack on the truck bed close at hand. The others did not know what to do with their weapons.

Arif walked into the lights. "Put down your guns."

The diplomat tossed a white-handled pistol from under his sweater into the truck bed. The lieutenant was slow to discard his rifle; he leaned it against a truck tire where he might get to it if he lived two seconds past the need of it. The Yemeni had no weapon; he looked lost and without purpose.

Arif approached the stretcher on the table of the lowered gate. The sergeant stepped aside. Arif leaned over Nadya to lay his bearded cheek against hers. She did not stir. He listened to her breathing, stricken by her breasts against his chest.

The sergeant tugged him by the shoulder to stand erect.

"I'll do my best. Let me get started."

"Is she conscious?"

"Not really, no."

"Did you give her more drugs?"

"I can't depress her blood pressure any further. She'll have to put up with some pain, if she can feel it."

"My wife is a strong woman."

"I don't know you well, pal, but I guessed that."

"Sergeant. You are aware you cannot fail."

"We understand each other. Now back up."

The sergeant laid open his heavy medical kit. Arif withdrew from the stretcher. His place beside the sergeant was taken by the young officer.

Arif continued to retreat, catching himself from a stumble.

In the formation of men around him, Arif knew the name of only one. He, Mahmoud, came to walk him away.

Chapter 38

Berko had said PJs don't work alone. But LB was alone with the weight of many lives across his shoulders.

He had only himself to turn to. He watched his own hands dig into the med ruck, grab the correct tools: forceps, a syringe pack, a vial of antibiotic, a bag of TXA clot inducer and an IV, a suture kit, sterile gloves, scissors, a headlamp. LB flowed through the first steps of preparing Arif's wife for surgery, making definite movements. He took heart from himself.

Stripping off his leather combat mitts, he jutted his nose at Khalil.

"LT. Grab him."

The big lieutenant spun the Yemeni to face the stretcher. Behind his black mustache the spy had gone white as the princess. He'd need evac within the hour, tango two. LB handed him a unit of blood, the third bag the princess would absorb, and a fresh sack of saline. Both drained into the same IV.

"Hold these."

"What am I doing out here?"

"Holding these. Shut up."

LB snugged the internal straps of the Stokes litter around the princess. He tugged the elastic band of the headlamp around his brow, then stretched the gloves over his hands. He tossed Berko a pair to do the same, gesturing at the syringe and small vial.

"Give her one mil ertapanem."

Berko tore into the syringe package. Quickly he drew from the glass tube one milliliter of the powerful antibiotic. The lieutenant stuck the needle into the princess's deltoid while LB rolled up the burqa's left sleeve to start a new IV for the TXA, tranexamic acid. The drug would promote platelets in her remaining blood to slow the bleeding during surgery and after.

LB wasted no time. Out in the open, with Arif and twenty-five guns watching from a close circle, there was nothing to be gained anymore by stalling for the Predators.

The team freq buzzed in his ear.

"Lima Bravo. Juggler."

LB hit the PTT with the back of his sterile hand.

"Juggler, go."

"LB, can you do this?"

"Probably not."

"Then what are you doing?"

"Trying."

Electronic silence wavered long enough for LB to think Wally had signed off.

"Lima Bravo."

"Go."

"Don't drown. Charlie Mike."

"Charlie Mike. Out."

LB inserted the new IV catheter into the princess's left arm, finding a vein more quickly than before. He plugged in the TXA, handing the 250 ml bag to Josh. The diplomat held his gaze for a beat.

"You get us out of this, I'll join the GAs. I swear."

"That supposed to be an incentive for me?"

LB left the big diplomat grinning uncertainly. He leaned close to the princess's moon-gray face.

"Can you hear me?"

Her head lolled to the side. She hummed a low meandering moan, but she wasn't lucid enough for LB to give her anything for the pain. She was effectively out of it.

"Okay." He said this to himself, though Berko and Josh echoed, "Okay."

He lit his headlamp. With the scissors, he snipped away the sodden gauze wrap, laying bare the bullet hole.

Bruised and serrated skin rimmed the entry wound, a larger and more jagged puncture than LB had expected. The princess had been in the back of the Mercedes when she got shot; likely, the round had passed through the car, which flattened the jacket before hitting her. On the inside of the thigh, he found the exit wound the same, a nasty oval tear from a flattened bullet.

Using his fingers, LB spread apart the lips of the hole. A purple-black jelly smacked inside: congealed blood. Using forceps he plucked out three sopping gauze pads stuffed deep. He released these to the sandy ground. Slowly, the hole began to fill again with blood.

LB dabbed a clean gauze pad into the puncture to dry it and get a quick look inside. The muscles of the princess's thigh had puckered, her body's attempt to close down the bleeding tunnel. LB levered in the forceps to pry the wound open, a blunt dissection. The princess stirred in the stretcher. Without being told, Berko clapped hands on her legs. The diplomat freed his own hands, giving the clot inducer bag to the Yemeni spy, allowing him to press on the princess's shoulders. Josh whispered to her a soothing, hushing noise.

LB paused, withdrawing the forceps. He looked up from the wound to exchange worried looks with Berko.

He'd come to the end of his paramedic skill; his unit did a few nights a year in a Vegas hospital ER, but never in the surgical suites.

LB was aware of his own heartbeat. Berko must have suspected this, because the kid nodded. "You're good."

LB couldn't just put on a show of cool to help a wounded soldier keep his; he needed more than fake confidence. He needed the tangible steadiness that came with the real thing. A slow pulse and an unwavering hand. Deadly composure. Or he had no chance.

He drew a long, slow breath and closed his eyes. LB recalled himself a young man staring down a rifle scope, hidden in a green and steamy tangle of leaves. The settling of his nerves, the unerring sense of the trigger, a different uniform, the one shot, a result every bit as bloody as what he opened his eyes to now. He reached back for more, the same, over and again in many jungles and years.

The irony was not lost on him. He was calling on the deaths he'd collected as a soldier for the calm as a PJ to save the princess, himself, and the men waiting for him to act. LB exhaled as he'd been trained to do twenty years ago as a shooter, soothing his pulse and breathing, pacifying his hands. He gave himself over to the inevitable, the old feel of the trigger pulled, the bullet away. He grew still, and his heart receded.

LB put those memories behind him, where they lived in a shallow grave.

"Okay."

Once more, Josh and Berko repeated this.

LB inserted the gauze pad again, soaking up the rising blood, then spread the thigh muscles with the forceps. With his left index finger, he prodded the wet walls to peer into the confusion of the bullet hole. He worked the forceps left and right, weaving his headlamp in search of the blood vessels, prodding at the layers of yellow fat and blood-starved meat. He steeled himself against the pain he must be causing; the princess groaned but lay motionless under strong hands. Was Arif being held back, too?

Less than an inch below the skin, two reddish-brown ropes crossed the wound's path. LB widened the jaws of the forceps to angle his finger deeper, to slip under and ease the pair into better view. The femoral artery traveled down the leg sandwiched between the vein and nerve. If either the artery or the vein had been sliced in two by the bullet, it would have retracted like a snapped rubber band, impossible for him to retrieve. LB held his breath and curled his finger, gently tugging both blood vessels into the beam of his headlamp.

The tubes were rubbery and flat, each a third of an inch wide, without enough blood to inflate them. Both were plainly vessels. One felt thin and pliable, the vein. The other was more brawny: the femoral artery. LB emptied his first relieved breath. Neither blood vessel had been cut. Next, he needed to determine the damage.

"Berko. Loosen the CRoC. Just a little."

The lieutenant backed off on the clamp, one turn, then another.

In the crook of his finger, LB sensed a feathery pulse. The thicker vessel came alive, swelling on the princess's desperate heart. The thinner vein remained unfilled, waiting to carry blood out of the leg.

LB strained the forceps as wide as he dared, risking a rip in the princess's flesh. Again she muttered. Across her shoulders the diplomat shushed and cooed. LB nudged the pair of vessels further into the light of his headlamp.

The warmth of blood dribbled over his gloved fingers. The artery had been rent by the bullet on the right-hand side, to the inside of her thigh, as it burrowed through the leg. A small flap, less than an inch long, rose and fell, mouthing blood with every quick pulse. LB tucked his thumb inside the tear to mark it. He waited more seconds for the vein to fill and stiffen, letting the princess bleed. In moments, the vein responded and swelled, showing no leak. LB let it slip off his finger back into the ugly hole.

"Crank it down."

Berko turned the CRoC's handle. The throb and bleeding in LB's hand halted.

His headlamp flashed across the anxious faces of the diplomat, Berko, and the Yemeni.

"It's the artery. The vein's good."

The diplomat asked, "How bad?"

"Seven or eight stitches."

"You've done stitches, right?"

On flesh wounds, on skin. Using both hands. Without his own life on the line, plus the lives of five others. With not so many guns aimed straight at him, from a lot farther away.

"Hold her leg down. Tight."

The diplomat shifted from the princess's shoulders to press down on her knee, while Berko checked the bags of blood, fluid, and clot inducer, all in the arms of the Yemeni. The LT located a pulse in her right groin, lifted her eyelids, then lay the back of his hand against her cheek to check her temperature, clamminess, color.

"She's hanging in. Like he said, she's tough."

Out of the suture set, Berko handed LB a curved needle trailed by twenty inches of white nylon thread. With the tips of the forceps, LB gripped the eye of the needle.

Keeping his thumb inside the damaged flap, LB wiped the wound dry with a sterile pad. The Yemeni leaned in close, a pinch to his eyes. Was this remorse for the princess, fear for himself, a lack of faith in LB?

"It's Khalil, right?"

"Yes."

"Khalil. Lean the fuck back."

The hand that moved the Yemeni away was Josh's.

LB tugged lightly on the artery to test its elasticity. If he pulled too far, the tear might lengthen and rip the vessel more. The artery gave him some play. It felt gristly, lined with muscle.

He exhaled, long-winded. The wound had filled again, but he could do nothing to stop it. Along with the artery, the bullet had slashed an uncountable number of smaller blood vessels. The leg was a reservoir of unmoving, deoxygenated blood, and though the CRoC was as tight as it could be, the wound would continue to weep. With gauze LB dried the jagged opening as best he could, then added to the crimson pile growing at his boots.

He eased his thumb from the cut in the artery. The flap closed. Quickly, before the blood could rise again and blind his hands, LB dipped the needle near the left extreme of the fissure. It had done him good to snap at the Yemeni spy; the sound of his own aggravation was a familiar thing and reassuring.

The needle pierced the shell of the artery. LB pushed it through delicately; if he shoved too deep into the collapsed artery, he might prick the opposite arterial wall. If this happened, he might sew the vessel shut. A practiced surgeon knew how to avoid this danger. LB knew only that he had to.

With caution he plucked the thick artery walls apart before curling the needle upward. LB gritted his teeth and sucked, trying to sense the needle entering the narrowed chamber. He worked carefully, too much so, and blood flooded the hole again. LB stopped.

"Mop."

Berko used a hemostat to pat a fresh gauze inside the wound. He dropped the pad under the truck gate.

LB urged the needle deeper, then, making his best guess, turned it up until the point emerged on the opposite side of the split. With the hemostat, Berko gripped the needle, gently lifting it clear.

"Pull all but two inches. Hold it high."

Berko raised the needle, tugging the nylon through the hole until only two inches remained. Using his fingers, LB tied a suture knot, looping the shorter thread around the taller post six times. When ready, he made a half hitch and pulled to begin setting the knot, trying to sense the correct pressure; too much and the knot would sink into the artery.

LB drew the ends of the thread apart, tightening, thankful not to be working on the frailer vein in such tight quarters. The artery stood up against his touch and the hardening knot. He stopped, then stood erect to rest his back. The first suture was in place. He had no idea if it would hold, if he'd sewn the interior walls together, or if his nerves were going to hold out.

"Okay."

Before Berko and Josh could repeat this, the princess thrashed.

Josh flashed into motion, heaving down on her knee. Though she was tied flat, she strained violently against the straps. Berko leaped for her shoulders. Holding the needle and thread out of the way of her shaking thigh, LB let the artery slip off his index finger to disappear into the wound and protect the lone suture.

The princess loosed a guttural howl. She arched her back, rising on her shoulder blades. She lacked the strength to lift more against the restraints and hands, and faded to the stretcher. LB leaned past Berko's wide frame to get a look into her face. Her batting eyes showed only bare consciousness but enough to sense what LB was doing. She'd surged into lucidity to shriek at the pain, then passed out again. The spasm released, she lay still, muttering, only her shaking head free to move.

LB had to make a decision. He couldn't have the princess bouncing around in pain while he tried to stitch her up. It was near impossible work even with her quiet. Her torso and leg needed to be completely still, more than the straps could do. If she jerked at any moment while LB was sewing, the sutures could rip, the needle could further tear the femoral, any number of calamities. Keeping the princess motionless would take two big men, Josh and Berko. But the wound kept filling with blood, and LB was forced to sew with only one hand. He needed Berko to handle the absorbent gauze pads. The diplomat couldn't control the woman alone, not if she kicked up like that again.

LB could sedate her with a shot of ketamine, but her blood pressure was already perilously low. The heart might stop altogether. What if he quit the surgery right now and demanded one more time that Wally let him go with the princess in the back of a pickup? LB would ask Arif to keep his word. If the Saudi tried a double cross, Wally and the team would still have a fighting chance, with Predators on the way.

The team freq chirped in LB's ear.

"Lima Bravo, Juggler."

"Juggler, go."

"What was that?"

"She woke up. Not happy. You close enough to hear?"

"We're just outside the ring."

"Stay there, Wally. No matter what happens. I need your word on that."

"You can't have it."

"I'm not sure this is gonna work. You've got to get Jamie and Mouse out if this goes south."

"Keep it north."

"Wally. No shit. Hold position. Don't compromise the team."

Before Wally could respond, Berko took one hand off the princess to tap his PTT with the back of a bloody glove.

"Juggler, Berko."

"Go."

"I agree, Captain. Hold position. Not much you can do for us. Exfil the rest of the team. We got this."

Somewhere on his belly in the desert dark, staring down a laser with the dot on the back of someone's head, Wally was biting his tongue.

"Roger. Out."

The transmission done, LB dragged a sleeve across his brow.

"Thanks. He can't stand not being the hero."

"What now? Knock her out?"

"It might kill her."

The young lieutenant peered into the wound, already opaque with blood. LB shrugged.

"You told Wally that we got this. What've you got?"

"Nothing."

Standing beside LB, still crushing down on the princess's knees, the diplomat piped up.

"We need another set of hands."

LB rattled his head, knowing where Josh was taking this.

"No. It's her fucking husband."

"Exactly."

"He's al-Qaeda. He's already threatened to kill us. I do not want him standing here the next time she screams. This is hard enough as it is. Get someone else. Him."

The Yemeni spy could barely keep his feet, with a round through his shoulder and a rotten attitude. LB waved off his own suggestion.

"Okay, not him. One of the tribesmen. Someone who doesn't know her."

The diplomat had already taken both hands off the princess.

"They're all Muslims. No one but her husband's going to touch her."

LB held the thread and needle and could not set them down to stop Josh from walking away. He opened his mouth to object at the diplomat's back but Berko stepped in front, nodding that this was all that was left to them and they would deal with it.

Josh strode directly into one set of headlights. This cast LB and the stretcher into his shadow. In Arabic, the diplomat called into the ring of men for Arif.

Chapter 39

Arif strained against the hands of Mahmoud and a Ba-Jalal brother. He did not fend them off; he wanted them to stop him. If he rushed to the screaming Nadya, he would sweep the Americans aside to hold her and that would achieve nothing. Better to be held back, chewing his beard, let the Americans have their chance, though his heart like a horse tried to pull him to her.

After her shriek, the diplomat walked forward to call his name. The elder and brother let Arif go, for he had stopped his efforts to go to her. She must be dead. The Americans were going to tell him this. Now the Ba-Jalal had to urge him forward. He spoke over his shoulder.

"Mahmoud."

"Yes."

"Be ready to kill them all."

Arif strode into the ring and the white lights. The Makarov rode under his T-shirt nudging him, ready to do its part.

The diplomat greeted him. Arif prepared a fist.

"She's fine. She's strong, just like you said."

Arif stopped in front of the diplomat. In his periphery, the circle of tribesmen whispered and weapons rattled into tensing hands.

"Then she is not dead."

"No. But she's in some pain."

"Relieve it."

"The sergeant will explain. We need your help."

Arif did not wait to follow. He brushed past the diplomat, until his arm was snared by a fast grip.

"Before you do, listen to me."

Arif held still. The diplomat was a powerful-looking man, wounded himself, and fearless. Arif recalled Russians like this, bears of men, hard to put down.

"What."

"Your wife has an awful wound. What they're doing is not easy to look at. There's a lot of blood. You need to let these men do their work. Stay in control, Arif."

"This, from the kidnapper of my wife."

"I want you to know I regret it."

"Regret. That is a Western notion. As if to ask for forgiveness is to receive it. Islam demands *tawbah*."

"Repentance."

"You must sacrifice to be forgiven. Now take away your hand."

Arif charged to the stretcher, putting the diplomat behind him. The sergeant blocked him from Nadya's wound. The man held a suture needle and thread. Both gloved hands were coated in red, as were the young lieutenant's beside him.

"Move aside."

The sergeant refused. "Not until I tell you a few things."

"Do not make me repeat myself."

"Or you'll what? Really."

Again, privately, Arif was glad of the restraint. The sergeant was right to slow him, make him check his emotions before seeing the damage.

"She is in pain. Help her."

The sergeant described the injury to Nadya's femoral artery, the complications he faced in drugging her.

"I need you to keep her quiet. Keep her still. Talk to her."

"Will she hear me?"

"Don't know."

"Let me see."

The sergeant moved aside. The wound confronting Arif forced him back. He'd lost the hardness of a mujahideen against blood and injury. The ragged hole was worse than he'd imagined. The harsh clamp, her snowy flesh, more spilled blood, the slow rolling of her head, all made him despair again for Nadya's life.

The diplomat positioned himself at her naked knee to press down with both hands. The Yemeni spy kept out of the way, holding intravenous bags and looking as if he might keel over. The big lieutenant eased beside the sergeant, who nodded at Arif to do what he'd been summoned for. Hold her down. Calm her.

Arif put his back to the Americans. He leaned across Nadya to hold her head in his hands, keeping his elbows on her breast should she convulse again.

The first time he saw Nadya at a party in Riyadh, he knew she was Al Saud. He, a gangly and fervent boy of twenty-one, had returned from jihad in Afghanistan, she from medical school in Paris. He did not for a second think himself unworthy of her. Perhaps that was why she'd picked him. Now he watched that girl fight the agony and fear that his missteps had brought her. Nadya was innocent of all but loyalty to him. Only at this moment, after a quarter century of marriage, after prison and exile, did Arif accept that he could no longer keep her.

Behind Arif, the Americans resumed. Nadya stiffened against their gory sewing. Above her, Arif lowered his weight. Staring into her flickering eyes, he lowered his voice and his lips, as if to kiss her.

"Would you like your favorite story? Yes? It's been how long since I've told it? Years."

If Nadya could hear, she could also feel the Americans jabbing inside her hip. This was awful to believe. But if so, she knew, too, that her husband stood with her.

"In the desert, Muhammad said to his young wife, Aisha, 'Let us race.' He had married her when she was nine and he was a young man, but now he was old and bearded. In front of his army, the Prophet ran a race with his wife and lost. He thought this wonderful. But he fed Aisha meat, and made her fat. When they raced again, he won. And he said, 'This for that.'"

Arif whispered to her of their home in Ma'rib, how he would make her coffee every day and bread if she would teach him to bake. He would put candles in each room and fan her while she slept. After she healed they would race in the desert. "And I will win, because I will make you fat."

Behind him, the Americans murmured and worked at her wound. Nadya surged against them once, they all held her in place, but she did not wake enough to wail as before. She collapsed into the litter, exhausted and fully still, as if that had been her final burst of life. Arif stopped talking and for minutes only stroked a rough thumb across her cheek.

A tap came at his back. Arif finally kissed her parted lips and turned. The American sergeant had put down the bloody needle and thread.

"I've done what I can. You want to see?"

"Yes."

With a forceps, the sergeant widened the wound's red walls for Arif to peer down. Arif hid his lips behind his sleeve. The young lieutenant dabbed a gauze pad into the hole to soak away the last shining beads of blood.

The white picket of a running suture marked the sergeant's efforts. All eight loops were sloppy and irregular, a few millimeters apart, but they appeared firm on top of the crimson artery. Arif looked away as soon as he'd satisfied himself that the sergeant had done what he claimed.

"Will it work?"

"I don't know. What if it does?"

"I will speak with the tribes for your lives."

"And if it doesn't?"

"Then I will not."

The sergeant held Arif's gaze a long moment. He seemed to imply a challenge: Let us make this only about you and me. When Arif did not accept, the sergeant shrugged as if he'd tried to take the burden for the others and failed.

"You understand. People are going to die. They don't have to."

"No one will die who does not have to."

Again the American stared at Arif, but differently, with an icy malice. The sergeant wanted to kill him on the spot as a way to save his men.

Arif indicated the patch on the man's arm.

"That others may live, Sergeant?"

"That's what it says."

"Then let us find out."

"All right. LT."

The big lieutenant moved beside the clamp. In slow turns he reduced the pressure on Nadya's pelvis. The belligerent sergeant broke away from Arif and used the forceps to widen the wound. He patted the wound with white gauze, then tossed the stained pad on the grim pile under the truck.

"All the way."

The lieutenant spun the handle. The sergeant dipped clean gauze again, inspecting his suture.

"There's some seepage."

He watched closely into the wound, then set down the forceps to walk to the end of the basket, at Nadya's feet. He laid hands on her cloth shoe.

Arif threw up an arm.

"What are you doing? Do not touch her."

"Little late for that. Fine. You come do it."

The American moved away from Nadya's foot. He instructed Arif to take off her shoe, then pinch the nail of the big toe.

"Squeeze hard. There. Now let go. Watch."

The flesh beneath the nail, already pale, blanched more under Arif's pressure. When he let up, the nail bed pinked.

The sergeant nodded. "We got capillary refill."

Arif set the shoe between her ankles.

"What does that mean?"

"It means she's got blood flowing through her leg."

"You have fixed her?"

"No. Come here."

The sergeant walked Arif beside Nadya's wound. He peered again into the wound. The torn flap lay flat under the nylon thread yet continued to weep crimson drops. The sergeant nodded to himself; this was the best he'd expected, and he may have been proud.

"She's still bleeding, but a lot slower. She needs a real surgeon in a real hospital as fast as she can get to one. We have to worry about that stitch holding for the trip, plus infection. Her blood pressure's still way too low. You got to let us take her out of here."

Arif backed several strides from the stretcher.

"Wrap her wound. Prepare her to travel. Then I will want a moment with my wife."

"Good. Okay."

Instantly the Americans busied themselves over Nadya. They dismantled and stowed the tourniquet clamp, plugged fresh bags of blood and fluids into the intravenous line, wrapped a clean white bandage about her thigh.

When finished, Arif waved them away from her. He pointed to the middle of the circle, into the crossing headlamp beams.

"Leave your weapons."

The sergeant rattled his head.

"That's hard to do."

"I intend to keep my word, Sergeant. It will be easier to argue on behalf of rescuers than *kafiri*[18] fighters."

---

18 nonbelievers, non-Muslims.

The young lieutenant walked away first. The big diplomat escorted the reluctant sergeant away from his leaning rifle. The wounded Yemeni shuffled alongside the Americans.

All the armed Abidah in the ring and in the earthen ruts, the Ba-Jalal brothers and the Sai'ar, the two armed Americans left in the mud hut—none knew what to make of this walk away from Nadya, into the center. Some tribesmen relaxed, believing the crisis had passed; others fidgeted with their guns, an ominous clacking. A few caught Arif's eye while they stuffed fresh qat leaves into their mouths to steady themselves for what was to follow. Arif found Mahmoud in the ring of weapons and asked for another minute. The elder dipped his long beard.

Alone, Arif moved beside Nadya. He lapped a hand over her bare calf, withholding a cry at her barely returning warmth and color. He lowered the hem of the burqa and replaced her shoe. Nadya lay peacefully in the litter. Plastic bags rested on her waist. Arif left the veil up to bring his nose just above hers. He did not whisper but spoke as if she were strides away.

"I bless you, my wife. I thank you. I thank Allah for you."

Nadya registered nothing. Without the strain of the surgery, the torture in her hip, she'd retreated deeper into her body, to rest beside the river of her flowing blood.

Arif pressed lips to her bare forehead. He stopped himself from giving the kiss all the meaning and memory the moment called for. If he did, he would stay too long. Arif let his lips touch her skin, found all his long marriage in this, and took it as enough.

He beckoned Mahmoud to come. The elder walked into the light, past the Americans and the teetering Yemeni.

"How is your wife?"

"She will live."

"Alhamdulillah."

"My friend. Do you remember the prayer for the dead?"

"No."

"Say what you can, when you must."

"What do you mean, Arif?"

"Thank you for everything. *Jazakallah*[19]. Please, go back. I will speak to the tribesmen."

Mahmoud walked away after a gentle push from Arif to send him on.

---

19 May Allah reward you.

Chapter 40

Arif called an elder tribesman to him. Josh stood waiting between LB and Khalil. LB remained bareheaded, his helmet in the truck bed. The spy wanted to sit, but Josh jerked him upright.

The ring of two dozen tribesmen eyed the four of them in the center. The qabili appeared unsure, twitchy. The surrounding desert and night sky were not evident under the glare of the headlights, and the evening cool had disappeared. The pangs in Josh's side and forearm had also vanished. He sensed only sight and sound and the slip of sweat down his back.

Berko murmured into his microphone, and several times he answered, "I don't know. Hold."

Khalil staggered. Josh jammed a hand under his armpit to right him. Khalil looked around confused, as if he'd just arrived.

"What is happening?"

"Hang on. We'll be out of here soon."

While Arif conferred with the old man, Berko kept up a narrative into his radio, tapping the button at his vest, describing the shifting situation.

Arif patted the old man's back to usher him off. He leaned to kiss his wife's forehead, then stood to behold the four of them lined up in the lights.

He beckoned for LB to come to him.

Berko held LB back.

"What's that about?"

"Don't know 'til you let me go."

The lieutenant unhanded LB, not liking him walking off alone. Berko asked what Josh thought was going on and got a shrug.

LB moved beside the stretcher, edging Arif aside to check the IV running into the princess's right arm free of the burqa. When he was done, he made room for Arif. The big Saudi planted both hands on the Stokes litter to hover over his wife. He lowered his face to hers, and in the shining headlights, a glistening tear dripped from him to run down his wife's cheek as if it were hers. He smoothed it away with his thumb, then spoke in English to her closed eyes.

Arif talked to her low and privately, with LB standing close. The ring of men and weapons waited; Josh began to fidget, taking on the anxiousness of the tribesmen.

Arif pushed away from the stretcher and tailgate. LB returned to his place beside Josh, while Arif strode to the middle of the circle. Josh nudged LB.

"What was that?"

"You wouldn't believe it. This guy."

"Tell me."

"Can't."

"What's he going to do?"

"We're about to find out."

Arif faced the four of them from several strides away. In Josh's grip, Khalil began to tremble.

Berko muttered into his microphone, "Hold."

Arif hoisted a wide palm at the unseen stars. He lifted his voice to match the hand, for the Americans and the spy and all the tribesmen to heed him in the heart of the lights.

"Abidah. Sai'ar. Ba-Jalal. Hear me."

Arif spoke, pivoting as if on a slow turnstile to address the tribesmen in the ring and hunkered around the hut, and the five men standing at machine guns in the beds of the pickups.

"You have shown me great loyalty, all of you. Men of the Abidah, you came at a call that a guest in your village, a man of the Kingdom, not one of your own, had his wife stolen from him. I thank you."

LB nudged Josh to have him interpret the Arabic. Josh shushed him.

"Qunbula Hossain. Three of your kin were murdered this night trying to stop the kidnappers. I respect your rights."

Josh bit his tongue, hard-pressed not to speak up. The gunfight at the roadblock had been set off by the Sai'ar's extortion. It hadn't been murder but escape. How was Arif arguing for their safety by saying this?

Arif scanned the circle again.

"Brothers of the Ba-Jalal. Men of honor. You have paid a harsh price for your father's vow to me. No man is worthy of such faithfulness, nor could he repay it."

Arif lowered the hand to aim it at Nadya.

"My wife lies at the gates to Paradise only because she did not leave me in Afghanistan. Or in the Kingdom. Or in prison. Or in Yemen."

Arif spread his arms wide to encompass all who had gathered around him. Skewered on the surrounding lights, in flowing clothes that made him seem greater, the bearded Saudi seemed a prophet, an angry one.

"You are here . . ."

He swung to confront Josh, the two pararescuemen, and Khalil.

"*You* are here . . ."

In a flash, Arif whisked from under his tunic a black pistol. He stuck it at the sky.

"For me."

Arif fired a round. Everyone jumped. Josh lost his grip on Khalil, who wobbled but stayed upright.

Arif held the smoking muzzle aloft, the way the Bani Yam and Josh had held their janbiyas only an hour ago. He thundered.

"I claim, for all of you, the right to tha'r."

Arif continued to pivot under the gun, glowering so intensely he seemed on fire. He demanded of any tribesman or brother to contest his right to take vengeance on their behalf. None answered.

Arif lowered the pistol to LB's chest.

LB drew back, then caught himself. One hand rose to his vest to push the talk button for his radio. He said only, "No. Hold."

The stocky sergeant took a stride toward the gun.

"Okay."

In the next heartbeat, young Berko moved up beside him, towering over LB.

Josh hauled Khalil forward into line.

Arif swept the dark eye of the pistol across the four of them. Inside his beard, his upper lip curled away from his teeth. The gun planed back across their lineup, settling again on LB. Arif kept his voice to the tribesmen loud.

"This American and his men are warriors. But they were not called to battle here. They, too, have taken an oath. They vowed to save my wife."

LB, with the pistol on him, urged Josh in a whisper. "What's going on? What's he saying?"

Before Josh could answer, Arif elevated the gun just above LB's bare head. He fired a round sizzling over the desert. At the bang, LB stumbled back a step, expecting the impact.

Without pause, the Saudi swung the pistol to Berko's big frame. Berko winced as Arif shot past his helmet.

"For her life, I give you yours."

Again, Arif held the gun high and rotated, a commanding figure.

LB and Berko both gulped hard, stiffening their legs. Berko rubbed his face and breathed into his palm. LB spit.

"What the hell was that?"

Hurriedly, Josh began to explain Arif's Arabic, the reprieve. All around them, the qabili were restless, mumbling but accepting so far.

Arif dropped the gun to his side. A different energy suffused him, the swelling performance over. Arif's voice turned intimate, not a pronouncement. He faced Khalil and challenged him.

"Who is your tribe, spy?"

Khalil licked his lips, eyes downcast. Arif asked again.

"Who is your tribe?"

Khalil shuddered against a chill only he felt.

Josh lifted a palm in Khalil's defense. Arif did not acknowledge this, and Josh let the hand down.

"Huashabi."

Khalil answered in a clear voice, his black shoes spread apart in the dirt, his wounded shoulders squared, "I am Huashabi."

Josh marveled how the man, twice tonight, faced guns.

Arif nodded.

"You drugged my wife. You kidnapped her."

"It was my mission. I am a soldier."

"You killed three Sai'ar on the road."

"I had no choice."

"Your mission."

"Yes."

Arif stepped closer. Two-handed, he whipped the pistol up. "This for that."

The bullet struck Khalil mid-chest. Standing close, Josh recoiled from the blast and the muzzle flash, the zip and thud that blew Khalil off his feet. The spy's arms flew up and for an instant he fell as if reaching for Josh to catch him. Khalil landed dead on his back while the noise fled and the qabili muttered in approval.

Josh searched for his footing. He staggered in front of the two pararescuemen. Needles burst in his rib cage. Behind him, LB and Berko quivered, too, but wanting to act.

Lowering the gun, Arif turned another circle, shouting to the tribesmen.

"The Huashabi have paid the Sai'ar. There is nothing beyond this."

The qabili bobbed their heads, muttering, Yes, it is fair.

Arif let their agreement percolate a moment before again raising the pistol high into the night.

The price was not to be just Khalil.

LB saw this, too. Josh reached back an arm to hold LB behind him.

Arif bellowed directly at Josh, directing the pistol with his voice.

"The Abidah have lost two brothers. They were American murders. They are an American debt."

Arif lowered his volume, only for Josh. He spoke in English.

"Afterward the others may go."

Josh, the bigger man, shoved LB away.

Chapter 41

The bullet spun Josh around and dropped him on his face. His hands clutched in the dirt; one knee tried to crawl.

LB bent at the waist, screaming.

"You gave your word. You son of a bitch."

From steps away, Arif trained the pistol between LB's eyes.

"I promised you no one would die who did not have to."

LB leaned toward the gun. He growled, rooted to the spot. Arif gazed back at him down the short barrel.

Berko moved between them. Arif followed the lieutenant with the gun. Berko ignored the pistol to kneel beside the groaning diplomat.

LB struggled against the momentum of his temper, Arif's betrayal, more spilled blood. Behind the gun, Arif seemed controlled, cold, and LB despised him more for that.

Berko rolled Josh onto his back beside the dead spy. The bullet had struck high and right in the torso, not a clean shot to the heart like Khalil. Berko tugged the knife from his ankle holster. Arif pointed the pistol at the back of the lieutenant's head while the kid sliced through Josh's bloody sweatshirt.

Berko exposed the wound only long enough to press both hands over it, oblivious to Arif's gun behind his head.

"LB. Get your med ruck."

Arif did not shift the pistol from Berko's head. LB hesitated, unsure what he would do if the Saudi pulled the trigger.

"LB. Snap out of it. Go."

LB ran for the pickup, still focused behind him, afraid to hear the crack of the pistol. He reached the princess, unconscious on her litter. He could easily snatch his M4 out of the truck bed. The image of the rifle in his hands blaring at Arif made him leave it behind. The gun could do nothing to save any of their lives right now. He grabbed his med ruck. When he'd turned to hustle back, Arif had walked away.

None of the tribesmen moved or took their hands off their guns.

The diplomat's wound was bad, but the bullet had missed the lungs and airway. Blood ran without bubbles; he was able to breathe. Tango two. Berko took away his hands and peeled off his stained plastic gloves. He gave over to LB the tending of the downed diplomat, to get on the radio.

LB stuffed combat dressing into the wound. Fired from close range, the round had drilled a neat hole; the big diplomat was so thick the bullet hadn't exited. LB couldn't guess where the round had stopped. After striking the collarbone it could have ricocheted anywhere inside the trunk. If the bullet wasn't sitting next to his heart or his aorta, if Josh left this place alive and made it to surgery, he had a chance. Along with the princess, he had a five-hour trip ahead of him. LB readied a fresh bandage and gauze wrap.

On the team freq, Berko hailed Jamie and Mouse out of the mud hut, to hurry forward with another Stokes litter. Quickly the young lieutenant briefed Wally, who was watching from the dark desert. Wally responded with "Roger." Berko was doing the job right.

Josh wheezed through clenched teeth, his color paled. He put a powerful grip on LB's forearm.

"Get out of here."

"We are."

"He said you could go."

"We're all going."

"Khalil."

LB reached over to check the spy's carotid pulse. He touched only silent flesh.

"No. Stop talking. It's not your strong suit."

Josh's groan pained him.

Mouse and Jamie joggled out of the hut carrying a second Stokes litter from the GAARV. LB tapped his PTT to tell them to go back for a body bag.

Arif's shadow crossed him. LB rose fast, and they almost bumped chests.

"Keep your calm, Sergeant."

"That's tough. Trust me."

"You will leave the spy's body."

"We'll take him."

"He is Yemeni and Muslim. The Sai'ar will bury him in the correct way. They will notify his clan."

LB let this go. It sounded better than anything he had to offer Khalil, just a plastic bag, a long ride in the dark, a cold locker, a wait to contact his kin.

"Why'd you shoot them?"

"To allow you and your men to go free. There was no other way. Others, as you say, needed to live."

LB indicated Josh, making it plain that Arif would have to go through him.

"What about him?"

"I've spoken to the Abidah. You may take the diplomat."

"Why'd you do that?"

"To put you in my debt."

LB tempered his tongue. Like his rifle, it could do nothing but claim more victims.

"For what?"

"So you will take my wife with you."

"That's the smart move."

"You'll keep her alive. You'll get her to the best hospital."

"As fast as I can."

"You'll save my wife, Sergeant."

"I will."

"It's very important you tell her everything I said to her. For her ears only."

"I will. And I'll tell her what else you did."

"If you must."

"Is that why you didn't shoot me?"

"Yes."

"Yeah. Well. Thank you."

Behind them, Mouse and Jamie trundled the diplomat on the litter toward the mud hut, to load him into the GAARV. Berko knelt alone in the ring of headlights, watched by the armed tribesmen. He finished tucking the spy into a body bag.

"You know the diplomat's story. You can fill that in."

"You mean the man you shot?"

"The man I did not kill, Sergeant."

Berko lumbered past. He bore the zipped-up corpse across one shoulder.

"You're still a murderer."

The Saudi faced off with LB, a head taller.

"Yes I am. You seem to want to judge me."

"Oh yeah."

"Have you killed, Sergeant?"

"It was never murder."

"Of course. Always in uniform. Always under orders."

"That's right."

"There is a man on the desert road fifty miles south who would argue otherwise, if he had not been reduced to ashes by an American mistake. My wife, kidnapped and shot, would be dead by a bungled CIA plot were it not for you. Forgive me, Sergeant, I am without the luxury of a uniform. I had to decide. Not someone else."

Arif held up a hand to stop LB from replying.

"Say it to my wife when this night is over. I trust her response to you better than my own."

Beside the princess, Arif and LB did not back off from each other.

"One final thing."

"Whatever."

"Will you drive north over the roads or the desert?"

"We'll stay off the roads."

"Could you go faster on the highway?"

"Sure."

"How much?"

"A lot."

"Then I ask you to follow me on the road. I will put one of the Abidah behind you. We will assure your safe passage."

"Let me check with my captain."

"My wife needs every minute."

"We all do, pal."

Arif dipped his head in solemn scrutiny.

"I believe you are a man who knows this to be true. Good-bye, Sergeant."

Chapter 42

Behind Arif, the American vehicles were invisible. Farther back on the road, Mahmoud's headlights occasionally winked, blacked out between Arif and the Ba-Jalal. The effect was discomfiting, like something crossing the moon.

Alone in the pickup, Arif drove 55 mph, the pace the American captain had specified. He was hard, that one, emerging out of the dark in his large, powerful vehicle, weapons trained, the sacked body of the Yemeni spy strapped on board. His tone was clipped, and he, too, seemed to want a fight with Arif. The captain and his stone-faced rescuers would have been elusive and dangerous if a running desert battle had happened. Arif was thankful it had not but was not moved to thank Allah more. He regretted this but could not change his heart.

Mahmoud had assured Arif that he'd arranged no more roadblocks ahead. The Ba-Jalal could not be confident that other Yemeni desert tribes or the Bedu had not set up their own obstacles to charge petty tolls. Mahmoud had given Arif enough money to pay and a Kalashnikov to be the final arbiter. If the Yemeni military had their own desert checkpoint, the Americans would take to the sand unseen.

The border with the Kingdom lay sixty miles ahead. Arif drove with an eye behind him, catching fleeting silhouettes, the last glimpses of his wife. He was grateful to the American captain for bringing his two vehicles onto the road. Arif was able to spend this final hour with her, watch her reach safety, know it was done.

He watched, too, the immeasurable sky for the stars to blink out.

Chapter 43

The blacked-out GAARVs zoomed north at top speed. Mouse, missing part of an ear, and Dow both lowered their NVGs to drive behind infrared headlights, viewing the rushing road in green detail. Out front, Arif's truck led the way, lighting up empty stretches of desert midnight. To the rear, the old tribesman hurried in a rickety pickup crammed with armed men. Overhead, *Kingsman 1* rumbled in low circles, keeping an eye on the procession.

LB sat in the windowless breeze, helmet in his lap, keyed up. Seated in front of him, Berko bent over the SADL display at his chest, tracking their position. In Team 2's GAARV, Wally would be alerting Torres in the ROC, the SEAL team at the border, the private Saudi jet in Sharurah, coordinating all the mission assets.

Nobody asked LB what Arif had uttered to the princess in his presence. They all knew LB well enough, even Berko; if LB wanted to tell them, he would.

They still had fifty miles to get out of Yemen, but the distance was flying by on the paved road. A few tractor trailers swooped south, but the GAARVs made no imprint on the dark highway. Nothing lay ahead but a black expanse, constellations, the border, another hour, and Arif.

Jamie rapped knuckles against LB's leg, excited, wide-eyed. He wanted to wind down, talk, begin the transition from guns pointed at them all. LB leaned forward to knock big Berko on the shoulder for his first rescue. He undid his safety belt and shifted to his knees to face backward into the litter cage.

Five minutes ago, roaring away from the mud hut, LB located no pulse in the princess's wrist. He tried again and found the faintest of beats, the slow return of blood and warmth. The gauze wrapping around her hip showed its first scarlet stains from the slow leeching past LB's suture.

The diplomat lay in the Stokes litter secured next to her. LB patted him on the hand and got no response. Mouse had taped a ketamine popsicle to Josh's thumb for him to suck on. This was self-medication; when the sedation grew sufficient, the thumb would fall away from his mouth, moderating the dose. Josh would drift in and out all the way to the Riyadh hospital. If the princess surfaced again in pain, LB and Jamie would decide if they could give her a pop, as well.

LB turned forward in the seat, strapping on his helmet. Jamie tapped his own chest, saying he would take over the patients. LB could ease off.

Time in the rumbling GAARV passed with the murky miles. Jamie pivoted every ten minutes to check on the patients in the cage. He plugged fresh blood and fluids into the princess's IV and chatted with a half-conscious Josh. Wally hailed over the team freq to say LB might have done something extraordinary back there. LB didn't engage, unable to shake his foreboding that the night was not done. Like the princess's pulse, he could barely put a finger on it. LB fixed on Arif's taillights holding steady thirty yards ahead.

Halfway to the border, the princess groaned harshly, louder than the GAARV's engine. Jamie whirled to soothe her. In the tight confines of the Stokes litter, he cuffed her to get a true blood pressure. She came out 85 systolic, still too low to sedate. The princess did not rock against her constraints but whimpered in pain for long passages. Jamie stayed on his knees until even he determined he could do no more, a hard choice, and turned away.

LB reviewed the things Arif had asked him to tell his wife. The man was sending her away to save her. He'd gunned down Khalil and wounded the diplomat, so the PJs could spirit her off to a royal family who'd had to steal her to pry her away from him. LB wished himself out of the GAARV and into the pickup truck out front, where he and Arif could continue their discussion about hard choices.

LB's thoughts cooled with the sweat under his armor. The strains of the last hour began to unhook. He wasn't happy that the PJs had been called into a kidnapping after being told it was a rescue, but he let this go as the taint of getting involved with anything CIA. You never got more than half the story from them, and half of that was a lie. From the sound of things, everyone had been suckered, even the princess, all of them, just a pretext to get to Arif. Were the Al Saud really eager to bring her home? Once they got her and fixed her up, how were they going to keep her away from him?

Lights flashed from the desert. Mouse tapped his brakes and the mission, so out of whack, slid into its endgame.

The GAARVs ground to a halt. Wally reported on the team freq that the SEALs had arrived to escort them over the Empty Quarter ten more miles, then across the border. Mouse and Dow idled on the road while communications flew back and forth.

To the rear, the old tribesman pulled his pickup off the pavement. He shut down his headlamps so that he would see nothing secret under the moon. Ahead, Arif drove on.

Mouse proceeded off the road, leading the way onto the silvery sands. Wally's voice zinged across the radio.

"Hold positions. Repeat, hold up."

Mouse braked to a jarring standstill, and behind him Dow.

"Juggler, LB. What's going on?"

"Just got word from Torres. She says don't move."

"Why?"

"She says one minute."

The SEAL team checked in to say they'd copied the order to stay in place far off the road.

By now, Arif's truck had stopped several hundred yards downrange on the vacant highway. He'd turned the pickup around to face south, and gotten out. In the shimmer of the headlights, his small outline dropped to its knees.

LB stepped out into the renewed chill of the desert. Berko emerged from the GAARV to join him.

Fifty yards behind LB, the door to the unlit pickup opened. The old tribesman joined him and Berko beside the road, transfixed.

Young Jamie called from the GAARV. "What's he doing?"

Wally left his vehicle to stand beside LB.

"Torres wants you to confirm that's Arif al-Bahaziq up ahead."

Far ahead, Arif's small silhouette touched his forehead to the road. Wally asked again.

"Is it?"

"Yeah."

Wally punched the PTT for his sat radio.

"JOC[20], Juggler. Roger. Confirmed."

Kingsman 1 banked away to disappear over the clear desert dark.

Arif prayed. As if in answer, a downward blur streaked to him out of the heavens.

The Saudi disappeared in a massive flash of fire and concussion. Inside the blast, he kept his oath to shelter his wife. Flames climbed over themselves upward and out, sprouting hot orange and oily black. The carcass of Arif's pickup flipped from the fury like a coin to land searing and gutted on its side. The princess would not come back to Yemen, would not share Arif's fate, because he was gone.

---

20 Joint Operations Center.

With nothing but desert and stars on all sides, the noise of the explosion settled quickly into the flitter of flames around the crater's rim and the greasy throbs of burning tire rubber and tarmac.

The old tribesman's voice rose out of the dark. He knelt in the sand next to the road and laid his long beard down to it. He chanted in the moonlight and the blazes of the missile strike.

Between the PJs and the wowed SEALs, the team freq became a babble. LB pulled out his radio earpiece.

He climbed into the GAARV and faced backward, to the princess. She remained oblivious. Gently, LB reached above her head to pull down the veil.

Chapter 44

King Saud Medical Complex
Riyadh
Saudi Arabia

LB let the limo driver get the door. The Saudis probably paid him twice what LB made.

He finished a virgin Bloody Mary, leaving the celery, and, with Jamie at his heels, stepped out. The driver closed the ebony door and like a daytime ghost floated in his long white robe to the driver's side. Without a word, the car motored away.

Jamie and LB stood before the facade of the biggest hospital in the Kingdom, on a pavement hotter than the desert. The massive medical building, all stone, steel, and mirrored glass, gathered the unrelenting heat and cast it off, herding Jamie and LB toward the front door.

Overnight, the al Faisaliah Hotel had laundered their green and brown field uniforms, dusted and oiled their boots, and knocked this morning with brunch trays and a note requesting their presence at the hospital by noon. The signature belonged to the same Saudi doctor they'd briefed in the emergency room last night, when LB and Jamie did the handover, while ambulance crews wheeled the princess and the diplomat in.

On the flight from Sharurah, she awoke briefly but not enough to talk with any sense. LB and Jamie took her vitals and decided she'd rallied enough to earn some rest and shut her down with a shot of ketamine. In the basket next to her, Josh kept knocking himself out with the popsicle.

In the frigid air-conditioning of the vast hospital lobby, men and women kicked past in white or black robes down to their shoes, plenty of shiny-haired men in business suits skimmed by, and only the women lacked mustaches or beards. LB and Jamie, plainly American servicemen, garnered nods all the way to the patient information desk.

"Joshua Cofield. He came in early this morning."

The slick Arab boy checked his computer.

"Eighth floor. Post-op recovery. Gentlemen?"

"Yeah."

"May I ask? Are you part of the Americans who brought back the princess?"

"I guess."

"Thank you."

"You know about that?"

"Anytime there is a member of the royal family in the hospital, we are all briefed."

Jamie gave that a hum. LB turned for the elevator banks.

On the eighth floor, LB didn't have to inquire where Josh was. Among the curtains, white linens, IV lines, monitors, gray faces, and baby blue scrubs, Josh's private room would be the one between two Saudi army guards wearing berets and automatic weapons.

"Fellas."

"No entry."

"Who says?"

The larger of the two guards smirked. "Who's asking?"

The door opened. A short, spectacled man dressed in khakis and a tennis shirt poked out his head.

"Sergeant DiNardo?"

"And Sergeant Dempsey."

"Come in."

The pair of guards didn't protest.

Josh lay on an elevating bed sitting up. He wore a yellow hospital gown and white sock booties and had a drip line in one arm and fresh dressing around his upper chest. The man who ushered LB and Jamie into the room extended a hand, introducing himself as Ambassador Silva from Sana'a.

"I was just leaving."

Jamie greeted him enthusiastically. LB gave a desultory shake. The ambassador smiled broadly, compensating for the lack of pressure in LB's grip and his eye-to-eye skepticism.

Silva grinned at Josh.

"I see why you like him. He's just like you."

The ambassador gave Jamie and LB pats on the shoulders along with quick, elusive words that included Good job and Well done. He swept out. The man had a definitive walk, like he knew where he was going.

Gazing down his cheeks, Josh considered the two PJs at the foot of his bed. His head tipped back and he looked a little loopy.

LB pulled up a chair on one side, Jamie on the other.

"How're you feeling?"

"Tuckered. Good. Morphine. I recommend it."

"That your boss?"

"Yep."

"What did he have to say?"

"I might be under arrest. I might not. I did kidnap a Saudi princess."

"Did he know?"

"He says he didn't."

"You believe him?"

"Don't care. He says he'll get me out of here."

"He probably will. I don't think the Saudis want you talking."

"Not my strong suit."

LB chuckled. Jamie joined without understanding the reference. Josh's voice carried a sweet drawl missing last night in Yemen.

"Silva thinks I'm a spy."

"Are you?"

"Jesus Christ."

Josh pushed a red button held in his fist. Two clicks sent more morphine dribbling into his IV. Jamie and LB waited for him to refocus on them. He gasped a little.

"No. I'm not. How's the princess?"

"We're on our way to find out."

"You did an amazing thing out there, LB. All of y'all did. I'm sorry for my part in it."

"No worries."

"When do you head back?"

"We got a commercial flight this afternoon."

"They dug my bullet out this morning. Guess where they found it."

"Where?"

"In my ass. My right ass cheek."

Jamie liked this. "LB's been ass-shot."

LB and Jamie didn't know Josh well, and though the awful event they'd shared bound them, it provided little for idle talk. They couldn't do more; LB and Jamie were both on lockdown from Torres until they got back to Djibouti for a debrief.

They rose to leave.

"You need anything?"

"Nah. I got morphine."

Josh flicked a hand to stall them.

"You seeing the princess now?"

"Yeah."

"Tell her I feel like a turd."

"Roger."

"I'm going to quit, LB. Do what I said. Join the PJs."

"It's not as easy as saying it."

"I'll make it."

"Did you tell Silva yet?"

"I'll send him a postcard from Louisiana."

. . .

The VIP wing on the sixth floor also had guns outside a room. These hung around the shoulders of three shining Saudis, bare-headed in white robes, trim beards, and sunglasses. LB asked Jamie to pick up a magazine. Jamie protested but LB stopped him.

"Arif's dead."

LB said it as if the fact shifted Arif to a different category, to whom keeping a promise was an absolute.

Jamie took a seat while LB presented the doctor's note to one of the guards. This one knocked, paused, then disappeared behind the heavy hospital door while the other two turned their shades on LB.

"You guys think it's too bright in here?"

"Go sit down."

LB had not awakened in a cranky mood, but the silent limo driver, the smarmy ambassador, guns in a hospital, Josh and his morphine, and these two chesty Arabs caused him to stand his ground. He waited, defying the goons' shaded glares, imagining a fistfight. The door opened and the third guard emerged, followed by a tall, thickset, older Saudi.

This man pushed across the polished linoleum. Broad, ringed hands extended from a black, gilt-edged robe. His round face, crowned by an ebony headpiece, sported a gray mustache and bulbous nose.

The third guard approached, but the big Saudi dismissed him with a flapping gesture, overly grand in the flowing robe. The guard did an about-face.

The man offered both hands to LB.

"You are the miracle worker?"

"Sergeant DiNardo. US Air Force."

"I am Prince Hassan bin Abd al-Aziz. Princess Nadya's father."

The royal gave LB's hand a hearty shake.

"How's she feeling?"

The prince squeezed LB's hand. "Speak with me privately."

Before LB could resist or remark, the prince pulled him away from the guarded door to a sunny, remote corner beside a potted palm. The prince held LB's hand longer, to press it again between his rings.

"Thank you for saving my daughter."

"It's my job."

"I understand. But many men would not have attempted such an operation under those conditions, much less accomplish it. The surgeons who repaired her artery found it equally incredible. She is alive and whole because of you. I do not know how to repay you."

"My hand."

"Of course, Sergeant. Pardon my enthusiasm."

"What can I do for you?"

"Beyond what you have already done, very little. Only one small item."

"All right."

"I will receive a full report after you are debriefed by your superiors."

"Okay."

"Before that, I have one personal question to ask. Only one."

"Go ahead."

"This is difficult to ask. Did you see with your own eyes the death of Arif al-Bahaziq?"

"You mean her husband?"

"Yes, Sergeant. My daughter's husband. The terrorist. Can you confirm it?"

"I already did that once. Why do you need me to do it again?"

"My business requires such morbid accuracy. I apologize. So?"

"Yeah."

"Good." The prince glanced at his feet, as though suddenly humbled. "I do not rejoice, Sergeant. I spent many years trying to bring Arif into my family. But he would not be tamed. Like you, I have responsibilities to my country. What you witnessed was, as you say, my job."

"I prefer mine."

"Of course."

"I'd like a few minutes alone with your daughter."

"I'm afraid that cannot happen. She is under strict isolation."

"I got an invitation to come here this morning. I'm pretty sure it came from her."

"I did not clear it. I will discuss that with her doctor."

"I would have come anyway."

"And I would have stopped you. Anyway."

"Prince."

"Yes."

"Arif and I had a conversation last night. After you kidnapped his wife. Before you blew him to pieces. He told me some things. He asked me to tell them to her."

"I will need . . ."

"And only her. I'll get debriefed first thing tomorrow morning. Military intelligence, State Department, CIA. I'm okay with keeping my word to Arif and telling just his wife, then leave it at that. Or I can do it your way and talk to everybody else. Which brief do you want to read?"

Abd al-Aziz ran the fingers and gold of one hand down his breast, smoothing the impeccable cloth of his black robe. The hand stalled at his gut, which he patted in thought.

"You know who I am, Sergeant."

"I do. And you don't know who I am. Let's leave it like that."

The old Saudi was dressed like death, in black with gold accents. When he grimaced, deeply carved lines set off his eyes.

"You do not avoid a conflict with me. Why is that?"

"I'm not looking for trouble, Prince. But I'm not looking to break my word."

"You have no fear?"

"I don't let it make my decisions for me."

Abd al-Aziz nodded, and when he smiled the creases beside his eyes bent upward, too.

"I suppose I cannot celebrate the man who defied the odds to save my daughter, who then defies me. You are a zealot, Sergeant. So was Arif. We have a few in the Kingdom, and it is my profession to deal with them. This is not a welcoming land for such men. You have two minutes."

The prince turned for his daughter's door. With another wave of a hand, the guards parted to let LB pass alone into the room.

The hospital room was immense. Even so, a single, gigantic floral arrangement filled one corner. In the bed, the princess lay awake, propped on pillows. A hand came to her forehead to tuck stray locks inside a hastily thrown-on silk scarf. The scarf did not prevent her black hair, touched with gray, from falling far past her shoulders. Behind pulled-up sheets and a long-sleeved gown, only her hands, face, and one IV-plugged arm were visible. She looked newly flush.

"How you feeling, Doctor?"

"Better. Thank you."

"The operation went okay?"

"I'm told it was successful. The surgeons were impressed with you."

"So you'll keep the leg."

"For all else I've lost, I will keep that. Please sit, Sergeant."

LB filled the chair already beside the bed. The prince had likely been sitting here, explaining himself. She put clear black eyes on LB, keen and focused without pain and drugs clouding them. She smiled in grief and gratitude together.

"I'm glad you've come. I wish to thank you personally."

"Ma'am, I'm sorry for your loss. And for all this."

"Thank you."

"I don't have much time with you alone. Your father."

"I know."

"Arif."

The princess drew a sharp breath, which caught in her lungs as if she'd inhaled a thorn. She struggled to release it and continue breathing.

When she could speak, she opened her mouth. Her lips stayed parted, her gaze strayed from LB. He said it for her.

"He's dead. You know that."

She blinked but dropped no tears. She bottled them to keep up her courage.

"Yes. I have been told how. And why."

"Arif asked me to tell you a few things. I said I would."

"He did?"

"I need to do it right now."

The princess scooted higher against her pillows.

"Yes."

"Just after he said he was sending you back with my unit, he had me stand with him while he talked to you on the stretcher. He had me listen. Do you remember any of that?"

"No."

"Okay."

LB had done his best to commit Arif's words to memory. He'd scribbled notes on the plane ride from Sharurah. He'd let this become important.

"He said he wanted you to forgive him. He . . ."

"Sergeant."

The princess extended a hand. LB left it ungrasped for an uncomfortable moment before he reached back. He laid her hand on the bed and covered it.

"Yeah."

"Please. If I may ask one final kindness."

LB closed his fingers around her palm, he put his thumb on the blue-veined back of her wrist.

"Okay."

"Speak to me as if it is Arif. Please. I want to hear him. Will you do that?"

LB looked away, past the hospital blinds to the scorching Saudi sky. When he came back to her face, the first tears had moistened her eyes.

This was what LB had won, this moment between the requests of the dying and the living. This was what LB did when he saved a life, let it go on.

"Okay."

She sniffled. LB spoke to her hand in his. He did not imitate Arif, just said his last words.

"Forgive me. When I believed you were going to die, or lose your leg, I was desperate for it to be beside me. Now that you will live, now that you will be whole, it cannot be with me any longer."

She wiped away a tear, leaving a gleam across her cheek. Arif had done the same with his rough thumb.

"Your father will not stop. Will we go through this again? I must send you with the Americans to save you from me. Go to your family. End your sacrifice."

The princess chewed her lip. She squeezed LB's hand as if she expected this was all.

"Thank you."

She said this in farewell, not to Arif but to LB. He spoke as himself.

"There's more."

"There is?"

"Yeah. This is tough."

"It is not the hardest thing you've done for me, Sergeant. Please."

LB released her hand, no longer her husband.

"Arif did not try to kill your father."

The princess reared her head, stricken. She flung both hands to her mouth, speaking behind her fingers.

"Tell me."

She showed no doubt. She granted the truth of everything before LB said it.

In short phrases, he explained the plot gone crazy. Arif had hacked into her father's computer. He let himself get convinced to hand the info over to an al-Qaeda named Ghalib.

She spoke behind the veil of her hands.

"The son of Qasim. Our landlord."

LB continued, quickly, before the prince interrupted.

Ghalib gave the information to an AQ bomber who used it to worm his way in to see her father at his home in Riyadh. The bomber blew himself up, framing Arif with a last-second cell phone call. The prince was sure that Arif was behind the attempt on his life. He made a deal with the CIA and the Yemenis to kidnap her, get her away from Arif before the CIA could target him in return. The Americans placed a diplomat in her car as a decoy, to make Arif's pursuit qualify for a drone strike. Ghalib, the one actually behind the bombing, got hit first last night, by mistake. Then Arif.

LB made no mention of Khalil's shooting or the remorseful, wounded Josh upstairs. Of course, the prince had probably been watching the CIA satellite feed live when Arif pulled the trigger. Right now, LB saw no need to tell Arif's widow.

She lowered her hands. Her mouth hung open.

"Arif did not do it."

"I don't think he did, ma'am."

She swelled, up off her pillows, the IV lines following, as if her big husband had entered the room and she could move in front of him, to protect him.

"My father had him killed wrongly."

"Looks like it."

Her face, sunken and pale no more, glowed red-hot with new blood and anger. Arif had been resurrected out of her shame.

"Send in my father."

LB raised a palm. "One last thing."

"Say it in front of him. All of it."

"Princess, listen to me. Then you make up your own mind."

Like she had after one of her bouts of suffering, Nadya settled against the bed, exhausted, drawn down by the efforts of living. She wasn't healed and wouldn't be for a while. In some ways, she probably never would be. She spoke to the ceiling.

"Yes, Sergeant."

"Arif asked you to keep this to yourself."

Against the pillow, she turned her head away. LB read in this gesture the beginning of his dismissal.

"Why on earth?"

"He knew you'd want to rip your father."

"I want to damn him."

A knock sounded at the door. They had to hurry.

"Sergeant."

"Yes, ma'am."

"Say it as Arif. Let me hear him say it."

She turned to LB a last time and rested her hand once more where he could take it. LB did not, should the door open too soon. Instead he leaned closer, lowering his voice, to lay the last secret like a wreath between Arif and his wife.

"Don't tell your father. Let him think I opposed him enough to want to kill him. Let this be one victory, a small one, for me over him."

The princess blinked shining eyes; the creases beside them were the same as her father's. She lifted a hand to LB's face for a terribly sad caress.

"Good-bye."

The door opened, and the prince swirled in with his robe flying. The room was large enough for him to need seconds to stride to the bedside.

In those moments, LB wanted to ask her, what will you do?

Instead, before the prince reached them, LB touched fingertips to the princess's hand against his temple. He smiled bravely in case she saw on him, at the end, Arif.

LB considered bumping Abd al-Aziz on the way out, but that would be looking for trouble.

Chapter 45

Camp Lemonnier
Djibouti

Wally went to fetch the second round. Half the team was not drinking, on alert tonight. LB and Berko were in that half. They puffed on Berko's cigars, blowing the smoke straight up to avoid bothering Major Torres. She told them there was no need and reached for LB's stogie to try. With a nasty face, she kept it.

It was hot as usual after dark in 11 Degrees North, but not so jammed. The camp's runway buzzed with flights; the aircrews who normally packed the canteen were occupied elsewhere. Most of the crowd was navy and marines, and contractors. The PJ team didn't have to shout to talk, and they were gabby tonight.

The cigars had the same kindly effect on LB and Berko, made them both quiet and observant. They smoked side by side with Torres. She was saying that she liked men and their ways, and when Wally swung six more beers onto the table, it remained clear that she liked him.

LB tipped his cigar into the night to the princess alone in her Riyadh hospital bed. In those moments when he'd been the visitation of her husband, LB had felt, though fleeting and not his, the power of the woman's heart. A lifetime of that, even cut short, must have been remarkable for Arif.

Torres and Wally could have that. LB raised his cigar to the major across from him. Okay. This was his family. It could grow. Torres looked back quizzically.

Berko nudged LB.

"That was nice."

"Don't know what you mean."

LB and Berko took puffs together. The others took swigs. Berko copied LB's gesture, lifting his cigar at LB.

"Something you said to me."

"And what was that, Lieutenant?"

"You've got time."

"I did say that."

"You do, too."

LB got to his feet, intending to walk off before this became a session about him. He rested both hands on his hips, cigar smoke curling around him. He backed away a step. The full PJ team and Torres seated around the table seemed puzzled.

Wally asked, "Where you going?"

"Figured I'd be alone for a little while."

The team objected. Torres joined him on her feet, bringing the cigar with her. She took a draw and still had a ways to go before she looked natural doing it. She smiled around the glowing stogie.

"When you could be with us, why would you be with just you?"

The team raised voices at him to stay. Berko and Doc shouted, "Good point."

LB sat. Out on the runway, behind the fence and in the dark, a plane, another mission, lifted off. The part of the PJ team drinking tonight lifted their beers to it.

Acknowledgments

One of the great thrills of writing a novel is the opportunity and responsibility to learn of worlds and ways both foreign and exciting, to bring home a powerful story. Along the path, a writer travels to incredible places, even if it's only through a book or a website. He meets remarkable people, even if these are the authors of related works, names and lives in a vivid history, or voices on the phone.

For this PJ series, I've read extensively, journeyed to remote corners of the globe, and spoken with dozens of folks who've been generous guides, deepening my understanding of my own stories. Each author, expert, and airline pilot, even if unknowingly, owns a place in my personal pantheon of gratitude. But a few helpers have stood out, a small cadre of living, breathing heroes who've taken me by my naïve, unknowing hand to guide me through the awesome world of the pararescuemen, the Guardian Angels.

They take my calls, stay patient with me, invent parts of the story for me when I falter, cheer me on, even sail with me, and bring me to earth. I am proud to know them as men and friends, and damned happy to have them in my corner as a writer: Maj. (retired) Scott Williams, USAF Lt. Col. John McElroy, Lt. Col. Sean Fitzgerald, Capt. Chris Baker, and Sr. Master Sgt. Jules Roy.

other key guide star for these PJ novels is my Machiavellian Bob Bigman. I can't tell you what he does for a living, but every time I think I've stretched the bounds of credulity, Bobby tells me more is not only possible but likely. Wow.

As always, as he has for all my books from the beginning, my old and dear friend Dr. Jim Redington walks me through every wound, bandage, pill, and medical trauma I write about. And he bought a house on the river, finally. Thank you.

I appreciate the Honors College of VCU for letting me learn and teach there, and the publishers of *Boomer Magazine* for giving me a platform for seven hundred words every other month. And Capt. Mike Beach for allowing Miami Beach to be my home away from home.

My copy editor, Kevin Smith, was again a marvel to work with. He was given to me by my publisher, Thomas & Mercer, and my editor, Alan Turkus, who have shown a refreshing belief in me and my writing. Thank you.

Lastly, my agent, Luke Janklow, and his super assistant, Clair Dippel, are irreplaceable components of my career. If you're a writer, make no mistake: talented, connected, and committed representation is as important as anything you put on the page. Thanks, team. And onward.

About the Author

David L. Robbins currently teaches advanced creative writing at VCU Honors College. He is the author of eleven action-packed novels, including *War of the Rats, Broken Jewel, The Betrayal Game, The Assassins Gallery*, and *Scorched Earth*. An award-winning essayist and screenwriter, Robbins founded the James River Writers, an organization dedicated to supporting professional and aspiring writers. He also cofounded the Podium Foundation, which encourages artistic expression in Richmond's high schools. Robbins extends his creative scope beyond fiction as an accomplished guitarist and student of jazz, pop, and Latin classical music. When he's not writing, he's often found sailing, shooting, weight lifting, and traveling the world. He lives in his hometown of Richmond, Virginia.